OVER THE EDGE

Carole T. Beers

W & B Publishers
USA

W & B Publishers

For information:
W & B Publishers
9001 Ridge Hill Street
Kernersville, NC 27284

www.a-argusbooks.com

ISBN: 9781635540826

Front cover over designed by Cheryl F. Taylor from a photo by Jenny J Jaks Grimm

Printed in the United States of America

DEDICATION

For my brother Mark, his family and others who've been at the edge.

ACKNOWLEDGMENTS

As always, the bulk of the credit for this book and the drive and time to write it goes to my Creator, with a nod to my earthly editorial guru, William Connor of W & B Publishers, without either I might be toiling away in query limbo. Plus a big shout-out to Richard Peterson, my husband, who provides love and "a clean well-lighted place" to write.

Thank yous, as well, to my friends and former Seattle Times colleagues Melinda Bargreen and William Dietrich – authors of note themselves – for their invaluable help and support. Authors J.A. Jance, Stella Cameron, Catherine Ryan Hyde, Anne Hillerman and Jo-Anne Mapson continue to inspire and occasionally offer a kind word of encouragement as do Western romance writers Laura Drake and Kari Lynn Dell.

My dear friend Tamara Chastain, along with trainers Mike Edwards and Patty Baker and her client Missy Neil, provided details of competing at World Shows in Texas. They also shared about some of the extracurricular (legal) fun to be had in Fort Worth.

Cousins, uncles, nieces and nephews make up my extended cheering section, for which I am profoundly grateful. Joy Luck Book Club, led by Cynthia Charat, is my self-appointed cheer squad. And dear friends on social media – especially in READING COUNTRY, a Facebook group I created for readers, writers and other fans of all things small-town or country (read: horses –) are treasured like rubies. Though I doubt I could I pawn them should book sales decline.

The Ashland-based Monday Mayhem writing group keeps me "moving right along." It forces me to focus on ways to omit commas and needless words, and to generally "make better." Kudos to authors Jenn Ashton, Sharon L. Dean, Michael Niemann, Clive Rosengren and Tim Wohlforth for editing proof books. Their "catches" have saved my book bacon more often than I can publicly admit.

No acknowledgment would ever be complete without an extended hurrah for my furred or feathered assistants. My horse Brad, dogs Billy, Dolly and Georgie, cat Velvet, and parakeet Peekaboo surround and fill me with hope, faith, love and laughter when the going gets tough. And when it doesn't.

PROLOGUE

Wednesday, November 9

What is it with me and bodies? They seem to stalk me, or at least pop up with alarming frequency. Especially lately.

Being a born snoop and obsessively curious ex-reporter as well as a high-energy redhead, after seeing a body I'm driven to know how it got that way – at whose hand, by what means, for which reason. Sometimes I know immediately. Other times not so much.

I saw my first dead body at eighteen, as a cub reporter on my college newspaper. I was sent to cover a campus car crash. Not pretty, blood enough for two. Telephone pole 1/Driver 0.

I saw my ninth body – or one as good as – little more than a week ago. It sprawled headfirst down the side of Southern Oregon's Table Rock, where I was horseback riding.

Horrified, I expected to see my tenth body within minutes of seeing that ninth. Except I wouldn't actually see that body, I would be that body, eyes clamped shut or frozen open. You see, killers don't like it when you're first at the scene. They want to silence you because they think you witnessed the deed. Sometimes they are right.

Obviously I did not become the tenth body. That dubious honor belongs to a person at the World Open Western (Horse Association) Show, or WOWS, in Fort Worth, Texas. I spied it just two days ago at the Will Rogers

Memorial Center, where I was showing my registered Paint to fulfill my dream of winning a world championship.

Though I'm no stranger to corpses, I still felt a jolt when I stumbled on that one. I buzzed with even higher voltage when police targeted me as a person of interest.

Two bodies separated by more than half a country and less than a month. With me smack in the middle of it, scrambling for my sanity, my reputation, even my life.

Writing now in the aftermath of these horrific events, hunkering in with my friends and lover in a cottage near the Texas death-scene, I'm relieved that it's nearly over. Punishment is being meted out. A final puzzle-piece is clicking into place. But I still feel uneasy, like I could have done more. I might have saved at least one person, if I'd been faster or smarter.

Seeing dead bodies was not unusual for a former big-city newspaper reporter like me – a short Reba McEntire-ringer named Pepper Kane. Especially after said reporter came crossways with a cranky editor, and got reassigned to writing obituaries and chasing night-cops after a sweet stint penning features on movie stars and upscale homes.

That job, like my second marriage, went south five years ago when I traded writing about the dead and the naughty – not mutually exclusive – for showing horses and selling tack near my childhood home of Grants Pass in Oregon's Rogue River Valley. Less lucrative but more fun. Plus I get to help my ageing parents, hang with horse pals, and ride the best river-mountain scenery this side of Paradise. Or how Paradise ought to look.

And, did I mention, to investigate the odd crime that crosses my path? People seem to expect it of me. I get a kick out of doing it. Plus, old reporter habits die hard. So to speak.

Much of which explains how I came to be in the wrong place at the wrong time when I saw my ninth and tenth bodies. When I looked into why they got that way, thereby pasting a target on my own back.

It's a twisted tale of betrayal, guilt and hurting hearts. But it's also a tale of redemption, faith and second chances. I'm still picking at the last knot, still staying awake rehashing things, hoping I made the right choices. It may help if I lay it all out. So I'll start at the beginning.

Chapter 1

Friday, October 21

"I just love your horse, Pepper," said the tall, thirty-something brunette sitting Grace, her pretty palomino Paint. "Such a nice Western lope. Slow, level, forward. Cute face, too."

"Thank you," I said, gliding by as if on a breeze-driven rocking chair instead of a saddle.

I knew the prizewinning horsewoman was studying me as I worked Chocolate Waterfall, my sweet chestnut-brown show horse in the outdoor arena. But until then, I was not sure if this newcomer approved or hated him and how I rode him. I thought Choc the greatest thing since cubed hay, and knew I rode him well. But I didn't expect everyone to feel similarly – with the exception of horse-show judges.

"Is he sired by Dark Superstar?" she called after me, a late-morning breeze ruffling coal-colored curls that had escaped her knit cap. She meant the world's most famous sire of winning, all-around Western show horses.

"No, he's by Chocolate Dandy and out of Zippity Goodbar," I tossed over my shoulder. Having top-tier champions in your horse's lineage was as important to the horse-show crowd as having pilgrim forebears or rich relatives was to the social-climbing crowd. In each case, a descendant should enhance ancestral advantage with wins of one's own.

Nevertheless, I glowed. She had singled me out from the other riders at our stable. It was her first real attempt to befriend any of us. It was about time.

Sandra Allende was a like a gush of fresh air through Brassbottom Barn, a settled little horse-show stable near Medford, where a dozen friends and I keep our show horses in training. Actually Sandra more closely resembled a whirlwind. Newly divorced and seeking new real-estate opportunities in the Valley, the statuesque brunette, her teen daughter and their two pedigreed ponies had moved up from California a few weeks earlier – the second equine recently purchased as a World Show contender for the girl.

From the start Sandra acted as if she owned the stable and everyone in it.

"I have some ideas about how to really put this stable on the map," she told Dutch and Donna Grandeen, Brassbottom's owner-trainers, and seven of us riders last Friday. We'd all rallied 'round the Mr. Coffee in our barn's western lounge. The daughter was MIA, taking a brain-busting test at the high-school.

As if the Grandeens wanted or needed help. They had three champion-caliber Paints and Quarter Horses in their string. And they were readying more for hopeful owners, including me, to vie for titles at the World Open Western Show in Fort Worth in November. They weren't the highest-profile trainers on the West Coast. But the couple produced results and had a ball doing it. We riders had just as much fun.

While we sipped coffee with a big dollop of skepticism that morning, Sandra spelled out her strategies: Advertise in high-end horse journals, partner with owners of stallions who'd sired some of our horses, and offer "monetary incentives", AKA soft bribes, to steal top contenders from other barns. As if the Grandeens would or could afford to do any of that.

I remember that Dutch Grandeen – all sexy, snake-hipped six feet of him in boots, jeans, navy hoody and Chicago Cubs World Champions cap – sat with outstretched legs on a canvas chair in the corner. His hazel eyes darted from Sandra to his leggy blond wife Donna, and back. Checking out Donna's reaction, which included eye-rolls.

His squinty Clint Eastwood eyes seemed to say what many of us thought: If Sandra were so smart and successful, why had she brought herself and her horses up from northern California anyway? A land of Mount Shasta, sweeps of forest and springs so clear that whole lakes'-worth wound up as bottled water. A land where Sandra, along with her ex-husband, the developer and artifacts-importer Max Allende, had ruled the rural real-estate world from Reno to Santa Rosa, before the real-estate crash of the late-2000s. The land from which she and her daughter could ride with any trainer they wanted. Ride with "The Bigs," as we liked to say.

I wondered why she would leave a good thing in Cali. Why she would choose the lovely but less horse-show-minded Rogue River Valley, home of the lower-key Grandeens. Unless she thought she could more easily make them do her bidding. In a higher-end stable there was always the possibility of playing second-fiddle to even wealthier riders.

Mostly I wondered why, until today's genuine compliment, I couldn't see more warmth behind her quick-to-smile eyes. She'd tossed generic kudos and polite asks about us and our horses. But until today, her efforts had seemed perfunctory, and hence fallen on deaf hearts.

Artfully coiffed, plucked and tucked, pretty Sandra already was causing a stir in the male populace in and outside real-estate circles. We'd heard her throw around names of several high-profile lawyers and businessmen she was "working with." That she'd scored a fabulous deal from one, on a silver Mercedes and extended-cab dually pickup to tow her luxe horse trailer.

She'd also leased a posh condo by a golf course with a killer view of Mount McLaughlin. Then turned around and, with her ex, bought daughter Jeanne the new horse and a mini-Cooper for her fifteenth birthday – which, as a student driver, Jeanne could use with an adult present.

Sandra's dimpled face already graced Rogue Valley billboards with the promise, "Properties to Die For."

How odd, I would think later. How prophetic.

I'd seen her type often in my twenty-five years as a reporter: driven, polished but brittle in looks and manner, and given to rubbing us ordinary peeps the wrong way.

Freddie Uffenpinscher, for one. That svelte, beauty-salon owner with the bald head, lush mustache and gazillion earrings said he didn't trust her as far as her horse could throw her. Fond of drama, but entertainingly so, our top English rider had a sixth sense about people – particularly poseurs.

"I know a snake when I see it," he opined, mustache aquiver, after last Friday's coffee klatch in the Brassbottom lounge. "Even when it's all safely curled up, and a li'l bit pretty."

Still, as the days went by, I had to admit I liked Sandra – especially, after today's warm compliment. She was becoming a barn buddy. The Sisterhood of the Horse and all that. A hard charger with high standards that I liked. We could all up our game by following her example.

But it was more than that. Beneath Sandra's glamour lay an air of sadness that made me want to reach out to help her somehow. Not to mention to befriend her daughter, Jeanne, who reminded me of my Chili at that age. Jeanne, like Little Stewie, our only other 18-and-under rider, rode after school and weekends. Rode quite well, considering her fancy new horse was hell-on-hooves.

Sandra often ragged Jeanne about her riding. But she also doted on the girl. Witness the new car and horse. Witness her pride pointing out Jeanne lounging poolside with another model in photos in real-estate flyers for multi-million-dollar properties.

A clue to Sandra's sadness emerged a short while after the compliment she'd paid me as we rode with other Brassbottom buddies in the outdoor arena. We'd been practicing for the World Show, mere weeks away.

Sandra and I led our unsaddled horses side by side back to their stalls.

"You had interesting ideas last week how the Grandeens can improve the business," I said. "Meant to tell you sooner, but we kept missing each other."

"Just trying to help," she said with a guarded smile. "They're good peeps. Probably can't afford to implement my ideas, but they might benefit in some way."

"So how're you liking the Valley?"

"It's good," she said, slowing.

"Is Jeanne happy, making friends?"

Sandra paused. A shadow drifted across her eyes.

"I assume so. She keeps pretty busy, though. Like me, that way."

"Mind if I ask you something?" I said. "As a friend?"

"Not at all," she said, stopping her horse, opening its stall door and motioning it inside.

"We're pretty drama-free here," I began. "We have fun, root for each other, have each other's back. But I've noticed something bothering you. Anything I can help with, answer a question about us or our trainers?"

Sandra stepped inside the stall, unfastened the halter and looked at me.

"I appreciate your concern, Pepper. You're sweet. But it's personal. It'll be fine." She hung the halter outside the stall, then went in to shake a stable blanket draped on the manger.

"No problem, Sandra," I said cheerily. "Have a good ride." I led Choc on down the aisle.

Sandra didn't tell me that day. The honor belonged to our buzz-cut, freckled youth rider, Stewie Mikulski. The nine-year-old had trailed with his horse behind us. Now he followed only Choc and me, because my stall was far down the aisle from Sandra's. His stall adjoined mine.

"I know what's eating her," he said, his voice and eyes conspiratorial. "Jeanne kind of accidentally told me yesterday. Wanna hear?" He cocked his head.

"Sure," I nodded. "But only if it's not supposed to be a secret," I quickly added.

He bobbed up and down, barely containing his excitement at sharing important news.

"I told her I was glad to have another youth rider at the barn, and that she rode really well. She said, 'Not as good as my sister.' Then she clapped her hand over her mouth."

"What?" I rasped. "Jeanne has a sister?"

"That's what I said. Jeanne didn't want to talk. But then she said, 'Oh, why not. I need to tell someone because it's killing me.' I guess her sister was almost eighteen, and ran away to be in the movies or something."

"Seriously?" My mind struggled to wrap itself around this news.

"Jeanne made me promise not to tell. They're trying to find her. But no one can know cuz it might mess up their search."

Little Stewie raised his chin importantly, as the bearer of special knowledge. A beat later he blushed, suddenly interested in his boots. "Um, maybe I shouldn't have told you."

"Maybe not. But it would've come out sooner or later."

My stomach thudded. Sandra had another daughter, one who ran away. No wonder she seemed sad. Anyone would be. I hoped Sandra was still in her stall, blanketing her horse, and hadn't heard us. The barn was oddly quiet. Almost as if the sparrows and mice were listening.

"One last thing. Did Jeanne say when her sister ran away?" I whispered, leaning in.

"Before they came here," he shrugged, kicking a horse turd with his boot toe. We watched it roll away down the aisle.

"Anything else, Stewie?"

"Jeanne said her sister fought a lot with her mom and dad. They said she was lazy and fat. Her parents hated her."

I shot Stewie a skeptical look, and lay a hand on his shoulder.

"No one hates their children," I said, wishing it were true.

Stewie produced a credible pout.

"Alls I know is what Jeanne said. Don't let on I told you, okay?" He squinted up at me.

"Sure. But I'm glad you told me. Maybe I can help. Remember, I was a reporter."

The boy nodded, and went to saddle his horse.

I looked back up the aisle to see Sandra leaving her horse's stall. Ducking into Choc's stall, I stood taking shallow breaths. When I heard Sandra's door slide shut, I waited a little longer, praying she had not heard Stewie and me.

In those moments I imagined I felt Sandra's sadness as if it were my own. I could relate to having a runaway kid. I knew how depressing and devastating it felt to fight with a child and then have him or her leave home before their time. I had two kids myself – my 35-year-old son Serrano, and 32-year-old Chili. During their tumultuous teens they'd left me for brief spells that had plunged me into depression and seemed to last forever. On one occasion, a friend of Chili's said she may have run off with a man who had a connection with modeling. Chili had wanted to be a model, so naturally, I'd thought the worst. That investigative story I'd done on trafficking was still fresh in my mind.

Thankfully my kids never went missing more than a week and always came home on their own. But during their gone days, I'd focused on trying to find them, and steeled myself against the possibility they might not return.

Sandra would blame herself for the runaway. She'd also be scared others would blame her. Shun her for being a bad mom. Maybe even withhold business. To this, too, I could relate.

I yearned to find a way to discuss the matter. I knew I could help her and that we could be real friends, not just horse-riding pals. Sandra and I had more in common than she knew.

Chapter 2

Friday, October 28

Making up my mind to learn more about the missing daughter, offer my help, and see if it had anything to do with Sandra's moving here, I looked for chances to talk. No one should have to bear what she and Jeanne did, by themselves, on top of a divorce and a move.

Constantly studying us other riders, making more contact, she told me yesterday of her desire to feel at home and make friends in the Valley. Despite having spent most of her thirty-nine years in Northern Cali, she said she'd grown stale, lost "so-called" friends during the divorce and generally worn out her business welcome.

"I have a sister-in-law, an artist and real-estate photographer, in Ashland," Sandra said as we rode together this morning, by way of explaining what drew her to the area. "We aren't close, but Jeanne adores her. Jeanne is artistic herself and designs jewelry for a few friends."

"My daughter Chili designs and sells jewelry," I said, warmed that Sandra and I had another thing in common.

Sandra also shared her desire to hook up with a good man, having ditched her husband for being "bossy and abusive." Again, I could relate, though not to the abusive part. My last husband was nosy and controlling but had not crossed the line into physical abuse.

In the five years since my divorce, I'd acquired a boyfriend, Sonny Chief – a six-foot-six, semi-retired tribal policeman from South Dakota's Standing Rock Reservation.

Sonny'd played basketball on an athletic scholarship at the University of Washington. After returning to the rez, Sonny occasionally returned to the Pacific Northwest to help with cases affecting Sioux people, to visit his adult kids in Seattle, and to spend time with me.

Our together time always left me wanting more. I wanted to wake up to his deep, slow voice, quick mind and strong body daily. Explore his spirituality. Be accepted by his family. Forever. The sticking point for him was that word, "forever."

So I could relate to Sandra's yearnings for a nice, interesting, forever kind of guy.

This very morning as we rode outdoors, Sandra said she'd met a "man of substance" (ka-ching!) who was "into horses." In fact it was the diabolically handsome developer who had built her condo community, Reginald "Reg" Stavropolis. His face graced his own billboards as well as TV ads. I'd had met him when a riding friend introduced him as a sponsor of a horse show. The guy was dark, tall, and sexier than a man has a right to be. His intense gaze chilled me to the marrow, though I couldn't say why.

Now I felt a flare of concern, but I brushed it off.

For bona fide legally unattached horsewomen such as myself, there were few phrases more compelling than "a man of substance who is into horses." Having caught and released several spouses who objected to my horse habit, I – like Tulip and other single Brassbottom buddies – forever sought the perfect man and perfect horse. Neither of which exists.

And yet here was Sandra on the edge of living the dream. She was a brave, glamorous and successful woman who could speak her mind and didn't offend others, unlike myself at times. A gal who could attract the likes of a Stravropolis, too. What was her secret?

When I asked, she threw back her head and laughed.

"You just speak your mind," she said. "The ones who appreciate straightforwardness will be your friends. That goes for men, above all. They rise to a challenge, excuse the pun."

"Hmmm," I said, knowing I fell short in the fearless-honesty-with-men department.

We rode beside each other wordlessly a full circuit of the outdoor arena. We had become the kind of comfortable that grows as much from sharing inner thoughts as from sharing a hobby.

"I am just so excited," she said, her diamond-stud earrings shooting off sun sparks. "Reg doesn't have a horse now. But a cousin, a job foremen, has a horse Reg can ride."

"Where are you going?" I said.

"Lower Table Rock," she said.

"What? The Nature Conservancy hasn't let anyone ride up there for years."

"Pfffft," she said. "Reg knows people who, with a nice donation, will look the other way. Besides. We're riding from Jim Dardanelle's ranch that abuts the Rock."

"The Grandeens know Jim. A long time ago he gave permission for any Grandeen clients to ride up there. But none of us have taken him up on it."

Sandra patted her horse's neck.

"The Rock has such a fabulous history. You probably know in the 1850s it was part of the last Indian reservation here. Before Chief Sam's people were marched to a rez up north."

"Why this area is called Sam's Valley."

She nodded quickly, and smiled, warming to her spiel.

"In the Thirties or Forties, developer John Day, whose family still has a ranch on the shoulder of the Rock, had movie stars like Clark Gable fly up to hunt and fish."

"I rode there a few times as a teenager, when anyone could ride there."

"John Day built the airstrip on the top of the Rock to fly in visitors to his hunting lodge, people who might buy properties. The strip goes to the cliff edge. Saw it on Google Earth."

She patted Grace while gazing across the valley toward two dark, eight-hundred-foot-tall mesas left eons ago when the Rogue River cut through hardened lava on its way from Crater Lake to the Pacific Ocean. The cool but dazzlingly bright morning made them seem near.

"So, Sandra, you score not only a forbidden ride on Table Rock, but are going with THE Reg Stavropolis?" Her plan sounded good, but it made me uneasy. Her riding out alone with a strange-to-her man struck me as a little dangerous.

I fought to redirect Choc's attention to our path in the outdoor arena. He avoided work by watching foals in far pastures edged by pine and oak, and framed by blue hills. Hills and mesas I hadn't ridden in ages, but that I yearned to ride again. Maybe I could ride with Sandra. I was so tightly wound readying for the world show, and could truly use a fun trail ride before facing the staged chaos in Texas. The Grandeens would haul our horses there next week. I might trail ride Bob, the bay Paint I kept on my own four acres a dozen miles away.

Sandra must have seen my worried look, the wheels turning in my brain.

"What, Pepper? Is something wrong with my riding with Reg? His divorce is final. He's one of the most eligible bachelors in all Southern Oregon. Plus we have business together. A huge land deal that could get me known nationwide. Very hush-hush."

"When are you going?" I said, also reining in. "You're not riding alone on a first date?"

"Well, yeah. So?"

"You just be careful. Two women were attacked in the Valley before you came here, out hiking or riding with men they barely knew. One died. Very bad business."

Sandra drew her eyebrows together. Then she shrugged, and urged Grace forward again.

"Riding out Monday, around nine," she said. "I hear there are tons of people hiking up there every day. Especially now with fall colors. But also in spring to see flora and fauna existing nowhere else in the world because the last glaciers stopped when they reached this Valley ten-thousand years ago."

"Whoa!" I said. "No one can say you haven't done your homework."

She smirked apologetically and kicked her mare into a jog. I sped up Choc until we again rode alongside her and Grace.

"Part of my job," she said, sitting her horse with practiced elegance. "Sharing with buyers how special the Valley is. Two hours from the Coast. An hour from Crater Lake. Nicely midway between the population centers of Seattle and San Francisco."

"Seems to suit you and Jeanne," I said. "What a lovely girl. And wonderful rider."

"Thank you."

There was that shadow again across her eyes. Like a vulture gliding between her and the sun. But it vanished almost as quickly as it had come.

"I don't mean to pry," I said. "But I heard you have another daughter?"

There. I'd said it. I felt my cheeks warm and my throat constrict.

Her head jerked toward me. Her eyes darkened.

"Um, yes. I do. That was the personal thing I mentioned the other day. I suppose Jeanne told you. That girl." She tisked, and shook her head. "Yes, it just kills me."

I said nothing. I hoped she'd fill in the blank.

"She ran away, something like that?" I said. "My daughter did that. If you want to talk —"

Sandra silenced me with a long sigh and rode toward the arena center. She looked back.

"I don't know what you heard. But Nancy left when the divorce turned nasty. She always wanted to be in movies. We heard she met a guy who had connections. Who may be somewhere in the Valley. Naturally I'd like to find her. But she is eighteen. Or almost."

Sandra began to work her horse through its show maneuvers. I noticed her spurs got quite busy, as did her annoyed horse's white tail.

I so wanted this conversation to continue. But this wasn't the time or place. Other riders already were mounting up, and more vehicles were pulling into the Brassbottom lot next to the Grandeen's white triple-wide ranch house.

Tulip Clemmons, my tall blond, Susan Sarandon-lookalike friend and horse-tack selling partner, rode into the arena on her horse. She waved dramatically, setting her ample bosom in motion beneath an aqua sweater. A short time later Donna Grandeen slid onto a stool at the arena's center to start a lesson on the finer points of horsemanship.

Today Donna wore a white crystal-dotted cap and hoodie with slim jeans. Faux leopard boots completed her rock-star cowgirl look. Donna had upped her game since Sandra's arrival. Like many another trainer's spouse, she kept close watch on her husband's heart — and other body parts.

I ran my horse through his slow show-circles and zigzags. His shoulders and flanks shone with sweat. The cool morning had become a warm noontime, coaxing odors of cured grass and hot horse from our country surroundings.

As I led Choc down the Brassbottom aisle to his stall, I stooped to pat Gracie, a kind old rescued Rottweiler. Interesting she had a similar name to Sandra's horse. But the dog seemed sweeter. I spotted Dexter, a marmalade-and-white tabby torturing a mouse in the open ended grooming stall. My gaze slid up from Dexter to Sandra, hurriedly brushing down Grace.

The horse tossed her head and pawed furiously at the rubber-matted floor, eager to go back to her stall. For her effort, Grace got a shouted, "Quit!" and a hard slap on the hip. Then another slap. One would have sufficed.

"Hey, Sandra," I said.

She looked over at me, anger at her horse still smoldering in her eyes.

"Yes?" Her irritation dropped away as she focused on me.

"You should put protective trail booties on Grace's hooves for that ride Monday. It's hard and rocky on Table Rock. I have extra booties and can lend you some."

"That's kind, Pepper. Thanks." She twinkled her eyes.

"Would you like company? Someone to ride shotgun with you and your hot new flame? I could use a trail ride. I'm fried. Been crazy getting ready for the show."

Sandra shrugged. Her dimpled smile stopped at her oddly attractive crow's-feet. Why didn't my own crow's-feet look that cute?

"No, thank you. As I say, Reg and I have business to discuss. Scoping out a project we'll see from the top of Table Rock. Plus, we might need private time, you know?" An overdone wink. She turned back to her horse. "Thanks, Pepper. I'm a big girl. I'll be fine."

I let it go. But I felt disappointed and still apprehensive. Sometimes I get a weird hum in my head, maybe higher blood pressure, when my reporter gene detects something else is going on, something behind someone's words. Often something ungood. Occasionally something purely evil.

Chapter 3

The afternoon was beyond busy at The Best Little Horsehouse in Oregon, the store Tulip and I run in the tiny town of Gold Hill, thirteen miles northwest of Medford. At times I forgot I was working. It was such fun to chat with customers and sell tack and apparel for people and their ponies that I spaced out on things unrelated to cowgirl commerce. I had no time to ponder Sandra's outing with Reg Stavropolis on Lower Table Rock, let alone fret over Sandra's poor gone girl.

And I almost forgot Tulip's and my worrisome need to make rent money, and make it yesterday. It was already many weeks past the first of the month.

Our landlord had threatened to chuck us out more than once for late payment. Tulip had a part-time gig as a receptionist at our Freddie's Manes 'N Tails salon in the river city of Grants Pass, ten miles to the northwest. But I had no viable options other than finding a sugar daddy, as likely as finding a Sasquatch – rumored to make their home in the mountains of Southern Oregon.

Having zero cash flow was a scenario I preferred not to contemplate. My present show horse alone cost a thousand dollars a month and then some, to keep in board and training.

I just tried to stay focused and smiling as I tended to the unusual and gratifying stream of customers. We were aided in our quest for calm attentiveness by old-time country music playing over the corner speakers that Sonny Chief-the-Fix-It King had found and mounted for us when

Tulip and I opened the store. The speakers that were way overdue for de-cobwebbing.

From time to time, whether Tule and I were tapping the cash register for a sale, or lifting a hanger with a blinged-out show shirt for someone to try on, one or both of us would bust into a line-dance sequence or a Texas Two-Step, eliciting laughs and mirror moves from our clients.

"I hope you're laughing with us, not at us," I told one amused woman holding a hoof knife. "Drop the knife! Join in." And she did, for a few beats.

As I said, there were plenty of buyers for what we had shelved, stacked or hung in our yellow cinder-block warehouse. Saddles, bridles, spurs, horse blankets, hoof-treatments, leg wraps and mud clogs. Visitors to The Horsehouse that day wanted all of it, with winter just around the bend.

I also tried to distract Tulip from flirting with every Tom, Dick, and Farmer John who entered the store. She was my friend from childhood, sure. Had advised me, long-distance, on raising my kids and losing two husbands during my time in Seattle. Joined with me in fun country-dance lessons and senior softball since I'd been back in the valley. So I owed her.

But sometimes my best friend, this sexy siren of a certain age, got to be too much even for me. She was easily distracted by the opposite sex, one or another member of which she was ever trying to reel in – especially if they wore expensive boots and drove a high-end truck.

Five years ago she'd lost her first and only husband, a taciturn, chain-smoking mechanic to whom she'd been married for thirty years. Now she was making up for lost time. Apparently being a merry widow agreed with her.

Store-bought boobs had been Tule's first line of offense. I about fainted when I first caught sight of those double Ds. Nothing halfway, for Miss Tulip. Pale-blond hair extensions, added just last year, came next. I didn't tell Tulip she looked like a dandelion puff on stilts.

This week it had been eyelash-extensions a mile long. Sixty dark hairs glued to the real lashes of each upper lid, and a scatter on the lowers. I'd said they made her resemble an alien.

I made it a point to rag her about the lashes again after we finally turned our shop sign to "Closed" and lit out for my western-decorated doublewide overlooking four acres, and miles of wooded hills across the freeway south of Gold Hill. That quaint town nestled on the north bank of the Rogue River along Interstate-5 where it turned before sweeping by Lower Table Rock. The town was named for a five-pound "nugget" found in 1850, which reportedly kicked off the famous Oregon Gold Rush.

On the way home Tulip and I grabbed salads, barbecued chicken and slices of mile-high chocolate-meringue pie at Katie's Kitchen. Once home, I let out my two Boston terriers and fed my old Paint show horse, Bob, along with Lucy, a boarder's Quarter Horse. Tulip mixed us a pitcher of mojitos. Then she and I collapsed into chairs on the deck overlooking pastures and hills bathed in the sun's last slanted rays.

It was balmy for late October. The dogs snored in a pool of sun. Tule and I tasted our mojitos before inhaling the chicken and pie. We ate like the starving cowgirls we were.

About halfway through, I brought up my concerns about Sandra, her runaway daughter, and the upcoming Table Rock ride.

"I can't get over that she's going alone with that guy," I said. "I've got a bad feeling about him. Have you heard anything?"

Tulip frowned, and looked over my shoulder as she thought about it.

"Isn't he the one who tried to run down an employee he caught trying to steal a piece of heavy equipment last year?"

"Oh, that's right. I forgot. He got off because he claimed the employee jumped in front of his truck. Stavropolis must have some temper. Be mean as a cut snake."

Tulip brayed with laughter, and nodded.

"And some high-dollar lawyers," she said. "I don't think I'd go out alone with that dude."

"I casually offered to ride along, said I could use some R and R, but Sandra blew me off."

"I wouldn't worry too much. She probably just wants time alone with him. You said they may be discussing a big real-estate deal."

"I really do need a recreational ride, Tule. If I rode up there and 'accidentally' ran into Sandra, what could it hurt? Plus I might tease out more on her missing daughter."

"Oh, Pepper," Tulip said through a mouthful of drumstick. "You're such a worrywart. Way too easily sucked into taking on other people's problems. I'll be all right."

Only a little stung by Tulip's words, I settled against my chair's cushioned back. I stared at her new eyelashes again and stifled the urge to snicker. To help with the stifling I poured myself another half-glass of mojito and took a swallow.

"I still can't believe the eyelash thing, Tulip."

"I am entitled," she said. A wounded look filled her baby blues as she batted lids overtaken by tarantulas.

"Shorter and thinner would be more believable," I said. "You look like you did a face-plant in a nest of spiders."

"I declay-er," she sniffed in the southern accent she sometimes affected. She'd spent her post-divorce summer with cousins in Savannah, and had come away with an accent she could summon at will. Now she placed a pink-nailed hand on her bosom. "You're just jealous. I'm telling you, these babies are man-magnets. Freddie said so, and he should know."

"Don't tell me he's getting faux lashes, too. His own make him man-magnet enough."

"Hey, I hear he's gonna hook up with that sexy Carlos Gutierrez when we get to Texas. Assistant to the big trainers Royce and Rogers? This Freddie-Carlos thing may have legs."

"Have to be long ones," I countered. "His bosses would never leave Texas." Fort Worth and nearby Pilot Point were the heart of Western horse country, a horse-show haven central enough to draw well-heeled customers from all over the nation.

"For sure," sighed Tulip. "Meanwhile, here's to my new lashes."

We clinked glasses. This time I broke into a full-blown laugh. Tulip still looked as if she were smuggling spiders.

Dolly Parton's voice rang out. I looked over at my cellphone, singing Dolly's country hit, "Here You Come Again." I'd meant to change that ringtone to something contemporary. I leaned over and put it on speaker mode.

"Pepper, honey? Whatcha doing?"

It was Mom. AKA Martha Mosley Kane, one-time champion barrel racer, distant cousin of the legendary Annie Oakley, and now a glamorous vintage cowgirl – though due to age and other conditions, she no longer rode.

"Hey, Mom. Just hanging at home with Tulip. Having mojitos. Been a hard day."

"Mojitos? Those fun Cuban drinks? Oh I love those. Now don't drink too much. You know how alcohol puffs up your face."

"Smooths out the wrinkles," I said, winking at Tulip.

"Can you hit the Wal-Mart in the morning and pick up some meds?" Mom said. "I called them in. Dad had a little wreck with the truck. Not too bad, just a dent. Truck didn't have much damage, either."

"Haha, good one, Mom," I lied. "I thought you weren't letting Dad drive. We might be getting closer to when we take his license away."

"We need those meds before noon, honey. Apple-pecan pie for your trouble?"

After we hung up, Tulip gave me one of her patented impatient looks.

"Pep, we need to talk more about finding your folks a good retirement home, and turning their place into a guest ranch," she said.

"My folks still have a lot of life to live independently, and we still have the store – which, by the way, filled our till to overflowing today. We'll make rent and then some. Things are trending up. Must be our sale ad in the Medford Mail Tribune."

I congratulated myself for having gone out on a financial limb that had held up.

Tulip raised her eyebrows and gave me another look, dramatized by the lashes.

"That ad was a fine idea. But this is just one day the store did well. One day. People, trends, the economy, are incredibly fickle. We all could lose that baby tomorrow."

Chapter 4

After Tulip and I drained the pitcher of mojitos, she split for her home a half-hour's drive away, between Medford and the artsy city of Ashland. She refused to move closer, saying that Ashland men enjoyed a higher average income – an average she one day hoped to tap into.

The night felt cold and lonely after she left. Somewhere an owl hooted. I thought again of Sandra and her missing daughter. I wanted to know more. When I'd worked on the prize-winning story about child sex-trafficking in Seattle, several mothers had impressed on me that if others – even bare acquaintances – had been vigilant before and especially after someone disappeared, shared even a tiny detail about a child's activities and associations, the trafficking would have been cut short or even stopped before it happened. Since then, I'd vowed never to pass on chances to help. I demanded the same caring commitment from my own children.

All Sandra had said was that her girl might have been with someone in the Rogue Valley. It was a big valley with plenty of places to hide. But for somebody wanting to be in movies, wouldn't it have made more sense to head to Hollywood itself? Not merely someone who'd worked there?

Still puzzling, I walked down the slope to the small stable where I kept Silhouettes Blond Dude, or Bob, nicknamed for the breeder who still owned his sire. Bob was a chunky bay with what horse folk call "chrome" – high whites and a blaze running across one blue eye. He was infamous for bucking me off and cracking my ribs when asked to lope. But I still loved him, occasionally rode him on trails, and was still proud he'd earned us Amateur Walk-Trot show honors in his day.

He and Lucy stampeded to the barn, neighing and raising dust all the way. Apparently the evening hay feeding needed supplementing. The horses, like most, perpetually were on the verge of starvation. Or wanted you to believe they were. I lifted the lid off the steel treats can, pulled out two apples and dropped them in mangers on the other side of the half-wall. When I turned out the light, I heard the horses happily slurping and munching.

Back in the house I tidied up, set the coffeemaker for morning and sank into Big Brown, my handsome leather recliner, to watch the late TV news. I played a little with the dogs, using a knotted towel as a tug-of-war toy that sent them into paroxysms of snarling. At ten-thirty I was ready to call it a night.

As I stripped for my evening shower, my phone sang. I picked it up off the counter.

"Hi Donna. How are you and Dutch doing? What's up

"We're in Eugene. Are you all set to do turnouts at the barn tomorrow and Sunday? Sorry I didn't call sooner to remind you."

Shoot. I'd almost forgotten. Our trainers had driven north to Eugene to judge and steward a small, charity all-breed horse show over the weekend. The stall-cleaners at our barn were doing morning and evening feedings, and stall tidying for the thirty-some horses that boarded or trained at Brassbottom. But I was in the barrel to lead stalled horses to their pens for their "me" time.

"All set," I said. "Thanks for reminding me, though."

"We'll be back before dark Sunday," Donna said. "I wish we hadn't committed to this gig so close to the World Show. Dutch and I are kicking ourselves black and blue."

"I know. Awful time to be away. But don't worry. We'll make it work."

I was getting chilly, standing there without clothes in front of my bathroom mirror, which did me no favors in the reflection department. My five-foot-four body was in fair shape from riding, and from having a fast metabolism. But a muffin top had made significant inroads.

"I hate saying this," Donna continued. "But now there's something even more awful." Her voice took a pinched tone.

"What's more awful?"

"Dutch just got a phone call from Dick Bradford, the big breeder and trainer in Texas who will serve as head judge over Dutch and the four other judges at the World Show."

"I know Dick, a little," I said. "Showed under him a few times."

"Dick said someone tried to run him down tonight at his ranch in Pilot Point. He'd parked his truck at the mailbox on the road. When he got out, another truck roared by so close he had to dive for the ditch."

My pulse ticked up a beat. Dick was one of the good guys in the horse business.

"How weird. He okay?"

Charlie, my frosty-muzzled Boston, nosed my leg. I patted his head.

"Dick's bruised from the fall, but okay. He doesn't think it was an accident. He saw a truck parked down the road. Like it was waiting."

"Whoa. Did he see the driver? Get a make or a plate? "

"All he remembers is that it was a white pickup. Those are a dime-a-dozen there."

"He call the sheriff?"

"They're keeping an eye out. But later he got a text warning him not to place horses sired by his stallion Superstar at the top of his judges' card at the World Show, or next time the truck wouldn't miss."

"No. I can't believe it, Donna. Why would anyone want to harm Dick?"

"You know there's always jealousy about a leading stallion. But I wouldn't think it would lead to something like this." Her voice got lower. "And it gets worse."

"How so?"

"Dutch and the four other judges got a similar text. Untraceable. Guy probably used a burner phone."

No way. Our head trainer's life might be at risk, and perhaps some of his clients' horses sired by Superstar were in danger, too. Dark Vader, the Grandeen's champion son of Superstar, was killed earlier in the year, though in different circumstances. I'd helped solve that mystery.

"Death threats are bad enough," I said. "That is, if they're real. But you and Dutch have three Superstar horses in training for customers. What are you, what are we, going to do?"

"Pray a lot," Donna said. "We're freaked. We we've notified the show committee. And we hope you'll do some digging. Your having been an ace reporter, and solved the Vader case."

"Don't know about the ace part, Donna. But I will do some digging. Put Dutch on."

After a moment Dutch's lazy cowboy voice came on the line.

"Hell of a deal, isn't it?" he said.

"Hate it," I said. "What do you think about the threats? Why and who?"

He filled me in on what Bradford had told him, and what the other four judges had said in brief texts or calls. They all had drawn blanks on the who or why. As if threats would really affect their placings. In fact, the judges might even be prompted to underscore their independence by swinging votes to offspring of another top stallion.

"Owners of stallions competitive with Dark Superstar," Dutch said, as if he had read my mind. "They might be trying to influence judging to gain an advantage for their sire. The breed association badly needs a broader genetic base than that of one stallion, even if it is Superstar."

"I'm with you on that."

"Or this may be due to some trainer who's laid everything on the line for world championships for his clients. Showing makes folks a little crazy."

"Or attracts crazy people," I said. "Forward that text to me. Then give me the numbers of the other judges. I'll try to get their take on it."

I grabbed a notepad and pen from my nightstand just through the bathroom door as Dutch was forwarding the threat text to me. He spoke the judge info and I jotted it down. I saw two judges lived in Texas, the others in Washington, Ohio and California.

"Now Pepper," Dutch said, "You and the buddies have to be super watchful of yourselves and the horses at Brassbottom. If you see or hear anything unusual, call the sheriff immediately.

"We'll keep everything safe at our end, Dutch," I said. We disconnected.

Immediately I re-read the text, which I'd only glanced at before:

"DO NOT place Dark Superstar horses at the top of your World Show judge's card. Doing so could be deadly."

I shivered as everything sank in. Some "crazy" making death threats. Out in the open, and to respected judges. How could we even travel to Texas, let alone compete in WOWS, with such madness needling our brains?

How could Dutch and Donna do their job, knowing danger might lurk behind any corner?

Before I turned in, I texted the other judges and the show chairperson, requesting ideas and information. I said the Grandeens wanted me to investigate the threats so they could stay impartial. I asked judges to forward me their texts so I could see scan them for similarities or differences, things that didn't line up, or wording that offered another clue.

I doubted that the other judges, like Dutch, knew anything concrete this early. But even a casual comment or observation could help me begin to understand the threats, and what or who was behind them. As if I needed more to stress about. I had to solve this, and fast, if I wanted to maintain any semblance of normalcy in my world show run-up.

Chapter 5

I slept poorly. I tossed, turned and got up several times to use the loo. Worry atop worry looped through my brain. Worry about Sandra, about her missing daughter, about Sandra's ride with Reg Stavropolis, a potential business and romantic conquest. Or it was the other way around?

Worry about the tack store not being able to sustain itself, despite our blockbuster day. About Tulip's oft-repeated suggestion that my folks find a retirement community so she and I could get out of the tack shop with enough money to re-imagine their farm as a guest ranch.

But mostly worry about Dutch, Donna and what dangers awaited them and maybe us, too, before or during the World Show. Donna's call last night had thrown a sinister veil over everything. An attempted rundown of a judge of the World Show, and texted threats to others including our own Dutch Grandeen, if they dared place Dark Superstar or any of his accomplished progeny in first place.

What had sparked that? The Grandeens had owned Dark Vader, a champion son of the sire. Also, my Brassbottom buddies Freddie, Lana, and now young Jeanne Allende – also owned Superstar horses, which were starting to make names for themselves.

Was another stallion-owner really behind the threats, hoping to enhance his own horse's reputation? Enhance, as in enable a big hike in stud fees because that sire was a producer of world champions. Bumping a $1,500 fee up to $4,000 or $5,000, multiplied by hundreds of mares impregnated each year, most by artificial insemination, would mean a breathtaking increase in income. My thoughts drifted to Royce and Rogers, owners of the top stallion Shiny Suspicion. A multiple world champion himself, he stood as the second-best producer of winning horses AND the main challenger of Dark Superstar's supremacy.

But I knew this thinking was a reach. Leading trainers and breeders couldn't risk making such dramatic efforts as death threats to judges. So maybe the goal was not to addle judges, persuade them one way or the other, but to rattle the owners of Superstar horses, so they wouldn't perform at their best in Texas.

Whatever was happening, it had my full attention and that of everyone else concerned. I was sure we still would travel and show. Dutch and Donna, on the phone, had not indicated otherwise. We all had too much already invested in it. But we would be under duress.

Only as a break as I lay in bed, only after I'd worked through as many worries as I could, did I allow myself to switch gears, feel a little pride. That, too, was a valid emotion. Pride that I had shown Choc to enough wins to qualify to compete in the World show, and pride that I had committed to trying for a championship in one of my six special events.

If I rode right and Choc went well, we could be World Champions. Simple as that. The best Western horse-and-rider in the world, chosen by top judges from a thousand competitors, some from as far away as Europe. God willing and the creeks didn't rise, in a few weeks in a Texas arena with flags flying and friends watching, we might just earn a title that would live forever on our resume.

It was mind-melting. Kind of like "Olympic Gold Medalist" so-and-so, but with fewer endorsement deals. Being a champion in Prime-Time (Over 50) Novice Amateur Western Horsemanship doesn't have the cachet of striking Olympic Gold in diving or gymnastics.

When it comes to horses, I consider myself a fair hand. I inherited that skill, or learned it from my mom and from my Aunt Connie, who runs a guest ranch in Washington. I'd honed it through nearly a half-century of riding horses of every western breed, with a half-Arab or Thoroughbred thrown in for good measure. I rode trails, competed in 4-H or open shows.

I learned how to perform with grace under fire. Almost anything a horse could dream up I usually can walk away from. Accidents left their mark, but taught me survival skills including how to avoid horse wrecks in the first place. What little knowledge I gained was dangerous. It spurred me to seek ever tougher events, and better horses, tack and horse-hauling rigs. I'd run headlong toward the oddly addicting horse-show world I inhabit to this day.

Is it normal for such hard, almost daily work, heart-stopping expense, consuming hope and daunting doubt to be so much stinking fun?

All of which helps explain why I felt proud as hell, and scared to death. Proud to have a chance at a world championship. But also scared I might not make it – this or any year. Not getting any younger or richer. Scared that bad things might happen to a friend, and my shop. Scared that my trainer had a death threat hanging over his head.

My thoughts circled like wolves until after 1 a.m. Finally I got out of bed and padded to the kitchen. I checked for any return texts from show judges. There were none at that hour, as expected. What I needed then was a mug of hot milk and a slice of buttery cinnamon toast.

Mission accomplished, I fell back into bed and slept better than a just-nursed baby. All I had to do in the morning was pull on my big-cowgirl boots.

I awoke after six, as daylight began to filter between the slats of the plantation shutters. I felt energized, which surprised me, after my restless night. Downing a cup of coffee and a hard-boiled egg jazzed with hot sauce, I jumped into jeans, boots and a favorite black hoody showing a medicine wheel, a souvenir of the Seattle Seafair Pow-Wow on a bluff above Puget Sound. I not only had to feed my animals, but also pick up and deliver my folks' meds, then jet back to our barn to turn out stalled horses as I'd promised Donna.

I also had to keep my eyes and ears open to spot any suspicious people or activities at the Brassbottom Barn. People who could have something to gain from sparking fear and uncertainty as Dutch, Donna and the rest of us prepared to go to Texas.

Before leaving the house I again checked my phone for texts. I was happy to see that all judges except Dutch had sent me one. Most were along the lines of, "We got the same text as Dutch. Notified show committee. No further ideas or information."

But two texts pumped me up a little. One was from Bradford, the judge nearly run down, the owner of Dark Superstar.

"Puzzled," his text read, "but not intimidated. Warned members of our stallion syndicate. Lot of jealous people out there. Take care. Don't put yourself in danger."

I thought his last sentences interesting. Was he just being a concerned citizen? Or was there more behind those words, which could be taken as a veiled threat.

The other text that morning was from a Quarter Horse breeder in Ohio who'd often placed me and Choc first or second in classes. I like people smart enough to like my horse.

"Got same threat," read her text. "One of our other judges has money in Royce and Rogers' Shiny Suspicion stallion syndicate. Try Grant Haverstadt."

I did. Again. Haverstadt's first return text was expectedly blunt: "Know nothing. Sorry."

This time I texted him about his connection with the Shiny Suspicion stud syndicate – the one that owned that horse's breeding rights. When he got into it, if he owned any offspring of Superstar's main competitor, mares bred to him, that kind of thing. It was bold, I knew. But if you're not bold, you risk not getting what you seek. I figured more detailed questions might produce a more detailed response. Or a reaction that threw light on something hidden.

I waited, did chores, lingered over my coffee. Waited a tad longer for that more detailed response from Haverstadt.

Or no response, as it turned out. No return text from Haverstadt. Was that because he wasn't that interested? Alternately, too busy? Or was his lack of response a statement?

At least Haverstadt and the others now knew someone was watching, that I was officially looking into who sent the death texts. I'd rattled their cages. Hopefully that would be enough to keep things related to the threats from escalating.

"Hopefully" being the operative word. I didn't put much stake in that, when it came down to it. The perpetrator could merely shake off my inquiries as lame meddling by a nosy nobody in their high-stakes profession. And then keep playing their game.

Chapter 6

I hopped into my red dually pickup, which I had re-named "Red Ryder," at Tulip's insistence, and hit the Interstate 5. That seventeen-mile drive north from Gold Hill to Grants Pass would give me a welcome breather.

Snaking at a smooth seventy-five among oak-and-madrone clad hills where the Rogue tumbled or lazed by the freeway, I shifted my mind into idle. Radio tuned to country oldies, I sang along with Vince Gill, Loretta Lynn, Willie and Waylon. Rocking new-country got my booty shakin'. But there was nothing like the classics.

I wished I could "Waltz Across Texas" with my Sonny, right now. I'd be waltzing there in twelve days. Maybe I could persuade my man to visit me at the World Show.

Grants Pass Walmart was the usual Saturday-morning zoo. The parking lot was jammed with vintage gas-guzzlers, RVs, and pickups whose beds overflowed with garbage cans, or with tired home furnishings looking for a forever home – like the dump. Many pickups also sported DIY security systems, or pit bulls. Second only to Chihuahuas as mascots of Walmart Nation.

I parked outside the garden section, blasted past people with using electric scooters or herding bouncy kids, and hurried to the pharmacy section. There was a line but it was moving. Miraculously I was out in under thirty minutes, even scoring a deli Italian sandwich for later. Had it wrapped in foil to keep it cold.

In ten more minutes I motored up the oak-lined driveway between pastures at my folks' forty-acre ranch, and pulled under the tree shading the porch of the yellow, hundred-year-old house. A grand-nephew of Mom's old sorrel barrel-racing horse, Cootie, stood asleep in the left pasture reaching from the road to a small covered arena and stable. A behemoth black-Angus steer grazed the right pasture. I was surprised to see him. Field-butchering usually happened in August, and here it was late October.

Chickens of every size and shade pecked near the garage and workshop off the rear left corner of the house. Beside the garage lay Dad's chili patch that had given up for the season. Long a chili grower with a still-respectable online chili-selling business, he'd insisted I'd be named Pepper, and offered a signing bonus if I'd named my own kids for kinds of chilies.

Visible through the open garage door stood Dad's silver F-250, "Lone Ranger," facing out. It sported a considerable crink in its front bumper.

I climbed the creaking porch steps and heard a tinkle of wind chimes. I spied pillows in fall colors on the swing and rockers. Old Heller barked a welcome behind the door. I'd have to take a minute to throw a stick. I backtracked to grab one. What was Heller, ten-going-on-one?

The door swung open with a clank of the cowbell inside a grapevine wreath tied with horse-show ribbons. Hot apple-pie smells drifted to my nose.

"About time," grinned Mom. She propped her bull-pizzle cane against her hip, and dried her gnarled hands on a kitchen towel. She was still unsteady after a small stroke that had scared me into making good on my threat to retire from journalism and return to Oregon.

Heller wiggled and grinned. I stroked his head and tossed the stick into the yard. He bounded down the steps and brought it back. I tossed it again. Same result.

Mom gave me the once-over. She'd pinned her white hair atop her head and put on black jeans and a white pearl-snap shirt caught at the waist by an ancient rodeo belt and trophy buckle. White moccasins and red lipstick completed her look.

"Are you putting on weight?" She pinched my upper arm.

I hugged her and handed her the sack of meds. No use getting into the old argument.

"Pie smells good, Mom. Must have gotten up before the roosters. Did you put pecans in?"

"Oh, you bet."

Her feet shuffled and her cane thumped on the oak floor as she hobbled into the kitchen with me behind. She was determined not to use a walker, though she probably should have.

Dad, in plaid-flannel shirt and jeans with red suspenders, hunkered at the round oak table. He was perusing the Friday paper over coffee and a bran muffin.

"Hey, Dad," I said, stooping to give him a hug. He smelled of Old Spice.

He looked up, paused, and then gave me a face-filling smile.

"Well, I'll be switched. Where you been? Run off with that war whoop of yours?" His rheumy eyes twinkled under frosty brows. His tan forehead wrinkled up to what had been a hairline but now was a shiny pate showing a purple bruise above one eyebrow.

"Dad!" I said, offended as always by his racist remarks. But I knew I'd never change him. He still lived in another era. Besides, he mainly did it to get my goat. Which he often did.

"Heh, heh," he chuckled.

"Heard you had an accident with Lone Ranger," I said, pointing to the bruise. "You're not supposed to be driving."

He raised one bony hand in a dismissive gesture.

"Gave as good as I got." He sipped his coffee, smacked his lips and eyed the newspaper.

"Had the bruise checked out?"

"Bruise?'

"On your head."

He looked confused. But then he touched his hand to the spot.

"Just a bump."

"So now our insurance will go up," Mom said from the stove, where she was wrapping foil around the plump pie in a yellow vintage-pottery dish.

Saliva squirted into my mouth imagining how that treat would taste. Buttery crust and gooey chunks of Honeycrisp apples interspersed with pecans. I'd probably enjoy it for dinner with sharp cheddar, bacon crumbles and vanilla-bean ice cream. My knees went weak.

A snap of Dad's newspaper brought me back to the present.

"I worry so much about you two," I said. "We should talk again about that idea Tulip has about turning the ranch into —"

"Had breakfast?" Dad said, patting an empty chair. "Set a spell, have a bite. Mom! Get Pepper the jar of chilies I canned this morning."

"I'd love to sit," I said, "but I have a million things to do."

Mom set the pie on the table. She gave me a sympathetic look, and then looked at Dad.

"You didn't can any chilies this morning, Gus."

"Well, get her some green tomatoes to fry up in butter."

Mom shook her head and smiled wanly.

"At least he's in a good mood today," she whispered. "He was at his desk early, banging on the adding machine. Like in the old days when he was the hottest CPA in town."

"Still am," said Dad, straightening. "Just taking a break. Might go help out at the college."

"Glad you're keeping busy, Dad," I said. "So what's new in that paper?"

"Same ole, same ole. Gary Gracey's back in the headlines. They're shutting down his strip club in Old Town. He'll likely concentrate on one of his other gigs, maybe the one up north near the Indian casino where there's less hassle."

"Quit is not in his vocabulary," I said. "Well, I must get a move on. Thanks for the pie."

"Save some for Tulip," Mom said. "And Freddie. Tell him I need a hair appointment."

Dad half-stood, one fist anchored on the tabletop. He squinted, cocked his head and waggled a crooked forefinger.

"You getting' yourself in hot water again, Pepper?" he said.

"Don't know what you're talking about, Dad."

"You got that look." His memory was shot, yet he didn't miss a trick.

"Dad, I got pie, I got you guys, and I've got a horse to ride. Life's good."

He held my gaze a beat longer, then sat back down and shook out his paper.

Nice try, Pepper, I thought. But he wasn't buying it. Neither was Mom. I felt her questioning gaze as I pretended to tighten the foil wrap around her pie.

Of course I had that look. Preoccupied, tight. Because that's exactly how I felt. And my look and posture were about to become even more intense.

Chapter 7

A herd of worries milled in my mind as I sat on Jeanne Allende's bay mare in the outdoor arena at Brassbottom Barn. It was just past ten. All was quiet, hardly anyone else was there. Only young Jeanne. I was glad for that.

The horse was a hot handful. Tossing her head and dancing, she'd been that way from the minute I toed the stirrup and stepped aboard. I knew she would be. I had seen the witch pull the same crap with Sandra's daughter, now slouched with a pout as she leaned against the fence. Oddly, the pout made her dark beauty even more fascinating.

How in hell could Jeanne possibly ride this dumb bronc at the World Show in less than two weeks? Let alone contend for a championship? What had Sandra Allende been thinking, letting her husband buy their younger daughter this "proven show winner?"

The horse was gorgeous. She had a chiseled head, long sweeping legs and nice body with a fist-sized white spot underneath. Having Quarter Horse parents and a body spot with pink underlying skin qualified her for registration in both the American Quarter Horse and the American Paint Horse associations. Double registry meant double value.

But the horse also was double deadly. A wreck waiting to happen. She trembled beneath me. Why in hell had I thought I could calm her down enough for Jeanne to ride?

The skinny brunette in pencil jeans, candy-pink cap and matching parka had stepped off, tears brimming, to beg for my help getting her horse under control. Being the only other rider at the barn, and having already turned the geldings into their outdoor pens, I'd reluctantly agreed.

Dutch and Donna were gone to judge that show in Eugene. Jeanne's realtor-mom was meeting a client. And my other buddies were MIA because Dutch Bros. coffee company – no relation to our trainers – was staging a "Buy One/Get One Free" flash special on caffeinated drinks and sweetly sinful pastries.

So I had taken the reins along with a deep breath. I'd ridden horses for forty of my fifty-some years, was fit from riding and dancing, and had the guts and gumption of a former big-town reporter. Plus I liked helping people. I, Pepper Kane, could do this.

The mare rolled her eye, taking my measure in her side vision. I settled deeper into the cold, hard western saddle.

Jig, jig, toss, toss. A rattling snort sent a white gob of horse snot hurtling toward Jeanne. She ducked. It flew by, hitting Grace the Rottie, who shook her head.

With one rein I pulled the mare's head halfway around to my knee. I circled her at a walk in each direction. Then I applied gentle pressure with my seat and legs, and fingered the reins, trying to persuade the horse to lower her head.

"Whoa," I said. "Easy, now. We're going to stand and catch our breath."

But instead of settling and exhaling loudly to show she had relaxed like she did when our trainers were aboard, the mare froze. So did I. This could signal disaster.

I knew then I was in way over my head. This horse's brain had been scorched with too much pressure, bad training, excessive showing, or all of the above. She probably was drugged or exhausted or both, when shown to the Allendes.

I could get killed. Or bucked off hard, and lamed for life. What was I thinking? Plus, if I survived, my well-meaning little "catch ride" would get back to the Grandeens, who'd hit the roof. As a boarder with my own horse in training, I shouldn't have agreed to help Jeanne. My twin flaws of pride and impatience had been my undoing more often than I cared to admit.

Shoulda, woulda, coulda. I should have declined to help Jeanne. I should have waited for Dutch. But it was what it was. Now I had to make the best of things. If the mare were allowed to get away with her naughty ways, she'd be even worse the next time.

The horse still stood as solid as an ice sculpture. All I could do was wait, heart in mouth.

"Shall I get a long line?" said Jeanne. "We could run her around on it to burn off energy. I've seen Dutch do that.

The mare began backing up. Oh, great. Now a backing runaway. I clucked with my tongue to urge her forward, and softly flagged her sides with my legs.

"Maybe," I said, kicking faster.

The bay hesitated, and then locked up again. I was in very deep doodoo.

Jeanne jogged to the barn for a twelve-foot whip and a thirty-foot, twisted cotton rope with a snap at one end and a hand-loop at the other.

The mare looked after the girl. Something shifted. I felt a slight relaxation as her attention was diverted. I tried to relax and, as our trainers always advised, just breathe.

Jeanne jogged back with the longe line. She clipped one end to the front of the noseband under the bridle, handed the other end to me, and headed back to the rail.

Since the mare was stopped and not at the moment agitated, I dismounted. Handling the line in one hand and the whip in the other, I sent her out trotting on a twenty-foot-radius circle around me. I focused on her hip, which encouraged her to keep moving. The mare bucked, getting out her frustration. But she finally lined out loping, ears forward, tail relaxed.

I was beginning to relax myself. I believed I'd dodged the bullet.

"She looks way better," Jeanne said, her pout replaced with smile, her eyes round and hopeful. "I bet she'd be okay to ride now. But would you try her first?"

"No problem," I said, faking my confidence before feeling it. I spent a few more minutes working the horse from the ground. I made her move away from a tap of my hand, or come up after being run around. No more bucks or backing. She had settled.

I stepped aboard again and urged the mare forward into a soft jog. Big exhale. I rode five more minutes, trotting and loping circles, then dismounted and handed the mare back to Jeanne.

"Star wasn't this way when you tried her?" I said as Jeanne adjusted the stirrups.

"No, not at all," Jeanne said, squinting back at me in the harsh, brightening light.

"Maybe the seller will take her back ..."

"Oh, no!' said Jeanne. "She's a Dark Superstar filly. Plus out of a leading mare. I just know I'll win a world championship on her. They guaranteed it."

My mind jumped. How could anyone guarantee anything, when it came to horses?

"She is pretty fancy. Must have cost a fortune."

"Oh, no. Breeder was asking a hundred K, but we got her for seventy. I so want to win at the Worlds. It's my life dream, and I finally have the horse to do it."

"She could if she were better minded," I said. "Bit of a burnout."

"We heard the best horses have the worst attitudes," Jeanne said. "The Grandeens will make her right.

Dutch is famous for fixing horses. Part of why we brought her here."

"Well, I hope your dream comes true," I said, not sure if even Dutch could fix this horse.

I felt something was off, though I couldn't say what. Just the situation, the desperation, the perhaps unrealistic hopes. Something more than a spoiled-rotten horse and a gently spoiled daughter. Something to do with threats including the name of this horse's sire, Dark Superstar. Yet those threats related to judges keeping Superstar horses out of the world show placings. Jeanne was going to be one very disappointed girl, if those threats got traction.

Jeanne swung aboard her mare and let it stand awhile as they got the feel of each other.

"Star feels okay, now," she said. "Hey, thanks, Pepper."

"Maybe you can help me with something, too."

"What's that?"

It was a long shot. I didn't know Jeanne that well. But I burned to learn.

"Your mom says your sister, Nancy, is a great rider, too. She could have had a wonderful horse for the Worlds. Are you in contact with her, or know why she ran away?"

Jeanne gave me a long, guarded look. In that moment she appeared like a young version of Sandra. Beautiful, warm and poised, but sometimes closed for too-personal business.

"Guess she had her reasons," Jeanne said, looking down. "She can come back any time, get a horse, go show. Her call." Jeanne drew herself up in the saddle and jogged away.

Again, I kicked myself. I had gone a little too far. But, as I often said, quoting someone famous, "If you don't go too far, how do you know how far you can go?" If I could tease out even a speck of a clue to the why of the daughter's runaway, maybe I could help her and her parents, even finger a possible abductor. At least I'd rest easier knowing I'd tried.

Jeanne rode and I hung on the rail, making sure she didn't get into trouble again. I felt things were going to be fine. At least from a riding standpoint.

But I also was spitting mad. Not at Jeanne or the horse. At myself. I shouldn't have taken a chance on getting hurt, or taken the time, period, to ride Star. I was already up to my thinning eyebrows in preparation for WOWS. I not only had to work long hours at my store next week to offset travel and show expenses nearing $10,000 for this one big gig, but also to ready my own clothes and tack, and my own horse, as well as stay mentally tight. My plane for the Southland left at o-dark-thirty in ten days.

The World Open Western Show. Only the pinnacle of the Western horse-show world. All I had worked toward. If I'd been hurt, all the blood, sweat, tears and money I'd spent readying for it would've been wasted. One bad injury from a fall could have dashed a lifelong dream. Maybe put it beyond reach forever. I didn't even want to think what would happen to Mom and Dad already barely getting by at their farm near the Applegate River outside Grants Pass. Although I loved my folks dearly, they did keep me hopping to fulfill their needs. Luckily Chili would be looking in on them while we were gone to "The Worlds" – the "s" added by competitors to give the phrase a fun slangy touch.

Jeanne rode over to the fence where I stood, about to go get my own horse.

"Thanks again," she said. "Don't know what I'd have done, without your help."

"No problem. Just stay centered, relaxed. Don't box her in with your hands or legs."

The teen edged the mare into a walk on a loose rein.

"Yell if you need help," I called over my shoulder.

Chapter 8

Choc greeted me with a nicker, a toss of his blazed chestnut head, and widened eyes that showed the whites. What a character. I pulled a baby carrot from my jeans pocket, and opened my palm flat for him to gobble the treat. As he chewed, I unblanketed him, and then led him to the open-ended grooming stall.

His shod hoofs on the concrete made a metallic clip-clop that sounded like clicking of a giant grandfather clock. Clip, clop, clip, clop. It made me hyper aware of time ticking away toward the Worlds.

Other sounds began to fill the barn. Jody and her husband Carlos scrubbed and refilled water tubs at the far end of the aisle. Horses that I hadn't turned out munched hay from floors and mangers. My Brassbottom buddies chattered like squirrels as they filed in.

"How's it hangin', Pep?" said the darkly voluptuous Victoria Whitfield-Smith III with a swish of her black mane and a bump of her full hips. Our barn vixen looked especially hot in a fitted red-satin jacket and poured-on black jeans.

"Closer to the ground every day," I grinned. I bent over, pulled one of Choc's hooves on my knee and used a metal hoofpick to chip out packed manure and dirty stall shavings. This daily chore kept wet, accumulated yuck from causing thrush, a crippling hoof-rot disease. Horses on pasture or in the wild did not have to stand on soiled bedding.

I felt another presence hovering as I moved to Choc's hind hooves.

"Hey, Pep. You turn out my horse already?"

It was Barbara Garber, the gum-smacking, grey-haired and pleasingly plump horse-show veteran on the verge of retiring from the competitive rat race. This might be her last Worlds. She lately had become more interested in raising her grandkids, foals and French bulldogs at her and her husband's farm nearby. Her last, best ticket to ride for glory was her liver-chestnut, Shiny Chocolate, a talented son of Dark Superstar's leading competitor, Shiny Suspicion.

Resplendent in a fringed red blouse, and clutching a grande Dutch Bros. takeout cup, Barb cocked her head. I wished I'd thought to grab some DB before coming to the barn.

"Yeah, Alfie's out in pen two," I said, referring to her handsome dark gelding who often dangled a wisp of alfalfa from his lips. Hence his "Our Gang" nickname, Alfalfa – or Alfie, for short. The Grandeens had made him a World Champion Open Western-pleasure horse. But our Barb, living with MS, desperately wanted a prime-time amateur-rider championship for herself.

That set me wondering. Did Barb want a world championship badly enough to threaten judges so her horse had a better chance at winning top honors? It occurred to me that reverse psychology like that would sway them to place the Superstars higher. Barb was a nice gal, easygoing, fun. But her competitive streak ran strong and deep. No one knew what went on behind closed stable doors.

"You set to win at the Worlds?" I asked as she turned to go get her horse. "Pretty big deal for all of us, but with your condition –"

"I'd better be set," she said, snapping her head and widening her eyes. "Lord know I've worked long enough for a world title." She popped her gum. "The MS is not making life any easier, Pep. Sometimes I can barely get out of bed. Doc says this might be my last chance."

I pondered her words as I watched her march down the aisle toward the back door. Her stride and posture seemed normal for one older and overweight, with a touch of arthritis. But I also knew she took meds for all that. Anything to keep going.

As I gave Choc final swipes of the body brush, Lana Holmes walked up. Her spiked, rainbow-streaked hair glowed under the skylights. Taking a hipshot stance, she pressed her purple-painted lips together and raised a painted eyebrow. Her green eyes sparkled with mischief. She was a frisky one, but was as true as the day was long.

"Y'all ready for Texas?" she drawled.

"Getting there, Lana," I said, reaching for Choc's pad and Western saddle on a rack. "Never enough time. How about you?"

"Think I'm set. But I'm jittery as a cow on ice, thinking about all those cute cowgirls down in Texas."

"I can imagine," I said, seeing in my mind's eye the hundreds of fit contestants in their crisply shaped hats, jackets or vests, and tight, fringed shotgun chaps.

"Showing does seem to be a Girl Thing," I said. "Except for roping and cattle classes."

"And halter," Lana said. "Where you pay some guy in a two-thousand-dollar hat to walk around with your fat fancy horse. A guy with a famous name who has an 'in' with judges."

"There is that," I chuckled. "Always the politics." I flashed on last night's call from Donna, and on threats now facing her husband and other World Show judges.

"Always," Lana nodded. She turned to stride down the barn aisle to get her horse—another Superstar. By noon the indoor and outdoor arenas hummed with riders putting horses through their paces. Straight down the rail or in the center, tracing circles and diagonals. Over poles laid out at different spaces apart to suit each gait, walk, jog or lope.

And through artificial gates — two wooden standards connected at the top by a rope with a loop over one post.

You had to smoothly approach the gate, lift the loop off the first standard, maneuver your horse effortlessly through the gate, turn and replace the loop. Working such obstacles showed judges that your horse could negotiate challenges you might find riding the range or a trail.

Yeah, right. A gate made of a looped rope. Like that would hold back stock on the range.

Anyway, the name of the show game was to demonstrate willingness, even good cheer, in your horse. Willingness to perform any maneuver you asked, ears forward and tail relaxed, rather than ears pinned and tail madly swishing.

As with any sport or discipline, you had to make the difficult look easy. And fun.

I rode Choc an hour, put him away and got ready to head for the Horsehouse. Tulip was subbing all day as a receptionist at Freddie's Manes 'N Tails salon in Grants Pass. I had put Little Stewie's mom to work opening the store. But I had to jet over there for what I hoped would be another afternoon's land-office business.

I lingered inside the barn doors, pretending to study the show photos on the wall. With my mind free of training issues, those worries about the judge threats, and Sandra's ride with Stavropolis, took center stage in my mind. As riders came back from schooling their horses, I'd toss them remarks that might point the way to answers to what needled me.

Va-va Victoria Whitfield-Smith III first came into view leading her black horse.

"How was your ride, Vic?" I began.

"So-so," she said, halting. "How about yours?"

"Good," I said. "I was thinking we'd see Sandra today, as she offered to help me with a few things about my riding. Her previous trainer has a different take than Dutch or Donna."

"That was nice of her," said Victoria, shaking her head to sling her thick dark hair over her shoulders. A breath of costly Asian perfume mixed with horse smell wafted past me. "You girls are getting pretty tight. Yah, Saturday's a big day for realtors. Probably doing showings."

"Vic, I'm a little worried about her riding Monday on Table Rock with Reg Stavropolis. You heard about the recent attacks on women out in the wild with new guys. I've heard Stavropolis has a bad rep with women, and a worse temper."

She wrinkled her ivory brow.

"Well, I do know his ex-wife filed a domestic abuse charge. Or two. Didn't come to much, since he has the best lawyers money can buy."

"Ok-aay." I waited for more. Old reporter trick. Leave an opening in a conversation and the one being questioned will want to fill it.

"A gal pal I know dated Reg, and said the dude made her wear little-girl school uniforms. And that he keeps whips, shackles and mink-handcuffs in his boudoir." Victoria raised a black eyebrow and slanted me a look.

"Oh, Vic," I laughed. "I hate the violence charge. But keeping sex toys is no crime. You, of all people, should know that."

Vic sniffed, pooched out her glossy lips, and led her horse away.

It was nothing more than gossip. But, I reasoned, where there's a smoke wisp of gossip, there's often a blaze of truth. So now I had added cause to worry about my new friend.

Jeanne Allende gave me even more reason. To worry not only about her mother and Reg, but also about our trainers, the Grandeens. And about her missing sister.

I stopped Jeanne as she led her mare, unsaddled and lathered from the workout, to the wash rack, an open ended stall with hoses, hot and cold water and heat lamps.

"How'd it go, Jeanne?" I said while she clipped ropes fastened to each wall, to each side of her horse's halter. "Star give you any more trouble?"

"She was good," Jeanne said. "Nice of you to help. Thanks, again."

"Our little secret?" I said in a conspiratorial tone. "No need to tell Dutch or Donna."

"Oh, no problem," she said, looking up from adjusting the hose spray to the proper pressure and temperature. "I can keep a secret."

"Dutch has enough to worry about," I said. "With the Worlds and all. You know, he and other judges were warned not to place Superstar horses too high."

Jeanne stopped and looked over at me.

"Really?"

"Since you own a Superstar horse, I thought you should know," I said.

"Huh." She paused a moment, then fiddled with the hose-sprayer lever. "That's weird."

"So, as Dutch and you and our other Superstar offspring owners are at risk, can you think why someone would want the Superstars placed low? Just brainstorming here."

She gave me a blank look and shook her head

"Not a clue."

"You and your mom know people in the high-end horse world. Trainers in California and Arizona, show people buying horse properties. Maybe some or all the judges."

I waited some more.

The bay mare stamped its foot and tossed its head, impatient to get on with things.

Jeanne chewed her lower lip. She looked up at me with an expression somewhere between disbelief and annoyance. Hard to read.

"I really haven't a clue. Wouldn't want to be in Dutch's shoes ... or boots." She gave a weak smile and turned to spray her mare, who threw up her head when warm water pelted it.

I waited until Jeanne shut off the sprayer and crossed to her horse's other side.

"I'm talking to everyone," I said. "Maybe you could ask your mom," I said. "I'm asking not only for myself, but for all of us. Donna wants me to help..."

"Oka-ay." Jeanne gave me a puzzled but slightly hard look from under her horse's neck.

"Just one more thing, then I'll leave you alone," I said, loud enough to be heard over the spraying water. "I know you'd both like to find your sister. I was a reporter. Maybe I can help?"

The spray cut off. A long silence in the wash rack made me hyper-aware of the whinnies, hoofbeats and bird chirps inside the barn.

"I think you'd better talk to my mom."

With that, Jeanne began spraying again. She had cranked the water pressure up to firehose strength. Our conversation – if you could call it that – was over.

But only for the time being. I'd put Jeanne off a little. What I wanted to know was if her anger were caused by my pushiness, or my questions. I had the distinct feeling she had something more to tell. That she had something more she might need to tell.

Now the trick was to find out which it was, and what lay back of it.

Chapter 9

I gobbled my Wal-Mart deli sandwich on the short drive to the Horsehouse. The spicy meat and peppers would give me heartburn, but they were just so freaking tasty. I thought of Mom's comment that I might be gaining weight. If she were so worried, why did she keep forcing to-die-for pies on me?

Parking the dually next to the long tack-trailer behind our store, I could tell the place was slammed the minute my pie and I walked through the back door. A happy hubbub rose above the smooth tunes pouring from the speakers. Some dozen people perused shelves and rounders. They tried on boots, held up blouses and gathered up grooming gear by the armload.

I washed up before slipping around the corner to greet the public and my Saturday help.

Karen Mikulski, Little Stewie's mom, rolled her eyes as I approached the counter which, for the moment, was devoid of customers. Her streaked chestnut hair looked more ruffled than usual. But her peach blouse and black leggings in short boots neatly traced her ample curves.

"Boy, am I glad to see you," she said, running a hand through her 'do. "I've got a PT customer in a half hour. Gotta run."

"Had to take my parents some meds and grab a quick ride, or I would've been here sooner," I said. "Sorry."

"How is Martha? We need to schedule her for another physical therapy session." Karen slung a black, suitcase-sized-handbag over her shoulder.

"Mom's good, Karen, but could use more of your magic touch. Hope your work here this morning wasn't too tough. Thanks again."

"We're good. It's been fun. See ya. Good luck."

She scurried out the door as customers circled like sharks around the checkout counter. I slapped on a smile and paddled over to meet them.

Just like that, my other worries floated away. New, shorter-lived ones rolled in – such as how to keep everyone happy while I filled the till and held onto my sanity. It was almost déjà vu of the day before. A stream of customers vied for attention, for this or that piece of tack, and for a discount, though we rarely gave them.

"I could just die for this saddle pad," said a familiar voice behind me as I tucked another customer's receipt in a Horsehouse-logo bag and sent her on her way. I spun around to see full-figured Sarah Banks, a tough little brunette barrel-racer with crystal studs through her eyebrows. She stroked a large woven rectangle of hot pink and turquoise wool edged with rhinestone crosses. The teen closed her eyes as if in bliss.

"Those pads just came in last week," I said, noting her blinged out, pink-and-turquoise boots. "They've been flying out the door. This is the very last one."

"Will you give me a discount?" Sarah said. "Please? I'm on a tight budget and have to come up with an entry fee for tomorrow's race ..." She gave me the puppy-dog eye.

Was she also pouting out that lower lip? Really? It had never worked whenever my Chili put the pout on me years ago. I was damned it if I'd let it work with Sarah, either. Teenagers.

"Well, honey, can't your daddy help you out?"

"He just helped me with a ginormous vet bill. But my horse and I are gonna make the pay window tomorrow.

Dash is running so good. Even my old high-school equestrian coach says so. Pretty please?"

My shoulders sagged.

"What price is on the tag?" I said, putting off the inevitable. I so knew the feeling of craving tack or show apparel I was convinced could make or break me in competition.

"Seventy-five."

"Seventy-five. Let's see ... I could do seventy ..."

"Yes!" She pumped a fist. "You're awesome."

A flush heated my cheeks. I smiled at three others standing in line to make purchases.

"Be with you in a minute," I said. "Thanks for your patience."

"I can put twenty down," Sarah said. "Pay the rest after tomorrow. I'll do an I.O.U."

Damn. The young lady was a barracuda. But I had other customers waiting.

"Okay. Just this once. But don't tell anyone."

I'd caved. But Sarah was a good customer. And I knew her father, Jesse Banks, that cute fireplug-of-a-contractor who did much work for me at my home. A mister fix-all on call, with benefits that included a quick friendly kiss or two, though he always angled for more.

I slid a notepad across the counter. Sarah slapped down a crinkled twenty. She scribbled an I.O.U, and then flashed a high-wattage smile, hugged the saddle-pad to her rounded bosom, and line-danced out of the store. Will to win, no matter what. Hey, I could relate.

The other sales that day were not nearly as taxing. Pretty straightforward: "This is what I want, here's my money, thanks a lot, see ya later." At five I turned the door sign to "closed" and made a beeline for Rogue Farm and Feed Co-op in Central Point. I'd buy dog food and horse supplement, plus a dozen bags of stall-bedding pellets. My home stocks had gotten low, what with all my time and attention going to work and worry.

Farm and Feed was slammed, too, it being nearly five-thirty on a busy fall Saturday.

Maxine George stood at register one, just finishing up with an old cowboy who had a blue-heeler dog glued to his side. Hard to tell where the denim ended and the dog began. The cowboy nodded at me and my heavy sacks as he worked his wallet into a hip pocket. After taking eons to secure it, he kissed to the dog, nodded to Maxine and gathered his sacks. Finally leaving the counter, he sauntered toward the glass doors.

No really, dude, I thought. Take all the time you need. Some people.

I hefted my dog food onto the counter.

"Hey, Pepper," said Maxine, peering warmly through her coke-bottle-lens glasses. "Long time no see." Her brown-streaked gray hair was in a loose topknot today, and she wore a fleecy gray top with faded jeans. Crystal-studded bronze Texas stars flashed on her earlobes – her only concession to fashion.

"How are you, Maxine?" I said. "How's Boo?" Boo George, a cousin of my darling Sonny Chief, worked for the sheriff's department in Jackson County.

"Can't complain," she winked. "But I will anyway."

I reached into a nearby cubby, snatched some sugar-less gum packets and tossed them on the counter. My sweet tooth had a craving.

"Heard from Sonny?" Maxine said.

"Not lately," I said. "But I hope to soon. He's been busy with that pipeline protest near the Standing Rock rez."

"It's a mess up there. Weather getting colder, and all."

I gave her a short list of my feed and bedding needs, which I'd pick up at the adjoining Farm and Feed warehouse on my way home. I showed her my store discount card and then swiped my debit card. She tapped the register and waited for the receipts to spit out.

"How're things at Brassbottom?" she said. "Aren't you headed for a big show in Texas?"

"It's good," I said, remembering that Maxine, a black-belt gossip gal, might help me with something besides feed and bedding. "We have a great new rider, that realtor, Sandra Allende, whose billboards are popping up all over?"

"Pretty gal," Maxine nodded encouragingly. "Don't know what's taking this freaking register so long. Must be made in China." She jiggled buttons.

"She's hooking up with that developer, Reg Stavropolis," I said. "You've heard of him."

"Reg Stavropolis," she nodded, though her eyebrows lifted. "Yeah. Very big dog."

"A big dog with a sketchy rep," I said. "They're riding on a first date Monday on Table Rock. Know anything about the guy?"

Maxine leaned in to whisper, ignoring other customers cooling their heels behind me.

"I wouldn't go near that one," she rasped. "Very bad news."

"How so?"

"I heard Boo and another deputy talking at a barbecue at our house this summer," she said. "Boo wondered how a guy like that who can buy any kind of action, would rough up his wife because she wouldn't have a threesome with some young girl."

Crap. Worse than I'd feared.

There was a cough in line behind me. I had to get going. But I wanted to hear more.

"Thanks, Maxine. Call or text if you hear anything more. Boo has my number."

"No prob. Your friend probably shouldn't go riding alone with that guy until she knows him better. If at all. Just tell her to be careful."

I picked up my supplies at the warehouse, and then hauled for home in a bigger cloud of worry than when I'd left that morning. I fed the horses, cat and dogs, and fried myself steak and eggs with steamed asparagus. I ate a little pie. Then I watched some TV news. I played with Charlie and Shayna. I even lingered in the shower, trying to wash away my harried day.

But I remained curious as a horse, to tweak a cliché. Would Sandra be safe out in the middle of lonesome with a seriously hot, seriously rich playboy who, in Maxine's husband's words, "could buy any action he wanted," yet still roughed up his own wife?

When you came down to it, her ride with Reg, on its face, was not my concern. None of my business. I didn't need to complicate my own life by getting involved in her affairs. I didn't have time, with the World Show coming up, and threats to judges to be solved. Sandra was, as she said, a big girl. She could take care of herself.

But in the short time we'd known each other, I had grown to care about Sandra, and she seemed to care about me. I considered her a friend. We had some important things in common – horses, daughters, the need for a solid relationship, a driving desire to win. We'd shared some riding tips, dreams and secrets – what makes a friendship blossom.

And once I make a friend, a "chosen sister," in another friend's words, I tend to care what happens with her. Not only care in my heart and mind, but also demonstrate it.

I couldn't help myself. My new friend was going out, in relative wilderness, on a first date with a mercurial, reportedly dangerous man: the infamous Reg Stavropolis. It just felt wrong. I wasn't going to let it go.

Chapter 10

I went about my normal routines, but underneath I felt agitated, as if something bad were about to happen. Maybe my makeup, or maybe my reporter's sixth sense. What would it hurt to do a little investigating? If I found nothing I could calm that agitation, and go on with my life.

First I'd check for any news items about Stavropolis' divorce circumstances, and his trying to run down that employee of his. But I'd also look into connection Sandra and her ex might have with Western horse-show elite, stallion owners and such, to shed light on why she would let her ex-husband buy a nut-case horse for her daughter – if they'd known it was a nut case.

I also should look into any stories about the missing daughter, that promising horse-show competitor who just gave up her family, wealth and privilege for a different life. Was starry-eyed Nancy merely a runaway, unhappy at home and low in self-esteem, who'd seen her chance at Hollywood and taken it? Or was there something I wasn't seeing?

After my shower that evening I dressed in comfy sweats, plunked down at my computer and prepared to scratch my ex-reporter's itch.

I was encouraged in this by Tulip, who had poked her nose in to good effect on more than one of my crime-solving capers. She called after dinner to ask how we'd done at the Horsehouse that day and to see if I'd be riding tomorrow at the barn. I spilled the gossip about Reg, told her I'd ridden Jeanne's wacko horse, and confessed my fears not only about Sandra and Reg's ride, but also about the death threats to Dutch and the other judges. That Dutch might be in danger or that he somehow was involved in the threats. At least one of his training horses – Barbara's, was sired by Shiny Suspicion, Superstar's main rival.

Tulip already knew about the threat to Dutch. She'd talked with Donna Grandeen when she'd gone to Brassbottom to check on her horse after working at Freddie's. She dismissed my blue-sky theory about Dutch possibly being involved in the threats.

"Pooh," she huffed over the phone "Grasping at straws."

But she sounded mildly surprised to learn the latest I'd heard about Stavropolis.

"Why not check him out in the papers and criminal-check sites, Pep? And call your fix-it friend, Jesse Banks. He's been in construction here for eons. May know a useful tidbit on Reg."

"Good idea," I said. "I'll call Jesse, and then jump online."

"Hey, Pep. Now that we're talking about Stavropolis, it's jogged my memory. Seem to recall that there was this guy here years ago, while you were in Seattle, reportedly into child porn or luring or something. And might not be him. But had a Greek-sounding name. Carl or Nick or something like that with a long-ass last name."

"Really," I said. "I'll check it out. Thanks, Tularoo. See you tomorrow."

A quick call to Jesse, my construction-worker pal, went to voice mail. I left a message.

Then I settled into my spare-bedroom office with the dogs curled around my feet, and checked Stavropolis out online. Maybe I would find something to tell Sandra. I'd check her out, too, long as I was checking. Just part of being thorough, and fair.

Reginald Stavropolis. Bonded and insured contractor/developer of long standing. Born and raised in California. Divorced, aged fifty, eleven years older than Sandra and a few years younger than I. Zero on him regarding any child porn or related crimes.

From the photos, Reg was as big, bony and black-haired as my invincible Sioux warrior and traditional Indian man, Sonny Chief. But considerably richer. Reg had pricey projects from Red Bluff to Roseburg, and out on the Oregon Coast. Couple of restaurants and bars connected to those developments. A dozen names, addresses, descriptions. He did get around.

I saw he was involved in controversial gold-mining projects on the Rogue, as well as on its tributaries including the vineyard-watering Applegate and pristine-green Illinois.

So he was successful. No news there. But he also was heavily litigated. Suits against him for everything real-estate, notably for permit-bending and for allegedly bankrupting a real-estate partner. Definitely not straight-arrow. Maybe he'd sought out our newcomer, Sandra, for his latest scam. With benefits.

About an hour in, wearying, I virtually jumped over to Facebook. I flipped through my news feed first.

I was surprised at a post from Rose Charging, another Lakota friend from my Seattle days. My heart did a flip as I saw the photo of my Sonny Chief, dancing in full regalia. Full throttle heartbreaker, his darkly handsome face and limbs gleaming with sweat.

"Sonny Chief won his category at the big Tacoma Pow-Wow," Rose's message began. "Women hanging on him like elk teeth and bugle beads. But he put it all into his dancing. He wore his new outfit and was amazing. Won a thousand dollars."

Amazing didn't quite cover it. Or my reaction to it.

The photo showed the statuesque Sonny, fringe and feathers flying, caught in a fast spin as the drummers raised their drumsticks and vocalized in the blurred background.

I saved, enlarged and printed the photo, leaning over in anticipation as the printer clicked, whirred and spat out the image on paper. Then I lay the page on my lap. I studied every inch of it, and ran my fingertip over the picture of Sonny's impossibly long, lean body.

What I could see of his muscular arms below the war-shirt sleeves, and of his exquisitely carved thigh and calf muscles below the ceremonial breechcloth, made my heart race. Not only did my heart race, but my nether regions tingled pleasantly. Man, I would have done anything at that moment to feel his warm, bronze skin in person. The weight of his body on mine. With me running my fingers and toes down the length of him as he fondled me with smoky, agonizing slowness. Slowness, that is, until the sparks caught and the wildfire flared, consuming us both.

I jerked involuntarily. As if awakening from a dream. Whoa! I had to have that guy in my life, somehow, some way. Maybe I'd try to call him.

Wait. Wasn't Sonny supposed to be in North Dakota? With the pipeline protestors?

I drew in a deep breath, returned to Rose's Facebook post, and checked the date and time. Okay. Right. It was a Facebook "One Year Ago Today" memory photo. Boy, I was losing it.

Last I heard, a month ago, Sonny was helping keep peace at the Dakota Access Pipeline Protest by people calling themselves water protectors. Since May they'd disputed the pipeline firm's plans to drill under Lake Oahe, their only water source.

Sonny had semi-retired from full-time to part-time policing for the Standing Rock people. But he had committed to work water protector camps for as long as it took to make the feds force the oil company find a safer route for that section of pipeline.

Whatever, I hoped Sonny was at last toeing the line – our line – and I'd see him again soon. Sonny hated being tied down to one place or one female. But he'd intimated more than once that I was the love of his life. Where that would go, I hadn't a clue. Still I always hoped we'd wind up together on a steadier basis.

Why was I so doggone addicted to the man? When I saw him rarely, but when I saw him, would give up practically all else to be with him. I had to address this. It didn't sound healthy or smart. Yet on some level it worked.

I sighed and stared at the photo one last time before filing it away in my "Sonny" folder. An actual manila folder, not an electronic file. I like hard copies. So to speak.

Well, our relationship was what it was. Maybe I actually liked being single, unattached, as much as he did. But single with a lifeline attached to one special person vested with what seemed like semi-permanent qualities. Was that it? And was I ready to accept that in myself? Questions for later. Much later. Right now I had more research to do. It was growing late.

I set aside Sonny's folder, and my thoughts about Sonny and singlehood, to do a little research on Sandra Allende. At least get a toe into it. I could finish tomorrow.

What I found, in the major papers and promos, was that she was remarkable for her creative, aggressive marketing, but also for her straight-arrowness except for one small story saying she'd been accused of "real-estate irregularities" years ago. Something about missing earnest money on a joint deal with her former husband. But she, or they, were never formally charged or convicted.

Disputed contracts, fees monkeyed with – so what else was new in the cutthroat, high-end real-estate biz? A realtor friend of mine recently had been through such a dispute, and called it, "Just another day in the life."

Sandra had successfully represented many Hearst Castle- and King Ranch-wannabe horse properties in Cali and Nevada in the 2000s. She'd won honors in Southern California horse shows under top trainers. She'd once even owned a champion bred by Royce and Rogers of Shiny Suspicion-stallion fame, before switching to the Dark Superstar offspring.

But clean as the proverbial whistle. Except the nasty, years-long divorce, of course. That had been finalized months ago, after years in the making. Among the divorce stories there was information about Sandra's ex, Maximilian Allende, a NorCal broker and investor, as well as an avid trader in American Indian artifacts. A one-time body builder who won minor titles. The father of Jeanne and Nancy.

My mind, if not my butt, was falling asleep. My eyes burned. I was about ready to give up and go to bed but I would follow only one or two more leads, jotting notes. That's when I came across a small, previously overlooked newspaper article from a Northern California community newspaper. The headline made my blood run cold:

HIGH-PROFILE REALTOR SAYS
TEEN DAUGHTER TRAFFICKED

I couldn't believe I hadn't come across this story already. Must've blown right by it. But there it was staring me in my bleary-eyed face.

The story from six months ago said that Sandra Allende, shortly after Nancy ran away, had tried to convince police in Redding and elsewhere that her daughter might have been lured away, perhaps by a slightly older man. An unnamed girlfriend of Nancy had come forward to defend Nancy's decision saying she was "no way trafficked" but had gone willingly "with a man she loved" who worked in or near Medford.

The friend was quoted as saying the man worked in "something like land." But also that he'd worked as a Hollywood stuntman. Aligned with what Sandra had told me.

I also printed out a photo of Nancy, said to be a "redhead with tattoos and piercings." Standing five-nine, weighing one-seventy. The height I got, seeing Sandra and Jeanne. And Nancy was only slightly overweight. Pounds that probably just made her "curvy."

Dressed in a black turtleneck, with long, poufy hair flowing past her shoulders, she stared into the camera, her eyes dreamy, yet haunted. She had a bit of the old-school glam movie-star look. What ended the resemblance was a huge diamond stud stuck in her right nostril.

I studied her eyes. They were outlined thickly and had long lashes, possibly extensions like Tulip's. Uber-fashionable girls did that these days, so she need not have troweled on the eyeliner and mascara. Her lashes, while not as thick as Tulip's, suggested an insecurity, and generated suspicion that Nancy hadn't thought makeup alone was enough to get her noticed.

My heart went out to her. She still had a touchingly vulnerable look about her. Insecure, dreamy, wounded. All excellent reasons for trying to make her own way.

There was another, much tinier photo reproduced from a real-estate flyer about a deluxe Nevada ranch. It was like the ones I'd seen showing Jeanne, but now I realized the other model beside the pools was Nancy, her curves stuffed into a bikini. The photo fit in with Nancy's reported dreams of modeling and acting.

The police, who farther down in the story identified Sandra as "the prominent realtor last year accused of real-estate irregularities," told the newspaper they had "looked into Sandra's trafficking assertion and dismissed her claims as unfounded." They'd turned up nothing indicating that the girl had left involuntarily. They'd put the case on the back burner.

Still, I wondered. I'd already known that Nancy might be in the Rogue Valley, or not far away, with a boyfriend from the area. Sandra had said she'd come here. The friend even said so. Could that be the real reason why Sandra had opened a second office and leased a condo here? Not only because she needed a new start after her divorce, but also because she was trying to track down her daughter here, or a possible abductor or seducer of her daughter? Now I burned even more with curiosity, and with more questions.

Before finishing for the night I printed out six copies of the newspaper photo of Nancy. I would try to squeeze out time to show them around, maybe at a few building sites, to see if anyone there recognized her.

That done, I changed into my coziest sleepshirt, turned down the thermostat, and snuggled into my queen bed. Soon the dogs and I were bagging Z's big time.

Halfway through the night, I awakened to feel Shayna, and then Charlie, wriggle from the covers. They began growling. Sprouting goosebumps and propped by an elbow on my pillow, I listened intently. Was one of the horses in trouble down at the stable?

Neighbor dogs down the road began to bark. That set mine barking. Not desultory watchdog barks, but rapid vocalizations that meant imminent danger.

I shuffled to the window and peered out. I could see nothing in the dark, nor in the beam of the security lights. Nor could I hear anything other than barking, which slowly subsided. Whatever had disturbed my mini-mastiffs was no longer an issue.

I used the loo, gulped down cold water and tried to sink once more into slumber. I reflected that my rural neighborhood, although host to a handful of marijuana grows, rarely entertained anything more exciting than a coyote, possum or raccoon. My neighbors said they'd recently seen a 'coon living in my driveway's conduit. That I should call an exterminator.

Yeah. A raccoon. That's probably all it had been.

Chapter 11

Sunday morning dawned bright. I slept until nearly eight, and awoke to a chorus of Boston-terrier whines indoors, and hungry-horse neighs down at the barn.

I hurried to tend to the critters and then wasted no time warming up Mom's apple pie. I mounded it with melting sharp cheddar, bacon crumbles and vanilla-bean ice cream that had a stratospheric fat content. That'd hold me for a day of relaxing, reflecting and riding – which I sorely needed and deserved. I'd done all I could for the time being regarding Reg and Sandra, Dutch and the Allende daughters. My store was closed Sundays, and my brain was fried.

For sanity's sake I would, to paraphrase Scarlett O'Hara's famous "Gone With the Wind" words, "think about that tomorrow."

I was tucking into my last helping of pie, when my cell phone rang with Dolly's vocals. Man, I needed to change that ringtone. Today, for sure.

The ID pane read, "Tommy Lee Jaymes."

Shoot. What had prompted a call from that handsome celebrity-tribute actor, a ringer for bona fide film star Tommy Lee Jones? Only this TLJ drove around the country in a fake, arrest-me-red Lamborghini, and appeared, with the real Tommy Lee's official blessing, at resorts and night clubs as well as charity galas.

"Hey, TLJ," I said. "Thought I deleted you."

"What's shakin', Reba?" he drawled, piling on the Texas twang that he probably thought might nick my resistance to him. I didn't let TLJ know that it did – despite my heart's belonging to Sonny. TLJ, who thinks I resemble Reba McEntire despite my Tinkerbelle stature, calls me every few months. He once even stopped by, trying to talk me into hitting the road with him and working as a tribute actor. Or something to that effect. To no avail.

"Up to my booty in a new case," I said, "that is a bit on the dark side, and probably none of my business."

"So what else is new, darlin'?"

I gave the CliffNotes version of my concerns about Sandra and Reg, and mentioned the missing Nancy, though they were strangers to TLJ. Thing is, he knew me, at least a little, from that stallion-killing case I'd worked on. He knew something about scams and shady dealings himself, having been a player in sketchy arrangements with auto sellers and film producers. Altered VINs. He was no Snow White.

TLJ made appropriate sympathetic noises.

Then I told him about the near-rundown of a World Show judge in Texas, and the threats to that man as well as to Dutch and the other judges we riders would be showing our horses to in a little over a week.

So far TLJ's side of the conversation had been fairly tame. Now he came to vibrant life.

"Y'all are coming to Fort Worth?" he said. "Great! Will Rogers Center is just a short hop from my ranch. I'll come root for y'all, and stake you to a steak at the Stockyards."

"We are going to be very busy, Tommy Lee," I said. "Thanks, though."

"Is your sexy girlfriend named for a flower, coming?'

"Tulip."

"That's the one. Put in a good word for me, will you?"

"Might."

"Where are y'all staying? We got a killer guesthouse at the ranch. A president's cousin stayed here once. And the real Tommy Lee Jones came to a barbecue. Now that was a hoot. People couldn't tell us apart. Story in itself. Remind me to tell you when I see you."

"I'm happy for you," I said, hoping my sarcastic tone wasn't too obvious, though it did amuse me. "Thanks. But several of us are sharing a two-bed cottage near the Will Rogers."

I mentally crossed my fingers he wouldn't key on the "bed" part.

"So what were you saying about a rundown of a judge, and threats to the others?"

I was glad he'd stepped off the innuendo train.

"Dutch's wife called me Friday and said Dick Bradford was nearly run down outside his ranch in Texas. He got a text saying he shouldn't place offspring of his stud Dark Superstar in first place in the show classes, or next time the truck wouldn't miss."

Charlie, my senior Boston Terrier, jumped back up on the recliner. He circled three times and cuddled between my outstretched legs. Shayna, my sweet, long-legged girl dog, jumped up to curl between my left thigh and Big Brown's padded leather arm.

"Well, I'll be," Tommy Lee was saying. "I know ol' Bradford. Nice guy. Lives in Pilot Point, not that far from Fort Worth. Hired me once for a charity function."

Tommy Lee, unlike his actor namesake, wasn't into horses that much. I figured the few he did own were pasture ornaments and publicity-shot décor. Or so I'd sussed out when Tulip and I met him at a cafe on our way to a California show. I didn't want to invite him into that horse world. The privilege was reserved for the truly dedicated.

"I might just give Dick a shout, see what's up. I wouldn't be too worried, if I were you, Reba. Ninety percent of threats are just that, scare tactics. Very few are followed through on."

"They sure feel real to us. And believe me, I'm going to conduct myself as if they are."

"Y'all don't worry, now. I'll do some digging. And call if I learn anything. Then see you in what, about ten days? How many of y'all's barn buddies are coming down here?"

"Eight, maybe more. Hey, if you really can help me with the judge thing, I'd appreciate it, Tommy Lee."

"Anything for a ... friend."

I appreciated his offer of help, but worried there was more behind it. Something ulterior. What was this guy to me? Almost a friend, but not quite. An amusing acquaintance, at best.

Then came the kicker.

"Say, you hear from your Indian warrior lately? What's his name again, Sonny Chief?"

I wondered when TLJ would get around to that. But I had a ready answer.

"You still married, Tommy Lee?"

"Separated, but technically still married," he chuckled. "Details."

"So still off limits, in my book," I said. "Alhough I can't speak for Tulip."

After we hung up, with TLJ safely ensconced, for now, at his Texas ranch and not bound for Southern Oregon, I sat down to do little more digging on Sandra and Reg. Having mentioned my concerns about them at the top of our conversation, I was newly focused on them. There may have been something I overlooked about Reg, the missing Nancy, or even her father. Sandra's ex. How did he feel about her disappearance? Had I missed a quote from him?

I did find an old police-blotter report from a tiny paper in the seaside town of Bandon, three hours northwest of Grants Pass. It said two girls walking near a Stavropolis condo build had been approached and offered modeling contracts by a tattooed, dark-haired man saying he worked in Medford but had Hollywood connections. They told police he gave them a long last name that sounded like "Stavropolis," but wasn't exactly it.

This probably was the incident Tulip had told me about. But it was five years ago, far away, and had merited no follow-up story.

Interesting but hardly damning. Smoke, long drifted away. And certainly no fire.

So, Reg Stavropolis: 1, Pepper Kane: 0.

I quickly reviewed stories of Nancy's disappearance. This time I focused on anything else I could learn about her father or his reaction to her running away. Could he have played a role in her decision?

"I have nothing to add," Allende was quoted as saying. "Only that we want Nancy back. She was on medication, and may experience complications from withdrawal."

There was also a business-column item noting Allende had traveled to Texas to pursue "leads on a possible expansion of his West Coast business." The end of the story alluded to a time three years ago when Allende, "whose wife and daughters ride," took a short break from selling NorCal properties to test the co-called waters in Texas, where he "had family."

Interesting. So Max Allende had ties to Texas. Did he know Dick Bradford? He'd bought Jeanne a horse sired by Bradford's Dark Superstar. Yet the threats demanded that judges block Superstar horses from wining. So how could Allende have anything to do with them?

By noon in the Rogue Valley the sun was fully high, and warm. My seat bones ached, along with my neck. I made up my mind to put the mysteries worries on hold. Downing an energy bar and filling a water bottle, I togged up and got set for a pleasant day riding with buddies at

Brassbottom Barn. I would squeeze the day for the rest and relaxation I needed.

Tulip and I had agreed to ride together. We'd practice show routines and mock-judge each other. I was sure other Brassbottom buddies would be doing the same. The atmosphere would be almost as charged as at a real show – an excellent setting in which to rehearse.

I went down to the garage, fired up the truck and drove out to my pipe-and-mesh gates. The diesel engine rattled noisily and belched out noxious fumes as I jumped from the cab to unwrap the chain holding the gates together. Anticipation flooded me. In less than twenty minutes my riding day would be underway.

But when I reached out my gloved hands to undo the chain, a thud in my gut signaled that something was wrong. The chains were not wrapped and snapped as I usually fastened them, in a tight figure eight. They were wrapped in a loose oval, the wrong way, with the snap dangling.

Somebody had been there, on my property without my knowledge. They had messed with or come through the gates during the night. So that's what the dogs had been barking about. An intruder, and not a raccoon.

An eerie chill swept through me. That weird, blood-pressure hum sounded in my head. Was someone whom I was watching, someone I was checking on or asking questions about, keeping an eye on me? Even worse, trying to frighten me?

Chapter 12

As I turned into the Brassbottom Barn parking lot, I saw half-a-dozen vehicles already there. Tulip's old pink Chevy pickup, "Peggy Sue." Lana's purple mini-SUV. And Freddie's black Land Rover. The sun made all the chrome shine, the dry oak leaves on trees around the house look brighter, and yours truly's mood lift considerably.

I scanned the vehicles for Sandra's big white dually pickup, but was disappointed not to see it. Today being a Sunday, she probably was busy, like she was the day before, showing properties or entertaining customers as part of her new local real-estate adventure.

Maybe I would see Jeanne, though. Despite my desire to enjoy the day of riding, I hoped to follow up on our talks from the day before, try to tease out more information or feelings. And maybe get myself back on her good side after having put her off by my prying. Surely she still appreciated my helping her with her horse.

The barn aisle was abuzz with people chatting, and grooming or saddling. Their horses stamped, snorted and whinnied. Dexter the cat made a beeline from the barn front to the back, racing between riders' boots and horses' hooves, oblivious to the risk of being squashed.

Gracie the Rottie lay in a corner warmed by sun pouring through a skylight. The warmth in the air intensified smells of leather, horses and alfalfa hay. My Chanel No. 5.

At Choc's stall I ran into Freddie Uffenpinscher, our bald and mustachio'd hair stylist and hunt-seat rider who looked far sleeker in breeches than did many of the female persuasion. His newly leased horse, a dark gray double-registered Paint Quarter Horse named Dark Hellza Poppin, was stalled next to my Choc. Another Dark Superstar horse.

"Hey, Pepperoni," he said, his multiple earrings and bald head catching the light. "You look hot today. Love the black jacket. Shows off your curves."

"Thanks," I said. "You don't look so bad yourself, Mister. Royal blue becomes you."

"Fit for a king," he said, attending to his horse in its stall.

"Or a queen," I muttered, haltering Choc.

"Hey. I heard that."

"Meant you to."

We led our horses out at the same time and tied them in adjacent grooming stalls vacated by other riders and horses. Close enough for us to converse as we tacked up. I felt mesmerized watching him work an assortment of brushes and combs to make his tall, elegant Poppin even shinier, if possible. The horse's charcoal coat was set off by a frosted mane and tail, and four high white stockings.

After the summer's death of his formerly leased horse, the stallion Dark Vader, Freddie had hustled to lease a new horse and hotfoot it to a Utah show to qualify for the Worlds. He'd barely made it. He'd threatened to commit hara kiri if he hadn't qualified.

Freddie had worked his whole adult life for a shot at a world championship, found the horse that could win one, and taken out a second mortgage on his new hair salon to pay for it.

Now he froze, brush clutched in one raised hand, and returned my pensive stare.

"What? I'm not brushing right?"

I laughed.

"You all set for the show? Excited to see Carlos again?"

"Yes and yes," he said, giving his horse's tail a few more licks. "You ready?"

"Ready as I'm going to be. If we're not ready after working all year, we sure won't magically make ourselves ready with less than a week left. Horses leave Thursday."

"Got that right, Girl. No, I meant, place to stay."

"Nailed that down as soon as I qualified last summer. Reserved a cute little cottage not far from the Will Rogers Memorial Center."

"Always prepared. That's my Pepper."

From the corner of my eye I saw a boyish figure leap behind me with a jingle of spurs. Choc jerked his head up as small, cold fingers clamped up over my eyes.

"Boo!" said nine-year-old Little Stewie, holding tight as I play-struggled. "Guess who?"

"The Cookie Monster?"

"No. But do ya have any cookies?"

"Is it ... John Wayne?"

Stewie's voice, deeper and more manly, belted out, "Fill your hand, you son-of-a-bitch!"

I spun around, broke his grip and shot him my meanest look.

"Stewie! What if your Mom hears you?"

"She's the one rented 'True Grit' for me last night. It's my favorite movie."

"Run along and saddle your horse so you can ride with us. We're working on trail."

I looked across at Freddie, cinching up Poppin's saddle.

"Kids are growing up faster and faster, and not always in the right ways," I said. "Blame the Internet. And hormones added to meat."

"True that," Freddie said, giving his horse a last swipe of the polishing cloth.

I studied Freddie's horse. For the first time I realized that the gelding had the exact same face markings as his sire, the prize stallion owned by Dick Bradford.

"Freddie, did you hear about the threat made Friday to Dutch, Dick Bradford and other judges set to work at the Worlds? To not give high placings to Superstar's offspring, or else?"

He looked at me. His eyes darkened and his lush mustache twitched.

"I did hear something like that. Tulip mentioned it yesterday at the salon."

"What are your thoughts? Owning a Superstar son, and all?"

"Kind of freaky," he said, rubbing his mustache with his thumb. "Bit unsettling."

"More than a bit."

"Especially since Royce and Rogers, my friend Carlos' bosses, own the majority share in their stud, Shiny Suspicion. His offspring are challenging Superstar's in the high-point standings. So it did cross my mind that Royce and Rogers, or someone in their syndicate, had something to do with the threats. Carlos got reamed out for voicing that opinion."

"Really. So there could be something there. Guess we'll have to wait until we get to the show to try to learn the truth."

He patted his horse before leading it out.

"Likely it'll come to nothing. Threats of one kind or another, rumors and such, always fly around a big show. Stakes are high, emotions higher."

He led Poppin into the aisle and toward the outdoor arena. I finished saddling Choc and led him up a few strides behind Freddie and his horse.

"So you're not too worried, Freddie?" I called.

"Not going to let it get to me. That's what they want. I'm just going to ride for the win. You know what I've sacrificed for it."

"Yes, I do. But what 'they' do you mean?"

"Whoever is making threats. And it might be totally unrelated to the two big sires. There are many other competitors riding horses by other great sires. People who wouldn't mind their horses doing better than the Superstars or the Suspicions."

My mind wanted me to go back home, study the stallions and their point placings, as well as their progeny's placings, in the latest issues of the Paint Horse Journal, the Quarter Horse Journal, and journals of other western horse registries such as Appaloosa, Palomino and Buckskin. But my body wanted to ride. It needed to ride.

And so I did. For two hours, off and on. Loping over white or striped ground poles set at six or twelve-foot intervals. Doing smooth, 360-degree turns inside a six-foot "box" made of poles, with not as much as a hoof-tap on any pole. Having Choc step onto a wooden "bridge" about a foot high and five feet long, then step down and over logs set and in an arc.

The ring was super busy as more riders came to practice. But, with the advantage of years of experience negotiating rings full of horses, we negotiated it all. Working one obstacle for as much as ten minutes, until I was satisfied with how we did it, kept other riders working other obstacles, or awaiting their turn to try mine.

Tulip and I coached and judged each other as we guided our horses in around orange cones set in a square, with ground poles – some elevated on blocks six inches high. It took a slow touch with heel and rein to run a pattern smoothly, with no hoof "ticks" on a pole.

"Lay the rein lower across his neck," she said, when Choc tilted his nose to the outside of one turn, signaling I'd cued him wrong. "Cluck, wave your legs, to make him turn tighter."

When I got it right, it was her and her horse's turn on the pattern.

"Use both hands on the reins," I suggested. "Bump his nose down, and drive him up with your legs. Make him collect and step smartly." She did so. "There."

Much of the "trail class" practice involved standing your horse at or in the middle of an obstacle. Often a horse who thinks he "knows" how to the maneuver will try to take control of the situation, do the obstacle on his own, and often in a rush, just to get it over with. Then you just whoa, sit back, take a deep breath and gaze out at other riders or the pastures. That resets everything. After a minute, you finish the maneuver and move to the next.

At one of those "rests", I let my gaze slide south to Lower Table Rock. It was, after all, such a prominent landmark in the Rogue Valley outside Medford. I'd recently hiked up it. The hard, flat, rocky top stretched out for miles, like a barren moonscape, edges softened by native trees and shrubs growing up the sides.

It gave you amazing views, especially from the steep, sharp southwest edge. Views of the Rogue River meandering through orchards and farms, views of big farms, old homes, leafy TouVelle Park, and yes, of the water-treatment plant with its "fragrant" settling ponds.

That was the view Sandra and Reg would see Monday morning on their ride. The ride that could be risky for Sandra. And the ride I shouldn't take, yet possibly might. To air out Choc's and my brain. Something like that.

If I did decide to go to ride, I definitely wouldn't take Choc. It wasn't worth laming him on the climb or on the rocks, even if I booted his feet. Choc was my potential ticket to a world championship ride. It was just too close to show time. The Grandeens would load our show ponies in their trailers on Thursday, so they would be settled into their Fort Worth stalls by Sunday for opening show-day Wednesday. It took a few days to acclimate them.

No. If I rode up Table Rock, I'd take Bob, my retired but far from retiring show horse at home. Hopefully Bob wouldn't buck me off as he had last winter. I'd only recently found nerve to get back on him and mosey around the hills.

As I put Choc away after our show practice, I felt a man's figure at my back. Before I could wonder who it was, I heard a familiar teasing voice. Dutch Grandeen's. He and Donna were back from the show they were scheduled to judge when they got Dick Bradford's frightening call and the anonymous, even more worrisome text.

I slid the stall door shut, fastened the snap and turned to face those teasing hazel eyes, tan face and lanky six feet of delightfully weathered cowboy. An impression he cultivated, much to Donna's consternation. But then, that svelte, savvy rodeo queen had her own flock of potential suitors though she rarely gave them the time of day. Stay inscrutable, cucumber cool, never let them see you sweat, was her motto.

"Thought I knew that cute booty," Dutch said, with a toothy grin and a wink.

"Damn it, Dutch, you scared me," I said. "Almost shut the door on my hand. Speak up when you're behind someone."

"I did," he said.

"How?"

"Body English." He did a quick bump.

I harrumphed and let it go. Because it was headed in a direction about which I had zero interest. But I knew it was in fun. Or, at least, mostly in fun. Trainers like him were well-nigh irresistible to love starved clients, who admired top horsemen as if they were gods. Who knew when they might get a random desire fulfilled?

Although I was fairly love starved at the moment, I was not in that league of worshippers, of ladies and gents seeking to improve the attention a trainer gave their horse – or themselves. I also refused to indulge in hanky panky with the mate of a friend, which Donna was.

Dutch knew that, or should have. I'd told him, and in exactly those words.

"How'd it go here this weekend?" he said, shifting gears, letting his fiery eyes cool down.

"Great," I said. "Nothing unusual. At least regarding the threat thing. Everyone here was pretty cool. We don't think the threats will amount to anything. And we had a great practice."

"Glad to hear it. Our gig went well, too. Plus we got the World Show committee to issue warnings that anyone making threats to judges or competitors will be disciplined up to and including being banned from the show. Or worse."

"Really?" I said. "So they are taking the threats seriously and promising action."

"They are. Takes some pressure off, that's for sure."

"So I guess we can concentrate on our preparation and showing, after all. I bet you and Donna are relieved."

"To tell the truth, Donna was more worried than I was. She's pretty protective of me."

"Regular Rottweiler," I grinned, seeing Gracie amble down the aisle toward me. ""I have some of that breeding, too. Can you at least give me an idea of who you think is behind these threats? I texted everyone, but got little. I understand that Grant Haverstadt is involved in the Shiny Suspicion syndicate, so there might be something there."

Dutch cocked his head and gave me his best cowboy squint. It held a challenge. His left cheek jumped with that odd tic he had when troubled. All he needed was a thin brown cigar, a flat brimmed hat and a striped serape to look like a spaghetti-western star.

"You fixing to play Miss Marple again?" he said, nodding. "Part-time lady sleuth?"

I considered a snappy comeback, then thought better of it.

"Been doing research, asking around. Both here and in Texas. You have to be aggressive with something like this. Let the threat maker know you won't take it sitting down."

"Well, I think it's handled," he said, his face becoming unreadable. "So relax, Pepper. I told Donna the same thing. The show committee's all over it."

I studied him. He was into his "Never-let-them-see-you-sweat mode." Probably so his clients wouldn't worry, as stress would affect their performance at the show.

"I hope you're right," I said.

He was quick to change the subject, and his features. Now he smiled languidly.

"You need a lesson on Choc tomorrow or Tuesday? Might be your last chance before we leave for Texas."

"We'll see, Dutch." I stroked Gracie's square head and ruffled her floppy black ears. "I might have plans for tomorrow."

"Who's minding your store while you and Tulip are in Texas?"

"My daughter Chili is coming down from Seattle. She'll look in on my parents, too. She's scoping out jewelry opportunities here, so she'll mix business with business, so to speak."

"That's how you get ahead," Dutch nodded. "Like mother, like daughter."

"Don't say that," I half-joked.

"Why not?"

"If she's like me, she'll find some way to annoy the dragon."

He folded his arms over his chest and arched an eyebrow.

"Speaking of," he said, folding his arms and looking serious. "I heard you rode Jeanne's horse while we were gone." He waited to hear what I'd come up with by way of an excuse.

I wracked my brain for a halfway acceptable one.

"No one else around, and she needed help, Dutch. You know that mare's a burnout, going to hurt her one day. Why do you let Jeanne go on with it? She needs a different horse."

He stiffened. He unfolded his arms. His hazel eyes turned dark.

"That's none of your business, Pepper. And neither is her training. No one should ride that horse if we're not here. Got that?"

Chapter 13

Late Sunday afternoon, I tossed in the towel. I'd had a great ride with the buddies at the Barn, been able to relax and was ready to hit the ground running on Monday. Freshly showered and full of herbed salmon and loaded baked-potato, I collapsed with the Bostons into Big Brown. I instantly dozed off.

I jolted awake when my cell phone sang out. The Bostons set up a terrible barking and jumped off the chair as I picked up the phone from the coffee table.

The ID read, "Sonny Chief." My heart leaped in happy surprise. I tucked the phone between ear and shoulder, and leaned back into Big Brown.

"Hey," I said in what I imagined was a casually sexy tone.

"Hell-o," Sonny said in his lazy, sing-song voice. "What are you doing out there in Oregon? Have a feeling I needed to call." Static crackled over the line.

"The spirits have been talking to you again?"

"Always." Someone mumbled in the background. Another someone answered. A truck engine revved. This wasn't going to be the easiest conversation.

"Still working the Water Protectors Camp in North Dakota?"

"So far stalling construction under Lake Oahe. Feds might stop that company digging in our sacred grounds and spoiling our water. We hear a Kennedy might come lend support on environmental and spiritual grounds."

"Washte, that's good, Sonny. Thank Tunkashila, Grandfather, for keeping you strong."

He was silent. But I could hear him breathing, could picture his large, handsome face, flat nose and wide, sensual lips close to the phone. His chocolate, black-lashed eyes would be half-closed. He probably was picturing me, too. I hoped.

I snuggled deeper into Big Brown's puffy, down-filled back while fantasizing about Sonny's warm embrace. Sonny's strong embrace. An embrace I thought would be tough to escape, should I ever want to. My heartbeat accelerated.

"Wish I could get away and see you, Pepper," he said in a lower voice, as if he didn't want anyone nearby to hear. "It's been too long."

"No kidding, I said. "Since summer, when the protests really got going back there."

"You all right? Spirits tell me maybe not."

So I spilled what I knew about the threats to Dutch and the other trainers headed to Texas for the World Show. Told him how it endangered lives and would affect us.

"We're pretty worried," I said.

"And not just about that," he said. "What else are you worried about?"

He knew. He always knew. Just like I seemed to know what he was thinking. It scared me at times. But it also felt like we fit, like we just belonged together, like some old married couple. So I told him as much about my new friend, Sandra, as well as what I knew or feared about Sandra's riding with Stavropolis, and about Sandra's missing daughter.

"Nancy is supposed to be up here in the Valley somewhere." I said. "But I read that her mom thought she was trafficked. I found a story online. Her dad supposedly thought the same. Police couldn't verify it though."

"Uh-huh."

"And," I said, "closer to home, I found my gate chain wrapped the wrong way today. Dogs had a barking fit last night. They were too crazed for it to be just a raccoon. I'm kinda worried someone's watching me because I'm asking too many questions about something."

"Just keep the shotgun handy in the house, and pack heat outside. Still got the Smith and Wesson revolver? The concealed-carry purse I gave you last Christmas?"

"That's affirmative, Officer Chief."

Again the silence, the cadenced breathing. I wondered if he were in a traditional tipi, or in a tent, as were many North Dakota campers. Maybe he was in the cab-over camper of his SuperDuty pickup, Black Beauty.

I heard scraping and ruffling as if Sonny were adjusting his sitting position. Charlie and Shayna did that now, circling and lying back down in new and improved positions. Light snoring commenced. From the dogs, not Sonny.

"Want some advice?" Sonny said.

"Can use all I can get," I said.

"You check on low-rent talent agencies, bars with dancing or strip clubs within a day's drive. Runaways often wind up in the sex trade along the I-5 corridor. Someone's nice to them, promises them careers, and it's easy money."

"I know, from a story I did," I said. "I was just getting to it." That was a lie but I would look into that major angle. Right now, my brain was cooked. But Sonny had a point, in that Nancy allegedly fit the classic trafficked-youth profile, being what might be considered as overweight, depressed, and convinced her mother hated her. Plus, the "controlling" father – Sandra's words. Even maybe an abusive father. Again, Sandra's word.

Sonny cleared his throat.

"One of my nieces was trafficked," he said. "Found her in a strip club. Sickening."

"It is," I said. "I wonder if, in addition to her other issues – competition, jealousy, weight – Nancy was physically or sexually abused at home."

"Could be. Then regarding your worries about that Reg guy? Big developer or contractor, but kinky? Bad temper?" You probably can contact local contractors who might know about him. How about that Jesse guy you hire to fix stuff around your place?"

"Left Jesse a message yesterday. Haven't heard back. Might give him another call."

Now my mind buzzed with even more to do.

"Just don't get too friendly," Sonny said. "I've seen how that guy looks at you."

I sat up straighter, interrupting the dogs' industrial-strength snoring. They gave me dirty looks, and went back to sleep.

"What way does he look at me?" Now it was my turn to needle him a little. It would do Sonny some good to think other men desired me. Couldn't hurt.

He laughed. A deep, slow, deliciously lazy laugh.

"Oh, Pepper, now you're all innocent."

"Like you're not."

I instantly regretted firing that remark. I'd forgotten to engage the safety on my mouth.

"Whoa whoa whoa," he said. I could just see him shaking his head. "Let's not go there. We've got it good. Don't spoil it."

I felt this was the time to say what was on my heart. With Sonny gone so long, nearly four months now since he'd said those magic words, "I love you," it was past time.

"Do we have it good, Sonny? If so, can we make it even better?"

Silence.

"It's better every time, Pepper. You're the best. I told you that. I meant it."

My mind whirled. I felt my cheeks heat up. I thought of a million things to ask or tell Sonny. Things I needed to know to keep love and hope alive. A glowing ember was better than nothing. But I craved a long, slow steady burn.

"Thanks for the call, Sonny," I said at last. This wasn't the time or place to dig deeper.

"When again are you going to Texas?"

"Plane leaves just after midnight Sunday."

"Have a cousin lives in Texas."

Of course he did. Why was I not surprised?

"You have cousins everywhere, Sonny. Real cousin, or pretend?"

"You have girlfriends, everywhere, too," I almost said, but didn't. Hopefully that life of Sonny's was long in the past. But you could never be sure.

"Martin Runs Fast," he said.

"Beg your pardon?"

"My Aunt Arlene's step-kid. Martin Runs Fast. Firefighter. Knows Dallas-Fort Worth like the back of his hand. Here's his number. Call him if you get in trouble or need anything."

He spoke the number slowly. I jotted it down with a pencil stub on a pad I kept by a lamp on the round glass coffee table beside Big Brown.

"I'm sure I'll be fine," I said. "Runs Fast, huh? Good name."

"But I know you," Sonny continued. "You'll worry big time. Just like you are over your friend going riding with the new boyfriend."

"That worry of mine might save someone's life, one day."

"Threats are usually just meant to scare you. Make you do something or keep you from doing something. Hardly ever followed through on."

"I've heard that," I said. "But it's the 'hardly ever' that scares me. It means there's a chance that at some point they could be followed through on."

Chapter 14

I wanted to say more, but this was not the time, over the phone, a thousand or more miles apart from Sonny. So I held my tongue.

"Pepper?" Sonny said. "You there?"

"Yes?'

"We'll be together soon, I promise. I need to taste you. Mmmm. And feel your hair."

I warmed up in all the right places. I imagined his hand sliding up my thigh, his hand cupping a breast, our bodies melding together. "I can't wait, Sonny," I sighed. "Meantime, take care. Hold me in your dreams."

"You read my mind, Pepper. What I was going to say to you." We disconnected.

I sat there staring at the TV wall, where an old oak hutch held family and horse photos that spilled over onto the pale brown walls on either side. My eyes came to rest on a photo of Sonny and me standing near a tipi on his rez in South Dakota. The plains reached clear to the bottom of the sky, which held everything safe under its azure dome. This photo captured his feelings about his home, its sacred rituals and places. It also signified that I had a place in that.

Two summers ago I'd taken a Greyhound bus to a small town outside a cattle ranch in South Dakota to see him sun dance, fast for a week, pray and dance to the haunting voices of singers vocalizing while beating a buffalo-hide drum. I had slept in a tipi at night, fasted in daylight, cooked over a campfire, stood under a shade arbor, and spiritually supported the seventeen dancers eight hours a day. Then gone to pray in sweat lodge in the dark.

I even had helped build that sweat lodge, carrying skinned saplings to a site a hundred feet outside the sundance circle.

I'd cut red cloth into one-inch squares, folded tobacco flakes into them and wrapped string around them every two inches to make prayer ties to hang on the cottonwood tree the dancers had cut and sunk into the center of the sundance circle.

Sacred times, sacred memories. I wondered if I would ever again be included in Sonny's traditional ways. Or if I wanted to be included. That was a something to ponder at a future time. Right now the hands of my antique gilded clock on the hutch pointed to nine. I marveled at that. The evening had gone by fast.

Before I tumbled into bed, I made another quick but fruitless call to Jesse Banks, my contractor buddy who might know something about Reg. Left another voicemail. I also jumped online for a moment to look for anything more on Sandra's ex. What could it hurt?

I did come across one personality profile about him in a national business journal. Born in Mexico and educated at UCLA, where he earned a business administration degree, Allende had launched his career importing boots, pots and blankets from Mexico, then expanding his trade to other Central and even South American countries.

The article said he'd also dabbled in importing South American polo ponies for some United States players, including Tommy Lee Jones. The real Tommy Lee Jones.

Now that was interesting. Seven degrees of separation, indeed. Small World Department. Max Allende and I not only had Sandra in common, but a connection, no matter how tenuous, to a certain accomplished Hollywood actor. One who, in earlier days, I'd had a major crush on. Let's face it, still did. Who didn't love seeing Tommy Lee Jones in classic films like "Men in Black" and "The Fugitive"?

I picked up my phone to check on Mom and Dad. We kept the conversation short. They were watching TV news. Mom had made a PT appointment for Wednesday with Karen Mikulski, Little Stewie's mom. Dad had finished another Louis L'Amour novel.

"I thought he'd read them all by now," I said.

"This is his second or third time around. He doesn't remember the endings."

A notice for Call Waiting popped up. I had thought it might be Jesse Banks, but there was no name, and I didn't recognize the number. If it were someone I knew, they'd leave a message.

"Well, have a good night, Mom," I said.

"Don't let the bedbugs bite."

After hanging up I called back the last number that had called me. I recognized the area code as being from California. I compared it with the numbers from the texts I had sent to the show judges. No match. I called it back. Disconnected. Probably a wrong number.

Yawning, I let out the dogs and took a slow, relaxing shower. As warm soft water pelted me, I reviewed my day, including the calls from Tommy Lee and Sonny Chief. I felt pleased to have such friends, such support. I'd see what happened in Texas. If anything developed from judge threats down there, I might use TL's help. Maybe Martin Runs Fast's help, too.

Toweled dry and rejoined by the BTs, I jammied up and made my way to bed. I paused halfway there to kick a large blue bumpy ball for Charlie, who attacked it and rolled it around the house. I grabbed a knotted towel and engaged Shayna in a tug o' war. She snarled like a wolf, shaking her head violently. These dogs were small, but as tough and tenacious as the bulldogs and terriers that they'd descended from

Letting things settle back down, I gave the chiming-clock its weekly windup, slipped into bed and pulled the covers up to my chin. That clock was quirky as me. Rather than chiming the correct hour and half hour, it chimed whatever hour it chose, which might or might not dovetail with reality. I'd tried to have it fixed, but it still went its own stubborn way.

I smiled in the dark, covers to my chin, dogs snuggled around me. I thought of Sonny, and felt warm and oddly happy.

Despite all your worries and troubles, there was nothing like a good call from your lover, a chat with your parent, or the antics of funny dogs to put things into perspective. After a busy day I anticipated a refreshing sleep. Because tomorrow I might enjoy R & R on Table Rock.

Dolly Parton sang a few notes. My eyes cracked open. I stared into the dark. Sighing, I slid aside a snoring dog and picked up my phone. It lit up with "One new message." I hit the buttons, saw again the strange California number and put the voicemail on speaker.

"Stay out of it, Sh...lock." Click. When I called back, there was no answer.

That voice, the words and sounds, had been just this side of unintelligible. I replayed the message, with the same meaning and effect. What was that last word supposed to be? Sherlock? But there was no question: The voice had been altered. Muffled, gender uncertain.

One thing was clear. Now I knew in no uncertain terms that I was being warned to drop or stay away from something I had been asking questions and doing research about. That could mean Sandra, Reg, Nancy or Max Allende. In the past few days I'd discussed my concerns and questions about Sandra and Reg, not only with Sandra, Jeanne and several other Brassbottom Barn buddies. I'd also reached out for information from people like Maxine at the farm store, Jesse my contractor-pal, and the elusive Sonny Chief. Not to mention Tommy Lee Jaymes.

Or did that cryptic voice mail mean I should not dig too deeply – or dig, at all – into the threats against a horse-trainer friend and other judges who'd work at the World Show? No secret I was trying to get information on Dick Bradford. And I'd also tried to reach Grant Haverstadt, tied to the Shiny Suspicion syndicate.

Who had made the threat call to me? Did it have to do with my wrongly wrapped gates?

A thought I'd had earlier now made my head buzz. It demanded serious scrutiny. My previous case investigating the killing of Dark Vader involved a son of Dark Superstar. Both present mysteries – death threats, a disappeared daughter – were connected to that same sire.

I drew boxes on my nightstand notepad. I wrote Dark Superstar's name in the center box and Shiny Suspicion's name in an adjoining box. In surrounding boxes I wrote the names of threatened judges, connecting those with interests in Superstar or Suspicion to their boxes.

To small surrounding boxes I added the names of each Allende family member, with lines running to Superstar from those connected to him some way. Stavropolis' box held a question mark, and a line labeled "business" running to Sandra's box.

I saw how many names were connected directly or indirectly to Superstar. But what did it mean? And how did these connections relate to each other? Which were significant, and which not? I hoped I was not merely conjuring demons in my desire to solve.

I doused the light. The house was eerily quiet. Outdoors not even a night hawk called. In my pre-sleep drift, before dropping off, I had to wonder if Dark Superstar, himself, were cursed.

Chapter 15

I awoke to mad Boston Terrier licks after six o'clock Monday morning. Although I'd had a full weekend, I felt good. I'd had a couple great rides on Choc. I might rest him today with only a last lesson tomorrow to put us in perfect condition for the World show next week. All I really had to do were house and barn chores, and work at the Horsehouse later. Tulip had the morning shift, as usual.

There was still time to decide if I would take old Bob, and go up for a little R&R ride on Table Rock, as well as riding unofficial shotgun for Sandra with Reg. I wouldn't worry about Bob getting huffy. The ride would tire him, and Sandra would be there if I ran into trouble.

I let out the dogs and fed them and the horses. Then I nuked a peanut-butter-slathered bagel, grabbed a mug of hot French roast flavored with salted-caramel, sank into my favorite recliner and switched on the early TV news.

It was five minutes into the six-thirty newscast. I wasn't fully awake, having done my chores on autopilot. But I snapped to attention at the story underway.

A blue-jacketed young woman was doing a recorded interview at a Stavropolis multi-unit building site near Bear Creek Greenway. That biking and running path ran between Medford and Ashland. The video showed mountains of bulldozed dirt, miles of chain link fence, a construction trailer and, along one side, a mobile-home park.

At the mobile-park the reporter talked with a fully-padded senior citizen whose oversized gold bangles, upswept hairdo and chic gold-and-white caftan bespoke a palmier past, possibly in a Southern Cali resort town. She commandeered the steps of a white single-wide guarded by an army of garden gnomes. Waving a cigarette-holder that left pearly-smoke trails in its wake, and ignoring a fluffy white poodle-mix yapping behind the screen door, Edna Montmorency ranted about dust, noise, and traffic generated by the project. Her clean, quiet semi-rural community, from Talent to Phoenix, was doomed if the massive Stavropolis project was allowed to continue. City councils had been put on notice, and a protest was underway.

She finished with a few choice words about the site foreman who'd reportedly harassed her twin fourteen-year-old granddaughters, Lacy and Lena. They were recently in her custody, she explained, but now on the streets because she had laid down too many rules. The foreman, claiming to be a former Hollywood stunt man, had approached them a few miles down the old highway, but they recognized him from the building project. He'd offered to let them ride his horses if they'd let him take photographs to show to producers and talent agents he knew.

That blood-pressure hum in my head started again. In Tulip's recollection and in my own research there was that man, two years ago near a building project on the Coast, whom girls had accused of soliciting. The man with a long, "Greek-sounding" name.

Thoughts and dots started to run together and connect as they often do in the minds of the too-curious, particularly one with a reporting background.

Stavropolis owned restaurants and clubs. Some that might feature dancers. He himself liked young girls. Nancy allegedly came here to pursue a friendship that might lead to movies. Today Reg was riding a horse loaned by a cousin who'd been a stuntman. Edna had said a Stavropolis foreman with film ties had approached her twin granddaughters.

I shot out of Big Brown, sending Boston terriers scrambling. I pulled on my boots and coat, reached for my purse and buckled on my right-hip holster bearing my S&W .38 revolver, then let my black parka slide back over it.

An editor once told me that, when it came to investigations, there was still no substitute for good old-fashioned footwork. Or no substitute for packing, when the going got dicey.

Rolling through a few stop signs and blowing through some amber traffic lights, Red Ryder and I reached the Stavropolis construction site by seven. The place already bustled with shouting workers and roaring Big Boy Toys, even this early on a dim, cool Monday.

I parked under an ancient monkey-puzzle tree – an anomaly in a community that ran to oak, pine, and second-hand stores. The white trailer with gnomes was easy to spot. I took a pen and pad from my pocket, climbed the steps and pressed the doorbell.

"Yes?" Edna Montmorency opened the door and spoke through a screen that let out a cloud of cigarette smoke. The white fluffy bounded up behind her to do his yappy thing.

"Sorry to bother you, Miz Montmorency," I began. "But I'm Pepper Kane, a newspaper reporter. I have a few questions on your opposition to the construction."

Edna drew hard on her cigarette in its holder. Her eyes looked like blue marbles set in skin the color of rose quartz.

"Already said my piece," she said, squinting through a smoke haze. "Why can't you people do something to stop their ruining this country?" In a dramatic wave of the cigarette holder, she gazed toward the smoke-belching loaders, graders and excavators.

"I'd like to hear for myself, your objections to the project."

"They can all go to hell," she snorted.

"You said on TV that one of the workers bothered your granddaughters?"

She kicked one gold-slippered foot back, touching the dog with her heel.

"Pavlova! Stop it." She turned back and drew on her cigarette in its holder, exhaling a chain of smoke rings that drifted toward the monkey-puzzle. Her face took on a puzzled look.

"The worker?" I prompted. "Your granddaughters?"

"Damn it. We have a right to be safe in our own neighborhood."

"I beg your pardon?"

"My grandgirls were walking along the highway before coming here. A man in a pickup slowed to talk to them. They thought he looked familiar, like they'd seen him at this site." She jerked her head toward the construction trailer. Her beehive spat out a hairpin.

"And?"

"This guy rolls down his window and asks them if they like horses. They were wearing the pink cowboy hats and boots I gave them last Christmas."

"Go on."

"He asks if they ever thought of being actresses, or models for horse magazines. Said he had Hollywood connections." She pinched out her cigarette and threw it to the gnomes.

"What else can you tell me, Ma'am?"

"They told him 'no way' and he took off. So I put my foot down. Said to stay away from the site, to not even watch from the fence. We got in a fight about their wandering around. They ran away for good. Gone a week now. Scared that if they need money they'll take him up on his offer or hook up with other men at the site. New ones come and go every day. Who knows their background? Could be a den of felons, for all anyone knows."

I thanked her, left her my number, and looked toward the white construction trailer just past the Stavropolis project sign. A glowing window showed the lights were on.

It might be a dead-end. Or a weird coincidence. Or not. For in experience, and in my reporter's heart, I knew this was no coincidence. With informed investigations there are few coincidences.

I touched my revolver under my parka. I had to play this slow and easy. But I should probably have run like hell.

Chapter 16

Accompanied by a symphony of heavy-equipment blangs, screeches, and roars, I walked purposefully along the site's chain-link fence and through open gates to the construction trailer. At the steps I paused and took a calming breath.

The next minute I set my jaw, climbed the steps and opened the door to a bright, stale smelling interior. The décor included a coat tree with a hardhat and Carhartt brown jacket, a gray file cabinet piled with papers, a wall of lists and charts, and metal chairs around a plastic table set with a coffeemaker and Styrofoam cups.

Also posted on the wall were several pinup calendars, plus a colorful western-movie poster showing a posse chasing a wig-wearing Indian on a pinto. A large, unreadable autograph had been scrawled along the bottom.

A dark-haired man who vaguely resembled the brave, but with elaborate tattoos showing below rolled-up shirtsleeves, slouched with his back to me in a chair behind a dented desk. He was talking on a cell phone and didn't seem aware I was there.

"Well, shoot me the info and I'll see what we can do," he said. "My cousin is out with a client. But I know the routine. Tell her it's a done deal." He clicked off the phone.

"Pardon me," I said.

The man swung around. His boyish face gave a startled look melted that into a smile that featured a toothpick poking out the side of a sneering-Elvis mouth. The guy could be forty, or he could be twenty.

His gaze raked the length of my body, finally stopping when it reached my face. He leaned forward, clasped his hands and rested them on the desk.

"What can I do for you, young lady?" he said with a too-white grin.

"Pepper Kane, a reporter," I began. "Are you the job foreman?" I studied the white plastic name plate on his desk. Carl Papadopoulos.

"Yeah. Why?" His smile faded, replaced by a wary look.

"I need to ask you a few questions. About the job, and other things you might be able to help me with." I pressed my forearm to the revolver's bulk under my jacket.

Carl kept his gaze steady. He rolled the toothpick to the other side of his mouth.

"Already talked to the TV and papers about the protests," he said. "I got work to do." He gathered a few loose papers into a stack, and slid them into a shallow drawer.

"Some people around here are concerned not only about the scope of this project, and its effect on the environment, but that some workers were bothering young girls in the neighborhood. You know anything about that?"

Nothing like being direct.

At first Carl looked blank. Then he smiled unctuously, rocked back and clasped his hands behind his head.

"Wouldn't know anything about that," he said. "There's always kids hanging around. We shoo 'em away. Attracted by the machines, looking for excitement."

"What kind of excitement, Carl?"

Feeling bold, I reached in my pocket, pulled out a folded copy of Nancy's newspaper photograph, smoothed it out and lay it facing him on the desk.

He looked at the picture, looked up at me, looked down again and drew back in his chair. His hands gripped its arms. His knuckles went white as he rocked the chair.

"Who's that supposed to be?" he said, arranging his face in an innocent look.

"Have you seen this girl, Carl? She's the daughter of a friend, and ran away with somebody up here in real-estate or construction. I'm just canvassing projects, and . . ."

The foreman frowned, folded his arms on his chest and rolled the toothpick back and forth.

"I knew you were no reporter. Just who the hell are you?"

I squared my shoulders, raised my chin and stared him down. My heart was about to beat out of my chest, but I hung in.

"Okay. Fair enough. I was a reporter. But now I'm investigating for a friend. I'm also in communication with Sheriff Jack Henning." That last was a stretch, but I'd talked with Sheriff Jack in the recent past about another case I'd worked on.

Carl glanced around and craned his neck to see out the open door. Then he rocked in his chair, took out the toothpick, steepled his hands and looked me up and down again.

"I don't know who you are, or what you're talking about, Lady. But you need to leave. I don't appreciate your questions. And you're trespassing."

"I'll leave. But I want you to think about this. Try to remember if you've seen this girl, here or somewhere else." I found a business card from my coat pocket and lay it on the desk. It was a Best Little Horsehouse card, but it was all I had.

He picked it up, rolled his eyes and grunted

"I don't like your implication, Miss … Kane," he said, glancing at the card. "And I sure don't like you. Get out or I'll throw you out."

Red-faced, he balled his hands into fists and lunged to his feet. His chair whirled back and clanked against the wall, fluttering pages of a calendar showing images of girls in schoolgirl uniforms and unbuttoned riding clothes.

"Get out," he roared, pounding one fist into the table. "Get the fuck out."

Sweat gleamed on his forehead and arms. Its smell mingled with the stale smell permeating the trailer, though the door was still partly open.

"Better clean this place up a little," I said, feeling even bolder, as I knew I had him. "You might be having some unexpected guests from the sheriff's office."

I snatched Nancy's photo off the desk, turned and jogged down the steps as quickly as pride would allow.

Chapter 17

Heart pounding, I scurried like a panicked crab to my truck beside Edna's trailer. Safely in the cold cab, doors locked, I tapped in Sandra's number. I wanted to tell her what I'd learned about a possible connection between Reg or his cousin with Nancy's disappearance. And to remind her she might be at risk with Reg on a lonely trail ride.

But the call went to voice mail. I left a hurried message. Then I called 911. I told the dispatcher where I was, what I'd seen and heard, and of my suspicions about Carl and Reg, and how Edna's granddaughters reportedly were approached by someone looking very much like Carl.

"Are you in any danger?" said the low, steady female voice.

"Not at the moment. But this man threatened me in no uncertain terms. I showed him a picture of my friend's daughter who went missing."

The dispatcher had me fill in the blanks about Nancy, and my concern that Reg Stavropolis or his cousin, or whoever the foreman was, may be involved. She sighed.

"We appreciate your concern, Miss Kane," she finally said. "I will pass your observation on to appropriate channels."

"Does that include the trafficking task force?"

"I am not authorized to say."

"Did Edna Montmorency, the grandmother of the girls approached by the Stavropolis foreman, report her concerns about him and the whole project?"

"Thank you for calling. If you hear anything more substantive, do call back."

When we disconnected, I felt deflated. I'd reached a dead-end, maybe even been suckered into a wild-goose chase by my overwrought mind. I needed to take that Table Rock ride more than ever. Not only for R&R, and to blow out enervating thoughts, but to alert Sandra to what I suspected about Reg and his foreman.

I had to leave Sandra another voice mail. She still wasn't picking up.

Running a few more stop signs and lights, weaving my way through traffic like a cop in some movie chase scene, I hauled arse home, and hooked up my trailer. I hoped to catch Sandra and Reg at the trailhead at Jim Dardanelle's ranch on the west arm of the horseshoe-shaped Table Rock. Or at least get onto the trail not far behind them.

Bob gave me the owl eye for dragging him out from his Life of Riley in the Gold Hill pasture. He loaded easily, but his eyes showed white. He neighed after I tied him in the trailer. He wondered what in heck was up at this crazy hour. An early vet call? A horse show down the road?

It was eight-fifteen, with the sky lightened to a soft pewter, when I drove out my driveway. At the gates, I noticed the chain and snap were secured as I had left them before. That was a good thing.

I raced my truck and trailer down the lane to the main road, as a pale yellow-gold band lined hills beyond the trees. Grass dotted with dewdrops caught the headlights like crystal. Two hares bounded in front of me, barely missing being turned into crow bait.

I hoped Sandra and Reg would still be at the trailhead, unloading, when I arrived. They'd planned to ride out by nine, if not earlier, to avoid hikers.

She hadn't called back. Was she out of range, out of battery, or ignoring me?

I reached the forests and farms abutting the west arm of Lower Table Rock at eight-thirty. I turned my rig right onto Jim Dardanelle's ranch road, past a long curve beyond Gold Rey Ranch Estates. A few yards in I stopped at a pair of iron gates decorated with a curleycued "D." I punched a code Dutch had given me into a box, waited for the gates to grind open, then drove my truck and trailer a quarter-mile up a gravel drive between sloping pastures dotted with ancient oaks. Ahead, to one side of the road approaching the house hidden in trees, I saw Sandra's white dually and long white trailer with its doors open.

The trailer was empty. But as I parked behind it, I noticed wet green manure littering the ground. I'd just missed them, but by much.

Heart hammering, I parked my rig, jumped out and unloaded Bob. Tacking up was tough. The cold, damp air turned my fingers into popsicles. Buckles and straps fought me at every turn. The trail booties were a bear to fasten over Bob's hooves.

But I finally swung aboard and legged my little bay up the steep, narrow dirt-and-rock trail heading up the northwest side of Table Rock. I looked back and saw we already were a good hundred feet above the valley floor. The woodsy smells of dry oak leaves, solitary pine trees and damp earth filled my nostrils. The peeling red bark on the trunks of madrone trees, distinguished by their glossy evergreen leaves, looked like skin ripped open to reveal pale, living flesh.

I noticed more fresh manure about a half-mile up the trail, which was overgrown in many places from disuse. Good. I wasn't too far behind my friend and her partner.

The trail became steeper, a profusion of sharp black rocks made the ride harder. But my plucky bay plodded on, ears flicking back and forth, his warm breath coming out in white puffs in the morning air. The trees thickened, then opened up. Dried grass and gravel crunched under Bob's hooves. We climbed steadily, twisting and turning, picking our way down a long dip before climbing up again.

We jogged over rock-strewn meadows and through copses of wild plum, oak, and manzanita like witches' claws. We rode for what seemed forever. Spectacular views of the valley appeared at every turn.

I looked at my phone. Nine straight up. I kicked Bob to go faster. He huffed an indignant snort and flattened his ears. He was out of shape, sweating hard, his sharp horsey scent mingling with the odor of oak, pine, damp earth and dry grass.

Hurry! I thought as we rode harder and higher.

When Bob and I finally completed a gradual bend to our right, out on the mesa's long arid eastern top, the sky opened up like an overturned pewter bowl. Table Rock's moonscape, barren and flat in every direction, was exposed to the universe in one stunning sweep. It felt like I was at the top of the world.

I jogged Bob forward onto the old dirt runway, I looked around, scanning the clumps of brush and lines of trees on either side of us. Where were Sandra and Reg?

That's when I heard shouts punch the still air. They came from some distance to the south. The snatches I could hear sounded mad as hell.

Chapter 18

Bob raised his head and stiffened his neck. I leaned forward, gazing to my right across the mile-long stretch of rock and weeds to where the mesa ended in thin air.

It was hard to see much in the dull gray light. Hard to see past the scattered brush, low hillocks and boulders along the way. So I pushed Bob into a fast trot for several hundred yards until we got a clearer view. I reined in near a scrubby oak.

Two people who from where I sat looked small as ants, grappled and twisted in a fierce fight at the edge of the cliff, some half-mile away. Two horses seen only in tiny silhouette, grazed unconcernedly to one side of the struggle. I thought one had a white mane, but could not be sure. That one raised its head, looked our way and neighed. It could only have been Sandra's horse.

I was sure the fighters would look, too. But they kept pushing and shoving. It was hard to tell more about them at that distance. I could only see that they were heavily engaged, doing a jerky conjoined dance fueled by anger. My premonitions about the danger in Sandra and Reg's ride had been dead on.

'Hey!" I shouted, pressing Bob forward at a trot as fast as we could manage given the rough, hard ground. "Hey!" I wanted us to be seen so the struggle would stop.

But it did not. If anything, it intensified. The fighters appeared not to have heard me above their own noise. Another high-pitched but unintelligible shout. Then, when I drew within two hundred yards, a distinct word reached my ears.

"Die!" The word was snatched away quickly by a rising wind.

"No!" That word came through clearly, too, as one person pummeled the other.

Bob and I clattered closer, shrinking the distance at an agonizingly slow pace. The horses near the cliff watched our approach and milled nervously, drawing away from the fighters. But the fighters appeared not to have seen or heard us.

I was afraid Bob would buck if I booted him into a gallop. But I booted anyway, risking my safety to try to save a life. He jumped into the speedy three-beat gait as if goosed. My body lurched violently in the saddle. Cold wind stung my face as we ran. Tears blurred my vision.

We galloped to within a hundred yards of the action I could see both Sandra and Reg wore black. There was a pause in their action. They still seemed oblivious as Bob and I closed the gap. Would we make it in time?

A woman's scream ripped the air. Then a gunshot. The sound ricocheted around nearby hills. Bob shied sideways and then stood rigid, focused on the scene. The couple stopped fighting. Then they took up the battle again, hurtling what sounded like curses.

What should I do? Hell, I didn't want to get shot.

I still couldn't make the fighters out clearly. They were both tall, slender, in black jackets and caps. Who was who? Which one had brought a gun and used it? They might use it again. Use it on me.

Wasting no time, hoping the shooter hadn't seen me, I kicked Bob to the right, down into a shallow ravine among young oaks. Pulling out my cell phone, I saw there was no service there, though there had been up top. Raw panic jittered my breath and pushed bile into my throat. I'd have to wait it out.

Peering between oak branches I saw the fight slow. Mostly pushing and shoving, punctuated by kicks. The fighters were tiring. Maybe it was over. Maybe they had made whatever points they were trying to make.

Suddenly one person sucked back, rushed forward and body-slammed the other, who sailed with a raw scream over the edge. That long scream, neither male nor female, but high and haunting, stopped abruptly. The lone figure at the edge glanced around, caught the nearest horse – which I now saw was black, not gold – and galloped right toward where I hid shivering in the ravine.

The small hairs on my arms and nape stood up. Was he coming for me?

I edged Bob even deeper into the ravine as the hoofbeats drew near. I felt for my revolver, keeping my hand on it. Bob pulled at the reins so he could graze on the sparse dry grass.

Long seconds I waited, barely breathing, calculating the closeness of the rider. But then the galloping hoofbeats receded, faded to nothing. He had kept going.

Still I waited. I waited until I was sure the evildoer was well gone. Waited until the only sounds and sights were of birds, small mammals, the wind and rustling leaves. He likely was headed back to the trailer, and either hadn't seen me or hadn't cared.

My loud heartbeat made me hyper-aware time was ticking. Not only for me, but for the one down that cliff. I could wait no more. She surely needed help. I hoped she needed help. Even if she were beyond help, I still had to go.

A check of my cell phone still showed no service. But the time was nine-twenty. Up top, nearer the cliff edge, there would be all kinds of service. Before heading there I made sure the .38 Smith & Wesson in its holster on my right hip was reachable.

Bob carried me quickly back up the rocky slope to the mesa top. The moonscape mesa seemed even more desolate now. And it reached out to all sides so I could see if anyone were coming.

I legged Bob into a jog, and pulled out my phone. Using my teeth, I peeled off one glove and tapped in nine-one-one. I hoped I wasn't too late.

"What are you reporting?" said the male dispatcher.

While I jogged, making sure I wasn't being followed, I used my left thumb and forefinger to pull the glove into my rein hand, and then stuffed the glove into the gullet opening below the saddle horn.

"Someone just fell over the southwest edge of Lower Table Rock," I said, sitting the jog. "They were fighting with another person, there was a gunshot, and –"

"Who are you and where are you?"

I gave the dispatcher the necessary information, words tumbling over each other.

"Will you send a Med-Evac? Don't know the person's status. May be deceased."

"Med-Evac. And first responders who'll hike up. Are you at the edge now?"

"Headed there. The other person in the fight rode his horse away. I don't see him but he may have seen me."

"Rode on a horse?"

"Yes."

"Do us a favor. Just stay safe, but near enough the fall site so we can find you."

I pocketed the phone and speeded the jog into a full trot. Hikers should soon be emerging from trees lining the public trail a hundred feet to my left. The hikers would seek killer views. Emphasis on the word "killer." Maybe among them would be Sam, a ninety-year-old dude who'd once told me he'd hiked every morning to the top of the Rock, in every kind of weather, for more than fifty years.

In a few heart-pounding minutes we arrived at Table Rock's black, rock-covered edge. At the precipitous drop-off, below which dozens of jagged black pillars jammed together to form a cliff wall. At the place that lured at least one drunk, or overzealous hiker, over the edge each year. Most were rescued alive. Some were not.

Afraid of what I'd see, I reined in, dismounted, and dallied Bob's reins around the horn. I stepped forward through pocked rocks to the precipice. Pebbles slid like marbles under my boots. I fell, skinning one wrist on sharp sand.

I cursed, stood up, inhaled deeply and pushed out a breath. There was no sound except for the wind. Bob stood quietly forty feet away, one hind hoof resting on its bootie-clad toe. Obviously exhausted from our mad morning dash.

But I still buzzed with adrenaline. Studying the remaining few feet leading to the edge, holding my arms out for balance, I sank the weight of each step onto solid rock or tamped dirt. I had to be careful or I might join that body down the cliff.

My pulse pounded. It was time to look. I squatted, braced one hand on a rough boulder, and stared straight down the columns, clefts, and clumps of red poison oak, buckbrush and straw-colored grass.

Some hundred feet below I saw the body. It sprawled face down against the rock, partly hidden in thorny buck brush. One long, jeans clad leg was extended beyond the brush. The leg ended in a black cowboy boot. The body was as still as the earth.

Chapter 19

"Hello?" I called down the cliff.

Silence.

"Need help?"

Nothing.

I felt chillingly alone. I also felt skin-crawly, as if I were being watched. A look back the way I'd come revealed nothing alarming.

A scrub jay landed on the thorny buckbrush. He cocked his crested head first to look at me, then to look at the body, as if evaluating its potential for lunch. He jumped over to another branch, ruffled his blue-and-grey feathers and uttered a raucous call.

"Scree! Scree!"

I clapped my hands. He launched himself as if he'd been thinking of doing it anyway, and flapped away.

Carefully I stepped a few yards to one side and down a few more feet through the rocks to better view the body. How it lay under the brush against the cruel pocked lava, and how its black-knit beanie hid its face and dark hair, I couldn't tell if it were male or female. But I knew it was Sandra Allende, fellow horsewoman, friend and mom.

The big mystery was, why she had fallen, or been pushed. Was it an accident? Or had Reg attacked her out of misguided passion, or from anger at a major real-estate deal gone awry? The other possibility was that Sandra had learned he figured into her girl's disappearance, and questioned him about it. My warning voice mail to Sandra possibly spurred her on.

Sandra's fall off the cliff provided an easy way out for Reg. Problem solved.

I continued staring as I reached for my phone. The body's long, jeans-clad left leg partly hidden by brush appeared caught in a crevice. The right leg was stretched straight as if in a leap. A puffy black parka covered the torso. Black-gloved hands frozen in a claw shape lay useless, stretched out to each side.

Looking around my booted feet, and further up the slight slope down which I'd come, I saw the rocks and dirt torn up fifteen or twenty feet all around. Hoof prints and boot prints, jumbled together with sharp rocks and uprooted weeds. Been quite a fight.

I shivered, feeling as if I might lose my breakfast. I looked all around again, even to the far trees from which I'd ridden. I still saw not one other human or horse. Nothing but open Table Rock hardscape bathed in air scented with sage and oak.

Despite what the dispatcher had said, I knew I should get out of there. The hum in my head sounded like ocean rollers. What if Stavropolis had seen me, and doubled back?

Lingering only a moment more, whispering a prayer for Sandra and for her two daughters, I remounted Bob and trotted back toward my hiding spot in the ravine. Who knew how quickly help – although too late for the dead one – would make it up there? Fifteen, twenty minutes if they sent a chopper. But officers with dogs and gear, and Search and Rescue, could take up to an hour to climb this andesite mesa.

I didn't want to wait around here. As I made for the trees, I felt my revolver bouncing under my jacket. It might become my best friend any moment.

Cold wind lashed my hair, snatched away my breath. I rode fast, Bob's hoofbeats matching my heartbeat. Sand

and pebbles flew from our path. When we reached our former hiding spot, where with a few strides I could ride up to check the mesa for responders, I hunkered in to wait. However long it took.

I had been there only about five minutes when I thought I heard hoofbeats. Those of a single horse. I rode deeper into the trees and scrunched lower in the saddle, as if that made me less visible. But I was on a horse. About as visible a target as there is.

I wondered again why I hadn't minded by own beeswax on this Sandra and Reg business. It had been an option. Not being able to keep my nose out of other people's situations was useful at times. Say, for helping them through a crisis, or for solving crimes.

But that behavior was going to get me dead, one day. Maybe even today.

Chapter 20

I tried to get more comfortable in the saddle in my chilly hiding place among the oaks. A slight breeze fluttered the dry leaves and scattered fallen ones among the grass and trunks. Bob grazed. I shivered, and tucked my gloved hands beneath my thighs.

The breeze dropped. It became very still. Bob raised his head, hearing something I did not. Were responders coming? If it weren't them, who was it? It had to be the responders, hurrying to the cliff. What was more urgent than a death?

I could wait no longer. I had to ride out. I turned Bob and headed out.

Overhead, through the treetops, I saw plank-like gray clouds drift away from the bright but unwarming disc of sun. Ravens croaked. A honking vee of Canada geese soared above, angled toward grass sloped along the river below.

I glanced around. Listened hard for any sounds coming from the mesa. Bob raised his head. Now I heard the sound of distant voices. Plugs of talk coming in blips. Sounds made by people hiking. Or likely the law coming at last on the Rock. Coming at last, though too late for poor Sandra.

I exhaled. Loudly. The wait was over. I could meet officers, and go home. Maybe cry myself silly. Call Tulip, to share what had happened. I might even call Sonny Chief. It would be good hear his soothing voice.

A crackle of twigs and dry leaves sounded among the trees just ahead. It startled me from my reverie. Bob nickered. Another horse neighed back.

"There you are, Pepper," said a low, heartstopping female voice. "Took me awhile. But I knew I'd find you."

Sandra, in a black jacket, hat and jeans, sat a black horse forty feet away, just inside the line of oaks bordering the mesa top. She pointed Reg's pistol straight at me.

"Sandra!" I said, instinctively halting Bob and reaching in my parka for my revolver. My cold fingers jammed as I struggled to unholster it.

"Drop your gun," she said, riding closer, still aiming the pistol. Her eyes darted from side to side. They flashed with an odd fire, turning her into a stranger.

"But you … I saw you down the cliff. At least I thought it was you …"

I wondered if I were having delusions. What were those voices I'd just heard? Must have been hikers. Or the law. Too far away to do me any good now.

"You may think you know what you saw, but you really don't," Sandra said, her voice shaking. She tried to control her lathered horse, agitated by her tension. Its prancing hooves scattered rocks and leaves. Clearly no show horse.

I was alone. With a possible killer right in my face. So it had been Reg, then, down the cliff. I shut my eyes to process this. I opened them and stared hard at her.

"Sandra. Stop it. You're still in shock over what happened."

"I know what I'm doing. Just throw out your gun."

"I called nine-one-one. Responders are coming. We have to go and meet them."

"We'll be gone by the time they miss us. You're coming with me. I need to explain something."

"What's to explain? You fought, and Reg fell over the cliff. Did you fire the shot I heard? Why are you carrying a gun?"

"Always carry. It can be dangerous for a female to show properties alone. And no, it didn't go down as you say. It was an accident. I think you're the person who's panicked. That's why we need to talk. Just toss out your gun. Now!"

I took my time, hoping if I delayed, she would calm down, and responders would be within earshot. But I wondered, as I tossed the gun into a pile of leaves, what in hell or earth had possessed this woman?

Sandra struggled to hold her pistol on me as she stepped off the horse. I briefly wondered where her palomino was. She swept up my gun, tucked it in her parka and bounced around on one foot while trying to hold the black still enough to remount.

"Whoa," she barked. "Whoa!"

Before she hit the saddle I grabbed my saddle horn and kicked Bob hard in the ribs. He jumped forward, bumping Sandra's horse. It spun around. We jammed past it and crashed through the last trees toward the open mesa.

"Stop," Sandra screamed.

A bullet zinged over my head. High enough to warn, not kill. So she was just trying to scare me. I bent lower in the saddle and kept on riding.

"Go, Bob!" I yelled. "Git, now." My legs got busy. Kick, kick, kick.

"Pepper, you have to stop!" Sandra shouted, her horse crashing after me.

I rode a zigzag in case Sandra really meant business. Bob's booted hooves ka-chunked through the rocks and brush. Twigs stung my face. But I was still alive, still horseback. When we scrambled out of the ravine, I kept him galloping toward the cliff edge.

Glancing back, I saw Sandra rein in her horse a hundred feet behind me. The black tossed its head and jigged. Sandra still held the gun, but it pointed at the sky.

Her face looked ashen. After a moment she spun and galloped away down the mesa.

When I slowed Bob to a jog, I heard chopper blades churning the air. I couldn't see it, but guessed the aircraft hovered out from and below the edge. I rode to within a hundred feet, dismounted, and held Bob's reins.

People in sheriff's uniforms or Search and Rescue jackets, along with a sprinkling of hikers, trickled across the mesa toward its edge from the public trail to the northeast. Sheriff Jack Henning, a grizzly-bear of a man, stood out in the approaching group, huffing and puffing from his climb. I'd had dealings with him before, not always to my benefit.

The chopper slowly rose toward the mesa top. It landed a dozen yards in from the edge, its blades slowing but still whipping up sand and debris. The whapping slowed.

I scrunched my eyelids as grit peppered my face, and then turned away. I saw a dozen hikers with children poking here and there across the mesa. They stopped and pointed when they saw the chopper.

The plodding team of responders, Sheriff Jack bringing up the rear, was now upon me. I braced for questions, thinking about how I'd answer.

I also said a silent prayer that the recovery and questioning wouldn't take all day. And Reg Stavropolis, by some miracle, were still alive.

Chapter 21

"Well, now, Miss Kane, we meet again," growled Sheriff Jack. He stepped up to me and rolled his shoulders like a Sumo wrestler. He took a pad and pencil stub from a pocket, licked the pencil tip and cocked his head while a walkie-talkie crackled on his shoulder. "What have you done now?" His lips quirked as if he'd made a fine joke.

I narrowed my eyes. Two could play this game.

"Hardly something to joke about," I said loud enough to be heard over the chopper noise.

"And how come you just 'happened' to be riding a horse where it's not allowed? And just 'happened' to see someone fall off the cliff?" He shifted the pad and pencil to his left hand and crooked his right hand into an air quote each time he said "happened."

His insinuations made my skin prickle.

"Special permission," I said. "I'll explain later, if necessary. But I called this incident in. Why would I do that if I had anything to do with it, as you imply?"

"I'll ask the questions, Miz Kane. Why were you here? You told the dispatcher two people were fighting. A shot was fired. Who fired it? Do you know the people involved? And where's the other one?"

"I knew Sandra Allende, as a riding friend. The other, Reg Stavropolis, is a real-estate developer, I knew only by name and reputation. Which is sketchy, by the way."

"Just answer the questions." He stopped writing. "Are you stonewalling me like you did with that killed-horse case last summer?"

Guilty until proven innocent. That's me, vis-à-vis Sheriff Jack.

"I don't know who fired the shot," I said, thinking it may have been Reg, though Sandra had a gun. "Sandra said they were riding here today on a first date, but also for business. They were riding here, I needed a trail ride anyway, so I went to meet them."

"And?"

"I also was worried about her because of the women attacked recently going out alone with men they barely knew. And Stavropolis is known to be rough with women, have a real bad temper."

"Then what?"

"I was late. When I rode onto the mesa I heard shouting at the cliff edge. Two people were fighting. I couldn't make them out but guessed it was Sandra and Reg. A shot, more fighting. Then one went over the edge."

"Go on. Which one fired the shot?"

I had to be careful now of what I said. Anything could be used against me.

"I tried to stop the fight by galloping forward. I was sure they'd see me."

"But clearly you didn't stop it." He paused to let that sink in. Did he think I was manipulating the story, hadn't tried to stop the fight, hadn't got my timing right?

"So where is this Sandra person? Why would she leave the scene?"

"I think she just freaked, and ran away to think," I said. "Or maybe she thought she'd get help faster that way than by calling it in."

"Do you know anything to support that?"

I was screwed. Sandra was screwed.

"She came back and told me it was an accident, that she just went nuts at what happened and panicked. Said she wanted to tell me what really had happened."

"And did she? Where is she now?"

"She was going to tell, but then she got scared again, seeing the massive response, and rode back toward Jim Dardanelle's ranch trailhead. Why don't you go ask her?"

Instantly I regretted that last retort. At least I hadn't mentioned her threatening me with the gun before she ran away the second time.

Sheriff Jack blinked hard and sighed. He put away his pad and pencil. He leaned forward and pointed his finger at my chest.

"I must caution you again, Miz Kane. Do not obstruct an investigation. Got that?"

"Oh, I think so. You've made that abundantly clear."

He rocked back, and pursed and unpursed his lips. Under his griz gaze, I felt like a fat maggot in a dead log. Yep. Bear bait.

"That so? And you say she is your friend. We'll explore this again. You may go."

Sheriff Jack bent over, keyed his walkie-talkie and spoke into it. The wind from the chopper blades snatched his words away from my hearing. I was eager to get out of there, or at least away from my annoying nemesis.

A horde of officers, EMTs, Search and Rescue and other personnel scrambled or stood talking at the cliff's edge. The Med-Evac chopper rotors sped up again, lifting the aircraft off, angling up and out from the cliff. A ladder and long basket hung below it.

Sheriff Jack took a military stance six feet from me. I was about to ask if I could leave, when a voice over his walkie-talkie said deputies had found "a person of interest" near the Dardanelle ranch.

"They caught her?" I asked him.

"They found your friend," he said. "That's all I can say, lest you interfere with police business again." He looked straight ahead.

"Didn't know it was police business until an hour ago," I said.

"You did say a shot was fired." He turned his head, pressed a finger to one side of his nose and blew mucous out the other nostril. He touched his nose to his sleeved arm.

There still was commotion at cliff edge where people worked feverishly with ropes, straps and the rescue basket to bring up Reg's body.

As before, shouts punched the air. Words tumbled over each other. But although sounding frantic, they also sounded hopeful. Words such as "Alive!" and "Hurry" were yelled, then repeated.

Sheriff Jack jogged as fast as his rolling bulk would allow the rescue staging area. He and everyone else peered over the edge, and babbled excitedly.

A tall African-American female officer motioned to Sheriff Jack.

"The victim is still alive, but unconscious, in bad shape," she shouted.

"Good to hear," yelled Sheriff Jack. "A rescue ... not a recovery. Makes my job a whole lot easier."

A jolt of joy zinged through me. Reg was alive, and hopefully would continue to be so. Maybe live to tell his side of the story.

At a signal from Sheriff Jack, the female officer strode up to me. Her name tag read, "J. Jenee." She gave me a warm yet professional smile, and extended one hand.

I shook it.

"Detective Jenee," she said in smoky tones. "I will be lead investigator. Are you Pepper Kane, who reported the incident?"

"I am."

"I'd like to ask you a few questions. Can we step away from here?" She led me a hundred feet away, near where do-not-cross tape had been stretched to keep away looky-loos. By now, it being late in the morning, there were plenty of those.

"Now tell me as much as you can about the incident and those involved."

I did so, happy to have a real, thinking and feeling human to tell my story to. As we talked, I decided to tell all because Sandra might be pressured to tell another version, sugar-coated to make herself look better.

"Any idea why Allende and Stavropolis were fighting?"

"She didn't say. But Reg has an awful reputation with women regarding violence, kinky sex. That's partly why I wanted to meet up with them."

"To ride shotgun."

"Yes."

The detective and I talked a bit more, and then she dismissed me.

"We may need to talk again later," she said.

"Happy to help," I said.

Because of his severe injuries, retrieving Reg from the cliff side took much longer than anticipated. More people, more cables and straps, more shouting and gesturing.

Jackson County Search and Rescue people lingered during the rescue. Among the onlookers, a toddler cried. An older youngster slipped under the tape, only to be hauled back by an officer. Adding to the excitement, a news chopper circled continuously.

I finally called Tulip, working the morning shift at the Horsehouse. I briefed her on the day's bizarre events, and asked if she could continue working, as I might be detained longer. She agreed. What a trouper.

By early afternoon it was done. The aircraft had left, responders and rescuers left after re-securing their gear. I was glad to see Sheriff Jack's back growing smaller as he trudged across the mesa toward the switchback trail to the parking lot.

Silence once again descended on Table Rock. Silence except for the calls of jays and keens of hawks, except for the lonesome whoosh of the wind. I was glad I'd stayed until the end. I'd hoped to learn more about everything, but was disappointed in that.

Drained and exhausted, crazy with questions, I mounted Bob. I reached in my saddlebag, gulped down a water and jerky, and lit out at a jog back across the mesa.

In thirty minutes I made it down to my truck and trailer. Sandra's rig was gone. She'd likely been questioned, and then left of her own accord. I wondered how she was doing, what was going through her mind. I ached to know what she had wanted to tell me. What was the thing that pushed her to panic, a thing she felt she could trust me with? There'd be no call from me to her today. I'd let the dust settle, try to talk to her tomorrow. Plus I wanted to know what had become of my gun. Still in shock, I loaded Bob and drove home.

My ranchita had never seemed so welcoming. Pride and gratitude washed over me as I drove through my gates, fastened them, passed the sweep of lawn and parked under madrones near my little, tan-and-white barn painted like the house. After tending the critters, I showered, reheated soup for dinner, flipped through magazines, watched a little TV to dull my mind, and fell into bed. Last thing, I powered off my phone. I didn't want to talk to anyone. I'd share and revisit today's madness, tomorrow. I just prayed I wouldn't nightmare about it tonight.

Chapter 22

The next morning, although flirting with a mild headache and still puzzled about the bizarre events of the previous day, I was good to go. I attended to barn chores, gave the dogs their due, and nursed a steaming cup of sweetened French roast.

Before calling Tulip to explain the incident on Table Rock, I sank into Big Brown. I settled the Boston Nation around me and switched on TV News. I wanted to see what they were saying about it all. About Stavropolis, about Sandra and maybe even about me.

Of course we were the lead story. Again the blue-jacketed young woman reporter. Doing a segment recorded yesterday in Lower Table Rock's parking lot. Interspersed with shots of the rock, and Reg Stavropolis and Sandra Allende – their billboard faces.

"Prominent developer Reginald Stavropolis suffered life-threatening injuries in a fall yesterday morning off Lower Table Rock," began the reporter. "He reportedly is in a medically induced coma at South Valley Medical Center. Early reports indicate the fall was accidental, but authorities consider Allende a person of interest. So, too, a woman who witnessed the incident."

No kidding, I thought. No freaking kidding.

The words I'd just heard sent a chill through my bones.

I took another slug of coffee. I savored the creamy liquid before swallowing.

But I almost spit it out when the reporter said, "According to the Jackson County Sheriff's Office, Gold Hill resident Pepper Kane was riding her horse on the Rock when she saw the couple fighting, and one of them fall off the cliff."

Fearing that the reporter would tell more about me and of my panicked run, I sat transfixed before the screen. But, thankfully, I was mentioned no more. The segment concluded with a request for information possibly related to the case.

Great. Soon my phone would be ringing off the proverbial hook. It didn't take even five minutes for Dolly to sing out.

"Hey, Tulip," I said.

"Tried to call last night," she complained. "And why the flake didn't y'all tell me before you went up there?" she said. Annoyance reverberated through every word.

"It was a split-second decision. Planned to be back to work by one. Then it all spun out of control. Too tired to talk last night, but I was about to call you now."

"Shoot. I would have gone with you, Girl. Called Karen to work. You know that."

"Didn't have time. Hey, you're working at the store this morning, right? I work this afternoon. Let's have lunch at Katie's and I'll tell all. Gotta get to the barn. Have a final World Show practice at ten."

"Can't take my eyes off you for a minute, but that y'all get your booty in trouble," Tulip whined.

I dialed the Sheriff's Office non-emergency line. I identified myself, asked about Reg, and Sandra, was put on hold and then was told the office had no information.

"That's all I can tell you," said the clerk.

"What is Reg Stavropolis' condition?" I quickly added, "Is this being investigated as a homicide?"

"I am not authorized to talk about any of that," said the woman.

But she had not reacted to the "H" word, so perhaps Stavropolis was hanging in there.

Still brimming with questions, I searched my contacts, found Deputy Boo's personal number and tapped it. Maybe Sonny's cousin would enlighten me on key points.

"Boo," said a breathy tenor voice.

"Don't scare me," I joked, instantly regretting my lame attempt at levity.

"Oh, hey, Pepper. Heard you were involved in that incident up on Table Rock yesterday. You're a big TV star now. Gone Hollywood. What can I do for you?"

He knew, or at least, guessed. Why else would I call someone I rarely spoke to?

"Let's cut to the chase, Boo," I said. "Being's how we're almost family. I need you to tell me what's up with Sandra and Stavropolis, and if the department is pursuing the child soliciting angle I called in yesterday re that foreman at the Stavropolis project?"

"Know zip about that last one. Didn't the sheriff interview you about Table Rock?"

"They did, on scene. But it was chaotic."

"Well, since it's already in the police report and will be in the paper tonight, I can tell you the dude's hanging in, but barely. Your girlfriend has had been checked out. But that's all you're going to get out of me. And you didn't hear even that."

"Got it. Thanks, Boo. One more thing."

"Isn't there always?" A chuckle.

"Reg Stavropolis. Your take on his history. Off the record."

"Seriously nasty dude."

"Facts to back that up?"

"Gotta go. Hey. Give my regards to old Sonny."

Well, what else had I expected? That Boo would divulge any further confidential sheriff's business? I was lucky to have gotten what I did.

When I hung up, I looked up Sandra's number and hazarded a call. She might not answer if she saw my name. But I had to try. It was ballsy, but I needed some answers.

Sandra answered. She sounded groggy and stuffed-up. Like she'd been crying.

"Wondered when I'd hear from you," she said. "Really sorry about yesterday."

"Not as much as I am. Pretty sure you were gonna kill me."

A small stretch of silence.

"Oh, no, I wouldn't have. I was just so damn frightened after he fell. Didn't know what I was doing. I panicked, knowing you'd seen something. Wanted you to hear me out. Come with me so I could explain things before the law got involved. I was only trying to scare you a little so you'd come."

"Mission accomplished. At least the scaring." I let her wait a moment. "Have you heard anything about Reg's condition?"

"Sheriff won't say, so I called the hospital and asked for his room. They said he's in the critical care unit. So that means he's alive," she said. "Thank God." she added.

"And how are you doing, Sandra? Did you get my voicemails?"

"Doing crappy. Got the voicemails. Thank you for trying to help."

"Why didn't you let me know? I was crazy with worry."

"I had lots to think about. Your message confirmed some things I'd guessed."

"Like, what, Sandra?"

She breathed rapidly. She blew her nose and sniffed. She definitely was crying.

My dog Shayna nudged my leg. Shayna had dropped a knotted towel at my feet. I tossed it across the room. She bounded after it and brought it back. This time Charlie joined in the chase, snarling and barking as he dug in for a major tug-of-war. I could barely hear Sandra's words over the commotion.

"Things about … Reg," Sandra finally said. "About him, and some others …"

Her voice trailed off.

"Want to meet for coffee?" I said. "Talk about it some more?"

Silence again.

"Why?" she said at last.

"You're a friend," I said. "A Brassbottom buddy. And, I'm curious."

"I can imagine," she snorted. "Everyone is. I do love small towns."

I waited a breath before voicing my next thought.

"Plus, Sandra, I think you owe me."

A deep exhale.

"Okay. Sure. I suppose we can meet. But let's keep it short, Pepper. I have lots to do today. More interviews. And I have a client. Several, in fact. TV coverage, even if it's not the kind you like, does bring out the curious."

We arranged to get together in an hour at Katie's Kitchen. I tried not to overthink things as I dressed in an expensively distressed royal-blue sweatshirt, cap and jeans. I then hopped into Big Red to head for town and shake down Sandra.

Afterward I'd hit the barn for Choc's and my riding lesson with Donna. It would be our last lesson before the horses loaded up for Fort Worth and the World Show.

How in God's green Earth was I – were any of us – going to do our best at that all-on-the-line competition, with our brains bursting with fear and suspicion?

I let the truck idle at my gates while I jumped down to unfasten the chains.

But before looking at how they were wrapped, it hit me. I knew they were again wrapped the wrong way. One glance confirmed it. Not only were the chains wrapped opposite to how I wrapped them around the crossbars, but now they bore a taped-on paper note inside a clear sandwich bag.

My knees felt watery. I opened the bag and stared at the words written in a block print with black marker on sheet of chili-pepper-red note paper:

"Back off, Sherlock."

I remembered with a jolt that mysterious voicemail from California. The "Sh....ck" I'd heard had been "Sherlock."

My skin crawled with unease and more than a little anger. These developments took everything to a whole new level. Someone was clearly steamed at me, and bold enough to repeat their warnings, in different ways, in no uncertain terms. Who knew where it would take them?

Chapter 23

I virtually trance-drove all the way to the café. Someone knew where I lived, what my habits were. Someone had been on, if not inside, my own property, and watching me.

When had the note been put there? Who had written it? And why?

It reminded me of the death threats posed to Dutch and other World Show judges. Meant to frighten, meant to paralyze. This could relate to my investigating that threat. Or, it could refer to my looking into people possibly involved in child soliciting. It may even have something to do with the missing Nancy.

Sandra was already seated at one of the worn, red-vinyl booths when I arrived at nine at the half-full café. She looked up with reddened, hastily made-up eyes as I slid in across from her, nodded at Katie and took delivery of a cup of creamy java.

"It wasn't what you think," Sandra said right off. Nothing like getting to the point.

I savored a sip of coffee before speaking.

"What do I think, Sandra? Tell me everything. You can trust me." I noticed a red-purple mark above her lips.

She looked down at her own coffee, stroking the mug with her brightly manicured fingers. I could almost hear her thinking, weighing what and how to tell me.

But I knew she would tell me.

"It was ... okay. It was my daughter. It was Nancy." Her shoulders dropped.

"Nancy," I echoed. "You know, I did some research. As I said in my voicemail, I found a man named Carl at one of Reg's construction sites, who –"

"I was just so damned angry, Pepper," she rattled on, either not hearing or not wanting to. "I was so crazy mad when I heard the guy had lured one of my daughter's friends to meet a man hiring models. I re-checked my notes. Then you called. Things added up. I've turned my notes and computer over to the sheriff. "

"Sandra," I said. "I tried so hard to stop you from riding with Reg. I showed Carl Nancy's picture and he went ballistic."

Sandra looked down at her coffee.

"As I told the investigator, I had already started to zero in on this Carl. Then I heard your voice mail. So on our ride, I confronted Reg about this. It was hard for me staying calm. I was shaking all over with rage."

I leaned in on my elbows toward her, and lowered my voice.

"So … you wanted to make Reg pay the ultimate price?" I widened my eyes as I stared at her, challenged her.

Sandra gripped the edge of the table. Her jaw clenched and unclenched. Her eyes darted to the windows, the bar and back to me again. She blinked rapidly.

"It wasn't like that, Pepper!" she rasped. "I just wanted him to tell me everything, but he refused. The gun went off. It was an accident. I swear. And that's what I told the sheriff." Spittle lay on her lips. She licked it off.

"Was it, Sandra?"

"What?"

"An accident?"

Sandra shut her eyes. When she opened them, they had the same strange fire I'd seen when she found me in the ravine.

"What does it matter?" she whispered. "Reg is still alive. And he did attack me when I told him what I knew. He screamed that little girls with big dreams often ran off to seek their fortune alone, or with a friend, if they had unhappy home lives. He said people who helped them fulfill dreams were often wrongly accused. What a crock!"

I sat back. I didn't know what to think.

"Unbelievable," I said. "That he would say that, be so angry. Unless ..."

"Unless what?"

"Unless he knew he was going to silence you."

She stared into her mug.

"I had to defend myself, Pepper. He tried to choke me, even bit me before trying to throw me off that cliff." She touched a finger to her upper lip. "But I somehow was able to turn the tables. I hadn't planned it. Then he just ... went over."

I nodded. I searched her eyes with mine. She had the look of a trapped animal.

"And that's where I came in," I said.

"It was him or me, Pepper. I have neck bruises, too, where he tried to choke me. They took pictures. I wanted him to pay, but through legal channels. Not ... that way."

I wanted to believe her. I needed to believe her. Maybe would believe her. But her statements begged the question.

"So why did you come after me?" I prodded. "That doesn't add up. Makes it seem like Reg's fall wasn't an accident. You threatened me with a gun. I thought for sure I'd be the next dead body. By the way, what did you do with my gun?"

The answers came quickly enough to be true. Or, almost quickly enough.

"I told you. I just panicked. Scared out of my mind. Didn't have time to think it through, wasn't sure anyone would believe me. Surely you've felt that way." Her eyes seemed to beg for understanding, forgiveness. "By the way, I hid your gun behind that big vertical boulder at the ranch trailhead. Didn't want it on me, if they came looking. Which they did. I had to show them my gun. They seemed to believe my story."

"O-kaaaay," I said. My mind spun.

"Thanks for not pressing charges against me for menacing. You could have."

I took a long swig of now-lukewarm coffee.

"You did go pretty crazy up there, Sandra."

Sandra nodded. She gave me a long, sad look. She began to shiver.

Café sounds of clinking cutlery and mumbled conversation filled the gap. I fiddled with the check for our coffees, and waited.

Her next words, uttered in a cold, low voice, made my belly tighten.

"It was my daughter, for God's sake. My daughter. But it was an accident. I swear. You've got to believe me." She closed her eyes and sobbed softly.

The café got very quiet. Other patrons were staring at us. It was some moments before normal sounds and conversation resumed.

I drained my mug and considered all she'd said. For now I would have to accept it. Accept it, that is, until evidence proved otherwise.

"I am so sorry," Sandra said, picking at her napkin, then touching it to her damp eyes and nose. "I didn't mean for all this to happen. It is so sad. I am sorry for Reg. But ... I just have to find Nancy."

"And you will," I said quietly, with an assurance I didn't completely feel. "We will." I lay my hand on hers. "As I said, Chili once ran away. I understand."

She fixed me with a long gaze. Regret, sorrow, fear showed equally in her eyes.

"Thank you, Pepper."

"Now you can do something for me. Tell me why you think Nancy ran away. News stories mention her Hollywood dreams, low self-esteem. But I also heard something about friction in the home. Was there something specific?"

Sandra waved her hand.

"Pffft! Every teenager has those problems," she said. "But, to answer your question, I can't think of anything particular. We did fight. So what else is new?"

"You described your ex-husband as controlling, abusive. Did he abuse Nancy?"

Sandra stiffened, and quickly glanced away before answering.

"Well ... not that I'm aware of. The police didn't turn up anything. I don't have any more to tell, that wasn't in the papers."

I let it go. My questioning had reached a dead end. I didn't want to alienate her, as she might eventually think things over and realize I was only trying to help.

"It may surprise you," she said, "but I'm glad you called today."

"No problem."

"Not many would have. I've been here such a short time and haven't made many real friends. I appreciate your hearing me out. Again, sorry for yesterday."

We stood, hugged and left the café to go our individual ways. I wasn't quite sure exactly what our relationship would be in future. But since we would be co-competitors at the World Show and its runup at Brassbottom, a relationship we would have.

I'd continue to dig for clues about Nancy and go about my own business. I just would be extra watchful. As if my life depended on it. Which it very well might.

Chapter 24

Later, at Brassbottom Barn for our last practice before Texas, I found it tough to concentrate. As I numbly guided Choc through our routines, with Donna giving verbal corrections to me and other riders, my mind spun with worry and conspiracy theories.

"Loosen the reins, give him some slack," Donna said. And, "And drop your shoulders, soften your neck."

I steadied my right hand holding the reins just above Choc's neck in front of the saddle horn, and got a decent lope along the fence rail. Hoots of encouragement erupted from my buddies sitting or maneuvering their horses at the arena's far end.

It was eerie to think I'd be doing this exact thing little more than a week from now in Texas in a desperate try for a World Championship trophy and purse. A purse amounting to several thousand dollars, which could help offset the seven or eight thousand it took to get me there. And help with tack store rent.

Again, I reminded myself, showing was not for the faint of wallet.

Finished with the run-through and satisfied that Choc was groomed and put away, I hurried into the parking lot. I'd spent too much time meeting Sandra for coffee, and had no time now to talk with Jeanne or our other buddies as I had hoped. Although it was a kind of blessing, too, as I was in no mind to discuss my ride on Table Rock, which had been all over the news and prompted curious stares. I had to meet Tulip for lunch.

I was so preoccupied getting to my truck, I nearly smacked into Donna, bound for her own lunch at the Grandeen's handsome triple-wide on a lush lawn on the property.

"Great lesson today," I said.

"Thanks," Donna smiled. "You did really well. You ready to earn a bronze trophy and some big bucks? This might be your year."

"I think I'm due," I said. "But they don't give you a trophy for just showing up."

"Did you hear? Just announced they're instigating that fun Preview of Champions class they talked about last year. During the Welcome Barbecue before real classes start."

I rolled my eyes. I didn't envy people who'd have to ride in a "public relations" event as they madly prepared for the big-money main events in following days.

"I know," she said. "Who'll have the time? But they say it will whip up interest in the show by spotlighting classes like your Western horsemanship. They'll have a drawing to decide who shows that night."

"Probably skew it to riders who are 'in' with judges. Any more on the threats?"

A lightning-bolt of worry appeared between her dark brows.

"Not really. I think we nipped it in the bud. Say, how are you after that horrible ride up Table Rock? We saw it on the news. You're famous."

"Not the kind of famous I'd like to be." I picked a bit of shaving off one sleeve, and stooped to empty my jeans cuffs. Barn debris was not an accessory I wore dining out.

"No," said Donna. She moved a step closer, and seemed to be trying to put a worry of her own into words.

"What?" I said.

She shifted her weight. Again the zigzag of worry.

"Do you think it really was an accident up there?" she said. "I've heard some very bad things about that Reg ..."

I glanced around as buddies drifted from the barn and approached their vehicles. For some reason, I looked down at my truck's door handle. It had a fresh dab of bird poop. I'd have to be careful opening that door.

"I talked with Sandra this morning, Donna. We had coffee. She insists it was an accident. I've looked into the situation, heard things about Reg, too. But Sandra might have her own reason to fight him."

"Like?"

"Like her missing daughter."

"Really? You think he had something to do with that?"

"Let's just call it a guess, Donna." I didn't want to go into my talk with Sandra.

Donna closed her eyes. When she opened them, the lashes looked damp.

"Let's talk later," she said. "I know you need to get going. But I might have some helpful ideas. Nothing solid, just things I've heard."

"Let's do it," I said. "After work tonight or some time tomorrow."

Opening my door handle with care, reminding myself to later clean the poop off it, I climbed into Red Ryder and lit out for Katie's Kitchen. Tulip needed catching up on developments. I needed a steaming bowl of Cowboy Goulash Soup.

On the way to downtown Gold Hill – its main drag flanked by low storefronts, old Victorians, a kayak outfitter, a budget store, a pizza joint and a post-office mall with a pot shop – I pulled into a side street and hopped from the truck. In less than a minute I was through the café door and into the warm mélange of tables, historic photos and cooking smells that was Katie's Kitchen. Where gossip was served up as hot and tasty as the food.

Tulip, looking fresh in a turquoise sweater that matched her eyes, sat nursing a glass of cola at our favorite window booth. She glanced up as I sat down on the red-leatherette bench opposite her.

"So," she said, looking me over. "The famous avenging cowgirl, in person."

"Wish people would stop calling me famous," I said. "And I didn't avenge anything." I grabbed a menu.

The café owner, Katie herself – a mountain of a woman with bright burgundy hair – materialized with a notepad and took our orders. She eyed me with curiosity, probably dying to know about my newfound fame.

"Second time you've been in today, Pepper," she said. "Shall I make up a bed?"

I chuckled. She lingered, as if waiting for me to tell her of my recent adventure.

"What?" I said.

"Do you think she did it on purpose?" Katie cocked her head.

"Who?"

"That lady you had coffee with. The hot new realtor in town. Sandra Allende. The one who was all over the news with you."

I studied her. Did Katie know something? The lady had her finger on the pulse of the practically the whole valley.

"Why would I think that, Katie?"

"I saw her up here a few months ago, before she moved here. She and that Reg came in for lunch. I heard they were thinking of combining some properties by Table Rock. For a super resort, something like that."

"You're kidding," I said.

"Oh, no. They stopped conversation. We don't get celebrities in here that often. Except you, of course. I've seen him here before. Usually with another man, probably a client or another business partner."

I felt a buzz in my head. Sandra told me she'd just met Reg. Had she forgotten their lunch at Katie's?

Tulip set her elbows on the table and cleared her throat.

"Now that's peculiar," she said. "I thought it was their first date."

"So did I," I said, my mind bubbling with implications. I turned to Katie, who tapped her pen on her order pad.

"What else do you know?" I said.

"Oh, that's it. And that he's a pretty bad dude with women, anyways. Probably did go after her up there."

"No, but why would you think the accident might have been on purpose?"

"Self-defense," Katie shrugged. "Seriously. Don't know nuthin' else."

Oh. Okay. Just fishing. Well, I wouldn't bite. Especially since I had no other helpful information. Which I wouldn't share with Katie, even if I did have it.

She left to give the kitchen our order. Tulip took a swallow of soda, leaned back and folded her arms.

"Y'all don't look any the worse for wear from your wild ride, I must say."

"Well, I feel it," I said, rolling my shoulders and shifting my seat. "I wrenched my back, and my arms are sore."

"It'll be all right," she said. "So, spill. Everything. What you did, what you think."

And I did. Filled her in on the run to the Stavropolis construction site, my hellfire ride on Bob up Table Rock, the warning note on my gate, my coffee talk with Sandra.

Part way through, Katie set hot fragrant bowls of Cowboy Goulash Soup in front of us, and poured Tulip a cola refill. We tucked in, me talking between spoonsful of fiery soup. I dabbed my mouth with a napkin, but pressed on briefing Tulip. Sometimes her insights were out of left field, but they could also be enlightening.

"Well, my Gawd," she said when I'd finished. "You do like to live dangerously. Gonna getcha killed, one of these days."

"It might," I said.

"What I want to know is, what Sandra's ex was thinking, buying that wild horse for Jeanne. And then not seeming to try that hard to find Nancy. From what you said of the news coverage, he just didn't seem that concerned."

She had a point.

Chapter 25

The Horsehouse was quiet when I got there after Tulip's and my lunch. Just me and the mannequins, serenaded by country music. I was glad. I could use the time to think about the curious events of recent days. But also to think about all I had to do before sending my horse and tack to Texas with the Grandeens and their big living-quarters trailer on Thursday.

Sipping a probiotic drink from the mini-fridge, I made lists and timelines. I wrote down and checked off what I already had gathered together for the show, and what I still needed to take to ready my country home for Chili's arrival Sunday.

It was already Tuesday afternoon, with time slipping away. I felt a jolt of anxiety each moment I thought about having less than two days to polish gear and round up grooming supplies into plastic show tubs and deliver it all to Brassbottom Barn.

I'd taken my show jackets, blouses, pants and vests to be dry-cleaned. But I had to pick them up. I also had to ready my everyday wardrobe for Texas. No doubt I'd want to dress up a bit for the show's parties and the buddies' outings to shop and eat. The Fort Worth Stockyards historic district was loaded with gotta-have Western clothes and home décor. The Horsehouse couldn't hold a candle.

My everyday riding gear was already in my tack locker at the barn. But I had to buy more bags of mane bands and jars of hoof polish. You never had enough.

And I needed to confirm my lodging reservations. Get cash from the bank. Make sure I had enough cash IN the bank and in hand. Call Chili to firm up our plans for her housesitting and parent-watching. Make sure the parents were stocked up on meds.

There was sure to be an all-nighter in it, somewhere.

As if that weren't enough, around three I got a call from Jackson County Sheriff's Department. They wanted me for a formal interview at four-thirty. Great. Just what I needed. I knew I hadn't heard the last from them, since I'd said a gun was involved.

I closed the Horsehouse early and made like a bat out of hell for the Jackson County Sheriff's Office. As traffic was sluggish, I made more like a herd of turtles.

Two nondescript sedans, a compact and one SUV patrol unit were parked out front of the sprawling, metal-roofed building north of Medford when I pulled into the parking lot at twenty minutes past four.

Straightening my shoulders, I pushed through the glass door. I entered a shallow lobby with a windowed counter. Seated back of the window was a woman with a square black hairdo and a crisp white blouse. Her glasses were for seeing, not being seen in. When she looked up, her lips formed a line so tight you could sign your name on it.

I cleared my throat. She regarded me as if I were keeping her from real work.

"May I help you?" she said.

"Pepper Kane, here to give a statement —"

"Yes," said the woman. She rolled her chair over to consult a computer screen, and then rolled back to open the smaller window in her booth. She slid me a clipboard holding a printed sheet. "Read, sign and date, please."

I did so and handed the clipboard back through the window.

She cued an intercom, spoke into it and told me, "Someone will be right out."

A door at the end of a short hall to my left swooshed open. A familiar-looking tall woman in a brown uniform raised one hand and opened the door of a room off the hall. Her wide eyes and prominent cheekbones made me think that if she hadn't gone into police work she could have been a model. It was Detective Jenee, from Table Rock.

"Please come in, Miss Kane," she said. She nodded toward the ten-by-ten room that held a table and two chairs. A small recording device sat on the table, along with a notepad and a box of tissues.

She was all business. Understandable, given the circumstances. Supposedly I was a witness, as I'd said Monday. But that was just my word. This detective had no reason to believe I was only a witness. I could have played a role in Reg Stavropolis' fall. A whole case could depend on her demeanor, her questions and how she asked them.

"We will record what you say, do you agree to that, or request representation?"

"Yes, and no," I said, knowing the need to keep things simple. The less you said, the less could be turned against you. Not that I was guilty. I just didn't want to appear so.

Detective Jenee turned on the recorder and stated her name, the date and her purpose. She asked me to state my own particulars, and then we proceeded.

"It seems odd to need a statement when this incident was an apparent accident," I said boldly, just to let her know where I was coming from, and also to shake loose any information I myself might find useful. "Especially when the man affected is alive."

She sat back and tapped her pen on the tabletop. Her gaze narrowed.

"How do you know it was an accident? Or that the man is alive?"

The beating of my pulse in my temples sounded loud as a grandfather clock's.

"It looked accidental to me," I said. "Possibly caused by an argument, as I said. But either one, Sandra or Reg, could have fallen. They were going at it pretty hard."

"All right. Let's try another angle, Miss Kane. Mrs. Allende told us you had followed her on her ride with Mr. Stavropolis. Why did you do that?"

"As I said before, I just needed to take a trail ride. Added to that, I was worried for my friend, what with the recent attacks on women and Reg having a nasty rep with women. Then I saw that connection with his foreman, who I think may be involved luring young girls. Which I called you all about."

Again the tapping pen on the table. She paused to jot a note. Then she looked up.

"Couldn't you have let the sheriff know about the couple's ride and your fears, when you called in the other incident?"

Damn. She had me. Somehow, in the haze of memory from that crazy morning, I thought I had indicated that. But I was in a hurry – a hurry to protect another woman, a friend. Maybe even save a life. My palms began to sweat.

"It all happened so fast, I just didn't think," I said, recalling with chagrin that Sandra had said almost the same thing about why she'd come after me on Table Rock.

Detective Jenee sat back and folded her arms. She gave me a sympathetic smile.

"I am sure this has been hard on you, Miss Kane. Why don't you just take a deep breath, relax, and tell me exactly how things unfolded Monday. Starting from when you woke up. Do you want water, or coffee or anything?"

There it was. The attempt to be reasonable, to empathize with me, to soften me up so I might reveal something I hardly knew, myself.

So I declined refreshment and told her everything that had happened, with no frills or editorializing. That's what I would want if I were on her side of the table.

She interrupted briefly to clarify timing or placement of people. When I asked about the progress of the investigation, the foreman, or Stavropolis's condition, the detective guided me back on track.

Finally we were done. She snapped off the recorder and looked at me neutrally.

"Thank you, Miss Kane, that's all for now." She stood, smoothed her trousers and extended her hand. "Thank you. We'll be in touch if we need more."

Very matter-of-fact, professional, yet cordial. I liked her approach. So unlike that of Sheriff Jack, who thought he could intimidate you with one blink.

Speaking of. We ran into The Griz himself in the hall.

"Well, we meet again, Miz Kane," he said, rocking back on his boot heels and giving me the suspicious glint from his shiny button eyes.

"Afternoon, Sheriff," I said.

"Remember anything more useful than you told us Sunday?" he winked.

Chapter 26

That night at home, having fetched my gun at Dardanelle's, I was jumpy as a cat. I focused on giving my best show bridle a final polish and checked my lists of items to pack for the World Show. One list of gear to go to Brassbottom Barn the next day, and another list of clothes and tack I would check through the airline when I caught my flight in the wee hours Monday.

I repacked extra show-grooming gear and other supplies into one large lidded tub to take to the Grandeens. That done, I refolded and repacked my outfits. They included a sparkly fitted vest, a svelte beaded and fringed Western jacket, two pair of black stretch show pants, two tailored cotton blouses, and my chaps and boots. My two custom hats, which had cost an arm and leg but were worth it for how they set off my face, went into a double hatbox with extra padding – all to be checked as luggage on the plane.

Oh, and the jewelry, of course – fabulous fake earrings with Tiffany dreams.

I was concentrating on Western classes for this show. I had enough to think about without adding English tack and outfits to my growing stash.

Feeling my stomach buck with hunger, I tucked the last jacket into a garment bag, slid up the long zipper, and attached the tiny padlock with contact information to the top. One of my recently manicured nails snagged and popped a crack. I don't wear long nails, but do like a nice French manicure. I would have to get this redone in Texas.

No time now, unless one of Freddie's gals could squeeze me in.

I was just settling down in front of the TV with my dinner tray, anticipating a late update on the Reg Stavropolis case, when my cellphone sang.

My heart skittered when I saw the name.

"Hey, Sonny." I couldn't quite believe that the love of my life, or at least of recent years, had called twice in the same week. Was he in trouble? Did he need a favor? Maybe he just really missed me. A girl could hope.

"Hell-oh," he sing-songed, his voice plunging on the second syllable.

"Long time no hear from," I said with what I hoped was a teasing lilt. "How are things going at the protest?"

"I wouldn't know."

"What do you mean? I thought you were up to your handsome eyebrows in keeping the peace out there."

"No more peace to keep. I'm more interested in making peace with you, Lady."

"Well, now," I sputtered, searching for a snappy comeback. "In that case, the white flag is out. I surrender."

My Boston Terriers exploded off Big Brown, where they'd been napping. They took up a barking station at the front door, creating such a commotion that I carried the phone with me toward the window, where I waved my arms and shouted, "Hey! Shut up!" I glanced at the shotgun to the left of the door.

"I thought you were happy to hear from me," Sonny said, sounding wounded.

"I meant the dogs." I reached down to push them aside, and reached to pull aside one window drape. "Hold on. Someone's here. I've been investigating the missing child case, and weird things are happening. Like my gate chains fastened the wrong way, and then a warning note."

I lifted a drape edge and peeked out the window. The glow from the yellow porch light showed a huge, dark figure, cell phone to ear, looming below the steps. My heart flipped as I recognized that figure. Flushing, I dropped the drape. The next second I unlocked the door and swung it wide just as Sonny jumped up on the porch.

"Damn you!" I said. My words came out muffled as one of Sonny's long, black-shirted arms pulled me tight against his unyielding torso. I trembled the length of me.

Emanating heat and a strength that never failed to shock me, he buckled my knees with a downward gaze and broad, sleepy-eyed smile. He searched my eyes, and then bent his head to press his wide, sensuous lips against my thin soft ones. My head angled back with the pressure, but he brought up his other hand to cradle it so he could kiss me more deeply. His tongue darted around mine while his mouth sucked it gently.

I felt warmth spread through my belly, and dampness grow between my legs. There was no stopping this runaway train. Even if I'd wanted to.

"Mmmm," he said, stroking the back of my head and ruffling my hair. "I love your hair. So – mm – silky."

As he kiss-walked me backwards indoors, he released my head enough to pull the door shut. Then he resumed walking me while raining kisses over my face and neck. I didn't know where we were headed but I was sure I wanted to go there. Not that I had any choice in the matter.

I was vaguely aware of dogs barking in the background. But after Sonny laid me down on my back on the long leather sofa, the barking stopped. There was only sweet, deep breathing. His, and mine. The weight of his chest on me. And the rhythm of his slowly grinding pelvis, his hardness, his jeans shooshing against my jeans.

His face changed its downward angle against mine, his teeth now play-biting my lip until I wanted to cry out, but not in pain.

One of his hands worked under my sweatshirt and cupped a breast, his thumb brushing back and forth over the hard nipple. The fingers opened to span both of my breasts, massaging them lightly.

I bucked and moaned under him, burning with a slow fire I had not known before. Why was he taking so long getting my jeans off?

Now ready to burst with desire, I fumbled with my zipper, helping his hands, and then worked on his zipper. We wriggled free, laughing as we did so. Then it was belly to belly again, both of us gasping. We were consumed in a crazy rushing blaze, unseeing, unknowing, feeling the heat but not being burned. Higher, higher, rose the flames until ... I hung high above, frozen, quiet, then suddenly plunged over the edge, whirling with joy until I came to rest quietly.

Pressed chest to chest, our hearts beat in perfect unison, my body sunk deep into the plump seat cushions of the now-warm leather sofa.

In a few moments I became aware of cool air on my arms and legs. Sonny raised up, as if he knew what I was feeling, and pulled down a fluffy throw to cover our bare parts. His long black braid, threaded with a wide red ribbon, fell across my face.

I laughed, and shook it aside.

"Welcome home, Sonny," I said, kissing his earlobe and his high cheek.

"Home is where you are." He sighed contentedly. His cheek lay against mine.

"That was one hell of a trick you played," I said, play-swatting his back.

"Pretty tricky yourself," he said, not moving.

"I mean it. I could have had a heart attack."

"But you didn't."

I lay there in my semi-coma a while longer before struggling out from under him, grabbing the throw and shuffling to the bathroom to clean up. Stopping in the doorway to my bedroom, I turned to look at him as he lay, now face up, on the sofa. He had zipped his jeans, but had left his shirt open, revealing his strong chest with its sundance scars.

He shot me another million-dollar smile. No wonder ladies fell over for him from one end of the country to another. Was I really so special? Or just another one of his unofficial "wives'? He claimed powerful men of every race – and he saw himself as a powerful Lakota warrior – had to feed their power often and in different ways, from athletic and business victories, to political and military conquests. But success with attractive, challenging women ranked first. Because genetically, that's what other successes were about: improving the gene pool and making their seed dominant.

Or words to that effect. We used to argue about it, in the beginning. Now I merely accepted it as part of having Sonny in my life. Which didn't say great things about me, I admit. But it's just how it was now. I needed him, he needed me. No questions asked.

"You hungry?" I said.

"Got any pejuta?" he said, meaning pejuta sapa, or black "medicine." Java. Coffee. Lifeblood of many Indian people. Lifeblood of me, as well.

"Can reheat this morning's," I said. "or make new."

"This morning's." He rose to pet the dogs, and go use the other bathroom.

God, I had forgotten how tall he was. Six-foot-six filled a doorframe. Or nearly.

After my wash up, I recombed my red mop, applied some peach gloss to my kiss-swollen lips and, for good measure, added a splash of perfume to my wrists. What a fine and delicious feeling to have someone to do that for. I was into delicious, right then. It had been a long, dry summer and fall.

I heard the back French door close and bouncy dog paws on the kitchen linoleum. When I walked into the kitchen, I smelled re-warmed coffee. Sonny sat at my vintage oak table, his long legs kicked out and crossed at the ankles. He looked at home there.

That's when it came back to me. His statement, casually whispered, while I was coming down from the outer reaches of lovemaking.

"Home is where you are."

That's what he'd said. It had pleased me at the time, but I hadn't been in the proper mood to fully appreciate it. Now I turned it over in my mind.

I filled my favorite Pendleton mug with coffee, dribbled in salted caramel creamer, and plunked down in a chair across from Sonny.

As if he guessed what was coming, he pre-empted me.

"Spirits said you were in trouble," he said, looking at me appraisingly. "You said some things on the phone Sunday. But I need to know more, if I am going to help you."

Chapter 27

I gave Sonny the update on all that had happened, and my role in it, with Reg and Sandra, the missing Nancy, my suspicions that her father may have played a role in her disappearance, possibly abused her. I also touched on the threats to Dutch and the other show judges. About who had a stake in the Superstar horses doing well, who did not.

Sonny listened without speaking. He merely nodded and murmured knowingly.

"You really put yourself out there," he said, "going on that ride on Table Rock. Witnessing what you did. Made yourself a person of interest in the eye of The Law."

"No kidding," I said, rolling my eyes.

"I wonder what that woman – Sandra – is to you. There are many things you have in common between you, you both admire each other. But I question if was this enough to put so much on the line for."

I felt busted. He was asking his typical indirect question, a traditional Indian way of gleaning information without directly asking, without putting someone on the spot.

"Not sure, Sonny. Can't quite explain it, myself."

"People can try. But only if they want to know themselves."

That was a curious statement. To know, for myself? Or to better know myself?

"As I say, there were the recent attacks on women out on first dates in the country with men they barely knew. Plus Reg's nasty reputation, and temper. Then his foreman, who I'm convinced has solicited young women, possibly against their will."

"Sometimes the imagination works too hard, sees problems when none exist."

I bit my tongue. Sonny knew me well. But he would never criticize me directly. His oblique method made me look inward. Criticize myself, if blame were to be laid.

"You may be right," I said. "But the informed imagination also can point the way to secrets that someone wants to stay secret. Maybe help prevent further mayhem."

His slow nod made me relax. I blew out a calming breath.

"I guess there's something else," he said, sliding his long fingers back and forth on the table. "Some things you and your riding buddy, Sandra, have in common besides horses, troubled daughters, the will to win."

I looked out the French door toward the hills. Fall color was making inroads.

"I suppose in other ways we are alike," I said. "Successful, confident, proud. People look up to us. We have curves thrown our way that would bring down lesser women – divorce, abuse, troubled kids. And I admit it. We're both kinda pushy."

Sonny said nothing.

"But I like who I am. I own it." I lifted my chin.

"Sometimes pushy is a good thing," Sonny said, a smile flickering at the edge of his mouth. "Might get you what you want." He held out a hand. When I took it, he pulled me onto his lap. I leaned against him, shut my eyes and felt the strong beat of his heart.

"I love feeling your heartbeat," I said. "Like the drum. Sending Creator's love through Mother Earth's beings. That how it goes?"

"A-ho," he said. "Yes." He rested his chin on the top of my head.

"Sonny? When we were making love, right after, you said something to me."

"Home is where you are."

He knew what I was going to say. Another of this man's talents.

"I wonder what that meant."

"I say what I mean."

"I know, Sonny. Just like last summer you said, 'I love you'."

The chin pressure on my head lightened but I felt him clench his jaws.

"I say what I mean."

I wriggled around to look him in the eyes. The skin over my temples tightened, and I felt the pulse in my neck

"Do you think you will ever want to make a real home, Sonny? Just you and me?"

The silence was deafening. I heard dogs snoring in the living room. The chiming of my gilded clock sounded like Big Ben's. Out on the road, an ATV roared by.

"You are my home, Pepper," said Sonny, running a forefinger along my jaw. "I come to you, I'm at peace. I have enemies – men who are jealous, women who use me. But I don't feel that with you. Never with you."

"And that means?"

"Can't see the future. Only the now. We obey our heart. We live where it is happy." His eyes were inky pools of mystery.

One of the dogs growled in the living room. The other barked. There was a sharp clang outside, followed by a grating sound, coming from where my driveway angled off the road. I launched off Sonny's lap and ran to the window. Pulling aside a drape, I saw, in a pale beam from a security light, one gate standing half open.

My breath caught in my throat. I didn't want to ask. I was afraid of the answer. But I had to. I looked back at Sonny.

"Did you leave the gates open after you drove in?"

He frowned, and came toward me.

"A ranch boy always leaves a gate as he found it," he said. "They were closed with the chain double-wrapped. I went through and I secured them as they had been."

Chapter 28

I knew what this meant. The person who'd messed with my gates before was back at it. Even likely knowing, at the sight of Sonny's truck, that I had company.

"You have a padlock?" Sonny said.

"Not one to spare."

"I'll secure the gates tonight as best I can, and get a padlock tomorrow." Sonny walked out into the semi-dark yard.

Mind whirring, I changed into my bedtime tee and sheepskin flip-flops. After Sonny returned, rubbing his hands from the cold, I served us the last of mom's pie, loaded. I could start my diet tomorrow. Now I needed serious comfort food.

Sonny sat down at the table. With his fork, he teased off a tiny portion of pie and nudged it to the edge of the plate. I recognized his gesture as a symbolic offering to the Creator and to departed souls. I hadn't seen him do this ritual in a while.

He saw my questioning gaze.

"Being at camp, praying with elders and going to sweat lodge put me back in touch with our traditions," he said. He shut his eyes. "We honor you who have gone before, all our relatives. Wopila, thank you for your help so that we may live."

Without further ado, he shoveled a big forkful of pie into his mouth.

"I could live on this," he said, licking his lips. "Your mom knows how to cook. Her pie is better than fry bread." His eyes sparkled. "She part Indian?"

"Mom claims we're descended from Annie Oakley, who performed with Indians in Bill Cody's Wild West shows. Her maiden name's Mosely, like Annie's real name. Oakley was a stage name she used, after a street she'd lived on."

He wiped his mouth with a napkin, and grinned

"You done any target practice lately?"

"No."

"You'd be smart to. Especially with someone trying to rattle your cage."

No kidding.

"Maybe I can find time," I said, "to plink some cans on fence posts." Though I'd been packing before and during the Table Rock ride, it had been awhile since I'd fired my Smith & Wesson.

Sonny and I slept like the proverbial logs that night, Boston Terrier bedmates notwithstanding. The next day he helped me load my truck before taking my gear to Brassbottom Barn, while he set out to connect with his deputy-cousin, Boo.

He'd spend a little time "scouting other contacts" who might yield intel on leads investigators were pursuing re Reg and his foreman. He told me not to expect too much, but at least get a feel for what was happening. His main plan was to drive to Redding, a few hours south, to check out Sandra's ex, and then return to look into strip-clubs and talent agencies in the Rogue Valley and farther north up I-5. He'd be gone all day.

All that was okay by me. I had a full slate, myself. Sonny drew me to him for a goodbye kiss, and left about eight.

I called Tulip to make sure she'd be working The Horsehouse that morning. When I told her about Sonny's visit, she blew a cork.

"That dog," she exclaimed. "Why doesn't he just marry you? He says he loves you, says your heart is where his home is."

"He loves his freedom more," I argued.

"Or he maybe just thinks he does."

"You may be right."

After our chat, I called the hospital to again try to learn about Reg's condition. Same result as before. Zip. I'd expected that. I decided I'd try to visit him, myself. I might get lucky if I poked around, casually spoke to personnel. Even though evil, he simply had to recover from his injuries. I felt sad I'd not been able to stop his fall – survivor's guilt, I suppose.

I also needed him to live so I wouldn't be a person of interest or even a suspect in a homicide, negligent or otherwise. Hopefully he would soon be able to talk about what really happened up on Table Rock.

First I headed out to pick up my dry cleaning, visit the bank and deliver my tack and grooming tubs to Brassbottom. I gathered a few other items from my locker there, and scored an invitation to early lunch with Donna in her triplewide. I'd wanted to talk with her, hear any news about the threats and tease out her theories on the Allendes.

As Donna bustled between her sink and refrigerator, I settled onto the cowhide-covered stool at her granite-topped breakfast bar. Oiled-bronze fixtures given to Texas-star and longhorn motifs graced walls, cabinets and drawers. An ivory valance over the sink window sported a coiled lariat at either end. A chandelier tricked out with fake pistols hung from the ceiling.

"Haven't been in your house for a while," I said. "Love your new décor."

"Cowgirl chic all the way," she smiled, spooning a mound of potato salad onto Indian-motif plates that already held tuna-salad sandwiches made with peasant bread. Donna seemed to do everything to perfection, from riding to cooking and decorating.

Bringing us each an iced tea in old-fashioned Coke glasses, she sat down next to me, and tucked into her sandwich. I followed her lead.

"All ready for the show?" she said, discreetly chewing.

"Pretty near."

"Saw you bring in your grooming tubs. We're loading the trailer tonight. There'll be enough to do tomorrow, before we haul outta here with the horses."

"What time do you plan to leave?"

"Eight or nine," she said. "Which probably means noon. Always last-minute stuff. Want to make Salt Lake City our first stopover."

I calculated in my head. The first leg of the drive would take about ten hours.

"Have you heard from Sandra? I saw her yesterday but forgot to ask if she's still going to the Worlds."

"She brought her stuff by last night," Donna said. "We assume she and Jeanne are still going. But if the sheriff wants her to stay in the area for further questioning, we'll have to take her horses and show them ourselves."

"Sandra probably won't let Jeanne go if she herself can't be there. Anything new on the threats to the show judges?"

"De nada. Well, that's not quite true. You know Royce and Rogers, head of the Shiny Suspicion syndicate, in Texas? Suspicion being second to Superstar as a sire?"

"Yes."

"Their dogs went to barking around midnight a day or two ago. Security cams showed someone using a pry bar on the breeding sterile-room door. They went out to confront him, but whoever it was must have heard them coming, and vanished."

"Who told you? What do you figure?"

"The guy was after frozen semen from their stallion. Probably to destroy it. The show committee texted us last night. Dutch is really upset. It seems we're all headed straight for a tornado in Texas. Who knows who'll survive it."

Each sunk a moment in our own worries, Donna and I ate drank in silence. This new development threw a monkey wrench into the works, already compromised.

"You want anything in that tea?" she said at last.

"No, thanks. My head is muddled enough. But I'd like to hear your ideas about Sandra and Reg, the missing daughter, or the judge threats. That was a super lunch, by the way. I want the secret behind your amazing potato salad."

"I soak the chopped onion in the vinegar-and-sugar for ten minutes before I mix in mayonnaise and other ingredients. My grandma taught me that."

Donna took our plates and took them to the sink to rinse. She looked out the window and seemed to be considering something.

"My thoughts on Reg are that he was a snake. I mean, is. Not all he seems."

"Any reason in particular?"

"Just a feeling, things I've heard. My thoughts on Sandra? She never talks about her daughter. I would, if I were in her position. I'd talk about Nancy to everyone I met."

"You may be right. But I do think she's deeply embarrassed, feels it somehow was her fault. Doesn't go with her polished, capable image. I think that's all it is."

"And I think that ex-husband of hers was a reason the daughter disappeared."

"Really, Donna? In what way? Why do you think that?"

"She did once say she divorced him because he was controlling and abusive. Maybe he abused the daughter."

"I've considered that," I said. "As a matter of fact, my boyfriend, Sonny Chief, was going to try to meet the ex and look into that today. Sonny came in last night."

"Really. He helped you on our other case, didn't he? I do know Sandra's daughter Jeanne really loves her new horse though it has been hard for her to ride. Hard for Dutch, too, though he's committed to showing it. It's great money. But he probably also still feels responsible for the death of Dark Vader, the mare's full brother."

I considered that. Dutch did seem committed to Jeanne's horse, despite its crazy, unpredictable ways. He had to know it wasn't the right horse for Jeanne.

Donna dried her hands and walked back to the bar as I stood up to leave.

"Don't tell anyone," she said, "but they pay us double to train it," she said. "No other trainer will take the horse. Why the breeder let it go at less than it's worth. Dutch seems to think he can fix it. His pride's a bit over the top, between you and me."

I hesitated, hearing Donna's words. All this was news to me. I'd wondered why Sandra had put Jeanne's horse in training at Brassbottom Barn. Guess it was the only game in town. And the Grandeens did need the money. Always needed money. Hard keeping a show barn in the red, anywhere. But more so in the laid-back Rogue Valley.

"Jeanne and her mom are more obsessed to win world championships than almost anyone we've known," Donna added. "And the ex-husband expects her to win the World High-Point Award, too. May have some money on that. Wouldn't be surprised."

Her words turned my thoughts in a new direction. The roots of obsession often tunneled into places they did not belong.

"The obsession is pretty unreasonable," I said. "Supposing Jeanne's father bought the hot new horse for her as a way to apologize for something, or calm her mother, who's scared Jeanne might think about running away, too. His promise of a generous gift, the new car, too, may have kept Sandra from being too hard on her husband in the divorce settlement."

Chapter 29

I went to The Horsehouse to work the afternoon shift. My mind still whirled with all Donna had said. About Sandra and Reg. About the Allende girls and their father. About a threat to owners of the stud that was challenging Superstar.

My mind focused on one name: Grant Haverstadt. The big shareholder in the Shiny Suspicion syndicate. I texted Tommy Lee Jaymes to see if he knew Haverstadt, having known Bradford and other players in Texas circles.

Tommy Lee texted right back: "Heard of but don't know Haverstadt. Will check."

It was no energy drain to keep the Horsehouse humming. I had few customers. I informed those few that we would be open limited hours the next three weeks, with my daughter staffing the store while Tulip and I were in Texas.

At a leisurely pace, dancing to country tunes on the music system, I caught up on sweeping and dusting, including ridding overhead speakers of five pounds of cobwebs. My least favorite pastime, although the results made the store sparkle. I even washed windows. Things had to be really slow for me to do that.

I also caught up on pricing and inventory, filled online orders, and called Mom. She surprised me with news that Sonny had stopped by their house that morning.

He'd met my parents but his visiting them without me was a first. Was he finally feeling more at home with my family? At home with me? Sonny usually had time only for me on his occasional, too-short visits to the Valley.

"That was nice," I said. "Maybe he's taking our relationship more seriously."

"I forgot how handsome that man is," said Mom. "And so tall! He talked to Dad, mostly, asking about his business, old contacts, and such."

"Really."

"Dad later said Sonny asked about nightclubs Dad had accounts with, or knew of his time on the City Council. Gus got a bang out of being needed. He was strutting around here like a rooster. Even drove to town without wrecking Lone Ranger."

"Sounds like a win-win," I said.

"I sent Sonny off with a tub of cold fried-chicken and poppers. I remember you said he loved those cream-cheese-stuffed jalapenos I sent you home with one time."

"Sonny loves all food," I said, quickly adding, "especially yours."

I smiled and clicked the phone off. That Sonny was sure a crafty one. Combining business with pleasure seemed to be his specialty. I was sure he'd also had made time to check in with his cousin, Deputy Boo George. They'd likely lunched at Katie's.

When my cell phone rang, I saw Grant Haverstadt's name in the ID pane.

"Sorry to be so late getting back to y'all," he said. "Been a zoo down here. Everybody needs something, like yesterday. Horse show fever."

"I can imagine," I said. "Hey, thanks for the texts earlier." Smooth the feathers, put the grillee at ease.

"I still can't give you any more info on the judge threats, or that break-in at Royce and Rogers' barn. Awful thing."

"What about that break-in? As a part owner of Suspicion, you must be fried. Any thoughts on who did it? Or why?"

He chuckled. "Some crazy trying to hurt Suspicion's bottom line, lessen the number of progeny, some Superstar fan. Pretty obvious." He chuckled again.

"Unless it's not," I said, taking a new tack. "The break-in could be an attempt to throw people off. Someone threatening judges who don't favor Suspicion progeny over Superstar's, might actually have skin in the Superstar game."

"How so? Don't follow."

"The break-in at Suspicion's breeding barn could have been someone using reverse psychology on judges warned not to favor Superstar horses. To subtly influence them to refuse to be pressured, to turn them toward the Superstars."

Silence.

"Hello?" I said.

"That's reaching," he said.

"Maybe," I said. "What do you think?"

"Listen. All I can tell you is that on Royce and Rogers' security cam, the person who broke into Suspicion's breeding barn was tall, wearing a raincoat, had a hat hiding the face. And that they definitely were trying to hurt Suspicion's breeding prospects."

"Thank you," I said. "Guess we'll just have to see what happens in Texas."

"Have a good one," he said, and clicked off.

So. Another dead end. Or, at least, diversion off my path to get closer to solving the mystery of the judge threats and now the break-in. Haverstadt had been cordial and not seemed upset. Maybe he was an actor, like Tommy Lee. I would indeed have to see what happened in Texas.

Late in the day I called Tulip and caught her up on what Donna and Grant Haverstadt had said. She had nothing new to add.

At five o'clock I closed the shop. I stopped by the supermarket to stock up on groceries before heading home in the evening's slanted light. As I drove up my semi-private country lane, I felt a sense of accomplishment from work and show prep, and from making progress, however small, in my mysteries – including that about Sonny's leanings toward commitment.

As I turned in at my gravel drive, I noticed the double gates were chained as I had left them. Good. But I still knew someone was watching me, trying to scare me. The note had squashed my earlier hope that the wrong-wrapped chains and the gate-opening were pranks made by a neighbor teen high on drugs – a common thing in semi-rural neighborhoods where police presence was lacking due to funding cuts.

I parked in the double garage, headed up with my groceries, and glimpsed Velvet, my black-and-white cat, slipping around a corner. In the forested hills beyond the pasture wild turkeys gobbled among trees shot through with low sunlight. A brace of brays erupted from the mini-donkeys where our neighborhood lane met the county road.

Comforting sights, soothing sounds. I even gratefully thanked the Creator for the earthy smells of autumn perfuming the air.

I loved this country life in Southern Oregon – so shockingly different from the crowded, caffeinated cacophony of Seattle. It was a gorgeous city, underneath all that. Hilly, green, poised on a strip between Puget Sound and the Olympic Mountains to the west, and Lake Washington, burbs, farms and Cascade Mountains to the east. But it somehow had lost its nobler, smaller timber-and-shipping-town identity to a younger moneyed microchip mentality.

After feeding the horses and dogs, and stocking my cupboards and refrigerator for Chili's coming, I sat down with a sweet iced-tea in Big Brown to watch a little TV news.

Still nothing for the public on Stavropolis' condition nor on the investigation of his foreman. The fall was still being called an accident, and given barely a mention except to say Reg still was in critical care. Still alive, in other words.

Also no news from Sonny. He probably was working hard in Northern Cali. Mom's fried chicken and poppers would have seen him through the dinner hour.

I fixed myself a hot French dip sandwich and side salad, and ate from a tray in front of the TV. I must have fallen asleep, because I awoke with a start about eight. I realized I should have heard from Sonny. I hoped he wasn't in trouble, with Max Allende or whatever Sonny was investigating.

I decided to give him a call.

"Hell-oh," he sang after the first ring. I could hear traffic noise in the background.

"Hey, Crazy Horse," I said. He wasn't fond of racial nicknames, but he used them sometimes himself, in a lighthearted way with people who would take no offense. "Think you might be home tonight?"

"Don't wait up," he said. "Your mom's chicken and poppers have me going."

"Where are you, Sonny? What's up?"

"Been about everywhere between Eugene and Redding today," he said. "I'm with my uncle near Mount Shasta now. The Holy man. Doing a little ceremony."

"Making progress on any of our cases?"

"Yeah. But right now there's something you can do for me. If you have time."

"Yes?"

"Run up to Canyonville. It's only an hour north of you."

Was he nuts? It was late, and that town was a little longer than an hour away.

"Now why I would do that, supposing I had the time?"

"There's a strip club there owned by Gary Gracey, the guy your dad put me onto. Owns another club north outside Grants Pass. Charged once or twice for using underage girls, some from Southern Oregon and Northern California."

"How do you know this?"

"Called him. Posed as another club owner seeking talent. Said I knew your dad."

"The hell you say."

"Take Tulip along. And the Smith & Wesson."

My heart thudded as I straightened in the chair. Charlie licked my free hand.

"What are you smoking, Sonny Boy?"

"Pretend you are madams looking for new hires. Tulip has the new boobs and the eyelash thing you mentioned, so she'll look the part. You could tart yourself up, too."

"Now I know there's loco weed in your peace pipe."

"Sacred pipe," he corrected. "Take the picture of Nancy. Say she's a girl of yours who called to say some friends there were looking for new work."

I closed my eyes and sat in disbelief. The Bostons pawed at my legs, but I pushed them away. Sonny had clearly flipped out. He knew I was ballsy, that I loved danger and a challenge. But not that kind.

"Ha!" he said. "Got you."

I sighed.

"You sure did. Damn you."

"Thought you could use a laugh. You just relax now, Pepper. Button up the place, hit the hay. I left you a new padlock. Under the planter on the back deck. Put it on the gates. I have another key. Catch you in a couple hours."

"So you're coming, I take it." I guessed I was glad, but he'd given me quite the shock. "Did you learn anything today from Deputy Boo?"

"They still don't have anything on Stavropolis or the foreman. Stavropolis is still in the coma. But my take is, they'll let the incident go unless something changes."

"Right. So I'm not really a person of interest."

"No. But for some reason the sheriff keeps pushing to find something on you."

"Figures." I patted my dogs. My feet by now were covered with puppy toys.

"So, Beautiful. Get your beauty sleep. See you later."

"What's on your agenda tomorrow, Sonny?"

"Gotta head to Seattle to see my kids, then back to North Dakota for my weekend shifts at the Water Protectors' camp. How about you?"

"Seeing my horse off to Texas, working at the store, cleaning up around here."

We signed off. I took my dogs, my flashlight and my revolver out to the gates to attach the new padlock. Back inside, I wasted no time showering, and hitting the queen bed. Horizontal felt so good.

I flashed on Sonny's fake suggestion that I check out that nightclub. Was it a veiled suggestion? Such a mission would waste time and put us at great risk. Low lifes such as Gracey would stop at nothing to keep their low lives going.

Chapter 30

I awoke to the heart-stopping sound of a metallic crash, followed by the sounds of an engine roaring and tires squealing. The Bostons jumped off the bed and ran barking to the door. I sat up and switched on the light. The engine sounds faded.

Running through the house I turned on all the lights, and tried to see out the front window. All I could see was the pale glow of security lights at the gate and garage. But I saw the gates were wide open, and bent crazily.

I snatched my cell phone off the bedside table. It was midnight, straight-up. And Sonny not here yet. I hoped he was coming. I called 911 and gave a report of what had happened and what had gone before. I was told someone was on the way.

My feet felt icy. My dogs milled from the front door to the back. I let them out into the back yard just to get their nervous energy away from me. I quickly locked the door after them and checked my other locks and windows. All secure.

Picking up my phone again, I looked out the guest-bedroom window. Then the other bedroom window. The neighbors' dogs continued to bark wildly. I heard my own answering with snarling barks of their own.

I turned up the heat, turned on the TV and tapped Tulip's number in my phone.

"Yeah?" she mumbled, understandably cross. "Y'all know what all time it is?"

"Somebody just crashed their vehicle into my gates and busted them all to hell," I said. "Remember the earlier problems with my gates, the warning note?"

"Want me to come on over?"

"Might be nice, Tule. Sheriff sending someone. Sonny should have been back by now, but he probably got hung up doing recon for me in northern California. Visiting an uncle in Shasta, last I heard, about eight."

"Better hope it's not some gal he has stashed in Shasta," she said. "Oops. That just slipped out. Sorry."

"Damnit, Tulip, I was just feeling better about Sonny's and my relationship. He told me that home is where I am. He visited my parents."

"That does sound like progress. I'll be over soon as I can throw together a duffle."

As we hung up, flashing colored lights filled my yard and driveway. That set the dogs barking again, and threw carnival colors around my living room. I opened the door to see Sonny's cousin, Deputy Boo George, stride up the steps. Almost as tall as Sonny, but walking with a slight limp and smelling faintly of cigarette smoke.

"Pulling night duty again," he said. "Must've upset the chief."

"Want coffee?" I gestured for him to come in.

He shook his head and looked back over his shoulder. I could see somebody in uniform moving around with a flashlight out there.

"You look good, but gates not so much," Boo said, wiping his feet and coming inside. "Jim's pulling paint samples from the metal, and photographing the gates and tracks. Someone rammed them pretty good."

"Sending a message that can't be missed," I said, shivering at the implications.

"After we're done, we can pull it back together and try to lock it again, best we can. Sonny coming home tonight?"

"Thought so," I said. Boo had said "home." I thought that interesting.

His shoulder walkie-talkie crackled. He keyed it, listened to the other deputy's report and mumbled something back. I shut the door. Boo drew out a pad and pencil. Then I told him what had happened. Mentioned the warning note. He wanted it, so I padded to my office and brought it back out.

"Got a plastic baggie?" he said.

I picked up my cell phone, snapped a picture of the note, and went to get a clear plastic bag from the kitchen. Boo bagged the note and read it through the plastic.

"So what are your thoughts about who's harassing you?" he said.

"It could be one of several people." I gave him the names and backgrounds, as far as I knew them, on Reg, Carlos, Sandra, Max Allende, and threw in the things with the world-show judge threats and the breeding barn break-in near Fort Worth.

"You tell anyone besides your horse friends and Sonny, about those threats?" Boo asked. "Talk it over with anyone else?"

"No ... wait a minute. Yes, I did. Had a phone call from a friend in Texas, near where the world show will be held. Mentioned it to him. He knew the judge who was nearly run down by a pickup outside his ranch gates."

Boo scribbled in his notepad.

I gave him my padlock key. He said that after relocking the damaged gate, he'd drop the key over my side of the fence, behind a fencepost one over from the gatepost. Before leaving, Boo told me to keep my phone and gun close.

I said I'd be okay, especially with Tulip coming for the night and Sonny probably headed my way, too.

"All good," Boo said, nodding. "But don't hesitate to call if you need us."

When they left, I locked the door and settled back in Big Brown to numb my mind with a little TV. A late-night comedy show was on. I was in no mood to laugh.

I jumped when my cell phone rang.

"How the hell am I supposed to get in? These gates are locked tight."

I picked up the flashlight and hurried out the door toward the gates. Tulip climbed back in Peggy Sue while I found the key back of the other post, and opened the padlock. Luckily the padlock wasn't damaged when the chain broke in the crash, but the gate frames were toast. At least there was enough chain to rewrap and padlock them after Tulip and her pink pickup drove through. I shut the gate and locked it.

Just as I turned to hop in Peggy Sue and ride with Tulip to the house, I heard a low rumble and soft honk. Behind me headlights flashed. I turned to see Black Beauty roll into view. Five-eighths-minus gravel crunched under the truck's big tires, which stopped turning abruptly just outside my gates.

"Pepper!" shouted Sonny through the window. "What are you doing out here?"

Even in the dim glow of his truck's dash lights, I saw an angry, puzzled face.

Chapter 31

"Oops," I yelled to Tulip, still waiting in Peggy Sue just inside the gates. "Guess Sonny came after all."

"Guess I can turn around and head back home," she shouted, inching Peggy Sue forward to turn her around.

"You're welcome to stay, Tule, since you drove all this way," I said.

"And be a third wheel?" she snorted.

"At least stay for a cup of coffee? May find you an extra maple bar, too."

"I will take you up on that," she said. "I've been dieting too hard lately, to fit into my show outfits. And you know what that does to the old top shelf." She scattered gravel as she gunned her truck toward the house.

Black Beauty stood grumbling behind the gates. The headlight glare partially blinded me, but I made out Sonny's face, and his forearm resting on the window ledge.

"Boy, am I glad to see you," I said.

"I see your gates trashed. And you got company. What's up?"

"I heard somebody crash the gate, called the sheriff and then Tulip."

"Said I'd be here."

"I wasn't sure when, though."

His sighed. His face looked inscrutable. What had I done? Insult his Sioux warrior pride? This was getting interesting. We hadn't really fought before. As an officer himself, Sonny couldn't really have expected me to call him first, or even second, with him who knew how far away. But he clearly looked hurt. I could press it, or I could ignore it.

"Guess the padlocked gates didn't hold up to a ramming," he said at last. "This guy's serious. I knew I had to get back tonight." He stared toward Tulip's pickup under the big tree by the front porch.

"Tulip's only staying for coffee," I said, now embarrassed at having been such a wuss that I asked her to come stay the night. "Boo and another deputy were just here. They checked it all out. Just left."

Sonny rapped his palms against the steering wheel while his truck continued to grumble. Then he leaned over inside the cab, opened the glovebox, jumped out and turned the key in the padlock. He took his time opening one of the crunched gates.

"You go on up to the house, get Tulip her coffee. We'll sort it all out later."

Here we'd been getting along better than ever. Now it seemed we had fallen back a step, getting on each other's nerves. Oh, well. We were both exhausted. And, wasn't it all just part of a growing relationship? Two steps forward, one step back?

Tulip had settled herself at the dining table with a day-old maple bar and a half-day-old cup of coffee. She'd filled a mug for me. She wore no makeup, and had finger combed her white-blond hair. The Bostons milled at her feet, angling for a crumb. I sat down across from her and filled her in on Boo's visit and Sonny's mood.

"Male pride," she said, making a dismissing gesture with one manicured hand. "You can turn that around in a heartbeat."

"I know." I straightened a small pile of magazines next to the salt-and-pepper shakers in a stylishly rusted holder, and gazed at the night-black front window. "I just wish I could read him – and this whole situation – better than I have."

"You know," Tulip soothed, speaking louder now, as the throb of Black Beauty sounded beyond the door. "I wouldn't worry about any of it, though. You – we – will work it all out. Sure of it."

The front door swung open. Sonny's black-clad form filled the frame. He smiled as if nothing were amiss. He walked in, closed the door and slouched with the dogs on the sofa. He turned his head toward the dining room.

"Hey, Tulip," he said. He looked tired. "Hell of a night."

"It is that, Sonny," she said. "Nice to see you. Now you're here, I'll just finish this coffee and be on my way." She raised her mug.

"Don't leave on my account."

Tulip touched my forearm.

"Here's the deal, Pepper," she said. "If someone really wanted to discourage you from snooping into one case or the other, and that judge thing is a long shot since you don't have any skin in that game, they'd already have silenced you."

She was right. A wave of nausea swept me. Too much excitement, plus late-night coffee. I pressed my lips together and leaned back in my chair.

"You're probably right, Tulip. But I can't relax until I get a handle on this. I think things may get a whole lot worse before they get better."

"I'd go with what Tulip says," Sonny said from the couch. "Take precautions, but don't let it get to you. It's not your job to solve everything. I'm here to help, at least while you're in Oregon. The law is on it. Your job is to be yourself. Stay centered. Then go win your championship at the Worlds."

It made total sense. Sonny was saying that he thought me capable, but also that he wanted me to realize my dream. Or at least my horse-related dream. His admission of admiration tempered with concern gave me a warm feeling. It'd be all right.

After Tulip left, Sonny and I fell into bed. But instead of indulging in pillow talk or play, we talked of his day, his trip to NorCal, things he'd learned that might be of use in our investigation into our mysteries. We'd covered much of it in our call that evening.

But then Sonny dropped the bombshell. We were lying on our backs, holding hands, as we stared into the bedroom dark.

"I did pay a visit to Max Allende, the ex," Sonny said, as casually as if he'd said he'd bought a new pair of cowboy boots.

I propped up on an elbow and looked at his face in outline, faintly blue in the glow of a nightlight in the master bath.

"My God, Sonny. Why didn't you tell me sooner?"

"I went to his warehouse headquarters. Guard said the boss had gone out with clients for a drink. Told him I was a supplier with an urgent delivery issue and hadn't been able to reach Allende on the phone."

"Good, good."

"It still cost me ten to learn he was at the country club. I drove out, flashed my badge and found him with a couple guys at a window overlooking the nineteenth hole. Classy place. Good thing I had the black leather jacket and turquoise bolo tie you gave me stashed under the truck seat."

Sonny rolled over and pushed his arm under my neck in a nicely possessive way.

"Had the Maitre D' introduce me as an exporter of Indian artifacts, on a short time frame, referred by the ex-wife with whom I had lunch after she showed me a property."

"Pretty creative story."

"He was wary but went outside with me for a quick smoke. I gave a fake name, and jived about my having to sell one of Crazy Horse's pipes. Said I was a relative of Crazy Horse. Which is true."

"Uh-huh."

"He looked at phone photos I'd set up beforehand, heard descriptions, said he'd think about it. I wrapped up by saying his wife and daughter in Medford are doing well, and wanted me to ask if you'd learned any more about their daughter Nancy, where she might be, if you'd been in touch."

I bolted into a sitting position.

"No. You went there, Sonny? What'd he say?"

"Threw down his cigarette, half-smoked, stomped it and said, 'Why don't you ask my ex-wife? She's been doing the research.' He got in my face. Told me I wasn't there to sell him any Indian crap."

"Oh, boy," I moaned. "Blew your cover. He sounded totally reactive, like he knows something. He can't track you, or link you to me. Can he?"

"Doubtful. I acted all innocent. Not sure he bought it, though."

I felt deflated. Still, the news stirred something in my brain. Could Max or Sandra suspect where Nancy was, yet not been able to pinpoint it? Worse, and still troubling, was the idea the ex might be at least partly the reason for her disappearance.

"Anything else, Sonny?"

"As we went back inside I tried to patch things up. I said Jeanne was excited to be going to the World Show on the new horse he'd bought her. I played on his pride, to see if I could squeeze more out of him about the daughters and their relationship."

"How'd that work?"

"He seemed to take the bait, and said the mare was guaranteed by the seller to be a World Champion."

"Interesting. I wonder if the breeder, or Allende himself, is behind those judge threats — a big maybe, but worth looking at."

"My impression, Pepper? He's probably not, or he wouldn't have gone on about the horse that way. I think he's blowing smoke. Full of himself. Mister Big, tooting his horn. Bragging on his kid. Wouldn't say such things if he doubted me or my motives."

The "thought was plickening," as Tulip said of events that turned complicated.

"Or maybe he bragged like that," I said, "to throw you off. Make you think he wouldn't say that kind of thing if he were involved."

"There is that."

"So. He's Mister Big. I can see that, with his business success, coming from the background he did. Need a T. Rex ego, and maybe help from a few friends, to make it from there to the top of the food chain."

"Just file it away, Pepper. All I'm saying."

He stroked my arm, which now lay atop the covers.

"So glad you're here, Sonny."

"Me, too. Let's get some rest. You've had long days, and so have I."

"Oh," I said, lifting my head. "What about that nightclub up in Canyonville? The one Gary Gracey runs, that you wanted Tulip and me to scout out?"

"Been there, done that," Sonny said with a sigh.

"What? You're kidding."

"Acted like a porn director looking for two NorCal girls that told me they wanted to do movies. Made up a name. Desiree. Then threw in Nancy. Showed the photo."

"And?"

"Guy said he might know the girls, but told me to call Gracey, the owner. Gave me a number. Called it. Gracey said he sold the club. They're doing a big resort development around it. A Reg Stavropolis project."

Chapter 32

The morning dawned way too early and way too bright. But I went with it and hummed a tune as I made coffee. I slipped a couple frozen biscuits-and-sausage-gravy breakfasts into the oven as Sonny tended the dogs and horses. The way it should be. I could get used to this routine.

When he came back in, he took off his boots and washed up. I set our coffees on the table and saw our breakfasts had twenty more minutes. Sonny grabbed my wrist and spun me around. My chest slammed against his.

"Oof," I croaked.

"Mmmm," he crooned, bending down to cover my lips with his and to dip into my mouth with his tongue. He smelled of cold air and warm male, with a dash of fresh cotton T-shirt.

My breasts tingled and my hips wouldn't behave. I was transformed from tense, worried cowgirl to sinful, needy slut.

"Damn you, Sonny!" I murmured between fast kisses. Now he was lightly licking my neck, sliding his tongue into the hollow of my collarbone and beyond, stretching not only the neck of my T-shirt, but what was left of any resistance.

"You taste so good," he said, pulling away for a minute. "I can't get enough of you." Then he fell to kissing my lips again, moving down to lift my T-shirt hem and nibble my nipples.

My belly warmed. My knees buckled. He caught me in time, and swept me up into the warm cradle of his powerful arms. The bulging biceps felt like rocks.

"Sonny," I said, "at least let me turn off the oven. Or our breakfast will burn."

He carried me to the stove. I reached over and turned the oven knob to "off."

"You're the only breakfast I want," he laughed, throwing back his head so that his braid slid over his shoulder. "Burning hot."

He carried me to the bedroom, kicked shut the door, and set me down as gently. Then he fell beside me, turned on his side and lay his head on the pillow.

"Tell me if this is not a good time," he said, a worry line denting his brow.

"So I take it you're not mad at me." I ran my hand under his tee shirt, feeling the hard tiny scars there. He'd pierced his skin with eagle claws tied to rawhide strips the summer I'd gone to the rez to watch him dance. He'd sought visions while being pulled up by his chest piercings toward the branches of the sacred cottonwood and suffered and prayed for the earth and his people.

Strange as they seemed to some, I was glad those traditions survived. They empowered those who took part. I recalled when we sundance supporters were invited into the sundance circle while grandmas in white buckskin danced by, telling us visions.

"Two husbands, two babies," said one wizened crone who stopped in front of me. She patted my belly with her eagle feather, saying, "No more." I'd wondered if she meant no more babies, or no more husbands.

Sonny chuckled, and cupped my chin in his hand.

"You think I could be mad at you?" he said. His long body slowly slid atop mine, and joined us like locking pieces of a complicated puzzle. The puzzle's picture swirled, but began to resolve into an increasingly sharp and beautiful image that hung in space. An image of love. An image of forever?

We lay together listening to each other breathe, feeling our racing hearts slow.

Then my stomach rumbled. Biscuits and sausage gravy were calling. Elemental need would not be denied.

Sonny and I freshened up and made for the kitchen and dining table. It took only a moment to reheat the coffee and breakfasts. We ate like a pair of starving ranch hands. I slipped each begging dog a tiny crumb of biscuit dipped in gravy. Which, from the way they snarfed it down, you would have thought was Steak Delmonico.

"So what's the plan for today, Sonny?" I said, savoring another forkful. "I'm seeing Choc off with the other horses, running errands, working at the Horsehouse."

"Sandra might be there this morning?"

"Affirmative, Chief Chief." I winked.

Sonny gave me A Look.

"You talk pretty big for a wasichu," he murmured, giving it right back by calling me a "fat taker" or "white man" – what early Sioux called those who killed for pleasure, taking only the best meat and fat, leaving the rest to rot. Unlike Indians, who used every part of the beast down to the tail.

"Got more nightclubs to call about," he said. "Not sure I believe Gracey sold his club. See if others have any leads on Sandra and Max's missing girl."

"Good idea." I put my hand atop his. "I can't tell you how much I appreciate what you're doing.I don't have the time or connections you do. I feel sometimes that men I'm questioning don't take me seriously. Got that as a reporter, too."

He looked me up and down.

"Oh, you do all right. If anyone doesn't take you seriously, they should. Plus you have other techniques at your disposal."

"You're incorrigible, Sonny." I leaned over and smacked him with his braid.

Chapter 33

The morning's warmth was offset by a stiff wind and sparse overhead clouds that raced above. I drove my pickup down Highway 234, following curves of the low, fast-running Rogue River. To my right the waterway played hide-and-seek below a line of trees. The Class Four rapids of Til'omick Falls tossed like manes of running horses.

It was a bright mid-morning. But I still I drove moderately and kept an eye out for deer. They could jump like rabbits from the brush onto the road, and be slammed in an instant. For every one you saw, there were often one or two more nearby.

I felt excited after my morning with Sonny and eager to see Choc off to Texas. I also was bone-aching tired. Lovemaking could do that. So could being scared out of my skin in recent days. I vowed to keep going at a calm yet focused pace. Big things on the horizon. I would need all the mental and physical energy I could muster.

The Grandeen horse trailers – a long, living-quarters rig with room for six horses at the back, and a shorter three-horse – sat hooked up to a tractor cab and one-ton dually like mine in front of Brassbottom Barn. Clients' vehicles were parked to one side. The trainers bustled in and out of the barn and trailers with bins, buckets, metal tack racks and padded saddle-carriers. Customers helped with loading, or groomed their horses before the long journey.

Sandra Allende's silver Mercedes stood out. Low sun slicing through a break in the clouds threw glints off ek lines, darkened windows and bright chrome. However, I saw no trace of Sandra or Jeanne. The girl must be in school. But Sandra, perfectionist that she was, had to be here, seeing to every detail before their horses' departure. This coming show, like the new horse, gave Sandra a great way not only to feed her own pleasure, but also offer a spectacular way to show love to her remaining daughter.

I still wasn't absolutely sure they were going, with recent developments. I aimed to find out. My chance came immediately after I greeted the Grandeens, and Little Stewie and his mother, at the open barn doors. Sandra, sleek in a quilted black jacket and flashy diamond studs, was schlepping her tack tub toward the large trailer. Then I heard Jeanne's voice inside the barn.

I walked alongside Sandra as she neared the tack-compartment's open door. Bins already were stacked inside, anchored by bungee cords clipped to hooks in one wall. The vagaries of driving at highway speed, with horses, over several dicey mountain passes between here and Texas, could turn even a carefully packed tackroom topsy-turvy, if things weren't strapped down.

"Saw your Mercedes," I said, adding warmth to my words to show I was making an effort to come to terms with our differences. "Thought you'd have brought the truck, since it'd hold way more show stuff."

There was no use carrying hard feelings about Table Rock into our show journey. Besides. She had apologized, and given a halfway understandable reason for her flipout.

"Wouldn't you know it?" she said. "Engine crapped out. Brand new truck. Like I don't have enough worries."

"No kidding."

"I called a mobile mechanic. But he couldn't come until afternoon, and I couldn't wait." She checked the lid on her bulging tack tub. "Now I know what Hannibal went through to take his army and elephants over the Alps." She grunted as she struggled to hoist her tub to the top of a three-high stack.

"Here, let me help." I stooped and put my shoulder against one end of the bin. Together, using all our Girl Power, we wrestled it where it needed to be, and then bungeed it to the wall.

"Thanks, Pepper," she said with a wan smile. "I've been to Worlds, but never to the Big Dance with a daughter. What was I thinking, taking that ride with Reg?"

"Yeah," I said. "I kind of wondered the same thing myself."

She put a hand on my arm and looked around before leaning toward me.

"So, did you hear?" Her eyes anxiously searched mine.

"Hear what, Sandra?"

"The news about Reg? I stopped by the hospital this morning to drop off a card."

"Oh, yeah? How is he?" I held my breath.

"Still alive. But a volunteer at the front desk, lady I showed property to, said Reg almost slipped away last night. There'd been an unauthorized visitor to the CCU."

"No," I breathed. "How could that happen? Why would it happen? He should be on 24-hour watch."

I wondered if someone with a major grudge had learned Stavropolis was in the hospital, and saw this as payback time. It could be an ex-wife, a business rival, or an employee. Maybe the foreman I'd met, or that employee he'd run down in his truck.

"Staff pulled out the stops to bring him back," Sandra said. "That's all I know."

"Did they get any security film, or a description?"

"No. But they thought it might be an employee."

"Or," I said, "someone impersonating one. Been known to happen."

She drew back, and blinked rapidly.

"Oh, my. I never thought of that."

I moved closer to her, aware of other barn buddies approaching with tack tubs.

"Be horrible if he died, Sandra. For Reg, in particular. But also for you."

"Tell me about it. I'm so stressed I can hardly function. Hey, what time is it?" She drew out her cellphone. "Shoot! I have to take Jeanne to her school to pick up homework she'll do while we're gone. Then we're heading for Cali to take care of some business, and driving to Fort Worth from there. See you in Texas."

Sandra bustled off to find Jeanne. Moments later they appeared, hellbent for Mercedes. Jeanne smiled as she passed me.

"See you in Texas," she said. "Slow down, Mom. My leg, remember?"

"You're the one who needs to slow down. If it's bad, I have Valium in the car."

Walking into the barn to say goodbye to Choc, and give him a grooming before his trip, I fretted over Sandra's news about an unauthorized visitor in Reg's room. Who could it have been? His foreman with the questionable rep that might be linked to Reg? Or someone else with whom Stavropolis had had shady dealings, some permitting honcho caught rubberstamping shady building plans.

I decided to pay the hospital a little visit, see if I could learn more. I had to be out that way before noon anyway to pick up crystal-trimmed sunglasses with prescription lenses I'd ordered months ago, but couldn't pay for until our recent success at The Horsehouse.

"Be a good boy, now," I told Choc as I stood him in the cross ties and brushed his red-brown coat to a blinding shine. "Just sleep through the trip. Be a piece of cake. You'll hit Texas, ready to win a world championship, before you know it."

Hey, a cowgirl could dream. As Donna says, "If you can dream it, you can do it."

Choc snorted, spraying my arm with green bits and pieces. I brushed them off. I love my horse. They say golf keeps you humble. But woods, irons and a dimpled ball have nothing on a big, warm, independent-minded horse.

In a half hour I was done with Choc, and the Grandeens were loading our horses. He was next to last in the big trailer. That was okay. He would be with his buddies, and situated over the trailer's wheels. He'd have a pretty comfortable ride.

I got cold chills when the rigs with our beloved cargo rolled down the driveway. Horses inside trailers neighed, and stomped around to get comfortable in their narrow stalls, poking their noses between window bars along one side of each trailer.

Dutch honked his horn and waved from the driver window of the bigger truck-trailer combo. Donna followed with the smaller rig. I stood silent in the barn doorway with other Brassbottom buddies whose horses were headed to Texas. A tear bubbled. This was it. The moment had come. They were off to the Worlds.

And I was on my way to a certain hospital, where a life hung in the balance. I burned to know what was going on, had gone on, with Reg Stavropolis.

Chapter 34

Traffic on the way to the South Valley Medical Center was a brick. But it moved. Kind of. Reduced to one southbound lane on Crater Lake Highway, it inched along past big-box stores and restaurants. Taking ten minutes longer than usual, I finally made it to southbound I-5 and drove the additional three miles to the South Bartlett Street exit.

Before reaching the hospital, stopped at a long light, I called Deputy Boo again. Sonny's cousin might be able to help me verify something he'd told Sonny.

"Hey, Pepper," Boo said. "No more problems at your place, I hope?"

The light turned green and I lowered the phone below the bottom of the window. I glanced around. No yellow license plates, no Smokies.

"All good," I said, driving extra carefully. "I'm headed to the hospital where Reg is. Just heard he had an unauthorized visitor last night."

Boo gave a long sigh.

"So it's out. You'll hear on the news, anyway. He took a bad turn after the visit and almost didn't make it. How'd you hear?"

I drove as slowly as I dared, keeping an eye on evolving traffic situations. Someone cut in front of me. I pulled into a parking lot so I could talk safely.

"Sandra said she went there this morning to give him a get-well card. Hospital wouldn't let her in the unit. But a volunteer told her what had happened."

"Thought Sandra was headed to Texas," Boo said. "She asked if it was okay to leave. We said fine, but to keep us posted on her whereabouts."

"At the barn she said she was leaving today, driving with her daughter, because she had business to wrap up in Cali. Probably some real-estate deal. Or something with the divorce. She didn't seem happy."

"When do you leave, Pepper?"

"Late Sunday. So, you have any leads on the hospital visitor, when he was there?"

"Around eleven-fifteen, right after the staff change, they reported seeing someone near his bed. When spotted, he took off. Lots of people coming and going. Good time for someone to grab a uniform and slip in."

"What about the security cams?"

"Recording shows nothing and no one out of the ordinary. We asked all staff and volunteers to review it. We need tips from the public and staff, and to send a message to the intruder that we're watching."

We disconnected. Conscious of time ticking away, I drove on to the hospital that occupied several blocks in south Medford. A hundred feet up a side road, I drove into the rear parking lot, dodging couples and wheelchair users. I still had to pick up my sunglasses. I would be late to the Horsehouse. I texted that to Tulip.

The visitor lobby was all glass windows, echoing tile floors and potted plants. A visitor's desk staffed by well-dressed, mature female volunteers, lay ahead. A kind-looking lady wearing a lavender pantsuit and looking to be a young 80, smiled and bobbed her cottonball-coiffed head at my approach. Her violet eyes twinkled.

"May I help you?"

"CCU?"

She swept an arm to her left. Her bracelets tinkled tastefully.

"Follow the signs, dear. Would you like me to start you out? It can be a little bit confusing."

"I'm good. Thanks."

I followed the signs and took an elevator. At the beginning of the hall leading to the CCU and several other rooms, a uniformed officer stood guard. Large and pale, he watched me walk up to the CCU door. I tried the handle. It didn't move.

On the wall by the door was a camera lens, a button and an intercom speaker. I pressed the button.

"Here to see Reg Stavropolis?" I said.

"Your name?" said a young-sounding male voice. I looked up to see a camera.

"Pepper Kane."

"I'm sorry, but you're not on the list. Are you family?"

"Cousin."

"Sorry, only immediate kin are allowed in right now."

"Can you at least tell me how he's doing?" I put on a disappointed look for the camera. "My children are devastated about his accident. He was like a father to them. They need good news, any news."

"I understand. According to our records he's still in here. But that's all I can say."

"Oh, thank you," I gushed. "They'll be so happy to hear he's being taken care of. He always played Santa for them at Christmas. Last year, gave them the cutest puppy."

The second the words left my mouth, I could have kicked myself. Now why had I added that? Usually I went light on the talkativeness, to encourage the other speaker. But not now. This person might be my best hope for getting helpful information. Who could blame me for pulling out the stops? Touch a heart. Make a friend.

"When he wakes," said speaker man, "I'll tell him you were here."

"What's your name?"

"Pepper Kane."

Out of the corner of my eye, at the end of the short hallway, I saw the officer straighten, his eyes still on me. He murmured something into his shoulder mic.

I felt his eyes on me as I hurried away, and back down to the airy, neutral lobby with the volunteer desk. I rested my elbows on the counter and smiled at lavender-pantsuit woman.

"Did you find the unit?" she said, in tones as mellifluous as a mourning dove's.

"Yes," I said, "thank you. By the way, I am a friend of someone else who came by today to see how Reg is. The realtor, Sandra Allende? Do you know her?"

"Oh, yes," said the woman. "Such a pleasant lady. She was so worried about him. Like you, she couldn't get in to see him. She left me a card to give him, though."

"That was nice. By any chance, with your connections, have you heard any more about his condition? Or an unauthorized visitor?"

"Not really. They had us all look at the security recording. Pretty hazy. All we saw were nurses and orderlies going in and out to check signs and refill drips."

I tapped my fingers on the counter. Then a thought came unbidden. I wondered how Sandra had worded her sentiments.

"Don't suppose you still have the card she left," I said. "Sandra has such good taste. I imagine it was gorgeous."

"You're in luck, as I haven't had a chance to deliver it," she said, reaching below the ledge. When she straightened up, she lay a large ivory envelope on the counter. The expensive kind of envelope.

"Would I be asking too much to see the card? Wouldn't want to buy a duplicate."

The woman tilted her head and looked thoughtful. Then she smiled.

"Well, I don't see that it would hurt." She picked up the envelope, teased open the folded flap, and slid out a thick, embossed card with artfully torn borders and a soft-focus photo of a lady on a white horse facing a spectacular sunrise.

"Lovely," I said, "What does the inside say?"

She opened the card and lay it on the counter. Its fancy script read, "Fond hopes and prayers/you rise to shine/again/ very soon." It was signed, "Praying for you/Sandra."

I drew out my phone to photograph the card and envelope.

"Lovely," I said. "Thank you." I glanced at her name tag. "Dottie."

"Happy to help," she said. "How again do you know Sandra? Are you a client?"

"We ride horses at the same training barn," I said. "She's an excellent rider. So is her daughter, Jeanne."

"Oh, how fun. I used to ride. Sandra was in a hurry today because she and her daughter are going to a big show in Texas. Are you going?"

"Yes," I smiled, turning to leave. "And I should be in a hurry, too."

Chapter 35

I wasted no time picking up my designer sunglasses at a vision center blocks from the hospital. Then I headed north to Gold Hill. I had to focus on work and customers, if any. My bank account was tanking. And I hadn't even started to "do" Fort Worth.

Tulip had turned the door sign to "Out to Lunch," and left to do errands of her own. I was glad for the relative calm of the shop. Gave me time to plan my next steps.

I was perched on the captain's chair at the counter, stuffing a cheese bagel in my mouth and a scanning the World Show Edition of the Quarter Horse Journal, when my cell phone rang. It was a local number.

"Best Little Horsehouse," I said. "Pepper Kane."

"What house?" a woman giggled. "I must have the wrong number."

"Horse. Horsehouse," I said. "We get that confusion a lot. We're a tack store in Gold Hill. I'm one of the owners."

"Gotcha! Hi, Pepper. This is Victoria."

"Oh. Vic. You rat. You weren't at the barn this morning. What's up?"

"Did you see the noon news? Someone tried to kill that dude Sandra went riding with Monday. At the hospital. Snuck into his room or something."

"All over it. But thanks."

"I just talked to his ex-wife. Apparently the sheriff called to interview her."

"No surprise. She would have known about Reg's fall. Police usually talk first to family, or former family, after a serious incident. I need her contact info."

"Name's Melissa Stavropolis. She been in L.A. all week modeling lingerie."

"And she told you what?"

"That she was shocked to hear what happened, because she and Reg were planning to hook up again. Which surprised me, considering how he treated her."

"I bet. Anything else?"

"Said Reg was excited to be getting into the biggest development of his career, an amazing resort with only a few pieces left to put into place. And that he'd changed. He wanted to get out of some nightclub gig they'd fought about. She was pumped."

"Where is it?"

"Sorry. She didn't say. Just thought you'd like to know that bit of information, since Donna says you're looking into the case."

Vic and I talked for a moment about the horse show, and then I thanked her. My call to the ex, Melissa Stavropolis, went to voicemail. I was getting a lot of that lately.

So the ex and Reg had planned to date again. And he reportedly was headed in a new direction. The operative word being, "reportedly."

I spent the rest of the afternoon reading up on and writing down, names of Dark Superstar's leading progeny and their owners. Since I had nothing better to do. Not one customer darkened the doorway. Tulip's note said she'd had only three sales. She had drawn a Sad Face at the end of her note, along with a dollar bill sporting wings.

This was all we needed. Terrible business just as we prepared for our show-debut in Texas, where we would drop more money than we'd earned here in months. How could we go on like this, treading the edge? My head began to pound.

On the way home after work I picked up more provisions – my daughter was a prodigious eater. I was no slouch in that department, myself.

As I drove up my road, I was shocked to see a pair of straight and shiny steel pipe-gates at my driveway. At the house, itself, stood Black Beauty.

Hearing me open the gates, Sonny poked his head out the barn door.

"Hey," he yelled. "Like the new gates?"

I remotely clicked open the garage door, drove in, cut the engine and walked with my bags to the little stable where Sonny stood. Bob and Lucy had their heads deep in their mangers. The stable smelled sweetly of horse, alfalfa hay and pelleted bedding.

"Like them?" I said, standing on tiptoe to kiss Sonny's sweat-damp cheeks and lips. "No. I don't like them, I LOVE them. Thank you so much."

"Wanted to surprise you," he said.

We swung our arms around each other and walked up to the house. The Bostons ran out the French door, jumping and barking as if they hadn't seen me in days.

Sonny washed his hands in the kitchen and poured us glasses of iced grape juice with a squirt of lemon. I washed up, stashed the groceries and went out with him for a late confab on the deck.

The hills looked beautiful in their gold-green late-October finery with occasional splashes of crimson poison oak. A pair of red-tail hawks soared overhead, trolling for ground squirrels. Somewhere out in the tall grass a pheasant squawked.

"How was your day?" I said, sipping juice and rolling an ice cube on my tongue.

"Busy. Gates took most of the morning. Made more calls to night clubs."

"And?"

"Caught up with Gracey in Grants Pass. Played the movie producer card again. Oscar-winning performance, if I do say so. Still owns that club in Canyonville, along with two others. Nancy used to be a headliner."

"Used to be?"

"Left for unknown reasons."

"Any way you can check further?"

"May stop at the clubs on my way to Seattle tomorrow."

"You're leaving so soon? I thought you'd stay until Sunday when Chili comes, and Tulip and I fly to Texas." I drank the rest of my juice in silence. Whining was not how you kept your man. Especially a man who loved his freedom.

He reached toward my chair arm, and lay his hand over mine.

"Promised I'd run up and see my kids before I head back to North Dakota," he said. "Besides. You have so much to do before you leave. Don't need me in the way. You'll be safe. Boo is doing extra night patrols."

"You're right," I sighed. "So give Lester and Renee hugs from me. And again, you've been the biggest help. I gladly accept what time and love you give."

"Nice," he said. "And I meant all I said. Home is where you are."

I let that sink in. It would have to see me through until we'd be together again.

Next I filled him in on my day. The unauthorized visitor to Reg's room in the hospital. My visit to the hospital to learn more. Victoria's news about Reg's ex-wife.

Sonny took it all in with a stoic expression and appropriate nods as he filed things away in his brain. When I was done, he offered to make a pizza run to Gold Hill. An offer I couldn't refuse. While he was gone, I entered notes about the past few tumultuous days in my computer. Reviewed my latest info, tried to see connections, none of which were obvious.

Discouraged at the slow progress I was making on my many mysteries, I donned my comfies, corralled my dogs, and settled in the lounger to watch TV news.

The bit I'd expected came up about the intruder in Reg's hospital room. Maybe I'd hear something new. I was all ears.

Chapter 36

The blue-jacket reporter was doing a live shot outside the hospital.

"Jackson County Sheriff's Office and a hospital PIO today confirmed Reginald Stavropolis, the Medford developer critically injured Monday in a fall at Lower Table Rock, was pronounced clinically dead late last night after an unknown visitor allegedly entered and left the CCU room during a shift change at South Valley Medical Center. Doctors revived Stavropolis after monitors showed a sudden change in vital signs."

She knitted her eyebrows together, then continued.

"He was revived. Stavropolis had been in a medically induced coma since being brought here after his fall Monday. Security video shows an unknown person in scrubs and a medical mask entering his room just after eleven, and standing near his bed."

I wondered why I hadn't yet received a call from Detective Jenee. Or if Sandra had received a call before she and Jeanne left for California. Or maybe I did receive a call. I had been in the shower or down at the barn. I hadn't checked my voice mail recently.

Blue Jacket continued her TV segment.

"The department is still investigating circumstances related to Stavropolis' fall. They are calling the fall accidental, but that may change as the case develops."

Henning, flanked by Detective Jenee and another officer, appeared on screen beside the department sign in front of the tan-and-brown, one-story department headquarters. A swoosh of traffic on Highway 62 made his words hard to hear.

But understand them, I did.

"At this time we now consider the Table Rock incident suspicious," said the sheriff. "Upon further review, and with supporting evidence, we may consider it a possible negligent homicide. Detective Jenee?"

A possible negligent homicide? Who had been negligent? Sandra, or me?

With a tight-lipped nod of his hat, Sheriff Jack handed over the microphone.

"Thank you, Sheriff Henning," said Detective Jenee. "We ask anyone with information on Stavropolis or a possible intruder, to step forward. Names and any information you give will be confidential." Numbers flashed on the screen.

The next minute the dogs exploded off the recliner. Sonny came through the door with a pizza box and a clinking sack of what I hoped was root beer. Or real beer.

"I could eat a horse," he said, carrying the feast to the table. "Sorry," he grinned.

I gave a half-smile, rose from Big Brown and robot-walked over to him.

"Sheriff may reclassify Reg's fall off Table Rock as negligent homicide. Meaning it may have been prevented."

A blank look froze Sonny's features.

"I wondered when they'd get around to that," he said.

I gave him details of the story as I set glasses and paper towels on the table. And I thought again about the ride on Table Rock. I felt Sonny's eyes heavy on me.

He now took one of my trembling hands, and pulled me to him for a hug. I closed my eyes soaked in his strength and comfort. A tear filled each eyelid.

"I know," he said. "He's evil. But he's also a human being."

"I tried to stop them, on Table Rock. But I wasn't able to. He could die."

"You did your best. You even put yourself at risk. They'll see that."

Sonny continued to hold me, and stroked the back of my head as I snuggled in the cleft of his chest.

My tears stopped as suddenly as they'd started. I pulled away, now feeling exhausted, and surprisingly hungry. Why was I always starved, after a crisis?

"Sorry," I said.

Sonny caught my jaws with his fingertips and tilted my face toward his. He kissed my forehead.

"Sit down," he said. "Have something to eat."

I sat, swallowed a few gulps of frosty root beer, lay a paper towel on my lap and chomped down on a thick slice of hot, spicy pizza. Pure heaven.

Sonny sat down beside me. After setting a dime-sized bit of pizza at the edge of his plate for the spirits, he ate quietly. He was formidable in a fight and indefatigable in an investigation, but he could be incredibly tender and respectful.

"Pilamaya, Sonny," I whispered, opening my eyes. "Thank you. For the gates, for helping me investigate, for, well, everything. For being you."

"Did you notice the sign?"

"Sign?"

"By the new gates. Up there in a tree. 'Warning! Security cameras on premises'."

I poured out more root beer and told him less important details about my day. He nodded or shook his head. He was a good listener. Another thing to love about him.

"And how again did Sandra seem this morning" he said.

"Stressed. She left with Jeanne for Cali around noon."

"Why'd she go to California?"

"Business, supposedly. What I want to know is whether the sheriff contacted her about Reg. She might have to come back. Be sad for them to have to miss the World Show after all their dreams and hard work."

"They might have her come back," he said.

I nodded, looking out at the pasture and hills, but not seeing them.

"They might have me come in again, too."

"They might."

"I should call her." I reached for my phone. I had to leave a voice mail because wherever she was now, she wasn't answering.

Chapter 37

I checked my recent phone calls and voice mail. Nothing from Sandra, or Reg's ex-wife. But there was a call I'd missed from the sheriff's office, made about five after I'd left the Horsehouse. I'd left my phone in the truck while I was grocery shopping.

"Miss Kane, Detective Jenee. We've been trying to reach you. Please contact the sheriff's office as soon as possible."

Now I returned the call. Even if my call only went to voicemail, it would let them know I'd at least tried to get in touch. I left a message that I would cooperate.

Sonny and I watched a little more TV. We caught the nail-biting end of a Seattle Seahawks game – thankfully they got the "W" – and then we showered and hit the hay.

Several times in the night I awoke from a nightmare, unsettled, damp with sweat. With Sonny touching my arm a time or two to awaken me, I was able to fall back asleep.

My first thought on awakening the next day was that Sonny would soon be gone. I already felt the hollow ache of missing him. I climbed out of an empty, still-warm bed. I saw no dogs, but heard water running in the guest bathroom. So Sonny had risen early. I didn't envy him his seven-hour drive to Seattle. But it was nothing, to him.

My first swallow of hot, doctored French roast was unadulterated bliss. Soon a calm energy filled me.

"Sleeping Beauty awakes," said Sonny, swinging his lanky bulk around the corner. He was a vision in black, from his sleek hair down to his ostrich boots.

"Don't know about the beauty part," I said, popping grainy bread into the toaster.

"You okay? You had quite the nightmares." He pulled out a chair and sat down. I caught a whiff of his spicy aftershave. It reminded me of the smell of the South Dakota plains and grasslands.

"Good as can be expected. This week hasn't been exactly conducive to sweet dreams." I caught myself. "Except for my incredible time with you."

I angled into the vee made by his outstretched legs, bent down and lay a deep, teasing kiss on his mouth. He rose to the occasion. I reciprocated with the female equivalent, sinking deeper into the kiss, wishing we had more time.

"Mmmm," he mumbled. "Hate that I have to hit the road. Rather hit on you."

"You (kiss) and me (kiss) both."

He raised his hands through the space between us. His hands brushed the sides of my breasts. I almost fainted. As our chests pressed together, our kisses slowed, each of us aware of ticking time.

That's when I had a new thought: Sometimes it was better to leave 'em wanting more. I pulled back. His dark eyes had glazed over, and his sensual mouth was wet. He made a goofy grin and took a deep breath.

"Damn, woman. What you do to me."

"No, man. What you do to me." This time I kissed him quickly and hard, pushing his head back with my mouth. We erupted into laugher, relieving our tension. It wasn't how I wanted to relieve our tension. But, again, it might be better to save something to look forward to for next time. Maybe he'd return to me sooner.

I poured orange juice, topped the warm toast with cheese slices, and brought our plates to the table as the dogs scratched at the door.

"Fed the livestock," Sonny said.

I let in the dogs and scritched their wiggly butts. They covered my hands with hot, soggy kisses.

"Wondered why I heard no noise from the barn."

I picked up the phone I'd left on the table the night before. I must have been super tired to have forgotten to bring it to the bedroom. No call back from Sandra or Jenee.

While Sonny and I ate, I glanced at the clock over the sink. A hair past eight.

My cell phone sang out with the new ring tone I'd installed yesterday at the store. The tiny speaker whumped and wailed with the deliciously danceable guitar intro to "Chatahoochee," a hit for the desirable Alan Jackson back in the day.

The ID pane said, "Jackson County ..."

I said, "Pepper Kane."

"Detective Jenee. Can you stop by our office this morning to answer a few more questions about the Stavropolis incident?"

"Can be there in a half-hour."

"Good. If you could be here around nine, that would be perfect. I have a meeting at ten that might go until noon."

I sat down across from Sonny to finish my breakfast. He was nearly done. I could tell he was anxious to start his 450-mile commute. He rose, hugged me, and then held me out at arm's length.

His eyes were blank, giving away nothing. But he pressed his lips together, licked them and looked away. I rose on tiptoe, touched my hands against his cheeks and pressed a tender kiss on his yielding mouth. When I dropped down from tiptoe, I felt a toast crumb on my lower lip. I flicked it off.

Sonny rolled back his eyes and laughed from his belly.

"So, I'm a crumby lover," he sniffed. He pulled me into a companionable hug. "Be extra careful, Honey. Already miss you."

"Wish I could go to Seattle with you some time, hang with you and your kids."

"You will," he said. "Promise."

With that, he hoisted his duffle, gave me a last long gaze, and was gone. I sagged as I stood at the door and watched him drive to the gates, open them, get back in Black Beauty and drive away. Who knew when I'd see him again? Sometimes we'd gone without each other for as long as six months.

The drive to the sheriff's office didn't take long. Neither did my interview with Detective Jenee. Standard questions, a review of my comings and goings the past few days, all routine. Then came the kicker.

"Say again what you did and where you were Wednesday night and yesterday."

I repeated what I'd said earlier, with no embellishment. I'd gone to the hospital to check on Reg's condition, because I was worried after the unauthorized visit and because officials were keeping mum. I said nothing of photographing Sandra's get-well card. If the detective knew, or wanted to know about that, she could ask.

"You made up a pretty creative story for the intercom guy," she said.

"I just wanted information on Reg's condition, since he'd had that visitor. Which probably would make you want to talk to me again."

Careful, careful.

But, I reasoned, if the detective knew anything about my other interaction, the one with the volunteer, she would have pursued that angle. I was sure she was just fishing.

She leaned forward on her elbows, and clasped her hands. "You appear unusually interested in him, as if you were connected to him in some way. Were you?"

"No. But I still care. I was there. I witnessed and tried to stop the fight. I've had nightmares. He's still in a coma, I assume."

I thought that last statement a good one. And it was the truth. She'd see that.

"That's privileged information."

I had to assume her words were affirmative. Otherwise she'd have shown a reaction, however small. Or answered differently.

Detective Jenee rose, shook my hand and thanked me for coming in.

Afterward I tried again to reach Sandra, but again failed. I spent the rest of the morning going again to the bank and checking on my parents. They were good on groceries and meds.

I kept surprisingly busy that afternoon at The Horsehouse, selling odds and ends of tack and clothing, and tending to last-minute details before Tulip and I left for Texas. My little barrel-racing friend, Sarah Banks, came by with the money she'd promised for the blingy saddle pad she'd bought for a competition last weekend.

"It brought me good luck," she said, eyes dancing. "Won first place with a time of sixteen-point-four. Personal best."

"Congratulations," I said, crumpling her I.O.U. note and pitching it into the wastebasket. "National Championship, here you come."

I closed the store at five, tossed an extra bag of mane bands into a sack – you could never have too many of those rubber bands to wrap at the roots of your horse's short trimmed mane to make it lie flat – and headed for home.

That evening, in addition to doing chores, I finally got a call back from Sandra.

"Hey, Sandra. I've been trying to reach you. Are you okay?"

"Why wouldn't I be?" Then a laugh. "Routine drive to Redding. Had to go fix a real-estate deal that went sideways with my ex. What's up?"

"I thought closing long-distance deals is why they invented FAX machines."

"Crazy client dispute over earnest money. Client wanted a face-to-face, attorney present. My ex tried to short me on my share. Ugh. Real-estate. No wonder they call us brokers. Something's always broken."

"Are you up to date on what's been happening up here?"

"Oh, yes. They wanted me to come back for another interview. But I said no way. Too much going on at my end. I did a conference call with them at the local station. Plus, we had to go to immediate care for Jeanne's leg. Turns out it's got a hairline fracture."

"Oh, Sandra, that's terrible. How did it happen?"

"She fell off our porch."

"Will she be able to ride at the show?"

"They're making up a brace for her. They'll FedEx it to Fort Worth, and we'll see a specialist there first thing Monday."

"That's good news, I guess. So. The detective here interviewed me this morning."

Her breath caught. I heard a rustling noise, as if she were shuffling papers.

"Why do they keep interviewing you, Pepper?"

"Because I was at the fall scene, and I because after I saw you at Brassbottom, I visited the hospital yesterday to learn more about the, um, circumstances."

"He must have some serious enemies. He's quite the barracuda, in business. Made more than one partner lawyer up. Then there's the vindictive ex-wife. They should be looking into her."

"Think they are. I hope we get answers soon. Meanwhile, have a safe journey. See you and Jeanne at the Worlds?"

"Unless something else bad happens. They come in threes, you know."

"Threes? Oh. The fall at Table Rock. Jeanne's accident. Your real-estate snafu with the ex. Wait. That's three. You're good to go, Sandra."

"Not really. The real-estate thing with my ex was no biggie. So I'm still waiting for that third thing. It better not be in Texas."

Chapter 38

The next day, Saturday, passed in a blur. In the morning, I hit my to-do list hard at home, at the shop and down the road. I scrubbed horse troughs, had a French manicure at Freddie's salon, and took my parents a few more groceries and meds. I also stocked up on travel toiletries. There were just so many details I'd let slide during my insane week.

At one o'clock, during the Horsehouse changing of the guard, I filled in Tulip on my latest doings regarding Sonny, Sandra, Reg and the others.

"Y'all ask me," she said from our store doorway before she climbed into Peggy Sue, "you should be looking more into that ex of hers. Pretty fishy, how he reacted talking with Sonny. Fishy, his buying that crazy horse for Jeanne. Fishy, how he's screwing Sandra on money for their real-estate deal, pardon my French."

"It's all fishy," I said. "It would not surprise me a bit to hear, with his abusive and controlling ways, his connections, and desire for a World Championship for his daughter, that he had something to do with the judge threats. The crashing of my gate to warn me off, and maybe Nancy's disappearance."

I was stunned to hear myself, in a casual, unguarded moment, coming up with all that. Apparently something deep inside my consciousness had pulled them up before my brain fully processed them. Was it informed intuition, or wishful dot-connecting?

The high-pressure buzz sounded in my temples.

Tulip just stared wide-eyed, doing some processing of her own.

"You're overtired," she offered. "Grasping for easy solutions. You're a person of interest. Concerned for friends. Preparing for the biggest show of your life. Super Girl Reporter, Avenger of Evil. You can't solve the problems of the world. Lighten up."

She'd nailed it. I was guilty as charged.

"Yeah," I sniffed. "You may be right."

"Not maybe," she huffed. "I am right, and you know it. Prioritize. Pick one path and stick to it. You've been running like a gutshot deer. Something will come to light. Don't force it. It'll be all right."

"I'll try. Thanks, Tule."

But I knew I wouldn't, really. I'd give it a shot, have a good drink, a good meal and a good bubble bath. But I'd never really let it go.

After my afternoon working at the Horsehouse, my head still throbbed and my body ached. But I'd accomplished some things, made some money, and scored a fresh peach pie from Mom. Bonus, my nails and hair looked great. You take your victories where you can.

I thawed and reheated beef stew I'd made a month ago using produce from my garden. I enjoyed a slim piece of pie – I had to leave some for Chili, after all. Then I lazed in a bath in the guest-room tub. Lavender-scented bubbles tickled my armpits.

Western guitar chords sounded in the living room. I should've brought my phone into the bathroom. Toweling off and lurching toward the coffee table, I left damp footprints on the rug and grabbed the phone. Not in time. Call went to voicemail.

The ID pane read, "Tommy Lee Jaymes." Now what did my cute Texas buddy want now? He would be seeing me in a few days at the World Show.

"Pepper, listen up," said his trained actor's-voice. "I got some news for y'all and y'all's horse-show friends. Call me."

I wrapped the damp towel around me and perched on Big Brown's arm to return the call. The Bostons worked to tongue-dry my ankles.

"Hey, Reba," he said.

"What's the news, Tommy Lee?"

"You probably heard about the break-in at the Shiny Suspicion breeding barn. Superstar's main rival. The one judge, Haverstadt, being a principal owner."

"Yes."

"So I looked into that problem with your other show judge Dick Bradford."

"Yeah, and?" A shard of fear ran up my spine.

"Well, he tells me he just had dinner with this new investor in his Dark Superstar syndicate. Dick's been down financially, owes back taxes, some folderol like this. So he can use the money. Still hasn't recovered from the downturn when horse breeding dropped off a cliff."

I put the phone to my other ear.

"So what else is new in the horse biz? I know you're on Texas time, but could you please get to it?"

"So this guy, some player from the coast who owns a few Superstars, a Mark or Mick, something like that, last name starts with 'A,' says he can do a deal on a sweet piece of land next to Dick's ranch, if Dick will influence the other judges to put the Superstars up top of their cards at the World. Dick being lead judge, and all."

"Really." A statement, not a question. I closed my eyes and sat back.

So. A wealthy investor from the coast with the initials "M" and "A." An owner of Supertar offspring. One who knew of Bradford's straitened circumstance. It finally was beginning to make some sense, regarding the judge threats. Could his investor be Max Allende, Sandra's troublesome ex, and Jeanne's doting father? Craving prestigious wins, and the money that followed them? Whoever, the news Tommy Lee shared clearly concerned an attempted bribe.

But this line of thinking also was confusing. The judge threats, the death threats to Dutch Grandeen and the others, were keyed to Superstars not placing at the top. What was going on?

"When was this, Tommy Lee? What did Bradford say?"

"He refused, of course, and told the guy he wasn't so desperate he'd risk ruining his reputation and all he'd worked for. And that he appreciated the investment in the syndicate, but no thanks to the offer."

"Can you get the guy's full name?"

"Thought I'd remember it. I'll have it when I see you in a day or two, in Texas."

"This is terrible, Tommy Lee. Even more trouble than we had with the threats I told you about. Those threats favored Shiny Suspicion. This bribe involves a different horse, Dark Superstar. Any help you can give with the guy's name would be great."

"No problem, Reba. You just take care. Hey, be sure and give my love to Tulip. Tell her I ran into Susan Sarandon on a shoot. Susie is interested in licensing her name to a new tribute actor."

I hung up, jittery and perplexed. With TL's latest news, the mysteries had taken a more troubling twist. Had whoever made the original threat used it as a smokescreen to throw investigators off the real issue, to sway placings toward Superstar?

One thing was clear. The trouble was escalating. And we were headed right toward its epicenter.

Chapter 39

My body ached. I didn't want to get out of bed. Great. I was now coming down with something. I had overdone it. Run on overdrive, taken risks, worried about my safety all week. Now I'd be sick the day before we left for Texas.

The dogs stirred when I rolled over to look at the clock. Crap. After ten. I must have needed the sleep. While I sipped coffee and ate cereal topped with berries, I heard horses neighing down to the barn.

"Don't nag," I told Bob and Lucy as I tossed them hay. "Horse joke. Get it?"

Back at the house, I promised myself I would not concentrate on worries, only attend to final packing, and get the guestroom ready for Chili's arrival in a few hours.

I could do this. I had to do this, so I could get to the show in one piece, ready to go. All I had to do was take one step at a time.

A fold-up suit bag for my show pants, blouses, vests and jackets, along with a big rolling bag for everyday clothes, jewelry and cosmetics, lay splayed open on my bed. A locking tub with a double hat-case and pairs of boots sat on the floor. I packed the togs first, making sure pieces for different events were in good repair and packed so as not to cause wrinkles. Then I tackled my everyday wardrobe.

Thoughts of winning a championship trophy and jacket plus other swag made my pulse speed up. But the idea of scoring a win check of a couple thousand dollars made be lightheaded. I could yank our tack store back from the brink of extinction and even hire a contractor to explore the idea of turning my parents' farm into a guest ranch.

At one-thirty I spread cream cheese, lox, capers and red onion on a French roll. Finishing up, I heard a honk at the front gates.

That would be Chili. My heart gave a little flutter. I hadn't seen my daughter in a year. My baby girl. All seventy skinny, redheaded inches of her. I grabbed the padlock keys off the coffee table and sprinted outside.

Chili's purple mini-truck sat outside the gates. It sparkled with a fresh wash. Her carrot-topped head decked out with jeweled sunglasses poked out the passenger window. She lay one pale forearm along the frame. Her nail-bitten fingers blazed with turquoise and coral rings.

"What's with the locked gates? And the sign and camera?"

"Explain later," I said. "We had a little trouble. It's settled for now, though."

I opened one gate and swung it wide for her to drive through.

"Hey, you made good time. Eaten lunch?"

She slowly rolled through the opening and toward the house.

"Yep. But if you have any of Gram's pie, I could use some for dessert."

"You got it, Baby Girl." I closed and re-locked the gate.

I hugged Chili long and hard when we got to the porch. The three Bostons made like jumping beans as we carried her bag, jacket, and footwear into the house. I busied myself in the kitchen while she returned to her truck for a huge tote marked, "Jewelry Samples." She put it with other things in her room. She changed into a new purple tie-dyed tee and ran a comb through her Medusa locks. Which affected them not a bit.

"Sit," I said. "Here's your pie with trimmin's. Want coffee?"

"I'm good," she said, leaning her elbows on the table and staring a question.

"How come you look so tired, Mom?"

"Long story." I sat down with more coffee and a sliver of pie, one crumb pushed aside for the spirits. I gave her the condensed version of my week. Her eyes widened as the tale unfolded, and then returned to normal size when it was done. Her blue eyes as large-seeming as a baby's, were framed in lush, pale-red eyelashes. She was a Nature girl. No makeup came anywhere near my Chili.

"Jeez," she whispered, tucking another bite of pie into her mouth and licking ice cream off her lips. You be good to show? I mean, your plane leaves at midnight."

"It'll be all right," I said. "Texas might actually be a break. With showing, shopping, and slurping fabulous food, you have no time to do much else."

After chatting a while longer – and no, I was sad to hear, Chili did not have a new man in her life, or better job prospects – we each lay down for a nap. She was tired from her trip, and I wouldn't know much sleep I'd get on the red-eye to Texas.

The afternoon and evening passed in a blur. Chili gabbed about her new custom jewelry venture, which she hoped to pitch to stores in the Valley including a half-dozen in Ashland. She showed me pieces with enormous chunks of turquoise and coral, which would play well in the upscale, tourist-rich town a half-hour southeast of us.

We watched TV news, eager for any news of Reg Stavropolis' condition, or of the intruder to his hospital unit. No news was good info. I figured the longer he held on, the better chance he might pull through. And then he could spill his tale.

My nerves got more jangled as the hour grew later. By ten o'clock I insisted on hauling my luggage and tubs to my dually, which Chili would drive to the airport. My heart tap-danced with anticipation in my chest. I could wait no more. I was on my way.

Chapter 40

Buckled in tightly, seated along a right-cabin window next to Tulip, I gripped the armrests so hard during the aircraft engine-runup that my knuckles went white. Flying was not my favorite sport, especially with seats narrowing and knee-space shrinking. In no time the only thing that would fit in them would be meerkats.

The engines roared, shaking the plane and us several hundred souls inside. Cool air blasted our faces from overhead vents.

Then we were rolling. The tarmac lights slipped by in the dark, lightened eerily – like the entire landscape – by a full harvest moon. We turned, and halted as the engines increased power. Suddenly the plane shot forward, raced down the runway, angled sharply up and leaped into the air. Changing cabin pressure messed with our eardrums. I swallowed, and swallowed again.

Lower Table Rock, looking ghostly in the distance under moonlight, loomed dead ahead. For a minute it seemed we were going to crash into it. It grew sharper and more threatening as we rolled into a left turn. I pressed my nose against the icy window. The vertical walls of the mesa came into sharp relief.

I shut my eyes, not wanting to see it. When I opened them, the plane's angle of bank had increased, blocking Table Rock from view beneath our right wing. Now only scattered lights lay below, and twinkling stars, above.

It was only a glimpse of Table Rock. But it was enough. It set my heart pounding, my blood pressure soaring. I'd flashed on the moment Monday when someone had sailed over the edge and I feared I'd be next.

Nightmare was the right word. Because awful as it all was, and although Sandra's and my issues might be resolving, it now seemed like a bad dream. Incredible. One of my life's most frightening times, and it now felt like a phantom vision.

I recalled my college psychology classes, even therapy I'd had while newspaper honchos were trying to fire me for the sin of approaching fifty. The prevailing wisdom suggested that after a horrific experience you came down with Post Traumatic-Stress Disorder, or you disassociated, disowned or compartmentalized the experience.

Whatever. I had to find a way to set the memory of that ride aside. To wish Reg a recovery. Sandra and me another chance at friendship, as we worked to learn what happened with Nancy, and if Sandra's ex or Reg were involved in the disappearance.

I might get answers, I might not. I'd keep pecking away. But my main focus must be on our weeks in Texas. At the moment I had myself and my horse to take care of, and a World Show that would devour all our time and energy.

Tulip jiggled my left forearm.

"Hey," she said while the plane banked left again, still climbing, and hitting air pockets here and there. "We're on our way. Can y'all believe it?"

I looked over to see her bosom undergoing aftershock from the turbulence. Served her right. No one willingly should have breasts that large. It certainly wasn't helping her horsemanship posture. Keeping her shoulders down and back, her spine ramrod straight must now hurt, with that extra baggage up front.

"Yes," I said, "actually I can believe it. We've done nothing but work and plan for the show for weeks, even years."

"So, Pep, will you be able to concentrate?"

"Think I'm good," I said. "Sonny's doing more checking, Chili's watching the home front, and I've got you and the buddies to keep me focused."

She nodded and looked across the cabin. Many of those Brassbottom buddies – Freddie, Victoria, Lana and Barbara, were on this flight. Dutch and Donna, of course, were driving horses and tack. Sandra and Jeanne were driving, too, though a different route than the Grandeens. It promised to be a full house in Fort Worth, virtually a Brassbottom bash on the road.

The plane began to level out. We passed through clouds, and felt more bumps. But then all went smooth. Before tipping back my seat and loosening my seat belt, I caught the eye of Little Stewie and his mom in a rear row. I gave him a thumbs up.

He nodded enthusiastically, his hair looking like a fuzzy flame under the overhead light. He gave me two thumbs and two feet up. What a little trouper. Scared of nothing. Or, if scared, saddling up anyway. A John Wayne-in-training.

"Well," said Tulip as she fished in the front seat-back pocket for reading material. "At least you won't have all that craziness with Reg and Sandra and the missing girl and crashed gates to consume every waking thought."

"That is something," I said. "The twenty-four-seven of the horse show should blot out everything else. But not quite."

"What do you mean?"

"I forgot to tell you. Tommy Lee called."

"He did? And?"

"Dick Bradford, the head judge? He told Tommy Lee he met with a big investor from the coast, who'd bought or offered to buy a piece of Dark Superstar stallion shares if Dick would help throw World Show results in favor of

Superstar progeny. Using his influence to persuade other judges. Dick's been in big trouble financially."

Tulip's eyebrows shot up.

"Slap your grandma."

"Sounds a lot like Max Allende, Sandra's ex. Same initials. M, A. Owns Superstar horses. In real-estate, ties to Texas. Tommy Lee's going to find out the correct name."

"What'd Bradford say to the offer?"

"Refused to play," I said. "That would be a game-changer. Stop this in its tracks."

"For sure. From what y'all said before, that daddy dude wants his daughter to win, a little too much. Did Bradford report him?"

"I'm sure he did, or will. We can ask Dutch and Donna at the show. Too late to call or text now. By the way, Tommy Lee sends his regards, and says he might be able to get you some Susan Sarandon lookalike work with him."

"Shoot," Tulip said. "I don't know about the work, but I wouldn't mind seeing ol' TLJ again. But that judge thing has me freaked. Who knows what will happen once we get to the show?"

I nodded.

"To quote a line from that old Bette Davis movie," I said, 'Hang on. It's going to be a bumpy ride'."

Chapter 41

Dallas spread out across the dawn-lightened landscape below like a lit-up toy metropolis. The Dallas-Fort Worth airport slowly came into view.

The sun already was up over the southeast horizon. I had stared out the airplane window to see it lighting the city and nearby Fort Worth for an hour. Almost there.

Yawning and stretching, I reached into my bag under the seat and pulled out a water bottle. I drank deeply, now that a decent toilet was in my foreseeable future. I sprinkled a few drops into my palm and patted them over my dust-dry face.

Groggy and cotton-mouthed didn't quite cover my condition. The joints could use a spritz of WD-40. We had only been sitting a few hours, and made one relatively quick transfer in Denver. But I might have spent the night in a cement vat, so stiff did I feel.

Baggage-claim was a sea of jeans and suits with cowboy boots and Texas accents, as well as "normal" outfits and lingo. Another line with a scatter of cowboy hats reached back from the counter at our car-rental place. But the lines moved fast. Before we knew it, Tulip, I and the Brassbottom buddies were headed our separate ways in an army of SUV's and mini-vans stuffed with us and assorted luggage.

Tulip watched the dashboard GPS and repeated its instructions while I drove. It wasn't easy negotiating apocalyptic morning rush-hour traffic in a strange town, along broad streets and unfamiliar highways, past high-rise motels, low-slung business parks and smug industrial buildings, along farmlands punctuated with the occasional quick stop, and then into the outskirts of Fort Worth.

Soon we spied the street signs for Will Rogers Memorial Center and followed them to our destination. The flags were flying over the sprawling tan complex. Horse banners were hung on some exterior walls, and the main RV parking lot in the two-hundred-acre facility was already filled up with white trucks, giant RVs with slideouts and a king's ransom in horse trailers. A few men and women reclined on lawn furniture outside deluxe motor homes. Others walked, or rolled by in a slo-mo stampede of golf carts, lugging human or horse apparel toward the central Burnett-Tandy building across a lane from the fully enclosed John Justin Arena building with its domed roof. That's mostly where we'd show our horses. More arenas, pens and stables fanned out around the main buildings. The Cowgirl Hall of Fame. A science pavilion. A park.

The Will Rogers was a city onto itself – like most venues when a horse show or rodeo hits the dirt. It surely had leaders, followers, tourists, worker bees and ordinary folks plus the usual cheats, gossips and connivers. It had a sushi bar, barbecue joint, fast-eat areas and well-appointed offices, first-aid stations, security and shopping spots. And major infrastructure – from surface roads and a big parking garage to underground rings and tunnels. Not to mention a thousand stalls and support areas for horses and cows.

And like a city, it had a million everyday tales, with occasional bursts of drama.

"Hallelujah," yelled Tulip, bug-eyed in oversized pink sunglasses that matched her clingy, low-cut top. She took it all in as she clutched the dashboard of our rented CRV. "Were Dutch and Donna going to park in this RV lot? Or another one."

"RV," I said. "Man, this is a huge lot." We inched down the rows of trucks, trailers and motor homes a block past the main Burnett-Tandy building where the Brassbottom horses would be stabled, fed and groomed.

My eyes burned both from lack of sleep, and from staring at shiny vehicles and buildings made brighter in epic sunlight. I'd lost my sunglasses at an airport shop before the flight. But I was so excited to have made it here, and to be soon seeing my horse, that I didn't care. I'd splash my eyes with cold water and take a nap when we finally escaped to our rental cottage.

Rolling down the window, I sucked in the hot, humid air and the smells of horse and diesel fuel. To me, right now, they were the greatest smells on earth.

Soon we spotted the Grandeen trucks and trailers. They were a few rows out from the main horse and tack entrances. Dodging people and golf carts headed to or from the complex's stalls, and feed and bedding areas, we wedged our vehicle in a narrow space between the two Grandeen rigs, and got out.

"Hell-o, Texas," Tulip shouted. She took off her sunglasses, threw back her head and spun in place, her arms reaching toward the sky. "Where everything is bigger."

"I feel bigger just being here, Tule. Not literally, though I seem to hear a couple Tex-Mex enchiladas calling my name. No. Bigger in spirit. I don't even care if I win a world championship. Just so glad to be here at last."

Tulip rolled her lash-heavy eyes and put her sunglasses back on. I now noticed the frames were shaped like valentines. Leave it to my bestie to wear her heart on her eyes.

"Now that's a flat-out lie, Pep. Y'all know you care like the devil. Wouldn't shock me a bit to hear you've already struck a bargain with Devil for a world title."

We locked our vehicle, leaned into the steamy breeze peppered with grit, and lit out for the Burnett-Tandy to find the Grandeens, our horses and our buddies. The show office likely wasn't open yet. The show's opening was tomorrow, when the welcome barbecue and show-preview classes were scheduled. And the show secretary wasn't available until Wednesday to check our horse's registration and association papers, and register us for classes. Long live the horse show mantra: "Hurry up and wait."

The thrill of being at the Worlds never left me as Tulip and I strolled into the big, bright, industrial-building's interior arranged with row after row of pipe-steel portable stalls. Sounds of shod hooves, hungry horses and busy riders echoed around the space. The bright colors of logo-imprint stable banners popped out from the end of each long stall row, and from drapes pulled back to reveal stalls tricked out with lounge chairs, flowerpots, coolers and snack-tables to serve riders and visitors.

A border collie ran past us, its nose to the ground, following some enticing scent. Horses pressed their heads against stall bars to check us out. Barn odors filled the air. Country music played softly over loudspeakers.

"There they are," said Tulip, making straight for the Grandeen's royal-blue-and-green logo curtain at the end of the fourth stall row. The chairs of a hospitality lounge, made by removing the partition between two stalls, was empty. But the coffeepot's red light glowed, and a box of maple bars and chocolate donuts lay open to reveal a few chunks. I stuffed one into my mouth. Our airplane snack had done little to curb my appetite.

Setting out down the stall row, I passed the tack room and dressing stall, looking to each side for Choc. Thirty feet down he peered out from between the bars of a ten-by-ten stall on the right. He bobbed his head and neighed when he saw me. I went up to say hello and rub his soft pink nose, freshly shaved. It felt soft as baby skin.

"How you doing, Handsome," I said. His pricked ears relaxed, and his brown eyes went to half-mast with pleasure.

Peering between bars, I saw that his shavings were clean and his water bucket half full. At least he was drinking water, which, in a strange place after a haul, was a good sign. Choc was an easy traveler, always ate and drank well. Colic was not a concern.

I heard a familiar, lilting voice accompanied by a clip-clop of hooves. I looked left and saw Donna Grandeen leading Freddie's saddled gray horse toward me.

"You made it," she said, opening Poppin's door and leading him inside. She replaced the bridle with a halter, and tied the horse to a ring on a wall. "Easy flight?"

"Not bad," I said. "Long night, though. Hope I can grab a nap later."

She greeted Tulip next door by her horse's stall. Then Donna turned back to me.

"I suppose you heard the latest about Dick Bradford," she said, lowering her voice as she shut the door. At a show, stalls were so close, aisles so open, that anyone could hear anything no matter how careful you were. We joked. "Even the stalls have ears." Anything said about a trainer, judge or competitor could be overheard and passed on, embroidered or exaggerated. Good gossip was the coin of the horse-show realm.

"Yes," I whispered. "I still can't believe it. That Tommy Lee Jaymes I know, the lookalike actor who lives here? He called last week and I told him about the judge threat. He knows Bradford. Was going to check around. He called with this latest, last night."

I told her about the mysterious investor Bradford had dined with, and the offer of ranch property or a big buy into the Superstar stud syndicate, in exchange for Dick's influencing the other judges.

Donna frowned and started to walk along the stall row to check that all stalls were latched and all water buckets were full. I trailed her closely.

"We heard a little different," she said. "Dick said someone possibly posing as an investor not only tried to bribe him, but says the dude threatened him, if he didn't play along. Maybe gave a fake name, too. Mark Abraham."

"Same initials as I heard, but did you say Bradford was 'threatened'?"

"Shhhh. Yes. Dick turned down the bribe, laughed in the guy's face. But the guy said he better rethink that or there would be 'consequences.' That's the word. With the fake name, there's little to go on. Just a description. Tall, and dark. Maybe Hispanic."

"So I was thinking it might be Max Allende, Sandra's ex, big realtor from the Coast, bought the Superstar horse for Jeanne, pressure to win and all."

"I can see that."

"But now, this is all just too bizarre," I said. "Hard to know what's going on. First they threaten judges to keep Superstar horses from championships. Now they're pushing to get them into top spots. Are we looking at two different threateners, here?"

"Your guess is as good as mine, Pepper. The show has put on extra security.'"

I touched her forearm.

"Do our other riders know about this development? You know how gossip can wreak havoc, lead to even worse things."

"Not sure," she said.

"What exactly did Bradford tell the mystery investor?"

"He said he would report the attempted bribe and threat."

I jumped when a horse kicked a stall wall. I'd brought my edginess to Texas.

"Any other judges approached?"

"No, no others. At any rate they've agreed not to be influenced either way. They must place horses as they see them in each class, each day. Their reputations, and the show's, depend on it."

She turned in at the Grandeen hospitality lounge, pulled bottled waters from the cooler, handed one to me and kept one. Just then Tulip in her Lolita-pink sunglasses rolled into view along with Freddie and his Texas pal, Carlos Gutierrez.

My mind did a double take. Not because Freddie was with Carlos, whom he'd met at a show in California that summer, but because Carlos was assistant trainer at the Royce and Rogers stables. The very barn that owned a majority share in the Shiny Suspicion stallion syndicate. The stallion who was Superstar's main competition.

"Carlos, nice to see you," I said, giving him a light hug. Though I did not know the handsome young man well, I knew his riding, his famous bosses, and some of their prizewinning clients.

"Looking good, Pepper," Carlos said, his dark eyes giving me the once-over. With one bronze arm, muscles flexing below the sleeve of his white tee, he drew Freddie close.

"Not so bad yourself, Carlos," I said. "When did you guys get here?"

"Yesterday," said Carlos, raising his eyebrows, which looked artfully waxed. "Our horses live near here. They don't have to get used to the place. Practically their second home." His smile revealed too-white teeth, and lasted only a moment.

"Where are you all stabled?" I said.

"Behind the Justin. Stop by if you get a chance. Our Suspicion babies are killing it this year." He looked down at an oversized watch on a crocodile band. "And I'm gonna get killed if I don't get riding."

"Before you go, what's your take, and your clients', about those judge threats? Pressuring judges to favor your horses?" Nothing like going for it.

A worry line sliced between his eyebrows. He looked at Freddie, and back at me.

"We're good," he said. "Just some crazy trying to throw their weight around."

"But Bradford was nearly run down."

"So he says."

"You think he made that up?"

"Not sayin' he did. But people can get creative when they're up against the wall. Good guy, but it's no secret he might lose the farm. So to speak."

Now that was an angle I had not considered. That Bradford might "get creative" because he was involved in something not quite aboveboard. Maybe even something concerning Max Allende.

He and Freddie air-kissed, then Carlos hurried off, flashing us the crystal-studded backside of his painted-on jeans. Freddie looked like he wanted to say something. But at that moment Sandra and Jeanne Allende came up leading their freshly bathed horses.

"Hey," said Sandra, smiling at Tulip and me. "You guys made it. Can't believe what fun we're having and the show hasn't even started, right, Jeanne?"

"Yeah," Jeanne said. "Lots of fun." She shrugged, rubbed her arms, and then managed a smile. What was up with the attitude?

She stood gingerly, favoring her left leg. She looked even thinner than usual, in a chiffon apricot tank and charcoal stretch-jeans tucked into the tops of tall black boots. Those boots were breathtaking – black-and-white tooled stovepipes with fashionable square toes and metallic copper insets.

She and her mother must already have hit the Cowtown stores. The show's own vendor mall, rumored to be a treasure trove, was not yet open. At shows like this, some riders came as much for the shopping as for titles. The tack and tog offerings here probably would put those at The Best Little Horsehouse to shame.

"How's the leg, Jeanne?" I said. "Will you be getting that brace so you can ride?"

"We got the brace this morning," Jeanne said. "So the leg's okay, I guess." She shot her mother a glance, and then settled her gaze on the snack table.

I looked again at Jeanne's boots.

"But you're not wearing the brace," I said.

"It's the latest technology, a soft brace like a second skin. Show them, Jeanne."

The teen leaned against a chair, pulled her jeans leg up above the boot top, and revealed a reinforced gel webbing that did, indeed, fit like a waffle-weave second skin.

She gently tucked the jeans back into her boot.

"Impressive," I said.

"It's okay."

Something in Jeanne's tone, her stance canted away from Sandra, and her giving me an odd look made me think more than her leg was bothering her. But what?

"You good to show, then?" I asked.

Jeanne went to the snack table, picked up a maple bar chunk, set it back down, and took a bottle of juice from the cooler. Looking at me, she drained it.

"Thanks for your concern, Pepper," she smiled. "We've got meds. I'll be fine."

Chapter 42

Sandra and Jeanne soon left the Grandeen lounge to go to their hotel suite and "decompress from the madness," in Sandra's words. Tulip and I nursed our bottled waters, and chatted up other Brassbottom buddies as they dribbled in.

Donna told us Dutch was still out riding Jeanne's horse, which refused to stop fussing. Donna herself left to ride Lana's and Barbara's horses.

Little Stewie whooshed in on a blue scooter ahead of his mother, who toted two stuffed grocery bags. He braked in front of me his eyes shining.

"I walked the whole place, and it's really huge," he beamed. "Those underground tunnels are supercool. And I'm gonna go visit that science thingy I hear is really cool. "

"Don't wander too far by yourself again, Stewie," said Karen Mikulski as she emptied her bags of apples, grapes, Cheezits, red licorice whips, and meat-and-cheese wraps onto the table. "Somebody bad could be waiting to grab a cute kid like you."

Stewie's eyes went big as jumbo grapes. He opened his mouth, but no words came. Instead he parked the scooter and filled a paper plate with goodies.

Tulip sprang up from a director's chair to fill her own plate.

My stomach growled. I'd best grab a bite. Soon it would be time to get going and settle in at our cottage. I couldn't wait to see it. In online photos it looked charming with an English garden outside and Victorian decor in parlor and bedrooms. Tulip and I would share the larger bedroom.

Barbara and Lana were sharing the smaller. It would save everyone quite a bit of money, over renting hotel rooms.

Two lunch wraps, a fistful of grapes and a can of sweet tea quieted my gut. Bidding farewell to the buddies, Tulip and I headed for our car.

"Don't forget," Freddie called after us. "Dinner at Joe T. Garcia's. The must-eat place. Meet there at six after we feed and water. Map on the wall. Be there or be square."

"Wouldn't miss it for the world," Tulip called back.

"We don't have to," I said. "We're at the World."

"Ha ha, hilarious," she shot back. "Hey. Nature calls. You go on ahead. I need to make a pit stop. Might take a minute or five." As she veered off in the direction of the restrooms, she put her cell phone to her ear and shouted, "Hey, Tommy Lee."

I'd been wondering when we'd hear from TLJ. But I thought I'd be the one to hear first. He was my pal, after all. In the recesses of my mind, one tiny renegade cell whispered that, if things with Sonny and me didn't work out – I silenced that voice.

But was TLJ really interested in Tulip, or in the acting work he might find her? She could be impulsive, both in romance and in adventures that might yield money. Or fame. She did like to stand out in a crowd.

Standing in the Grandeen lounge, while I touched up my lipstick and ran a comb through my red-and-gold locks, I wondered how much time Tulip would take chatting with Tommy Lee and doing her restroom business. Sometimes she took forever. She always seemed to have a plethora of clothing and cosmetic adjustments to make.

I decided I had time to do some horse-show recon. I wanted to familiarize myself with the layout. And, if I used good old-fashioned reporter's footwork, who knew what clues to my mysteries or their characters I might run into?

Of course my boots were made for walking – sorry, Nancy Sinatra – walking out the door and across the street to the John Justin building, with its below-decks stalls reserved for horse-show high rollers such as Royce and Rogers. It would be interesting to see how the Other Half lived.

Having familiarized myself online with the Justin's layout, I went straight through the doors. To my left on the mezzanine was the first-aid station, and windows looking down into the stands and arena of an auction pavilion below. There were also multiple food booths and vendor booths. Fascinating, this multi-level Taj Majal of the Horse.

I pressed on, and soon found a staircase leading down to underground tunnels and the fancier stalls. When I came out in the horse area back of the enclosed arena, it didn't take long to locate Royce and Rogers' stall row and hospitality lounge with its fancy, purple and gold drapes. Potted palms and leather furniture drew my eyes.

So did the presence of Jeanne Allende, who glanced up from talking with another pretty teen. It was Honey Carpenter – the tall blond daughter of famed competitor, Patsy Ann Carpenter. The mother owned a son of Dark Superstar. However, her daughter's main ride was a son of Royce and Rogers' Shiny Suspicion.

I'd remembered Jeanne saying she was going back with her mom to their hotel. Clearly she'd been sidetracked. Meeting up with show friends from around the country was always fun, at a show like this.

"Jeanne, I didn't know you knew Honey," I said, smiling at her and stepping up to greet the other girl, in tan English breeches, tall black boots and a low-cut white lace tee with a flowing hemline. Honey dabbled in Western events, having bought a saddle from The Horsehouse. But she preferred English riding. "Hi, Honey, nice to see you again."

"Nice to see you, too," she said, looking past my left shoulder. Her pouffed lips turned up slightly.

Jeanne recrossed her legs, causing me to look again at her glamorous black boots. They must have cost a thousand dollars or more.

"I used to get beat by Honey all the time," Jeanne said as I took a chair beside her. "That's when I showed my old horse." She leaned toward me, eyes brightening. "Now it's my turn to ride to the front of the lineup. I told Honey she's been served. Grace and I are gonna beat her and Calvin's butt." She raised her chin and shot Honey a smug look.

I basked in the warmth Jeanne radiated toward me. Maybe she'd rethought our conversations, and how much I'd put on the line to help her, back at Brassbottom.

Honey raised her own chin and worked her prodigious pout.

"Fake news if I've ever heard it," she sniffed. "That uppity bitch-horse of yours gonna buck you clean off. Can't take the pressure like our Shiny Suspicions can."

I smiled, hearing the trash talk, words I might have issued once or twice myself.

"Well, I wish you both good rides and good luck," I said, filing away what they'd said. Jeanne owned a Superstar daughter, and Honey, a Suspicion son. Given the current atmosphere of death threats and attempted bribes to the judges, especially if one of them were acted upon, one of these young women was sure to get burned. Likely suffer emotional or financial loss whichever way the judges ruled.

Secretly, my money was on Jeanne. She was my fellow Brassbottom competitor and, I hoped, a developing friend. A buddy whom I was increasingly sure had more than winning a championship going on behind those sultry eyes. Hopefully I could tease that out of her, take off some pressure for her, help make her world championship more doable. She didn't need doubt and worry dragging her down. None of us did.

"How's that saddle you bought from me working out?" I asked Honey.

"Okay," she said. "I've had lots of compliments. Thank you for selling it to us."

"My pleasure. Say, Honey, I wonder if you could help me with something."

"Yah?" She shook back her blond ponytail over one ivory shoulder.

"Royce and Rogers own a majority share in Shiny Suspicion, right?"

"That's the word. Far as I know. Why?"

"You no doubt heard of the threats against judges who favor offspring of Superstar, then the attempted bribe of Bradford, head judge, Superstar's owner?

"Everyone's heard that." She blinked dramatically.

"What's your take?"

"Just some idiots trying to throw everyone off their ride." She lifted her eyebrows and swung her gaze to Jeanne. "Someone in particular."

Jeanne, sitting next to me, pulled herself up and shook back her hair. Almost as if she drew power from me. Just as she had that day I'd helped her with her horse.

"Pull-ease," Jeanne said. "No one's fallen for any of that crap, Honey. That means when I win, it will be fair and square, and on the way better horse. Prepare to lose."

Jeanne picked at a pine shaving stuck to her jeans. Stall bedding and other bits from a horsey life had a way of showing up when you least expect it.

"Well, ladies, I'd best be on my way," I said. "Again, good luck. Jeanne, I think Dutch is spending extra time today adjusting your mare's attitude."

"He'll make her right," she said. "Do you want to go with me, and watch?"

"I'm meeting Tulip to scope out our rental cottage. Catch you later. Nice boots."

Jeanne smiled. But Honey squinted her eyes at me, tilted her head, and scowled.

Chapter 43

After leaving the girls, I picked up the pace, hotfooting it back to the mezzanine of the John Justin building. I had to hustle my assets out to the parking lot. I'd allowed Tulip more than enough time to take care of her business.

My cell sang out. Of course it was Tulip.

"On my way," I said. "Five minutes, tops."

"No hurry. I've laid back the seats, cranked the A.C., and been drifting toward a power nap."

Guessing she'd be good for five more minutes, I peeled off my path and hurried to one of the spectator entrances for John Justin Arena — that high-ceilinged, dirt-floored palace where champions were made or broken. The place where I'd show Choc. The place where I hoped to make my dreams come true.

As I pulled open the nearest door, air rushed at me. My gaze swept down over a steep bank of blue seat-rows. I began descending the concrete steps toward the ring, a very deep story below. Its gates connected to the tunnels Little Stewie had seen.

A tractor harrowed and watered the arena footing. Its deep engine roar, combined with clanks from the drag, reverberated through the big space. Driving the rig was a tall, good-looking cowboy. He steered the tractor in slow ovals, pleating and smoothing the footing to a level, fluffy consistency.

Mesmerized, I stopped six seat rows from the rail, I studied the far fence plastered with advertising art. There were ads for everything from horses to horse insurance, boots to barns, and everything in between.

As I took it all in, my pulse quickened. Yes, I could see myself out there, in a western pleasure class. All dressed up in stretch pants and sparkly jacket, creased hat, shined cowgirl boots and silver-studded saddle squeaking rhythmically, I'd be jogging Choc along the rail among thirty other riders. I'd try to keep us well back from horses ahead, riding in an open slot where judges could have a long, unobstructed look at us. Understood: If you don't get seen, you can't get placed.

In the stands behind me, and in seats across the arena, an audience of other riders, owners and trainers would be watching. Donna Grandeen, seated or standing at the rail as I rode by, would softly say, "Loosen your reins," or "Breathe, have fun."

If I could imagine it, I could do it. Make that would do it. Easy as store-bought pie. Just like we did it at home. At least that's what our trainers always said.

I turned to climb back up the steps and go out to catch up with Tulip so we could find our lodgings and freshen up before hitting the Stockyards for dinner. Almost to the top, something caught my eye seven or eight seats in to the left. I hadn't noticed it going down, so hypnotized was I by the sights and sounds in the arena below.

Why was a boot lying heel up over a seat back? Was this some kind of joke?

Filled with growing apprehension, feeling chilled, I stared at the boot. I moved into the space between rows for a better look. But even before fully focusing I realized that boot had a leg inside it. What I saw after that stopped my breath.

A man's body, its long right leg caught at the ankle by the seat back, and the bent left leg caught on the seat itself, lay jammed at a forty-five-degree angle sideways on the narrow concrete floor between rows.

My heart hammered. Heat rose to my cheeks.

From the look of him, he'd been tall. Black-haired and muscular, he wore a brown tailored Western blazer, starched jeans and upscale, reptile boots. A tan cowboy hat, the expensive kind, partly covered his head.

It struck me that this man, whoever he was, may have had a medical event such as a heart attack, flailed around, and tumbled into that position from the aisle, or a row or two above. Whatever, it had been some fall.

I steeled myself to look more closely before calling for help. I braced one hand on a seat back ahead, and took two steps toward where he lay between rows. Immediately I shrank back. What I saw at close range made goosebumps pop on my arms and neck.

He was still. Too still.

Fighting an urge to vomit, I squeezed my throat to keep down my bile and half-digested lunch. The effort only partly succeeded. The inside of my mouth tasted bitter.

I shook my head to clear my vision as well as my mind. Surely I was dreaming. This couldn't be real.

But it was real. He was real. And he was dead.

Chapter 44

His head lay on its right side on the cold concrete, most of his left cheek obscured by a white shirt collar. His eyes, at least the one I could see, were glazed open.

In an instant I knew it was Max Allende. Sandra's ex, Jeanne's father. The large, tall frame that, in newspaper photos, resembled Sonny's. The black hair in a bronze face. The wide, fleshy nose. And of course, the ring with the initials "M" and "A" framing a large diamond set in a gold band that grazed his knuckle.

Impossible hope rose in me that he, like Stavropolis over the cliff at Table Rock, was only unconscious. But that cold feeling in my gut, the weight in my shoulders, did not lessen. Like many people, I knew dead when I saw it. But, unlike most people, as a reporter, I had seen it more often than I'd liked. Felt it in my bones as if it were me.

To make sure again I weren't trapped in a nightmare, I inched forward in a half-crouch, and pressed my fingertips into the cool neck under his jaw.

Nothing.

I slowly rose, backed into the aisle and glanced around. I saw the tractor nearing the center of the arena, and shadows of people in the opening of the announcer's booth above the gates at the arena's far end. Plus three unknown people with a brownish lap-dog in the stands across the arena. Squinting, I picked out a plump brunette in a fur-trimmed denim jacket. She held the dog. Beside her sat a thin, middle-aged man in a blinding white tee. With them sat a man in a sharp chambray Western shirt, sharply shaped straw hat and, from what I could see, starched jeans. This one nodded and gestured with expressive hands, from one end of the arena to the other. Trainer enlightening clients about the arena, and how to show in it.

The tractor banged and roared on. Its ovals got smaller. Usually I could ignore tractor noise, but not now. It had given me the granddaddy of all headaches.

I quickly ran through my options. The first was clear. I reached into my shoulder bag, drew out my cell phone and tapped in 911. I trembled, and still felt sick to my stomach. I studied the body while I waited for the dispatcher to pick up. Four rings. Then a man's voice said in a Texas twang, "Nine one one. What are you reporting?"

My gaze now picked up something different with the body. Something even more upsetting. There was a red-rimmed bullethole in his upper back, and blood inching out under him, outlining his chest and one shoulder against the concrete.

"Are you they-er?" the voice said in my ear. "What are you reporting?"

"Sorry. Pepper Kane, Will Rogers Memorial Center. The horse show? I just found a man's body in the grandstands. John Justin Arena. There's blood. He's been shot."

"What? You found a body? He's been shot?"

"Yes. And I think I may know who he is."

After a few more questions, the dispatcher asked me to stay there, touch nothing, and wait for responders. We disconnected.

I was relieved to see the noisy tractor and drag finally roll toward the arena gates. Once outside, its roar quickly faded. The resulting quiet came as a huge relief. My shoulders relaxed. Maybe my headache would fade.

As I sat down across the aisle from the body, I took a deep breath and let it out slowly, counting, trying to calm my runaway heart. Then I called Tulip. While I waited for her to answer, the grandstand doors above me banged open. I turned to look up. A sturdy-looking policeman trailed by EMTs jogged to where I sat.

"Where are you?" whined Tulip in my ear.

Her voice on the phone startled me. So did the noise of sirens wailing in the background. I pressed the phone tighter to my ear.

"Listen. I just found a body, I think it's Max Allende. In the upper stands at the Justin. Responders just came. Gotta go."

"What did you just say? "You—"

I hung up on top of her words. Then I powered off. I needed to concentrate. All hell was breaking loose, with me in the middle. Glancing anxiously around, I saw the people across the arena were gone. For how long, I hadn't a clue.

The policeman, a tall blond with long, pale hands and a ring of light hair showing below his hat, touched his badge as he stared at me. He keyed the mic on his shoulder.

"Yeah. It's here. Second row of the stands, east side of the Justin. EMTS on it."

He coughed, and pulled a pad and pen from his shirt pocket. He clicked the pen, preparing to take notes.

"Jim Dale Bond, police. You the one who found him and called nine-one-one?"

Hearing the man's name jerked me out of shock. I almost said that I didn't know British superspy Double-O-Seven rented out for horse shows. Miraculously, for once, I reined it in.

"Yes. I'm Pepper Kane. From Oregon. I'm showing a horse here." I followed that with my other particulars, as well as how and when I found the body. During this, one medic confirmed the death, while a young woman stretched yellow tape around the scene. A few looky loos poked their heads through the door above.

"The arena is closed," shouted Bond, waving them away. The lookers backed out, and Bond shut the door after them.

The next minute more officers and staff arrived. Bond motioned me deeper into my row across from the body. He confirmed I'd turned off my cell phone, and set to grilling me in depth, while his crew photographed, outlined and otherwise processed the scene.

The arena and stands became eerily still. During pauses in our interview, I could hear every cough, footstep and whisper of the investigators. While choosing my words for accurate answers, I also kept track of what was happening around Allende's body.

An older white woman I assumed was the medical examiner began working on and around it, while a young black man worked near her, holding evidence bags.

"D'Shon," she said to him. "Look for shell casings. We got what looks like an entrance wound on the back."

I shut my eyes. We were looking at murder. No way around it. I'd thought it might have been a heart attack or medical incident when I'd first seen the body. But noticing the wound and the blood had revealed the shocking truth. The M.E. had confirmed it.

Officer Bond interrupted my thoughts.

"Tell me again, Miss Kane, about the reported threats and bribes you heard about, and who you heard them from," he said. His face was professionally neutral, yet also was sympathetic. I told him again what I'd heard. Of course, he and staff would check everything against what others said.

After he was done, he said he'd be in touch. He motioned for me to walk out ahead of him. At the door I looked back to see workers readying a body bag and stretcher. It all seemed surreal, almost like being underwater with no air supply.

Once outside on the mezzanine, I saw a mob of whispering people gathered not far from the arena doors, guarded by a deputy. Some talked on cell phones. Others just stared. A blonde with a large microphone and small cameraman hurried forward.

James Bond materialized, lunged in front of me and held up his hands.

"Please, everyone, stay back. No reporters. There was an accident. We're asking you not to go into the arena."

"If it was just an accident, why the police presence?" shouted the reporter.

Bond was all over it.

"Standard procedure. I don't know what y'all heard on the scanner, but disregard. If we need to issue a statement, we will."

He looked down at me.

"We'll be in touch, Miss Kane. You may go."

I nodded, powered my phone back up, and watched him walk toward the exterior doors. Through them I saw an ambulance, a van and other official-looking vehicles. Traffic was being redirected.

Onlookers still gave me curious looks. I felt dizzy. But I pulled myself together and headed for those doors.

Tulip bumped into me, and grabbed my shoulders, stopping me with a lurch.

"What the hell's going on?" she said, leaning in. "What'd you do now, Pepper? Somebody die? What I heard. Judging from the response here, it wasn't accidental."

"Can't talk here. Let's go back to the stalls, and I'll tell you about it."

We pushed through the doors and headed across the street, weaving among people and vehicles. The heat pounded down and radiated up, increasing my discomfort. When we reached the Grandeen stalls, we saw Dutch leading Jeanne Allende's bay mare down the aisle. The horse was lathered in the flanks, and hanging her head.

Dutch halted in front of the mare's stall, unsaddled her, and handed me the tack.

"Jeamne's gonna be shocked," he said. "Her mom's gonna be shocked."

"Why's that?" I handed the saddle to Tulip, who schlepped it to the tack room.

"I think their horse has given up the fight. Plus, I gave her a little shot."

"Whatever it takes, long as it's legal," I said.

He tossed a sheet over the horse and tied her in the stall.

"Dutch," I said, "I have something to tell you. Let's go sit down."

Just then Sandra Allende walked up. She gave Dutch her broadest smile.

"I watched it all," she said. "Star looked terrific. I knew I could count on you, Dutch. No way we can't win, now."

"Sandra," I said. "Sandra."

"What, Pepper? You look like you've seen a ghost."

"It's ... it's ... didn't you hear?"

"Hear what? Forgot my phone, been so busy with Dutch."

"They called you over the loudspeakers."

"Don't think they were working over where we were. Why would they call me?"

I struggled with how to tell her. There was no good way. But I tried to ease into it.

"It's Max. Your ex-husband, Sandra. He ... there was an accident."

"What? Max? What kind of accident? How'd you find out? Where is he?"

I touched her shoulder, looked into her eyes.

"Sandra. He's here. And he's .. he's dead. I found him in the Justin minutes ago."

"What? Here in Fort Worth? He said he wasn't coming until Wednesday. Did you say, 'dead'?" Her eyes looked moist.

"Yes. I'm so sorry."

Her gaze swept from side to side. She clasped and unclasped her hands.

"Max. No. It can't be. You must be mistaken."

"The policeman might still be outside the Justin. At least he was a minute ago."

"Then it's true." She lay a trembling hand on my shoulder.

"Yes," I said.

"Oh, God," she whispered. "How did he die? Are they sure it's him? Does Jeanne know?" Her words rushed out. Before hearing answers, she was gone, racing toward the Burnett-Tandy exit.

Dutch, Tulip and I watched her disappear around the corner. Our mouths hung open. I shook my head, angry at myself at having told her so bluntly.

"How did you find out?" Dutch asked, eyes wide. "How did he die?"

"I found him," I said. "A half hour ago. I went to check out the arena, see what it would feel like riding there, and saw him at the top of the aisle. Lying on his face."

"Did he fall?" Tulip said. "Have a heart attack or something?"

"Bullet wound in his back. He was shot. They were searching for a casing."

"Shot?" Dutch and Tulip said in unison.

Tulip seemed to shrink. She shook her head.

"To die is bad enough. But to get shot ... unbelievable."

We all looked around, to see if anyone were listening. So far, so good. "Now the questions are," I said, "who would do that. And why?"

Dutch readjusted his ball cap, and worked his jaw.

"It sounds harsh to say," he said. "But Allende was the kind of guy who had no shortage of enemies. Abrasive, real hard-baller in business. If he's the one who tried to bribe and threaten Bradford, there'd have been hell to pay. Bradford has lots of friends who'd come to his defense if they knew someone was messing with him."

"Then there's Haverstadt," Tulip said. "Who has that interest in Shiny Suspicion. If he got wind Bradford might favor the Superstars, he could have tried to eliminate the person making the bribe. Even make one of his own."

We were silent as we contemplated the possibilities.

"So I wonder if Sandra and Jeanne will still show," she said.

"Nobody'd blame them for scratching," Dutch said.

We ducked into the Grandeen lounge. Dutch sank into a chair and shoved back his cap to reveal his receding hairline. He picked up an open cola can and drained it.

"What are we going to do, Dutch?" I said. "What are you going to do?"

"The committee might delay or cancel the show," Tulip offered, shuddering.

Dutch crushed the cola can and lobbed it into a white wastebasket. "Sorry, ladies. It sounds harsh. But the show must go on."

I spotted several barn buddies who'd come to muck out stalls down our aisle. I dreaded having to share the news. Maybe many of them already had heard. Soon there would be a Texas tornado of gossip. A tornado I couldn't avoid. Because I, as finder of the body and likely a person of interest in the death, would be at its epicenter.

Chapter 45

I looked out beyond the lounge. Horses stood tied in the aisles, riders grooming, saddling or unsaddling them. Someone was forking old bedding into a wheelbarrow a ways down our aisle. But nobody was within fifty feet of us. Shouts, neighs, stomped hooves had helped mask our conversation.

Dutch said what Tulip and I wanted to.

"It all comes back to who needed him dead," I said. "I think it comes down to the two we mentioned."

Dutch pulled down his cap so that his eyes were partly shielded. But he glared at me as if I might be responsible for the crimes. That's right, shoot the messenger.

"With Max's death," I began, "right after the break-in at Royce and Rogers' barn, coming after the previous attempt to scare judges into not placing Superstars up top, we may be looking at two criminals, or groups. Warring stallion syndicates."

"Yeah," Dutch said. "Could be."

"We're all pretty sure the bribe attempt was made by Max Allende. At least it sounded like him, from my friend Tommy Lee James' description."

Dutch considered this.

"Not surprised. Allende is, or was, fairly intense, judging from what few dealings I've had with him by phone or email. He's the one who sends the checks for Jeanne's mare's board and training."

"You haven't actually met him?"

"No. But what evades me is who made the original judge threats. So you think maybe Haverstadt, or one of the other Shiny Suspicion people?"

"Possibly."

"All I know is, it's damned peculiar. All this reminds me of a time before you put Choc in training, when there was a horse-show death that looked accidental, but wasn't."

"What death, Dutch?"

"When we were at the Western All-Breed Congress, Ron del Santos, a big Texas trainer, died of Xylazine poisoning after he hired a stall-cleaner, an illegal, to inject the drug into horses owned by clients of his competition."

"Oh, yes, I did hear of that. It took a while, but they finally nailed the guy."

Dutch's cell phone rang. He reached into his shirt pocket and pulled it out.

"Yeah." He listened for a minute, and then stood up. "Be right there." He looked down at me. "Show committee calling a judges' emergency meeting."

With that, he reached into the adjoining tack room, swapped his cap for a sharp western straw, and strode down the aisle, his spur-bedecked boots jingling.

"Whatya say, Tulip?" I said. "We'd better go find our house. There's nothing we can do for now. Besides. I'm ready to pass out."

We grabbed our purses and headed to the steaming-hot street outside the Burnett-Tandy. Several police units still stood outside the Justin, but the crowd had thinned. We made fast time to the RV lot. When we yanked open our car's doors, we were hit by a blast furnace. We gingerly settled on the molten seats, fastened our seat belts, and turned the AC to flash freeze.

I pulled the directions to our rental cottage off my phone. I read them to Tulip as she drove. We had been so close to the Will Rogers, within walking distance, that we'd turned up the short driveway to the little yellow house before I could say much more about the death. All I managed to say was how I found the body, and how I so wanted to find the mystery couple across the arena.

"I don't suppose Dutch knows what's behind this, but isn't saying," she offered as she set the brake. "Like y'all say, you have to look at every possibility."

"Why would he be involved, or know something and not say it?"

"He could have an interest, or else an agreement with another owner or trainer."

"Hmm. Now your imagination is working overtime, Tulip. Grasping at straws."

"Like yours isn't. What else do we all have to grasp at?"

"I guess it's something to consider."

I considered. But I came up empty. Unless he had somehow been involved in the Superstar syndicate, because he had several of the stallion's progeny in training, and had owned the Superstar son killed last summer.

I told Tulip as much.

She turned off the car's ignition and looked at me, her sunglasses reflecting my worried face, complete with lens-enlarged elephant nose.

"You know what, Pepper? They still could cancel the show over this."

"Oh, I doubt they will, Tule. Too many people have spent too much money to enter, and have come too far. They'll figure something out."

"But it casts a pall. How can we even show, with this hanging over us? We've got to find the killer. Dutch and the other judges may still be at risk. You could be, too."

"Just like at Table Rock last week. I called about the body. The killer knows that, wonders what I saw beforehand, and guesses I'm hot to finger him."

"Plus the law in both cases considers you a person of interest."

"That is true."

"Tell me about those witnesses, Pep. The people you saw in the stands across the arena. And the tractor driver you said was cute."

"Those other people left before the sheriff came. Probably only there a short time and saw nothing. The tractor guy was so involved in his work and making so much noise, he probably wasn't aware anything happened. But I'll try to find them anyway."

"Good luck. Needles in a haystack. Thousands of people at this show."

"Let's get inside the house," I said, opening my door. "This heat is killing me."

A glance around the cottage and yard, where an ancient elm shaded the porch and yellow roses rambled in the garden, told me we'd have a needed sweet retreat away from the show grounds. Neighboring houses stood close. But they were well kept, their shades drawn against the mid-afternoon sun. A poodle mix yapped behind a picket fence in a side yard to the right. Other than that, all seemed quiet.

Tulip found the key under a ceramic toad tucked among shrubs beside the porch. Toting several bags, she put a key in the old-style lock and opened the door. I followed.

The living room was warm, but not objectionably so, fairly dark, and smelling of lilac air freshener. The plantation shutters had done their job. We wandered wordlessly through the house, dropping bags in the larger bedroom, using the red-tiled bathroom.

Barb and Lana had not yet arrived. The second bedroom bore no sign of them.

Canvassing the black-and-white vintage kitchen Tulip and I filled clear tumblers with tap water, and flopped on the parlor's floral-print sofa and chair.

"This'll do," I sighed, closing my burning eyes. But instead of calming blackness, all I saw against the backdrop of my lids was Allende's body crumpled between seats on the grandstand floor. I began to shiver – with the reality of it, and the possible danger to me as the crime finder, sunk in. I'd been too busy up to now to realize its effect on my psyche. I had no idea how I'd get through the coming days.

"This place is just perfect," Tulip purred, leaning back and closing her own eyes.

I must have drifted off to sleep. I awoke with a start. Bass-guitar riffs pulled me fully wake. I reached for my phone.

"Reba, you're one tough senorita to reach," said a familiar baritone voice.

"Hey, Tommy Lee," I croaked, barely awake from my power nap. "Had the phone off. Want to talk to Tulip?" I'd forgotten to ask about their earlier conversation. I put the phone on speaker mode, so Tulip could hear, if she were awake with eyes half-closed.

"I just heard somebody was killed at the Will Rogers," said Tommy Lee. "Y'all know anything about that?"

"How'd you hear that?"

"Contacts in the police department. Not much I don't hear, sooner or later."

"So you know someone died. And probably that I was the one who found him."

"So it was you. Man. That's tough. I just heard some lady at the show had found him. That she's a person of interest. Talk about wrong place, wrong time.'

"Got that right."

He was silent for a few ticks.

"Awful business. For the guy, but for y'all. Maybe I can help you unwind, or put that scare on ice for a little while. Join Tulip and me for dinner out. We can hash it out then. I might have information of use."

"If you do, I assume you told your police contacts."

"Hell, yeah. But you should know, too."

"As a matter of fact, all of us from our barn were planning to have dinner at Joe T. Garcia's. Why don't you join us? Around six?"

Tulip's eyes sprang fully open. She must have been awake since my phone rang.

Tommy Lee chuckled in my ear.

"There's better places. But hey, you gotta do the tourist thing. I get it. I'll pick y'all up. Joe T's is great. Fantastic gardens. Did a tribute gig there. They all know me."

"Who don't you know, Tommy Lee?" It was naughty to say, but fun. "I'm anxious to hear your information. Give me a clue?"

"At dinner."

Chapter 46

Scented, showered and poured into jeans as snug as our skin – but with fewer wrinkles – Tulip and I sat on the edge of the cottage's sofa and chair. Tulip looked seductive in a low-cut pink top that revealed just enough cleavage and matched her sunglasses. I fluffed up my hair, and smoothed the folds of a red-chiffon tunic I'd purchased online and saved for Texas. The tunic that cleverly hid my muffin-top.

Barb and Lana still rustled about the bath and second bedroom. They'd come in with groceries, and reeking of horse, later than Tulip and I. They'd meet up with us and the rest of our Brassbottom group at Joe T.'s, but drive their own rental car.

I looked at my watch. Five-forty-five. By my calculation, Joe T's was a fifteen-minute drive away, but probably longer, with rush-hour traffic. As I finished texting Donna to let her know we'd be late, I heard a deep-throated rumble in the drive.

Tulip and I shimmied out the door. Tommy Lee was just stepping out of his fake red Lamborghini – with the real Lambo body over a Chevrolet chassis. Fooled the girls, and cheaper to maintain than the real deal. As TLJ was to the real TLJ.

Wearing aviator sunglasses, a navy blazer over an open-necked white shirt, sharp Western slacks and a belt buckle the size of Texas, he hooked his thumbs in his belt and gave us the once over. He wolf-whistled.

"Whoo, ladies, y'all look ready for the Red Carpet."

Tulip fluttered a hand at her bosom and regarded TLJ through her pink shades.

"Not chopped liver, yourself, TLJ," she said, with a provocative head-tilt.

"Wait, let's get a selfie." I grabbed my phone from my bag.

We leaned together, made faces and assumed varied poses, with me recording our hamming for posterity. Then Tommy Lee folded Tulip and me into the front seat – the only seat – where I, the smallest, bent in two and squeezed onto Tulip's lap.

'"Ouch!" she squawked when I squashed her bosom. This was going to be one interesting ride.

After twenty minutes of juking and jiving through thick traffic, horns blaring and middle fingers hoisted in our wake, Tommy Lee and his angels pulled into a darkening street fronted by bars, shops and tattoo parlors. Judging from the storefront signs, this occupied the heart of a barrio.

Several times I flashed on Max Allende's death. I saw over and over his large tan face pressed against cold concrete. Saw in my mind the bullethole in his jacket, the blood beneath. Trembled once more with horror, as well as with fear for myself, Dutch and my Brassbottom buddies.

Tulip leaned to one side and wrapped a sisterly arm around me as Tommy Lee swung the Lambo off the main drag, and onto a side street.

"Here we are, " he said, giving us a show-stopping smile as he tooled past a nondescript white ranch house modestly displaying a sign reading, "Joe T. Garcia's."

"That's a restaurant?" Tulip shouted.

"You wanted to come here," Tommy Lee said. "And hey, it's great. You'll see."

We drove aways further, circling for a few minutes before we found a parking spot under a streetlight where the Lambo wouldn't attract dents. After we parked, Tommy Lee helped Tulip and me disentangle ourselves and leave the car.

I heard a text alert on my phone. I looked at the screen.

"Mind your own business, Sherlock. Or die." The text came from some unknown number starting with an unfamiliar area code.

Icy adrenaline surged through me. I stared in disbelief at the phone as if it had more to say. It did. The time the text was sent was six-straight up.

I re-read the message. Twice. When Tulip and Tommy Lee began walking away, motioning me to follow, I looked at them as if I'd never seen them before. I became aware of my heart compressing, as if squeezed by a giant forceps.

Tulip stopped. She turned back.

"What is it, Pepper? What's the matter?"

"I just got texted a death threat," I mumbled.

"What? A death threat?"

"Yes."

She hurried back. I showed her the message. She held up the phone for Tommy Lee to see. He leaned in and frowned, shaking his head.

"Trying to scare you," he said with a dismissive wave. "Don't let it get to y'all. They'd never go through with another killing so near the first. People are on high alert, security cams working overtime. Just keep on keeping on."

"I hope you're right," I said. "But what gets me is that this text is worded almost exactly like the note on my gate back home. 'Back off, Sherlock.' Likely written by the same person. I have a feeling they may be here, now, watching my every move."

I hugged my concealed-carry purse close. The .38 added weight, but might save my life one of these days.

"Call the police and let them know," said Tulip. "Try not to let it get to you. Then whoever is doing this, will win."

"Easy for you to say." I took a deep breath to calm myself, and blew it out slowly.

"Wait just a daggone minute," Tulip said. "Let me see that text again."

I handed her the phone.

"Well, shoot," she snorted. "It was sent yesterday."

"What? But it just came though. Let me see it again."

Sure enough. It had been sent Sunday. The day before Max Allende died. So it could have been him who sent it. Weird. A voice from beyond, or before, the grave.

But then everyone occasionally has received an email or text sent earlier but not for some reason delivered in real time. Blame Internet glitches, servers, damaged apps. Fact of modern life.

"We've got your back, Reba," said Tommy Lee, giving me an affectionate pat on the back. "Nothing will happen if you keep people around. Let's go eat. Try to have fun. That's what you're here for."

Pigeons pecking for tidbits on the sidewalk flew up with a clatter of wings. Across the street a man shouted at a mini-skirted girl. "Mary! Over here."

We headed down the still-warm sidewalk while long shadows gathered. The two blocks to Joe T's made for pleasant walking. I willed myself to feel a good vibe. Just as in a horse-show, where other riders ache for you to mess up, but you keep your cool, focused only on yourself and your horse. You play the winner for all you're worth.

Chapter 47

Joe T. Garcia's was a tantalizing mix of scents before it was a sight. An odd little ranch house fronting the street before it was revealed to be a lively mix of rooms and lighted gardens inside. And a not-unpleasant assault on the ears, before the crowded, iconic restaurant became etched in memory.

Tulip, Tommy Lee and I swung through the restaurant's main entrance. What lay before us was a modest, earth-toned Tex-Mex room with diners happily doing their thing. What was the big deal?

But I knew, because I'd scoped it out on the internet. It was the gardens out back, the leafy ambiance and sparkling lights outside, as much as the delicious food and giant margaritas. The website showed an array of rooms, patios and gardens that could seat a thousand. The restaurant was old as the Texas hills, or at least as old as 1935, when the Garcia family opened it as a small café. Garcias still ran it.

Led by Tommy Lee, we made our way through the main dining room to the end of a short line of patrons waiting for tables in the patios and gardens. Through the open door I could see what they were waiting for: a chance to dine in a paradise tricked out with lights, tables, plants and trees around a glowing turquoise pool with a bubbling fountain at its center. Cozy trellises and pergolas, along with outdoor heaters, kept everyone comfy.

The Grandeen bunch, at tables on the left side of the pool, hailed us the moment we walked outside. Tommy Lee, Tulip and I waved, and walked forward. Heads swiveled and chatter died as we progressed. I heard "Tommy Lee Jones" spoken.

An old cowboy-wannabe in a field-worker's hat, too-short jeans and a store-bought belt-buckle jumped in front of us with a cell phone, and snapped a flash.

I jumped back, thinking "gunshot." My nerves already were raw, my imagination working overtime. The back of my head collided with Tulip's chin. Stars filled my eyes.

She patted my shoulder.

"It's only a flash photo. Take it easy, girl."

I heaved a sigh. Tommy Lee stepped in front of us. He looked around, and raised a manicured hand at the star-struck fans at nearby tables.

"Folks, I appreciate the attention, but I'm not the real deal," he grinned. "I just look like him, do tributes AS him." He leaned down, put an arm around an attractive brunette, and let her shoot a selfie of them. He repeated this gesture with a grandma nearby, and with a big man in small shorts.

It only took a few minutes. Then Tommy Lee pulled business cards from his jacket, and handed them around.

A little tacky, I thought. It was called working the room. We weren't here for that. But I could hardly blame him. His livelihood depended on getting tribute gigs.

Moving forward toward again, I heard the voices of the Brassbottom buddies, most of whom raised frosted margarita glasses and motioned to us. A few hooted, as Tulip, TLJ and I made it to the tables.

I re-introduced Tommy Lee, who elicited an excited clucking among the women. I then guided him to our new girls on the block, Sandra and Jeanne Allende. So Sandra and Jeanne had come to dinner, after all. Which surprised me. I had thought that, with Allende's death, they would give it a miss.

Jeanne looked quiet and subdued, as if she'd rather be somewhere else. But she was trying to make the best of it. I wasn't sure how close she'd been to her dad. But he had been her father, after all.

Sandra turned especially demonstrative at meeting Tommy Lee. Her lips opened in a broad smile, her eyes flashed. She scooched her chair against Jeanne's in an attempt to open a space for the tribute actor to sit beside her.

"I'm sure you're in regular contact with the real Tommy Lee," she said. "My ex ... sorry." She cleared her throat. "I understand the real Tommy Lee owns polo ponies imported to Texas from Argentina. Do you play polo, Mr. Jaymes?"

Jeanne blushed, steadied her straw and sipped at what might be a virgin margarita.

Tommy Lee gazed at Sandra, a professional actor's smile on his face.

"No, Ma'am, afraid I don't do polo. But I've watched TLJ play. He's quite good."

"You should try it. Some time. You look athletic." She arched an eyebrow and unleashed another smile.

I felt for Sandra. I hadn't really seen her in action, with a man. She was trying a little too hard to be the merry ex-widow. But I imagined that many women got giddy meeting this TLJ. I had, when I first met the guy. Tulip still did it, bless her heart.

The restaurant employee trailing us pulled over untaken chairs from another table, and motioned us to them. We three jimmied ourselves into the Brassbottom formation, ordered jumbo margaritas and braced for a Texas storm of questions.

Before it could get rolling, Donna picked up a knife, tapped her water glass and shooshed everyone. And before she got talking I dove in.

"Where's Dutch?" I said. I was temporarily distracted by the arrival of the margaritas. I took a few frosty swallows, and immediately felt more relaxed.

"He'll make it if he can," Donna said. "But after the judges' emergency meeting, and the sheriff's interview, he was going to install security cameras on our stall row."

She gave us the condensed version of how the sheriff had issued a press release about Allende's death. It was being investigated as a homicide, the cause not disclosed. She said the show committee had resolved to hire extra security, and advised judges to put cameras on areas where horses they owned or had in training, were stalled.

She also reported that she heard the arena tractor driver had been interviewed, but that the spectators whom I'd seen, and told police about, were still being sought.

"The show is offering a thousand-dollar reward to anyone providing details leading to an arrest," she concluded. "Do you want to tell us exactly what you saw, Pepper, and what you have learned, if anything?"

The buddies swiveled their heads to me.

"Well," I began, trying to make myself heard above chatter at the nearby tables. "I just got a threatening text. Sent yesterday, but somehow delayed."

There came a burst of surprised exclamations around our tables.

"Really?" squeaked Little Stewie. He had a green frothy youth-drink in one hand.

"No way," said Lana, shaking her spiked-hair head.

The buddies began to buzz excitedly.

I was interested in reactions not only of owners of Dark Superstar horses, but also of one who owned a horse by Superstar's rival, Shiny Suspicion. That would be Barbara. She was still something of a mystery to me, despite her joking and confident ways. I knew my other buddies like I knew the back of my horse. But what did I really know about her?

For that matter, what did I really know about Sandra? The nitty gritty. Yes, we had much in common. Yes, we'd spent time together and she'd called me a friend. But we hadn't become the kind of close that besties had. There was still the matter of the incident on Table Rock.

Yes, she'd said Reg's fall was accidental. Yes, she'd apologized for her impulsive actions after. And yes, she'd conveyed genuine concern about her daughters. She wanted to solve the mystery of her gone girl, and to help the remaining one bring home a world championship. Could that motherly concern be so extreme that she'd found a way to manipulate her ex-husband to try bribery, while spurring his attempts to find Nancy?

"I had that happen once with a text," Sandra said. "Got it a day after it was sent. Probably a server glitch."

"You had other threats, didn't you?" put in Freddie. "Because you're heading our investigation of the judge threats ... and other things."

"Yes," I said. "Somebody crashed my gates, left notes, voicemail. The Law's doing extra patrols past my house. Worry a little about my daughter house sitting."

"What'd that text you just got say?" said Little Stewie.

"'Back off, Sherlock, or die'," I said. "Referencing Detective Sherlock Holmes."

Barb stiffened, raised her margarita glass and took a long drink. I realized she looked older tonight, her face more lined, her eyes sunken in her plump face. She'd mentioned that her M.S. was flaring up. But it might be something else. Something connected to wanting a championship before she could no longer ride.

Jeanne took another draw on her youth-drink straw. She looked out from lowered lids and twisted her napkin.

She must be tormented, just having lost her father. I felt bad for her. I wished there were something I could do for her.

"Could we all just chill?" she said. "Take a moment of silence, for my dad?"

Chastised for conversing of things other than the sobering fact of Allende's death, we all fell silent. Sandra put an arm around Jeanne's shoulders, and drew the girl to her in a tender hug. A tear glinted in Sandra's eye as she murmured something.

After a moment, Freddie Uffenpinscher rose to his feet, lifted his margarita glass and dramatically cleared his throat. Old actor skills never die. He still played small roles in community theater productions.

"I say we make our own resolution, take our own pledge," he said. "We condemn what has happened. We agree to share useful information. But we of Brassbottom Barn — especially those with horses related to the top sires — hereby resolve to go show," he said. "Not only go show, but show like we've never shown before. Not let this beat us down. And win those world championships we've worked so hard for."

He looked around the table.

"I've worked so hard for," he emphasized. "I don't need to remind you that I was robbed of my chance for a world championship last summer after Dark Vader was sold out from under me and then killed."

It got even quieter at the tables. The splashing of the nearby fountain sounded like that of Niagara Falls. Freddie drew in and exhaled a monster breath. He slowly sat down and flipped his napkin back over his lap. People at adjacent tables leaned closer, pretending not to have heard.

Tulip stood, breaking the awkward silence.

"Hear, hear," she shouted, raising her margarita glass, slopping some on her bosom. She dabbed the spot with a napkin. Then she quietly sat back down and sucked on the wet corner of the napkin.

Tommy Lee grinned at me and shrugged as if to say, "That's our Tulip."

Normal conversations slowly resumed at our table and around it.

Freddie, now with a new margarita before him, tapped his glass for a final word.

"Carlos told me something that I am supposed to keep secret," he began, eyes shining. "Of course I won't. He says he heard his bosses say a realtor offered Grant Haverstadt a piece of land he was dying to annex to his ranch if he'd influence other judges to favor Superstars. Also tried to bribe Royce and Rogers to scratch some Suspicion horses from a few classes."

"Hold on, Freddie," I said. "Did you tell the police?"

"Well, no. I just heard it before I came here."

"Big rooms have big ears. Will you step over to that corner with me?" I motioned with my head to a secluded spot where there were no tables. "We'll call the police from there. Tommy Lee, you come, too. You said you had something to tell me."

Donna half stood, arms akimbo. A stern look tightened her features.

"I need to be in on this," she said. "My husband and I may have a stake in it."

Tommy Lee, Dutch, Donna and I rose and scooted our chairs from the table.

Suddenly Jeanne Allende slanted toward her mother, and pointed toward the door.

"Mom," she said. "Look over there, in the other corner. There's Dick Bradford, that judge who owns Grace's sire."

Chapter 48

I looked where Jeanne Allende pointed. Sure enough. Sixty feet away, wearing a dress Stetson and dark blazer, his silver hair licking his ears, was the man whose stallion inspired such jealousy and intrigue. Intrigue enough that someone had paid for it with his life. Dick Bradford. The head show judge.

Four other judges, the bewhiskered Grant Haverstadt among them, stood beside Bradford as he looked across the patio. Bradford spotted us, nodded, and then followed the maître d' to a secluded pergola several yards from the door.

Tulip crowded me and jerked her head in their direction.

"There they are. The big guns. Man, do I wish we could ask them questions."

"You and me, both. This might not be the time. But opportunity trumps time. I'll figure out something."

The judges settled into a table flanked by giant cacti. I felt a sudden urge to use the Ladies Room. "I'm scoping out how to be a fly on a wall," I murmured.

Freddie Uffenpischer rose and came up to me.

"I need to tell you what else Carlos told me," he said.

"I'm all ears."

"Carlos heard one of their clients, maybe it was Patsy or Honey Carpenter, say some California big shot had approached them and their trainers, about getting in on a betting pool for their stallion, Shiny Suspicion. It had to be

Allende, trying to work another angle. On the sire whose offspring won the most championships."

"Allende sure walked the edge," said Tommy Lee. "No wonder he got axed."

Tulip gave him a look. He raised his eyebrows in answer.

Donna leaned over.

"I'd heard that rumor about the double betting pool, too, Freddie," she said. "God, I hate this part of showing. There's always some talk about something illegal, or flat-out dangerous going on behind those smiling faces. Luckily most of it is just that. Gossip."

Tulip and I nodded, and headed toward the Ladies Room inside the restaurant.

"You go on," I told her, glancing at the judges at their table. She gave me one thumb up and slipped through the door.

I pretended to admire the giant cacti near the judges. Then I looked over at them.

"Oh, hello, gentlemen, and ma'am," I said cordially. "See you're a fan of Joe T's, too." Cue smile. "Pepper Kane. I have a horse with the Grandeens?"

Bradford nodded at me. The others gave obliging smiles. Fraternizing with judges at a horse show was frowned on. But this wasn't really fraternizing. More like fishing.

"Hello," said Haverstadt, giving a small wave between sips of margarita. His wide whiskered face with its long nose and close-set eyes reminded me of a wolf's. "Aren't you the one who found the body?"

Nothing like getting right to it.

"Why, yes. Such a scare. The ex-husband and father of a couple of our riders."

"And how are they doing?" said Bradford, glancing toward our tables.

"As expected," I said. "But soldiering on."

Sympathetic nods and murmurs went around the table.

"What's the buzz on who might have killed him?" said Bradford.

"That's the million-dollar question," said Haverstadt.

"Lotta theories," I said. "Any of you prefer one theory over another?"

Haverstadt grabbed two tortilla chips, dunked them in salsa and stuffed them in his mouth, chewing rapidly. Bradford blinked as if he had something in his eye. He touched a fingertip to it.

"A few," Bradford said. "But nothing I'd bet the ranch on."

I thought that an interesting statement.

"Your best guess?" I said.

"Allende was in real estate," Bradford said. "Land deal gone wrong? I had dinner with him Saturday. He seemed like a regular guy. Real nice."

It wasn't what we'd heard, but I held my tongue.

"So you didn't really know him? His daughter is showing a horse by your sire."

Bradford leaned back. A frown pulled at the corners of his mouth.

"We were just discussing a piece of land I was interested in ..."

He looked at the other judges. They were busy with chips and drinks.

"Well," I said. "I hope you... we... all can still have a good show, have fun and make some money, in spite of what happened."

"Should have a great turnout now, for those preview classes at the welcome barbecue tomorrow night," said Bradford, smoothing his napkin on his lap.

"Hear, hear," said Haverstadt, raising his glass.

Chapter 49

When I returned to the Brassbottom tables, my mind whirled with what the judges had or had not said. But my stomach demanded filling.

Mercifully, our food had arrived – gorgeous, plentiful plates and bowls of it, from big, round tortilla chips dabbed with refried beans, and condiment cups arrayed around them, to hot, fragrant enchiladas and fajitas, large tortillas melting with cheese and oozing with meats and savory sauce.

Our Brassbottom group immediately halted the chatting and launched into eating. Speculation and gossip took a back seat to the important business of gorging. When flans and other desserts arrived, we savored them more slowly. Sated and happy, we finally waddled back through the restaurant and slipped out into the cooling Fort Worth night.

We found the Lambo and drove, silent and stupefied by the food and margaritas, about a mile back down the road. Tommy Lee insisted that we see Fort Worth's famous Stockyards before we called it a night. We could make it a destination, some other day.

We drove beneath the rustic Stockyards sign. Tommy Lee regaled us with tales of how, to the delight of tourists, cowhands ran a small herd of longhorns down the street daily, and staged a rodeo every Friday night. There was fun to be had at Billy Bob's, music to dance to, beer to enjoy.

Long live Texas history, was the general idea. Vintage buildings, cobbled streets, antique and western stores, noisy bars and dance halls blaring music surrounded us as we drove at a parade pace. Colors, smells and sights were rich and memorable. It almost made me forget the day's tragedy at the Will Rogers Center.

Tulip squealed, as Tommy Lee pointed out the White Elephant bar, and other attractions with memorable music and décor. I sighed as we passed store windows promising Western shopping heaven.

In the dark lit by neon and moonlight, somewhere beyond the bars and stores that Tommy Lee, Tulip and I rolled by with windows wide open, I thought I heard a longhorn low. Was it only my imagination? I made a mental note to see the longhorns herded down the streets some time during my Fort Worth stay.

Finally back at our cozy cottage near the Will Rogers, I stepped inside the house to hear Barb and Lana busy in the bathroom and their bedroom. I undressed in Tulip's and my bedroom, while she and Tommy Lee lingered in the car. Maybe his marriage really was on the rocks, as he claimed. Or else he was the hound dog I thought he was.

Tulip entered our bedroom with its twin beds shortly after I did. I heard the Lambo rumble off down the street.

"What a night," she sighed, tossing her purse down and peeling off her clothes.

"You can say that again," I answered, "but please don't."

Once the bathroom was clear, we took turns cleaning up. Then we hit the rack. I had forgotten how good being flat felt.

We were up and at 'em by six. Though jet-lagged, I'd been awake since five, lying in bed and reviewing the previous day's events, being horrified all over again.

This was going to be a very long day. Not only did I have to have to exercise Choc to take the edge off him, but also have a lesson on him with Donna at nine, and a grinding day of prep for my first elimination class tomorrow. If I made the final cut of that class in western horsemanship, made the top fifteen, I was in like Flynn for a show jacket embroidered with the words, "World Show Top 15" on it. Final championship classes were scheduled for the following week.

So after our morning lesson, my busy day would continue with bathing Choc, sanding and polishing his hooves, using a powder spray to whiten his white blaze and stockings, and maybe practicing tying a full, fake tail into his own tail to dramatize his elegance in the ring. Horse showing, as I've mentioned before, is not for the faint of wallet, or those lacking in time or energy.

I also hoped to find time to hunt down the couple and trainer I'd seen across the arena yesterday before spotting Allende's body. Who were they, what had they seen? More important, whom had they seen? The sheriff sought them too, but I hadn't been able to provide a very good description. Just what they wore, their look. Plump, older brunette with a fur-trimmed denim vest and a brown dog. And her male companion, possibly her husband. Skinny, white tee. Plus the trainer, in a hat, chambray shirt.

By six-twenty that morning, Tulip and I were slamming down breakfast in the vintage kitchen of our cottage. Poached eggs on toast, coffee, cream.

"Are you up for watching the World Preview Class tonight?" she said.

"Might give it a pass," I said. "I am beyond beat. And there's tons to do today. My first class is tomorrow."

"Be fun to watch the Preview. It should attract more spectators to the show. The announcer's supposed to explain classes that can be a mystery unless you know what judges are looking for. Big buckle and jackpot money will sweeten the pot."

"I thought the committee would have drawn for the preview contestants by now."

"First thing today. The last-minute surprise is part of the fun."

"Doesn't sound fun to me. You need time to prepare. What're the classes, again?"

"Showmanship, Western pleasure, horsemanship, trail and reining."

I felt for, but also envied, the half-dozen or so show participants who'd be chosen at the last minute, to show off at the preview. They'd get a leg up, to repeat an equestrian expression, on making an impression on judges before the real championship classes began. That impression had better be a good one.

Tulip took her mug and plate to the sink.

"We need to get a move on," she said. "Stalls to clean, horses to longe, and our lesson with Donna at nine. She's got the horsemanship pattern we'll use in our class tomorrow. And who knows what will be going on related to Allende's death."

'No kidding," I said, fighting back a bit of nausea. My emotions were a mess, and the brew coughed up by the ancient Mister Coffee just wasn't doing it for me. I missed my salted-caramel creamer, and hoped to score some today in that store I'd seen along the way to the Will Rogers.

Before leaving I took a call from the police. It figured. They wanted to interview me again. We set a date for eleven-thirty at the show grounds. I was sure they considered me a person of interest if not a suspect in the death. It would be hard getting that out of their heads, but I'd do my darnedest. The key was finding one or all the people I'd seen across the arena before finding Allende.

It was a short drive to the grounds, but took a few minutes longer because we stopped to buy creamer and a few more grocery items to stash in the Grandeen cooler. Amid a growing crowd of trainers and competitors, Tulip and I cleaned our stalls, haltered our horses and miraculously found spots to lounge them in a warm-up arena.

I had been running Choc around me for ten minutes, when I thought I glimpsed the mystery couple, minus trainer, leading a tall black horse outside the arena. I jogged over, Choc in tow, and shouted at them. But they disappeared into the crowd.

"Do you know who those people are?" I asked Donna, who sat Jeanne's bay mare nearby, warming up the horse for Jeanne prior to our practice.

"Don't know who you mean," Donna said, staring into the crowd.

My heart sank. But at least now I had another clue. The couple had a tall, black horse, probably part-Thoroughbred. I'd tell the investigators at our meeting.

Time seemed to race by, leaving me little time to fret over events of recent days. Shows can do that for you.

By eight-fifty, Choc was warmed up and saddled. By nine, I was riding with other Brassbottom buddies toward the practice ring. By nine-fifteen, Choc and I were wrapping up a horsemanship, or western equitation, pattern before Donna's critical gaze. Having worked Jeanne's horse, she sat on a stool in arena center, as a few dozen other riders and trainers had their own practice sessions and stayed out of our way.

Donna gave Choc and me double thumbs up. Resplendent in a fitted lime-green jacket and cap, she smoothed the blond hair poking from under her cap. She'd silently watched me ride Choc at different gaits, plus stopping, turning and backing a set pattern among orange cones set in a triangle. But her critical gaze had spoken volumes, making me tense from the mental noise.

I also felt tight from the questioning stares of other buddies lined up to take turns in our lesson. Luckily, I had avoided questions about my discovery of Allende's body. Just like I'd evaded their questions about my Table Rock ride the previous week.

Now I slapped on a smile and walked Choc back toward the others.

"Now that's what I'm talkin' about," shouted Lana.

Sandra, sitting her palomino alongside Lana and her horse, nodded in agreement.

Jeanne Allende sat silently aboard her fidgeting mare on the other side of Sandra. Jeanne's face was stony under a hat pulled low. So far she'd managed to control the mare, and keep her own counsel about her father. What a trouper.

"Try to relax more," Donna shouted as I steered Choc into one end of the lineup and turned him to face her. "But I think you'd make the final cut, with that ride."

I patted Choc's neck and allowed myself a small gloat as I sat, shoulders back, in the lineup. Choc mouthed the bit and flicked his ears forward with pleasure. This horse, like many, not only worked for carrots, but also for praise. Discipline or corrections had to be applied sparingly, or he'd be offended. Most horses just want to get along, please their leader.

"Lana? You're next," shouted Donna.

Lana squared her shoulders and legged her chestnut Paint toward the cones. She stopped at the first cone, her horse's shoulder three feet out from it.

Dust motes hung in the bright air above the hoof-marked dirt. Several horses snorted, clearing airways. Country music played over speakers, creating a calming atmosphere. We riders looked calm. Inside, we were anything but.

"Lana!" shouted Donna as our buddy rode her pattern. "Don't look at the cone. Just feel where it is. Know your horse's stride enough to halt right at the spot."

I, too, had seen Lana's gaze slip sideways to make sure she was properly lined up at the cone. Such a gaffe could knock you out of the placings. This was a game of inches, even centimeters.

Little Stewie, on his buckskin Paint-Quarter Horse that looked too big for the boy's frame but was a compact mover, edged closer to Choc and me.

"It's the regular amateur pattern, right?" the boy whispered, inclining his head topped by a too-big tan cowboy hat.

I kept my hand still and my eyes straight ahead, wanting to avoid Donna's wrath. No talking, fussing or slouching in the lineup, no horse adjusting. And certainly no texting on the cell phone, if I'd had one with me. Other days, other lessons, that was okay. But not in a World Show practice or class. It just looked tatty, unprofessional. Every minute you are in or near the arena, you are showing. A judge might catch a glimpse of you for the wrong reasons, and delete you from placing.

"Pepper?" Stewie prodded.

"Yes," I whispered. "Not your Youth pattern. This one's harder, but it will make you better. Suck it up."

Donna's head swiveled our way.

"Remember, everyone," she said. "You are now at the World. Treat it as such."

She returned her attention to Lana and her horse, now loping a large circle.

I studied Lana, hoping she was prepared to ask her horse to switch its leading legs around the inside of the circle, at the right spot, as they headed the other way. I did see, though, her circle was symmetrical, ridden at a rhythmic cadence. All good.

She switched her horse's leading legs a stride past where she should change.

"Late!" barked Donna.

Lana rode on, halting sharply at the final cone, and then backing her horse the four prescribed strides. She halted again, then turned and jogged her horse toward us.

"Woohoo!" I shouted.

"Way to go, Lans," said Sandra.

The other buddies clapped. Besides being all about tight focus and grace under pressure, horse showing – like other sports – is about mutual support even in mutually competitive circumstances.

When practice was over, we rode or lead our horses toward our stalls. I looked back at Sandra as I led Choc. She had dark circles under her eyes, and a zigzag of concern between her eyebrows. Jeanne led Grace several yards behind us.

"How're you doing today, Sandra?" I said.

"Medicated," she replied.

"Whatever it takes."

"Max's death was quite the shock. Poor Jeanne is devastated."

"Nobody would blame her if she scratched," I said.

"Plus her leg injury is acting up. I told her to ride through it. It will make her a better person. This is the show she's dreamed of her whole life."

"I'm sure she'll get through it, Sandra. I've seen her cowgirl up before, like when I helped her with her horse. I'll help cheer her up. We all will."

"Thanks, Pepper. Appreciate it." Sandra angled off to go to her stall and Jeanne followed, sliding me a glance.

"Wishing you well, Jeanne," I said. "It's a tough time, but you have my support."

She paused to give me a wan smile. She seemed to be about to say something, but she murmured, "Thank you," and moved to put her horse away.

I led Choc up close to Freddie, leading Poppin. Freddie looked sharp in a shiny black vest, checked grey shirt and black jeans.

"Lookin' good, Fredster," I said, giving him the once over. "Had a good practice."

"Pretty sassy looking, yourself," he grinned, adding a wolf whistle. "For someone whose middle name is trouble. Maybe I shouldn't get too close."

I tossed him a cross look.

"Funny. So. You and Carlos getting along?"

"Not so much," he said, tugging one of his bejeweled ears.

"There a problem?" I said.

"He had a big fallout with Royce and Rogers," Freddie said, dark brows drooping. "Don't know how that's going to shake out, but he asked what they knew about Grant Haverstadt, his rep for gambling, and about the rumored betting pools on the Suspicion and Superstar horses. "

"Really." I said. "Pretty bold of him. And that's news. That Haverstadt gambles."

"Royce told Carlos employees should butt out of things that didn't concern them. He reamed out Carlos pretty hard. His job might be on the line."

"That seems over the top. Maybe they are or were involved in the pools? "

Freddie shrugged.

"Your guess is as good as mine. Wouldn't be surprised if they and Haverstadt have a little something going along those lines."

"That might explain the earlier threats against judges placing the Superstar offspring high."

"Exactly."

"Maybe why Allende was killed," I said, thinking aloud. "Remove competition."

We reached our stalls, tied up our horses and loosened their cinches so they could rest before Dutch or Donna tuned them up. We'd bathe and prep them after lunch.

I filed Freddie's intel in my brain. More trouble with stallion owners. Hopefully no additional evil would ensue. But with emotions this high, and bank accounts on the edge, anything could happen. One man had paid the price. Who might be next?

Chapter 50

I calculated I had about an hour before I had to meet with investigators for my interview in the John Justin Arena where I'd found Max Allende's body.

This block of free time was my chance to try to track down the spectator couple. Changing from boots into tennis shoes, and unfolding the Will Rogers floor plan I'd stolen from our tack room, I began walking the stall aisles. I'd look in every cubicle, every arena, for a certain tall black horse, ready to jot owner and trainer names in my phone's Notes page.

I made it down only two aisles when my phone rumbled.

"Pepper!" said Donna. She sounded breathless. "Hope you're sitting down."

My pulse sped up.

"They find Allende's killer?"

A pause.

"Sadly, no. Not that big.'

"Then what?"

"You're in the barrel for tonight. The horsemanship class. In the new World Show Preview they're staging as part of the Welcome Barbecue."

"You're kidding." I stopped as if I'd hit a wall. It was the last thing I'd expected. My heart did a flip.

"They just drew your name for the class. You're one of five. We're beyond excited. Great publicity for you and for Brassbottom Barn. They expect a thousand spectators, TV coverage, the works."

"This is insane, Donna. So last-minute. We have only hours to prepare."

"I know. They wanted everyone to just treat it as a formal practice, and have fun. The good news is, it's horsemanship. Your best event. Lucky we drilled in that this morning. There's a World Show title and some money to go with it."

"No pressure," I said. Like hell. This could make or break a rider's success once the main show got underway. If you did well, a judge would remember you. If you did poorly, a judge would remember you.

"You'll be great," Donna said. "Dutch just got Choc out to tune him up. But you need to get back here as soon as you can. We'll help bathe him, tidy his mane bands, and do whatever else we need to do."

I rattled out a sigh.

"Shoot. I'm trying to find that couple with the black horse. The people I asked you about who were across the arena before I found Allende's body. And I have a sheriff's interview in a little while."

"Just get back here as soon as you can. Remember, that Preview Class can be your ticket to a world championship."

"Or not, if I tank," I said. "Like I need any more on my plate."

When we disconnected, I felt as if I'd had the wind knocked out of me. But I pulled myself together. I walked faster up and down the aisles, and into other buildings such as the Moncrief, in search of those possible witnesses.

At each stall with a black horse I paused, studied the animal and checked out the stall card on its door, which often had a pedigree and owner information. I knew which aisle, which stalls, were designated for which trainer. So if I found the right horse, the right trainer, I had a clue to the horse's owners.

It was as Tulip had said, like searching for a needle in a haystack. But pure-black horses were fairly rare at any show. After looking into a couple hundred stalls, I'd seen only six pure blacks. And they weren't tall or elegant like the one I sought.

At eleven-twenty, sweaty and footsore, I was in the air-conditioned Justin. I hit a food stand and picked up a hot bread-bowl of chili. I took it and a cold sweet-tea to a nearby table and chowed down.

Then I kept my appointment with Officer Bond. We met at the door leading to the top of the stands, just outside the aisle I'd walked down before finding the body. He offered a cool hand and I shook it, trying to appear relaxed. Now his speculative looks were a hundred-eighty degrees from his looks of the day before, and worlds apart from Detective Jenee's sympathetic ones back in the Rogue Valley.

"We have information that you had a friend of yours check into the deceased's recent associations, like dinners out, that sort of thing," he said. "Why did you do so?"

"I was acting at the behest of my trainers and friends, as I told you before," I said.

Bond's eyebrows hitched up under the band of his policeman's hat.

"And you still swear you had nothing to do with the injuries suffered by the man who went over that cliff in Oregon," he reiterated. "It just seems odd someone would be involved with two suspicious incidents within the same week, and connected to the Allende family, and to horses."

The pulse in my temples pounded when he told me again what he'd learned about the Table Rock fall. He was just doing his job, trying to connect dots. But it annoyed me. Some dots might not be connected, as Sonny would say.

"So I suppose you've interviewed Dick Bradford and Grant Haverstadt, and their associates," I said. "Or at least are aware of them. Since word was, each had a lot to gain with offspring of their stallions winning world championships."

"Miss Kane, we are exploring all possibilities. Let us do what we are hired to do. Please remember that my job is to learn as much as I can from you."

"So am I considered a person of interest, here? Or a suspect?"

"Your words, not mine. We just want to solve this case."

Chapter 51

After the interview, I hurried back to the Grandeen stalls in the Burnett-Tandy to help prep Choc for my class in the evening's World Show Preview.

Shoot. I really didn't have time for this. But I would have to put one boot in front of another, regardless. For myself and for Brassbottom Barn. I had no choice. And, who knew? I might be a star. Yeah, right. And armadillos might fly.

Donna already had Choc in the aisle crossties. Standing with each of her feet on a stepstool, she worked at re-banding his short, flax-frosted mane. He looked damp but incredibly shiny.

"Got here soon as I could," I told her, stashing my purse in the tack room.

She glanced back, her hands holding a thin section of mane and her lips gripping a tiny brown rubber band ready to go around that section, pulling it tight to the neck crest. She'd already banded three-fourths of the mane from poll to withers. There would be at least sixty tiny banded sections, when she was through. A job that could take an hour.

"Mmm," she said, returning to her work. "I already bathed him. I couldn't wait."

I inspected Choc, gave him a pat and grabbed my grooming bucket. I set to work smooth-sanding a rough spot near the heel of one of his hind hooves. It was already smooth enough for applying clear polish. But I wanted to be doing something.

Soon I was brushing him to a blinding shine. I finished off with a light toweling, and a spritzing with a spray that repels dust and adds shine. To finish, I'd wipe lemon-scented fly repellant over his face, and spray it on his legs and whole body. The Texas flies were big, bad and biting, to which a rising bump on my right arm attested.

The hours-long grooming done, and the faux tail matching his own tied under his tailbone, I led my pretty boy back into his stall. I arranged a stretchy nylon neck-sleeker and body sheet on him to keep him spotless for the evening class. We'd feed him right after Dutch tuned him up, and then we'd wipe off any green stains around his mouth.

Donna handed me a sheet of paper. It was a drawing, with text, of the pattern I was to ride in my class. Holding it in one hand as I studied it, I traced its circles and straight lines with the other hand, memorizing every change of gait and direction.

I was aware of other riders coming and going in nearby stalls and aisles, but not paying them much attention. I looked at Donna.

"When do you think I'll go?" My heart stuttered as I said the words. My debut on the World stage drew closer. But I had to stay calm, and concentrate. I took a few deep yoga breaths and let them out slowly while Donna calculated.

"Dinner starts at five, two hours from now. You're on about six-thirty or seven. A few classes before you. People will eat dinner and watch from the stands."

"Think I'll go chill for a few in the lounge," I said. "Maybe grab a power nap. Then clean up in the restroom, get my outfit on. Who else is scheduled to ride in my prime-time horsemanship?"

"Patsy Ann Carpenter, for one." Donna named three others of the five who were to compete in the horsemanship class in mere hours.

My stomach jumped. Not Patsy Ann, only one of the best, richest show girls going. A client of Royce and Rogers. Owner-rider of a winning son of the fabulous Superstar. The sire at the center of a swirl of trouble. The hits just kept on coming.

I headed to our lounge to guzzle the contents of a water bottle. Slouched in a chair, my cap pulled low, hoping to catch a nap, I drained one bottle, downed a bare bagel, and nibbled grapes. Then I pulled out my cell phone. I'd been so busy, I'd forgotten to see if Tulip had heard my news.

"Hey!" Tulip's voice beside me made me jump. "All set for tonight?"

I jerked my head toward her and lifted my cap brim.

"Hey," I said. "As much as I'm going to be. What've you been up to?"

She dropped into the chair beside mine.

"Emergency manicure," she sighed, holding out her left hand with shiny new hot-pink gel nails that matched her lipstick. "Gal over at the Justin has a table for that. You should check her out."

"If I ever get time," I said, examining my French manicure, which looked decent. I'd worn surgical gloves when prepping Choc. I had a huge stash of them in my grooming tub by his stall.

"I think I saw that couple you were looking for with the black horse," she said.

I sat upright.

"Really? Where? When?"

"Five minutes ago. Watching their trainer warm him up in the Justin. He might be in a Preview Class tonight. Looked like Western pleasure. Came here as fast as I could."

I jumped up as if stung by a wasp. Tulip tagged after me as I threaded past the stall rows, avoided a few slow-moving golf carts and pounded across the street to the Justin. I may have set a record for city running as I threw myself into the crowded building, which now smelled of deliciously blackened ribs and spicy barbecue sauce. Crowds blocked each step.

Pulling the nearest grandstand door open, I stopped at the top of the steps and stared down to the arena. I was too late. The last horses who'd been warming up now made for the exit gates, while a tractor engine throbbed beyond them. Not one black horse in sight, no witness couple, and no hope for me to solve Max Allende's murder before I had to go into the Preview Class.

As I strode back toward our building, my phone thrummed. I dragged it out of my purse. I saw the call was from Tommy Lee. I thought he was calling Tulip these days.

"Hey, Reba. Great dinner last night. How are y'all doing?"

"Okay, I guess." Get to it, TLJ.

"How's the investigation doing? Any way I can help?"

"Just keep your eyes and ears open, Tommy Lee. Use all the help I can get."

I kept walking, right through the Burnett-Tandy toward our stalls.

"I heard y'all are fixin' to be a big star tonight."

"Tulip tell you about my make-or-break class?"

"Sure did. Hey, you sound in a hurry."

There was a pause.

"Sorry. Million things on my mind. You gonna come cheer me on?"

"You bet your booty, er, boots," he chuckled. "And I understand Tulip's bringing you a surprise."

"What is it, Tommy Lee? I need some good news about now."

He snorted.

"Then it won't be a surprise. Good luck tonight, Honey. See you soon."

Honey? When had I given TLJ permission to use that term of endearment? And what was the surprise? Hopefully it was the clue that would solve our mysteries.

Chapter 52

I stared into the Grandeen dressing-room mirror. Who was that Western-togged movie star in Hollywood makeup staring back?

The sharp-creased black hat set off my glossy red lips, high cheekbones, blue eyes and Hope Diamond-dressed earlobes to perfection. The crimson fitted show-jacket with giant crystals and black fringe did credit to my figure, plumping up my bust and lengthening my torso. All finished off with black custom chaps and boots.

But those eyes. As if I were facing the guillotine.

I pushed aside the dressing-room curtains and out into the aisle, where Tulip and Tommy Lee applauded. Hearing the commotion, Donna peeked from Choc's tall, where she'd been tacking him up with a red Indian-patterned pad and my silver-studded saddle.

"Gorgeous," she breathed, nodding approval. "Now to make your ride match that winning image."

"Easier said, than done," I grinned as she led my red-brown boy into the aisle.

The sight of Choc took my breath away. He always looked handsome to me. But now he resembled a horse on the cover of a prestigious show magazine.

"He looks fantastic, Donna," I said. "Thank you so much."

Donna smiled and held out the reins. I took them.

"Good luck," she said. "You look great and you'll do great."

Dutch popped out of the tack room and greeted me.

"Not nervous, are you?" he winked.

"A little," I lied. I should have said I how I really felt: scared spitless, my mouth dry as the cow-country outside Fort Worth.

"Good," he said. "A few butterflies always make for a better performance."

I folded up my chap cuffs to keep them from dragging through the dirt, and led Choc toward the entrance to the tunnels leading under the street toward the Justin warmup pens and arena.

Zombie walking. That's the only way to describe how I felt preparing to show at the Worlds. Even if this were only a preview class, I reminded myself that this was my chance to impress judges who'd determine my horse-show fate in coming weeks.

Breathe, just breathe, I told myself, walking the claustrophobic slant of the lighted concrete tunnel. Relax your shoulders. Stay calm to keep your horse calm.

Choc's hoofbeats clattered like an overachieving metronome. I heard other horses clopping ahead of and behind me. Neighs and snorts bounced off the wall. Soon I was out into the underground maze of the John Justin's warmup and sales arena and stalls.

Donna beckoned at me from the gate of a small arena bustling with more than a dozen horses and riders. Disembodied voices echoed around the space. In the background, the main arena announcer called out over speakers.

"A big ol' Texas welcome to all you spectators and contestants at the World Open Western Horse Show Barbecue and Preview Classes," said the voice in an exaggerated Texas drawl. "Are you ready to have yourselves a great time? Because not only is everything bigger, in Texas, but it's ten times ten more fun."

More fun – and more frightening, I thought, for a Southern Oregon rube like me.

Hands trembling, I took Choc's reins from Donna. She looked a bit tense, herself. Dutch was nowhere to be seen, having to fulfill his judge duties. He was able to do so, as were others with clients or horses in classes, because he'd taken an oath of impartiality, strictly adhered to unless he wanted to risk losing his judge's card, if not his clients. It was an odd system, but oddly it worked. Unless someone let themselves be bribed, threatened – or killed.

"Now just walk and jog in your little circles," Donna said, giving me a twinkly grin, and laying a hand on my thigh. "Don't tighten up, stay soft, and smile. That will help you and Choc relax. You look great. Everything's going to be fine."

It wasn't easy. But I had a lot riding on this class, this show – money, time, life dreams. I'd done it before, I could do it again: Put my fears on hold and do as I'm told. Be a perfect little soldier.

I circled and jogged in my own small space among other riders warming up. I did it a long time, with Donna watching, lined up along the rail with other trainers.

Tulip and Tommy Lee came up to the fence, greeted Donna and gave me thumbs ups. They then disappeared, probably to find seats in the sure-to-be crowded stands.

I lost track of time. I just circled and jogged, reversed and repeated, hearing the announcer describing the rules and expectations of classes ahead of mine. My heart lurched as I heard my class was next up. Those five of us in the horsemanship class filed out of the pen and made our way toward the entrance gate at one end of the main arena.

Patsy Ann Carpenter, riding her fancy, dark brown gelding, looked back as she led our small procession. She wore a blingy purple jacket with chocolate chaps and hat.

"Good luck, Pepper," she said, giving me an almost sincere smile.

"Good ride to you, Patsy Ann," I answered, trying to quiet my butterflies.

Our back numbers were announced, along with the expectations for the class. I was number six-oh-four. Set to demonstrate my winning horsemanship form right after the western pleasure class, and before the trail and reining.

We rode at a walk into the vast, echoing arena, and lined up our horses, as per the announcer's instructions, forty feet inside the gate. I almost fainted from the excitement. There were so many spectators up there in the stands. Six judges in blazers and Stetsons, and six stewards, clipboards in hand, sat in folding chairs along the right wall.

My breath caught. Heat rose to my cheeks. I had to focus only on myself and my horse. I kept my shoulders softly back and down, my hips tucked under, my legs soft but straight, with the balls of my feet pressed lightly into my stirrups.

The announcer boomed out course instructions, reinforcing them in our minds. Then he explained how our rides should look effortless for both horse and rider, our eyes always focused where we were going, our backs straight yet supple, our legs and hands relaxed as they applied invisible cues to our equine partners.

I was last to go. That was good, as I had a chance to watch how the other riders did it. The arena was still as each competitor rode their pattern. At the end of each person's ride came shrieks and applause. The last rider was finishing the pattern.

Then it was my turn. Showtime.

My skin prickled and my pulse pounded. I tried to steady my hands and legs as I urged Choc at a soft, confident walk toward the start cone. Just as his shoulder neared the cone I squeezed him with my calves and he stopped sharply yet softly five feet to the right of the cone. Perfect.

To prepare him to jog out forty feet from there, a difficult start to pull off, I put light tension on the reins in my left hand a few inches above the saddle horn, clucked imperceptibly and flagged my lower legs almost invisibly against his sides. Although lazy Western-two step music played over the arena speakers, I heard only my breath and the squeaking saddle as we jogged forward, and then accelerated into an extended trot for the next forty feet.

Then I halted, backed four steps, made a perfect, 360-degree haunch turn to the left, and set off at a collected lope across the arena toward another halt point. Stop, haunch turn the other way, then lope a diagonal on the new lead halfway to the start cone.

Change leads at the lope. Halt on the near side of the start cone. Sidestep right midpoint to the other cone. Do a forehand half-circle to the left. Halt, nod at the judges to show the pattern was complete, turn, and jog back into the lineup.

Wild applause and a few hoots broke like waves over me. Electricity rippled through my muscles. I had a feeling. That was the best ride of my life. I knew it even before I heard my high, winning score announced five minutes later.

A World Show buckle would be mine.

The announcer confirmed it by saying Chocolate Waterfall and I were first under all six judges. I knew it but still had a hard time believing it. I believed it when I stood at the front of the placings line and flashbulbs exploded in my face. I believed it when they held up the oversized, thousand-dollar check, and handed me a bronze trophy. I believed it when I took a loping victory lap around the arena, waving at people I knew.

Patsy Ann Carpenter congratulated me just outside the gate.

"Great job, Pepper," she smiled, this time looking genuine. "I'd happily take second any time, if it was a ride like yours that beat me."

"Thank you, Patsy Ann," I smiled, feeling buzzed. It was a once-in-a-lifetime win, I knew. Nothing like that would likely happen again. But I'd take it.

Tulip, Tommy Lee and a flock of Brassbottom buddies came down to share in my glory as I led Choc toward the tunnels leading back to our stalls.

"You're golden, Pepper," Tulip gushed, hugging me with one arm as we walked.

"Fantastic ride," said Tommy Lee.

"Never seen you ride better," glowed Donna, patting my shoulder and taking the trophy. "Got it all on video. You can watch later." She held up her iPad, and waggled it.

Sandra, Jeanne, Lana, Barb and Little Stewie nodded as they trailed alongside and behind us through the tunnels. I was glad Sandra and Jeanne had come to watch. It must have been hard, with what they were going through.

Tulip had snagged me a to-go box of barbecued ribs, corn and salad from the welcome dinner. As we came up inside the Burnett-Tandy, she held it up triumphantly.

"You can sink your choppers into barbecue, after you put Choc away," she said. "You must be starved. Then we have another surprise."

"People keep saying that," I said. "I have had enough surprises, thank you. Just tell me now."

"No, no," said Tulip, wagging a finger. "You have to wait a while more."

I let that go. I had to eat. My stomach felt like it was doing somersaults. I hadn't felt hungry until now. I also hadn't felt tired. Now I was both – from desperately trying to solve a mystery, and from riding like my life depended on it.

At the stalls, the buddies expressed their final congratulations, and drifted away. I unsaddled Choc, stripped off my chaps and show jacket, pulled on sweats and gave him a quick groom before locking the door. Even he looked tired. I tossed him an extra flake of alfalfa, made sure his water buckets were full of clean water, and bade him good night.

"Good job, Buddy," I said, watching him attack his late dinner. "Love you more."

I saw Sandra lingering alone outside my stall. Jeanne must have left. I wouldn't blame her, in the physical and emotional pain she must be feeling.

"I'm so happy for you, Pepper," Sandra said. "Jeanne told me to tell you congrats. I knew you could do it. I knew your horse was amazing first time I saw him."

"Thank you," I said, heaving a sigh. "It was quite the challenge, what with what's been happening here."

"By the way, Max's sister, Gloria, in Ashland, is dealing with his final arrangements. She talked with Jeanne a long time last night."

"That's good. How is Jeanne doing? And you, Sandra?"

"Jeanne's pretty depressed about losing her dad. Plus her leg is really bothering her. Me, I'm okay. Max and I were never that close. Still, it's sad."

"Yes," I said. "Again, my condolences to you both. So will Jeanne still try to show tomorrow?"

"She didn't want to," Sandra said. "But I told her she has to. It's not only that we've paid a small fortune for the horse, the training, the show. But that this is her lifelong dream, she's worked hard to make it come true, and her father would have wanted her to show."

I pondered this.

"Tell her good luck for me," I said. "Jeanne is totally capable of making that mare the star she was bred and trained to be."

"I'll tell her. Thank you, Pepper."

Sandra chewed her lower lip, and then fixed me with her beautiful eyes. I wished I knew how to apply makeup so artfully.

"So. Do you know any more about the investigation into Max's death? If they have any suspects?"

"Police aren't saying. I'm not supposed to talk about the case, either."

"Yet you have. At dinner at Joe T's. And I heard through the barn drums that you were trying to find some witnesses."

"I'm not sure there were any," I said. "I imagine the sheriff is looking into that. He has to cast a wide net, you know."

"But you found the body, Pepper. Did you see anyone else there?" She cocked her head and narrowed her eyes.

"Not really," I lied. The couple had gone when I found the body.

"Well, just let us know, okay? We're very anxious to find Max's killer. Or killers. Jeanne and I need closure."

I nodded, and we said goodbye.

After she left me, Sandra sped up, shook back her dark hair and put her phone to her ear before she disappeared around a corner. I got the distinct feeling she knew more than she was saying.

Chapter 53

As Tulip and I, plus the barbecue-dinner she'd snagged, made our way back to our cottage, I studied the Preview Class video on the iPad. But I didn't need to study it because every move was etched in my brain in high-def detail. Even if I hadn't won, I would have been thrilled with my ride. One for a lifetime. I thought it a harbinger of things to come. Judges in the show proper would remember me, and in a good way.

We turned onto our street. The streetlamps and porch lights cast a cheery glow, the small houses promising quiet safety and unpretentious comfort.

Then I saw something that wasn't right: The biggest, baddest black dually truck was parked in front of Barb and Lana's rental car at our yellow cottage.

That only meant one thing: Sonny Chief.

I grabbed the dashboard to steady myself as I leaned forward while Tulip parked in the remaining bit of driveway behind Black Beauty.

"Is that my surprise?" I said, incredulous. "I forgot all about it."

"That would be it," she said, with a breezy wave of her hand. She set the brake and turned off the engine. "It was pretty hard keeping the secret. He got delayed. He wanted to see you in the class. Some wreck on the highway outside of town."

The cottage door swung open, and there he stood. All six-feet-six of him, in black, wearing his trademark cap with eagle feather. I fell out of the car, and raced up into his outstretched arms. They were warm, he was warm. I tipped my head back, gripped the sides of his face, and kissed him like my life depended on it.

"I take it you're happy to see me," he whispered, working his face around so his lips nibbled my earlobes.

"Can you believe he's here?" Tulip said, sweeping past us into the house.

"Quite the shock," I said, throwing one arm around Sonny as we went inside.

But I could believe. Sometimes this predictably unpredictable man just appeared out of nowhere, when least expected. Or seemed to teleport from one spot to another without your seeing him move. He claimed it was an old Lakota warrior trick. It kept enemies – and us lovers – guessing. Added to his mystique. Conveyed power. Or something like that.

We three headed for the kitchen where I grabbed utensils and prepared to dive into my barbecue, maybe split some with Sonny, while Tulip made decaf. As we sat down for our late-night repast, Sonny told me about his drive.

"I thought you were tied up on the Rez," I said. "To what do I owe your magical presence, now, at the exact time I really need your help? Not the spirits again?"

"No-o-o," drawled Sonny, giving me a mischievous look from under those thick, lazy eyelashes. "Though my cousin is a spirited kinda guy."

"Martin Runs Fast," I said. "Your cousin who's a firefighter."

"That's the one," said Sonny, setting down his coffee mug. "Called me to say he heard about a death at the horse show. I'd told him you were there. And I knew you'd probably be in the thick of it."

I should have been insulted, by his implying that I couldn't keep away from dangerous situations. Or at least, pretended to have been.

"So you came to see if you could help," I said. "Well, Sonny, I've got a shocker for you. It was your friend, Max Allende. Who you talked to last week. Sandra's ex. Jeanne and Nancy's father."

"No kidding." Sonny rocked in his chair as if he'd been slapped. "Max Allende. He looked like a guy who might have some enemies. Details?"

I told him what I knew and what I suspected, about ties to judges, betting pools and the like. And that Sandra and Jeanne were both devastated. That Jeanne might not want to show, but that her mother was insisting.

Sonny took it all in, shaking his head from time to time.

"I contacted Gary Gracey again," he said. "Pretty sure he's gonna help me find the missing daughter. That should cheer up Sandra and Jeanne."

"It would," I said. "It surely would."

Sonny grinned, beckoned me over, pulled me onto his lap, and held me tight, rocking me slightly.

"So sorry you had to go through what you did, finding the body and all," he said. "Dealing with the aftermath."

"So how'd you find time to get away, Sonny? Thought you were busy at camp?"

"Things have slowed down a lot. At least for now. I'm a part-time cop, anyway. Lots of other young bucks want their chance to play the big man."

"Well, I'm glad you're here," I said. "Not sure how you can help with the murder investigation. But I could use a nice back rub. To help me relax."

Sonny and Tulip shot each other looks.

"What?" I admonished, frowning at Tulip and rising from Sonny's lap. "I'm way too tired for hanky panky tonight."

"Don't look tired now," Sonny said, licking his lips and looking flirtatious.

"Hey! Sonny! Did Tulip tell you? I won. A world championship. Wait until you see the trophy. And the thousand-dollar check."

"No kidding," he said, eyes widening. "You can buy me dinner tomorrow. No, she didn't tell me." He looked at Tulip and back at me. "Really. You won. Thought the show started tomorrow."

"They held preview classes tonight. A new thing. I'll explain later. It was only a World Show Preview class, Sonny. But it's a world championship, for real. I have the video, the trophy, the check to prove it."

"A murder, crazy happenings that would flatten anyone else."

"Beyond crazy."

"But yet you showed, and won your championship."

"A girl has to do what a girl has to do," I said, tweaking the line from an old John Wayne film. I'd have to remember to tell Little Stewie the line, but with "man," as in the original, if the lad got jitters before entering a class.

Sonny rose, stretched and crushed me in a hug. Then he held me away from him and looked sweetly into my eyes. I felt that look to my marrow.

"Congratulations, Lady. I am happy for you. Knew you could do it."

He stroked my hair, and leaned down for a slow, sweet kiss. His feel, his smell, his body made me dizzy. Maybe I wasn't as tired as I thought. At very least, a back rub.

Tulip sniffed, and stood up.

"I'll just get my things and make up the couch."

Chapter 54

Morning came too soon. Even with Sonny's amazing back massage, my body felt run over by a truck. About midnight, I'd taken a long shower, watched Sonny drag the twin beds together in the larger bedroom, arranged the bedding so there was nothing between us, and lay down for what I thought would be a blissful sleep.

It was all that. There just wasn't enough of it.

Sonny, Tulip and I, following the lead of Barb and Lana, downed coffee at six, and beat feet for the Will Rogers. If I'd thought things were busy and crowds were big the day before, it was nothing, compared to Opening Day. The first real classes, halter conformation events, began at eight. I had showmanship that afternoon. And so did Jeanne. If, she chose to show. Maybe, like me and other competitors, she could put emotions on hold when the world-title chips were down.

Brassbottom buddies filled our stall row. They mucked stalls, groomed horses and polished tack like crazy. They also wolfed down delectable pastries chased with copious amounts of coffee or Red Bull. They gobbled apples and oranges for fiber and Vitamin C.

Sonny settled in to make calls, and have a last hit of coffee in the Brassbottom lounge stalls. Victoria carried around a luxuriant new faux ponytail to add to her own luscious locks showing below her spangled ballcap.

Sandra and Jeanne prepped the bay mare, saddling her for what must be a warm-up ride and showmanship lesson. Sandra's mare, already sparkling, her white mane tamed by a nylon neck-sleeve known as a "sleazy," nibbled hay in her stall.

I hurried over. This might be our only chance to converse with Sandra and Jeanne before classes. I could gussy up Choc and myself later. My prime-time showmanship event did not start until early afternoon, a good hour before Jeanne's.

"See you're showing today, Jeanne," I said. "Way to go. How's the leg?"

Jeanne stopped picking out Star's feet, and gave me a tired smile.

"Fine, thank you. Yes, I'm showing." She glanced at Sandra, combing out a black faux tail for Star. Then she looked back up at me and straightened. "Congrats on your ride in the Preview Class last night, Pepper. It was amazing. Considering."

"Thank you, Jeanne. I know you and Star will be just as amazing today. Dutch seems to think she's turned a corner. Good luck."

"We'll need it, Pepper. I'm a little jittery. But thanks."

She went back to another of Star's hooves, and then checked her cinch. "Well, gotta go. Donna is giving me an early riding lesson, because Dutch is judging."

"Good luck. In your class, I mean."

I turned to Sandra, who was headed for the tack room.

"Jeanne's a trouper, Sandra. Raised her right."

"She can be tough, when she has to."

Tulip and I set about cleaning our stalls, getting it done before the heat of the day. Sonny offered to help, but I refused him, so he disappeared to do some digging of his own. He planned to talk with police and other first responders, as well as owners of leading Superstar and Suspicion offspring.

"Sounds good," I said, tossing a forkful of horse apples into the cart.

"Might turn up some juicy nuggets of my own," he grinned. "Catch up with you around noon." He gave me a quick kiss, and was off. I paused to watch his high, tight backside sway as he strode away, cell phone to ear.

Then I wheeled my full cart to the dump area outside the Burnett-Tandy. Along the way I took more congratulations for my performance the previous night.

"I can hardly believe how it all came together for you," Freddie said as I passed him returning from a warm-up on his horse. "Jealous."

"You'll get your turn," I grinned, giving his horse, Poppin, a pat. "Hear any more from Carlos? Like about betting pools and who's involved in them?"

"Carlos did mention the betting pool thing, and Allende's possible connection. Only a theory. A few other names, too. You should ask Carlos."

"I might do that." If I had time.

Finally plopping down in our lounge, I checked my phone. There was a text from Chili, letting me know things were fine at home and with my folks, but also asking what was happening at my end.

I chided myself for not keeping her abreast. She'd be thrilled to hear that I'd won my championship. But not so happy hearing about the murder. I tapped her number and looked forward to a short chat with my Baby Girl.

"Hi, Mom. What's up in Texas? I've been worried, after I didn't hear from you."

"I have good news and bad news." I filled her in first on the bad news, trying to fake her into thinking I was in little danger. Which I didn't believe. There was a killer loose, one who knew I was looking for him, so I was in ridiculous danger. I didn't tell Chili I'd found the body. That would totally freak her out.

She was freaked enough out as it was, at my bad news.

"Somebody was killed? Who was it? How were they killed? Do they have any idea who did it?"

"Probably some jealous lover, or competing horse owner. But the police are all over it. We have cameras in our area, people around all the time. Think we're good."

"You're not in danger, are you?"

"Lots of people around. Increased security. Plus I have my own personal policeman. Sonny came down when he heard about the killing."

"You better take care. Let me know if they catch the guy. So, Mamacita, what's the good news?"

Swelling with pride that was safe to show to family, I brought her up to speed on my winning the world championship.

"Awesome," Chili said. "Good job, Mom. So now I'm the daughter of a world champion. Should put it on my resume."

We talked some more, about her showing her jewelry and that of other designers around the Valley, about my folks having her over to dinner, about a coveted property possibly coming up for sale between my folks' place and the river.

I knew the place. Its overgrown acres included not only riverfront footage, but also a beach, but also an unlicensed marijuana grow and a rundown shack. A shack that, when we were little, Tulip and I had played in. We had dubbed it "Ghost Ranch," because we were convinced ourselves it was haunted.

Just the kind of place that, if added to my folks' property, would make a perfect Western resort.

Like that would happen. Dream on, Cowgirl.

Before signing off, I asked if there'd been any trouble at my place.

"Nope," Chili said. "Everything's cool. And I have the Bostons to guard me."

"Some guard dogs," I laughed. "They'd lick a criminal to death."

We disconnected. I contemplated the snack table before I redoubled my efforts to find the Allende-killing witness couple who owned the tall black horse. Since Monday I had searched the crowds for them, looked at every face, in every stall. So far I had come up empty. It was such a large place, with too many arenas where a horse could be, too many buildings and hidey-holes where its owners could hang out.

But first I needed fuel for my increased effort, and for my real show class later, the prime-time novice-amateur showmanship – a class in which you're judged on how well you lead and present to judges your immaculately groomed horse in set poses and movements at the walk and jog.

I poured myself a cardboard cup of coffee, and savored the shockingly sweet taste of a warm fresh maple bar. Someone had just brought the big box over. Probably Little Stewie's mom. Karen Mikulski was a caring gal. I had to ask how her PT session with my mom had gone.

A loud clatter of hooves on concrete shattered my reverie. Then came a scream that turned my blood to ice. Its shrill notes ricocheted through the building.

"WHOA!" shrieked a female voice. A scared-to-death voice. Jeanne's voice.

I jerked around and looked eighty feet back down the aisle. Jeanne's mare danced and reared in a blur of fury, the teen barely clinging to the saddle. The horse rose and fell repeatedly. Her hooves raked the air. The bridle reins whipped like snakes toward stalls on either side, and flew toward the high ceiling.

The drama unfolded in Slo-Mo. I was scared to go toward it, as I might upset the horse further, if that were possible. Or get trampled myself. A raging, twelve-hundred-pound monster with death-dealing hooves and teeth is nothing to mess with.

But get up and run, I did.

Jeanne still miraculously hung on the pitching horse. She had her right foot in one stirrup, the other hooked over the back of the saddle. But as the horse reared and bucked, the girl slipped sideways, ever closer to the concrete floor.

The mare grunted with each effort to dislodge her rider. Sparks flew from her shod hooves as she lurched and scrambled.

"Help!" Jeanne cried, plunging a knife of fear into my gut. "Help!"

The hell with danger.

I flew forward to one side of the crazed horse. Freddie stepped out of his stall and dove for the other side. Onlookers materialized, looking scared. Trying to avoid flailing hooves, I grabbed at the reins, but they continued to whip beyond my reach.

Jeanne's cries intensified.

"No! Whoaaaa!"

The mare shook her head, and then folded into a deep bow before rising porpoise-like into an explosive buck. Her body arced into the air, all four hooves off the ground. They came down with a screeching clatter, dropping the mare onto her left side, head forward, Jeanne's leg pinned beneath her bulk. The already injured leg. Jeanne's head briefly brushed the ground. Her cowgirl hat spun away.

Wild eyed, lathered and panting, the horse lurched to her feet. She looked around dazedly at the small crowd gathering. Freddie, Lana, Victoria, Little Stewie and his mother, along with an older man holding a whining red-heeler dog by the collar.

Jeanne lay still.

Emotion choked my throat. I swallowed, and then sprang into action.

Freddie grabbed Star's reins and led the prancing mare back to her stall. I knelt by Jeanne, who lay on her left side. I was aware of others moving close as I studied her body and ashen face. I felt for a pulse in her neck.

There was one. But Jeanne lay still as a stone.

"Jeanne?" I said softly. "Jeanne. Can you hear me?"

No answer.

I half-rose, snatched a horse blanket off a bar on a nearby stall door, and threw it over Jeanne's curled, painfully thin body. Her eyelids quivered but stay shut.

"Somebody call or run to the First Aid Office," I said, looking around for Sandra. Or Donna. Sandra must be working her own horse somewhere, and Donna with her.

Lana stepped forward and bent toward me.

"I'll contact Sandra," she said. "She and I were meeting for an early lunch today at the sushi joint." She held her phone to her ear as she bustled away toward the outside door. Her round bottom bounced in black sweatpants – a horseshow-girl's best friend, after she's worn tight breeches or jeans much of the day.

I looked down at Jeanne folded in a fetal position on cold concrete. Tears dampened my lashes. I lay an arm over her. She was so quiet under that blanket.

"Jeanne," I said, my mouth close to one of her ears. I pushed away a few strands of ebony hair from her eyes, and felt the petal softness of her cheek. Many times I'd touched Chili that way when she was young, and in some crisis.

The teen's eyelids trembled again. She'd heard me. It was something.

"Mmm?" she croaked. "Pepper? Is that you?"

My heart skipped a beat. She might be all right. She would be all right, if I had anything to say about it.

"Honey. Jeanne, yes. It's Pepper," I said it with a confidence I hoped soon to feel. "Hang in there. Take a deep breath. Help is coming. Lana went to find your mom."

Jeanne shivered under my arm.

"No," Jeanne rasped. Her eyes opened part way. Her gaze was intense. "No. Not my mom."

"What? Why not?" I said, confused.

Jeanne was addled from the fall, not in her right mind. I didn't want to stress her more. I would have to let her come around at her own speed.

"She'll say it's my fault," Jeanne whispered, her body shaking. "Mad at me enough as it is." Then she moaned.

"No, she won't," I soothed. "She knows the horse is unpredictable. I'm sure you did nothing wrong."

Excited chatter stuttered down the aisle, coming from near the Grandeen lounge. It was accompanied by running footsteps. The next moment, Sonny's long shadow fell across Jeanne and me. Tulip was at his side.

I turned and sprang up. With his eyebrows in an inverted V, he knelt beside Jeanne. I shimmied back to give him more room while Tulip squatted behind me.

"What happened to Jeanne?" she said.

"Her horse bucked and fell on her. EMTs coming. Lana's gone to find her mom."

"How's the horse?"

"OK, for a nut case. Freddie put her away, but called the show vet."

Tulip nodded.

I watched Sonny murmur questions to Jeanne, and gently manipulate her hands and feet. She cried out when he touched her left lower leg.

Of course. As a police officer, he would have EMT skills. I recalled he'd used them on me, once or twice, when push came to shove, and I'd been the shovee.

A few moments later a pair of medics appeared at Jeanne's side. Sonny rose to meet them, explaining who he was. They peeled back the blanket, asked Sonny and me a few questions, brought out a backboard, and set about sliding the girl onto it.

"I'll have them call for Jeanne's mother over the P.A. system," said a man. He began talking into his shoulder mic.

Where was Sandra? A good ten minutes had passed since Jeanne's accident, and Lana had been gone most of those. In an era of instant accessibility via cell phone, I couldn't understand why someone, Lana, hadn't found her mother. If it were me, I'd have been there almost before the accident. Had Sandra powered off her phone for some reason, or left it somewhere?

Then I remembered what Jeanne said when I'd told her Sandra was on the way. She'd said, "No. Not my mom." With an exclamation point. That still seemed weird.

Sonny wrapped me in his arms. With my nerves stripped and my brain tangled, his embrace had never felt better. His chin pressed down on my head. I wished that the safe, comforted feeling I felt with him would last forever.

He dropped his arms and asked again exactly what, step by step, had happened with Jeanne and her horse. Before and after. I told him. There wasn't that much to tell. They'd had a wreck. Jeanne was scared her mother would be mad.

Sonny shook his head.

"She wouldn't be mad, she'd be concerned," he said. "Wasn't that the same horse you tried to fix for Jeanne back in Oregon? Who'd buy her such a crazy bronc?"

"Her dad. With mom's approval. Guaranteed world champion. As if you could guarantee a thing like that. And he reportedly was running a betting pool on it, tried to pay off a judge of two. I've been trying to run that down. You probably were, too."

A few onlookers lingered at the accident scene.

"Let's go sit down for a second so I can catch my breath," I said. I led the way to our lounge. Tulip and Sonny took chairs either side of me.

"Who've you talked to today, Sonny?" I said. "Any leads regarding Allende's killer, threats, etcetera?"

"Talked to Bond. Good guy. But he can't say much, even to a brother. He did let it slip, though, that a judge or somebody dressed like one, with the navy blazer, tan hat and slacks, was seen dashing through the Justin in a hurry ten or fifteen before your call."

"Really."

"An elderly lady reported him because he knocked her down so hard she went to the First-Aid office to get herself checked out."

"Which judge, do you think? Did Bond give a description?"

"Lady told him the guy had whiskers, looked a little like a wolf."

"Grant Haverstadt," I breathed. "I knew it."

My heart thumped. Grant Haverstadt, the majority owner of Royce and Rogers' stallion, Shiny Suspicion. One who'd have a lot to gain by offing the major investor in Superstar. Someone who knew who I was, my phone number, what I was looking into, where I lived.

Chapter 55

"Haverstadt can't be reached immediately because he's judging halter," Sonny said. "But probably will be available during lunch break. I'll go ask around the stabling area below the Justin, where the Suspicion people hang out. Try to catch Haverstadt around noon, before Bond does."

"You can call on your acting skills again," I said. "Pose as a potential bettor."

Sonny left the lounge, and I got up to give Choc his daily bath. When I stepped into our aisle, I saw a man in a chambray shirt and black vest lead a shiny yearling into the aisle several rows down. The horse pranced and danced, as overfed, over-fit halter horses are prone to do. So different from our laid-back Western pleasure mounts.

Tulip startled me when she tossed her empty cup into a wastebasket. It made a hollow-sounding thunk. I had forgotten she was there.

"I think I'll try to track down Sandra," she said.

"And I need to go check on Jeanne in the First Aid office. I hope she wasn't hurt badly enough to be taken to the hospital."

Moving fast, legs pumping like the quarterback for the Seattle Seahawks, I wove from side to side, trying to negotiate horses and a wave of people coming in and out of the Burnett-Tandy doors. Seeing an opening, I lunged forward, smiling at the middle-aged brunette in a fur-trimmed denim jacket who moved to let me pass. She carried a jittery brown dog, and was accompanied by a thin man in a white tee.

I stopped, paralyzed with recognition. It was the couple I'd seen sitting with that trainer across the arena before I'd found Allende's body. The people I'd been frantic to find for two days. The people whom the police department, having only my sketchy description to go from, also sought for questioning.

There had even been announcements over the loudspeakers: "May we have your attention. Will anyone who was in the John Justin Arena early Monday afternoon please report to the show office as soon as possible."

"Oh," I now said as I stopped in front of the woman, and smiled. "May I speak to you for a minute?"

The woman nodded. But her intense green eyes held a question.

"I suppose so," she said, stepping just outside the crowd near the door. Her husband, a preying-mantis fellow with large sunglasses and hands thrust in his jeans pockets, gave me a questioning look, but followed her to one side.

I introduced myself, mentioning my name and that of my trainers.

"Sally and Sherm Donaldson," said the woman, idly stroking her dog. "We have a horse, actually two of them, with Jack Jurkovski."

"Let me get to the point. I am the one who found the body on Monday."

They tilted back at the news. The woman stroked her dog faster.

"Oh, dear," she said, looking at the man, and then looking back at me. "She's the one who found the body."

"I don't understand," said the man. "Why are you telling us?"

"Because you were there," I said. "Across the arena that day. With your trainer."

"We were?" said Donaldson, looking at his wife.

"We might have been," she said. "About two o'clock?"

"Yes. Didn't you hear the announcements over the loudspeakers? They are looking for you as potential witnesses."

"Really?" she said. "We didn't hear that. Yesterday we took the courtesy tour to Pilot Point, to see all the horse ranches. They call it Horse Country USA."

"Yes, well, you need to go talk with the police. But before you do, I must ask if you saw any other people in the stands while you were there?"

"Well, let's see," she said. "Sherm, didn't we notice someone who looked like Pepper here come in right before we left? Oh, now I know who you are. You won the horsemanship Preview Class last night. Congratulations."

"Thank you," I smiled. The group blocking the doors had nearly dispersed, most having moved outside and let in a blast of hot, humid air.

"What exact time did you sit Monday, in the Justin?" I said.

"Oh, two to two-fifteen or so," said the woman. A startled look filled her plump face. She wrinkled her brow and glanced at the man. "Sherm, when we first came in the Justin stands Monday, to scope out the arena, wasn't there a tall brunette talking to a big good-looking man in the stands across from us?"

He scratched his chin.

"Why, now that you mention it, I believe there was," he said. "A very tall man. A tall, pretty brunette talking to a tall man in a cowboy hat and brown blazer."

Now I was momentarily confused. A woman talking to Max Allende? Not a man?

"We got to talking with our trainer about how we would show our horse," the woman said. "But we had to shout and repeat ourselves to be heard over the tractor."

"Yes, that's right," said the husband.

"When I looked back over there that couple was gone. You came in after that." The woman's eyes grew larger as she put two and two together. Her dog growled.

"No," she breathed. Her eyes locked as it hit her. "You don't think …"

But I did think. It must have been Sandra with Max. He'd come to town early. She'd not gone to her hotel room Monday as she had said. It was only her word she had seen Dutch ride her horse. She'd been angry at Max about something, or several somethings. Just as she had been angry at Stavropolis and had gone after him. It had to have been Sandra who killed Max.

My heart beat so hard I almost fainted.

"I want you to go tell the police what you just told me," I said. "Hurry! I have to run. One of our riders was injured in a fall."

Leaving the couple looking stunned, their mouths open, I was through the doors and out in the dazzling sunlight on the sidewalk when my phone sang. When I looked to see who was calling, and I felt a punch to the stomach. The ID pane read Jackson County Sheriff's Department. In Oregon.

A heavy sense of dread poured over me. I took the call, but kept walking, dodging cars and golf carts in the street. I heard sirens in the distance.

"Pepper Kane."

"Miss Kane, Detective Jenee, from Jackson County Sheriff's Department. I'm afraid I have some very bad news. Reg Stavropolis has died."

That was the last thing I expected to hear. My stomach dropped.

"No." That didn't begin to cover it.

"We've issued a press release. You'll find it on our website. But we need to talk to you as soon as possible. And to Sandra Allende."

My temples pounded. Then I willed my legs to keep walking, as the horrible news sunk in. Stavropolis was dead. And I might have prevented it, but didn't. So in a way, it was on me. Even if he were evil incarnate. Even if it were an "accident."

"You there, Miss Kane?"

"As you know, Detective Jenee, I am at a show in Texas. I've paid thousands to enter. I can't leave. Can I talk to police here, in a conference call or something?"

Sweat streamed down my face and back. I stopped in the street to let a silver pickup roll by. Then, still holding the phone to my ear, I rushed into the John Justin Building, thankful for the cooler air inside.

"That might be possible. Let me check, and call you back," said Detective Jenee.

In a daze, trying to deal with the news of Stavropolis' death, I looked around the brightly lit mezzanine. Making a hard left, I entered the First Aid Office.

A young woman with blond hair in a high ponytail looked up from the counter.

"May I help you?"

"I was with Jeanne Allende, who just fell with her horse in the Burnett-Tandy," I said. "Which room?"

"To my right," she said. "But the ambulance will be here any minute. Her mother just left. Are you family, too?"

"Her aunt," I lied, on my way to the room she indicated. Jeanne lay on a table. A medic in green scrubs stood over her. He had his back to me. Jeanne looked over, eyes half-closed, likely from moderate sedation. I rushed to her side.

The medic turned. He dropped his clipboard with a clatter and bent to pick it up.

"Jeanne," I said, touching her arm. "It's Pepper. Where's your mom?"

She looked up, her eyes blinking rapidly.

"She's gonna get the truck and follow the ambulance to the hospital. But I was right. She said it was all my fault about the horse. And Nancy. My fault, too."

"Jeanne. What do you mean?"

The medic held up his clipboard and stepped between us.

"Sorry, Ma'am," he said. "Unless you're family you have to leave."

"No!" Jeanne shouted. "My friend. Need to tell her something."

I looked around the medic at Jeanne, now raised on one elbow. But the man stepped in front of me.

"Please, Ma'am," he said. "Don't make me call security."

I sucked in a breath and ducked around the medic.

"Jeanne," I said. "What are you trying to tell me?"

The medic grabbed my arms. He tried to guide me toward the door. I pulled away.

Jeanne's next words rattled like machine-gun shots.

"My sister and I were in real-estate photos. Men started calling about us. No. One man. That Stavropolis guy. Dad knew him. Right after that, Nancy ran away."

"What?" I shouted, trying to put it together as I dodged the busy-handed medic. In our spastic waltz, the medic and I kicked over a metal trash can. It clanged to the floor and rolled toward a corner.

"Let go," I spat, bobbing around to keep my eyes on Jeanne. "What else, Jeanne?"

Words gushed like water from a fire hydrant. The medic paused as if stunned.

"I knew Dad abused my sister, but was afraid to say anything. Mom didn't know until last week, when she ...

when she rode on Table Rock. I let Dad buy me off with the horse and car. Mom thought it was just to get me to not run away, too."

The medic broke out of his trance, and grabbed my arms.

"Go on, Jeanne," I rasped, trying to wrestle free from the medic's hold.

"I was jealous of Nancy, thought she'd made her own decision. That way I didn't have to feel too guilty."

"It's not your fault, Jeanne." More wrestling. The medic's hold tightened, and he pushed me toward the door. I leaned in and resisted.

"I'm so sorry, Pepper," Jeanne said, a sob choking her voice. "Please don't hate me. You're the only one I can trust."

"I never could hate you, Jeanne."

"She'll kill me if she finds out I told. I'm so afraid. She pushed me off the porch. She's crazy."

The medic gave me a hard shove. I threw an elbow into his gut. When he doubled over, I hopped sideways to kick the trash can back across between us.

"Jason! Get in here," shouted the medic through the doorway.

"Help me, Pepper," cried Jeanne. "And find Nancy." Then she fell silent.

Another young man entered in the room. Both men clamped me by the torso and dragged me outside. The examining-room door slammed in my face.

"Y'all have to leave," said the young blonde at the desk.

Still stunned by Jeanne's revelations and the manhandling, I stared at her as if she were an alien. Then I spun around, bit my lip and headed for the Justin's exterior doors. Smells of cinnamon rolls and bread bowls filled my nose. Crowd chatter rattled my ears.

My gut contracted. Weakness coursed through my legs and body. I felt I might collapse. It wasn't hunger, though I was half-starved. No, not hunger. It was fear of imminent death, possibly my own.

As I ran, I stared at the faces in the lobby of the John Justin, thousands of miles from Medford, millions of miles from normalcy. I pushed through the doors onto the hot street, where an ambulance now stood, EMTs opening the rear doors. I pounded toward the RV parking lot where I'd seen Sandra and Jeanne the day before. The day before my world – and Jeanne's – flipped upside down.

Hopefully Sandra was still there now, or just leaving. I had to stop her.

Panting in the 95-degree heat, soaked with sweat, I pounded down the Grandeen parking row, working my way toward the end. It's where I figured Sandra had parked that silver Mercedes she and her daughter had driven here from California.

A hundred feet from the back, a white, chromed-out dually crawled toward me at an exaggeratedly slow pace. I slowed to a walk and moved to one side, then to the other. But the truck always matched my direction and blocked my way.

I now saw that the big, grumbling white pickup had a badly dented grill. A dually that was supposedly in the shop near Medford for repairs. A dually with an all-too-familiar, jaw-clenched woman's face showing above the steering wheel.

Chapter 56

I halted and held out my hands, palms forward.

The truck also halted, idling noisily. Its diesel exhaust swirled like hell smoke.

I coughed, and went around to the driver's side window, which was rolled down. Through it I saw, floating atop a female body, my distorted face staring back from the mirror lenses of crystal-trimmed sunglasses with frames the same black as her hair.

"Hello, Sandra," I said.

"Pepper," she purred. Her diamond ear-studs flashed almost in time with the tapping of her blood-red nails on the pigskin-wrapped steering wheel. Only the best would do, for Sandra Allende. Armed with glamour and dangerous with cunning, she could use her daughters, whip rivals in business, or make a killing at The World.

Perhaps even two killings.

She shot me a dazzling smile.

"Where are you going in such a hurry? Don't you have a class or something?"

"I could ask you the same question, Sandra."

"I'm going to the hospital where they're taking Jeanne. Where else would I go?"

"I just talked with Jeanne. She told me some things. Things you might want to deny, or run away from."

"Heat must be getting to you, Pepper. Don't know what you're talking about."

"You have to turn yourself in, Sandra. You killed them, didn't you?"

She raised her left hand and flipped it dismissively.

"Jeanne has a concussion. Not in her right mind. What do you mean, 'them'?"

"Jackson County sheriff just called. Told me Reg Stavropolis died."

"I told you it was an accident," she said, spittle lining her lips. She licked it away. "Why doesn't anyone believe me? Now you've turned my own daughter against me."

I stood taller, tried to look bigger, in my hot spot a few feet away from the truck.

"Right after the accident, when I told Jeanne I'd get you, she acted really afraid. Now, in First Aid, she told me about your husband's abuse of Nancy and how she ran away. Jeanne knew about the abuse, but allowed your ex to buy her silence with a new horse. Then you learned the truth about him, how he practically gave her to Reg."

A fly worried my eyelid and nostrils. I swatted at it, and then blew it away.

"Is that so," said Sandra, chewing her lip. Then she reached down her right hand and brought up to a handsome silver pistol with a silencer fitted to its muzzle.

"Nice piece," I said, feigning nonchalance. After all, it was high noon in a public parking lot. She wouldn't dare do anything rash. "You seem to have a gun for every occasion, Sandra, this being more dressy than the one on Table Rock."

"Shut up," she snapped, gesturing with the gun. "Go around and get in."

"Now why would I do that? You need to answer some more questions, Sandra. About your daughters. Reg, and Max. And then turn yourself in."

She pursed her lips, glanced around and lowered the gun just out of sight.

"I'll just bet you'd like me to do that," she said. "Not happening."

"How could you do those things, Sandra? Attack Stavropolis. Then turn around and kill your ex-husband?"

"Are you demented? Reg's death was an accident. He attacked me."

"To defend himself."

I watched two people in a golf cart roll toward the RV lot exit three rows away. Someone else came out of an RV the next aisle over, briefly looked our way, and sat down with a drink under an awning of their motor home. Otherwise all was quiet.

"And for your information, I had nothing to do with Max's murder, either. I think it was one of the other judges, something to do with a betting pool. Max liked to gamble, and so did some other horse show people. I was napping in my room when it happened."

"You weren't napping. You were at the show grounds and you had been with Dutch. But witnesses saw you at the arena with Max on Monday."

She stiffened.

"I think you're bluffing." She raised her chin. Something had shifted, and not in a good way. "Tell you what, Missy. You've been a friend. I'll answer any question you have. But not here. It's too public."

"Just put down the gun, Sandra, and give yourself up. Be easier that way."

She rubbed a nail along the window frame, stopping to pick at a baked-on bug.

"Oh, I can't do that. Who's going to believe Jeanne, anyway? She's hurt, and she has always been neurotic. Has an eating disorder. On meds. Just like her sister."

"The acorn doesn't fall far from the tree, Sandra."

"You said you hadn't been to Fort Worth before, Pepper. But my ex and I did business here once, so I am quite familiar with the area. Especially places few others know about. Get in."

My mouth was already bone dry. At this command, my tongue attached itself to my palate. Sweat poured down my spine and chest. I dug in my heels. There was no way I was going with this witch.

"I don't think so, Sandra. You can't shoot me here in the parking lot. Too many people around." I saw a couple wandering among the RVs over by the street.

"Don't bank on it, Pepper."

"Reg died. The police want to talk with both of us."

"As I said, I got the memo."

The diesel fumes were making me nauseous. I fought the impulse to gag.

"This is ridiculous, Sandra. I'm calling the police."

I fished my phone from my purse, and turned so my body shaded the viewing pane from the sun's glare.

The next moment the truck door whooshed open. Sandra lurched out, hair flying. She slammed her pistol-butt into my hand holding the phone. Pain exploded in my fingers. My phone arced away, and skittered across the hot asphalt.

I screamed, but one of her hands clamped my mouth, and the other grabbed me by the hair. Her fingernails stabbed my scalp. She jerked me sideways, and then hauled me back and up through driver's doorway until I lay panting across her lap. I bucked like a bronco.

This was not supposed to happen. But it was so happening. I'd been careless.

"No!" I yelled, my scream muffled against her sweating palm. "Helllllp!"

I kicked and thrashed as she wrestled me headfirst, on my back, across her lap and the console, halfway onto the passenger seat of the leather-scented cab. I knew this woman was strong. I'd just had no idea how strong.

Banging into the console, the dashboard and the passenger door, I battled to free myself from Sandra's grip, but also to put a hurt on her. One foot bumped the steering wheel. I tried to hook my foot in it, so I could lever myself into a sitting position.

But the back of my head banged the steel and hard plastic of the center console. The shock and pain slowed me enough for Sandra to yank and shove me fully into the passenger seat. One of her hands tried to contain my scissoring legs. Her other hand, holding the gun by its muzzle, flew to my face.

Stars exploded in my head as the gun butt thudded into my left temple. The dove-grey headliner above me disappeared. All went black.

Chapter 57

While I floated back to consciousness, I heard a jaunty country tune playing in the distance. I seemed to be slumped in a truck seat and gently bouncing along. My legs were dropped into the foot well. Beneath the music rumbled a diesel engine. Inside my temple throbbed red-hot pain.

Then I recalled how I got here. I figured I was on my way to being dead.

Carefully opening my eyes, I raised and rotated my head. Sandra Allende, all in black, was driving. The mirrored sunglasses hid her eyes, while her lap supported her right hand with the little silver gun aimed straight at my heart.

I felt a small surge of relief. She hadn't seen me come to. And she hadn't fastened my seatbelt. Maybe I could do something about my predicament, and her gun. Keeping my eyes slitted, I raised my body in small increments, hoping she wouldn't notice. If I sat up too much or too fast, I was a dead woman.

Treetops, power poles, and roofs of trucks with containers slid past the darkened dually windows at regular intervals. Then only power poles against a white-blue sky. I had no clue how long we'd been driving, or to where. But it was a good bet we were not going to a hospital or sheriff's office. Wherever we were headed, it wouldn't be good.

My cell phone was long gone, dropped as Sandra yanked me into her dually at the Will Rogers parking lot. My purse had been lost in that struggle, too. How long ago was that? Hopefully, someone had witnessed my abduction.

Hopefully, a license plate or truck make had been reported, and help was on the way.

Hopefully, but not likely. I figured I had been out of it quite a while. I glanced at the dashboard clock. One straight-up. I'd been hijacked about half-past noon.

I looked down to see my wrists bound in a long white zip-tie. Probably like ones Sandra used to attach a fake white horse tail to her palomino's own tail, for showing.

Now I pulled and twisted at the ties, trying not to attract her attention. I knew you could break those ties, if you gave them the right hard yank at the right angle, over your ribcage or another solid surface.

Sandra's profile in dark glasses looked stern. Her jaw pulsed from grinding her teeth. All was quiet for the moment. But I had to get her talking. It might distract her enough that I could try to free myself.

Or not. If I were going to die, I was going to die with answers.

She must have seen me reconnoitering. Or else read my thoughts.

"Don't try anything," she said, glancing sideways as she drove. Her left hand tightened on the wheel, and her right hand raised the gun barrel toward my head.

We appeared to be on some county road or small highway well outside the city. Basically ranchland. Traffic was light, mostly pickups, semis and SUVs. Nondescript buildings and a gas station or two relieved the monotony of the flat, dry landscape.

"Just tell me your story, in your own words, before you kill me, if that's what you're planning," I said. "I need to know."

She tapped the red nails of her left hand on the steering wheel. As I waited, I studied the configuration of the wheel and the buttons on its flat, wide spokes.

"Tell me again what you think you know," she said, still holding the gun on me.

While I considered how to put it all into words, maybe somehow even finding a way to excuse what she'd done in order to encourage a more complete confession, I examined the dashboard. As if it might be the last thing I'd ever see. My eyes kept returning to the glove compartment.

Without knowing exactly why, maybe just operating on instinct or informed intuition, I raised my zip-tied hands and opened the glove box. The lighted interior revealed an owner's manual, black gloves, papers. I pulled out the papers and flipped through them as best I could with zip-tied hands.

"What are you doing?" Sandra roared. "Put those back." She waved the gun.

I held up a chili-red note pad with writing on it. A list of names, addresses and phone numbers, including those of the show judges. Both the handwriting and paper looked familiar. I'd seen such writing on the red note on my crunched gate, and in the cream-colored get-well card at South Valley Medical Center, where Reg had been. Of course the note paper and the handwriting were hers.

And I'd now seen the big dent in this truck's bumper. From crashing my gate.

Sandra, Sandra. Why didn't you just report what you found out about Reg, about your ex, to the police? Maybe Jeanne is right. Maybe you are crazy.

With deliberate slowness, I put the booklet and papers back.

"I only want you to tell me one thing, Sandra," I said. "Why?"

"Why what?"

"Why everything. I know why Nancy ran away, why you bought Jeanne that mankilling horse. But why kill Reg? And then your ex-husband?"

"And now why I am about to make you disappear," she said calmly, as if it were just one more thing on her to-do list. She sighed.

I waited some more, knowing what I must soon try to do, but dying to hear her answers. So to speak. I chided myself for my need to see humor in even dire situations.

"Both Jeanne and Nancy have poor body image and low self-esteem. My ex was abusive. Both girls were stressed. I thought it was the pressure to succeed."

"And?"

"Jeanne is realistic. More like me. But Nancy is a dreamer, and wanted to be this big star. I flipped out when I found out about Max, Reg and Nancy. I couldn't believe Reg had his cousin, that guy who used to work as a stunt man, be the middle man. Of course, Reg had his own reasons. He liked how Nancy looked in my real-estate photos. Just his style."

"So you killed them both. Why not go to the police?"

She looked over, holding her gun on me, and gave me a stern look. The Botox was wearing off. Those crow's feet didn't look so cute and harmless, now.

"Do you want to listen, or make snide remarks?"

Sandra's right foot depressed the gas pedal, and the truck sped up. We approached a beat-up sedan going much slower, and passed it at a breathtaking clip, swinging hard back into our lane before a semi sped by in the opposite direction.

"Reg tried to make it look like I was the one who arranged for him to take Nancy. He and Max had it all figured out. I'd used the girls in photos. Sex sells, right?"

This was just unbelievable. But I had to keep her talking. It might prolong my life.

"Then Max showed up here, started messing with judges so Jeanne could win, and threatened to tell how it was I who kept back earnest money in our real-estate deals. So it was simpler if Reg and Max just went away."

"If you kill me, it won't be simple. There's still Jeanne. And Nancy."

She glared at me, taking her eyes off the road for too-long seconds. I felt hot under her gaze, as if the AC couldn't keep up with the terrible Texas heat.

"Who's gonna believe them? On meds, neurotic. I'll just move someplace where I'm not known. Start a new life. This will blow over. I set it up for that Haverstadt to be blamed for Max's death. And they still can't prove I meant for Reg to fall."

"But you had everything, Sandra. Money, a great career, two beautiful daughters. "They would have found Nancy, you could have prosecuted Max. Why risk it all?"

"It looks great from the outside. That's the image I cultivate. But things weren't all that good."

She sniffed, chewed her lip, and looked from side to side, as if to see if we were being followed.

"Max was cutting me off. But I still held a policy on him. With him gone, and the insurance money, I could move again, entice Nancy back, keep Jeanne with me, and everything would be fine."

Fine? What would be fine about it? How could this she-monster think that?

My thoughts flew to Jeanne. Hurting in body and mind, she'd gone along with all this for almost a year, endured untold suffering. She clearly had wanted to tell me all along, but not found a chance until an hour ago. Not been desperate enough.

Why hadn't I found a way to get her to tell me sooner? I had won her confidence and friendship. But I hadn't tried hard enough. If I had been successful, at least one life might have been saved. Possibly two. Just like at Table Rock. If I had been fast enough, aggressive enough – .

Sandra cleared her throat.

"We done?" she said.

Again, the stomach churn.

"What about those judge threats?" I prompted. "Max's alleged bribery attempt?"

Sandra jutted out her jaw, and looked over at the side mirror. I looked in mine, as well. A State Police vehicle had materialized a half-mile or so behind. But its flashers weren't on. Sandra slowed her truck but drove on.

"Reverse psychology," she said, her eyes back on the road ahead. "To influence them to pin Superstar horses at the top of their placings. Then my damned ex rolls into town and screws everything up with his own deal, offering Dick a bribe."

I didn't know what to say. Instead, I worked at the zip-ties. They hurt my wrists.

Sandra drooped her head for a moment and pounded the steering wheel. Then she raised her head and looked pointedly into her rear-view mirror. She accelerated again, until we were travelling twenty miles over the speed limit, such as it was out this far.

"Look back," she commanded, jerking her chin toward the cab's rear window. "Is that truck following us? Shit. Now there's a smoky."

Seeing her distracted, I saw my chance. I rotated my torso, jammed my hands down hard on each side of the console, and popped the zip-ties. With my right hand I ripped the gun from Sandra's hand and pointed it at her. With my left hand, I reached out to punch the steering-wheel's "Neutral" gear button. The truck dropped speed. Using my last ounce of strength, I steered the truck manually with my left hand. It rolled some hundred feet more, and then bumped slowly down to stop in a ditch. A sedan and two other trucks roared by, horns blaring.

Chapter 58

The next moment, still clutching Sandra's gun, pointing it at her as she slumped in her seat, I threw one of my legs over the console, raised up, pressed the "Park" button and yanked the keys from the ignition.

"Look in the mirror, Sandra. They're coming. It's over."

I lurched out my side of the truck into the heavy, white-hot afternoon. I stood holding the gun on Sandra. For good measure, I squeezed off a round into a tire.

At the *blang!* she jerked as if she'd been shot, and collapsed against her seatback, her head dropped on her chest.

A mean-looking black pickup that moments before I had given up hope of ever seeing again, pulled to the shoulder several yards ahead. Two patrol vehicles, light bars flashing, drew along and behind Sandra's truck. A helicopter whapped the air overhead.

Diesel smoke belched from the trucks. Other traffic roared by in an almost-steady stream. Radios crackled from open doors of police SUVs. But to me, at that moment, the hyped-up scene was as comforting as a picnic by a pond.

Sonny unfolded from Black Beauty. He strode toward me, his eyes shining from beneath the brim of his pow-wow cap with its eagle feather and beaded brim.

I now tasted blood in my mouth, from crashing into something on my escape from Sandra's truck. But bloody or not, I ran forward and opened my dry lips into a smile so big it hurt. Everything was bigger in Texas.

Sonny and I collided in a bone-crushing embrace. We leaned heavily on each other. I felt intoxicated by his manly smell, and rubbed my cheek on his T-shirt.

Behind us, officers talked on radios, to each other, and with Sandra. Only snippets came to me, but I shut them out. Right now I only needed to hear Sonny. And the healthy throb of my own blood humming. As in, I was still alive.

"You okay?" he murmured in my ear.

"Oh, yeah," I murmured back, pressing kisses into his chin and cheeks. Their smoothness and warmth shocked me, as it always did. Lucky Indian men. Skin like babies. Many didn't even have to shave.

We pulled apart. He gazed down, holding me lightly. Out of the corner of my eye, I saw two uniformed EMTs with blankets and other gear, bearing down on us.

"You didn't have to risk your life," Sonny said. "You must have seen us coming."

"Wasn't sure it was you, wasn't sure anyone was coming. Took long enough."

"Didn't know you'd been kidnapped for more than an hour," he said. "Tried to call but no answer."

"Lost my phone when she grabbed me," I said.'

"Jeanne was gone for emergency surgery. First-Aid said you were there but then took off. Finally someone we talked to remembered a loud argument in the parking lot, around a white dually. We went there, found your phone and put out the all-points."

"It was a bad deal, for sure, but I kind of had it handled," I said.

"You did."

"But I am glad you're here."

The EMTs reached me, sat me down, and asked questions about my injuries. An officer who bore a faint resemblance to actor Tom Hanks, but with mirrored sunglasses and a Smoky hat, stepped into view.

"Excuse me," he said, introducing himself. "I need to ask a few questions."

I licked the last of the blood from my teeth, turned, and spat as discreetly as possible into the ditch. Then I faced the officer.

"Ask away," I said. "But could we please do this in your unit? It's hot as hell. And I want this man with me. He's been with me through a lot of this."

The officer wrinkled his forehead above the wire-frame sunglasses glasses, and tilted his head, addressing Sonny.

"Show me your badge, and I think we can do that."

Once in the SUV with the AC cranked, Tom Hanks studying us from the driver's seat, and Sonny and I seated in the shady back, looking through the bulletproof window ventilated for sound, I collapsed into my core.

"Do you have any water?" I croaked.

The officer rotated back around, grabbed a full plastic bottle, held it up and said, "My brother in Oregon sent me a case of this stuff last week. Straight from the Upper Rogue River."

I looked at Sonny and he looked back.

"No way," we said together.

EPILOGUE

I lay on my back beside my lover and stared up into a dark void, awakened by yet another nightmare of me riding for life – mine and someone else's – at the edge of a cliff. Always too late. Always seeing another dead body. And screaming, always screaming.

Or squeaking as I tried to scream, until I awoke to someone stroking my arm.

"Pepper. It's only a dream. I'm here. Come to me."

I was already there, of course. Already safe with Sonny Chief in a pretty bedroom slowly lightening on another hot Texas day. Already satisfied with answers to twisted tales, and that Sandra Allende was behind bars. Satisfied, that is, except for the final question: What about Nancy?

But that question, too, would soon be answered. Wheels were in motion. Sonny and I shared all we knew in a long, Internet-aided confab and conference call with police in Texas and Oregon. By midnight they'd checked a lot of things, including us, and confirmed they already were pursuing leads on the last mystery, with "very promising" results.

A lost girl would be found. Nancy, betrayed by her parents and conflicted about herself and her place in the world, was being contacted at a club near the Oregon casino Sonny had identified. She could be her own person again.

Make choices out of wisdom, not fear, shame and half-formed dreams. Maybe celebrate her eighteenth birthday by breaking out of sexual slavery. A club where the name Gary Gracey showed on tax records along with the name of a partner, Reg Stavropolis.

On a lesser note, I, along with my Brassbottom Barn buddies, would now be free of fear and worry, free to concentrate on riding our horses in a variety of events that could score World Championships. Real championships, not like the one I'd earned Tuesday in the Preview Class. Although that was glory enough for me.

As I had missed today's showmanship class, my first proper event, prime-time amateur horsemanship, would be tomorrow. I had almost a full day to prepare. I could just feel the heft of the trophy in my hand, and the sizeable prize check in my pocket.

"You awake?"

I started at Sonny's voice, so deep was I reviewing our mysteries, and imagining my next arena triumph. But I did not flinch when he rolled over and pressed his warm, virile body against my nude right side. In fact I pressed back.

"I'm awake now." To soften any possible misreading of the lame joke, I ran my big toe up and down his long, hairless calf. How could muscles feel as hard as steel? A whiff of his dusky scent rolled over me. His left arm came out from under the sheets and descended slowly across my breasts. I felt him swell against my thigh. I dragged a lazy finger across his high, round buttocks.

In the next dizzying moments, all else flew away. Worry. Slivers of leftover fear. Even vague thoughts that Tulip, probably dreaming that Tommy Lee was with her on the living-room sofa, and thoughts that our other friends in the second bedroom, might hear. We would be quiet. So quiet that our lovemaking would be a thrilling game. No words, grunts or screams of pleasure allowed. Just fingers, toes and tongues exploring each other in the dark. Waves of damp heat coursing through us, centering in our bellies. Hearts racing, breaths coming quick and fast. Silence is overrated.

~*~*~*~

Meet our Author

Carole T. Beers

Born in Portland, Ore., to descendants of Oregon Trail pioneers, Carole T. Beers fell in love with writing as soon as she could read, and with horses as soon as she could ride. After earning a B.A. in Journalism at University of Washington, she taught at a private school, wrote for true-romance magazines and worked 32 years as a reporter/critic for the Pulitzer Prize-winning Seattle Times newspaper. Several of her pieces won awards.
Along the way she competed on a women's shooting team and earned a pilot's license. She also worked in marketing and retail – great sources of story and character ideas!

Carole now lives in Southern Oregon, where she enjoys writing mystery books and stories. Her debut novel, "Saddle Tramps," centers on two 50-something women who show horses and solve crimes. These sassy ladies are ever seeking the perfect mate and the perfect horse, neither of which, they suspect, exists.

Over the Edge, a sequel to *Saddle Tramps,* forces the plucky, modern-day cowgirl-sleuth to find a lost girl and solve a pair of murders half a country apart – aided by Sonny Chief, her Lakota policeman partner in crime-solving ... and romance.

In the pipeline is *Ghost Ranch,* a third book in the Pepper Kane Mystery series, as well as *Blood Rider.* The latter is about a horse-loving teen and a circuit-riding minister who's her triple-great grandfather. Each hunts down a killer a century apart.

Soon Carole will publish a 16,000-word novella, "The Stone Horse," inspired by Zuni carvings of spirit animals. Years ago she mentored Indian youth, sang on a drum and danced in pow-wows, with the support of Lakota, Cree and Northwest Coast friends. She still holds these friendships dear to her heart.

Carole's free-time pursuits include dancing, playing games and watching the Seattle Seahawks along with her husband, Rich Peterson. She also likes to attend Bethany Presbyterian Church, visit friends, hang with her Boston Terriers, and ride her American Paint horse, Brad. Though retired from showing, she still rides as if she may show next week.

You may reach Carole at:

www.facebook.com/caroletbeers

www.caroletbeers.com

Made in the USA
Columbia, SC
15 March 2018